KILL YOUR DARLINGS

KILL YOUR DARLINGS

Terence Blacker

St. Martin's Press
New York

www.stmartins.com

ISBN 0-312-28329-6

First published in Great Britain by Weidenfeld & Nicolson

First U.S. Edition: December 2001

10 9 8 7 6 5 4 3 2 1

To Xan and Alice

A Note to the Reader

I have included throughout extracts and quotations from several of my previously published works, notably *Limber: Daily Exercises for the Fiction Writer* (1989), *Appointment with an Angel: A Writer's Affirmation Calendar* (1992) and *A Muse of Fire: The Writer Speaks* (1998). Certain additional statistics have been taken from *A Book of Literary Lists*, which has yet to be published.

As T S Eliot once pointed out, it is only by going too far that you find out how far you can go.

GK

London, 2000.

I

He was no Chatterton, that was for sure.

The hair was dark and matted, splayed across a grey, stained pillow-case. The skin on his face, once so lumin-ously pale, was now blotchy and flushed beneath an uneven growth of beard. Dimensions which, when contained and clothed, had conveyed an air of distracted intelligence (as if his unusual tallness had allowed him to breathe a purer air, less contaminated by everyday life), spilt across the bed in an almost comical attitude, a lanky man running away from life. On his stomach and chest, there were flaky psoriatic blotches of purplish red. Only his eyes, light blue, gazing at the ceiling with a sardonic disdain, as if trying to outstare his Maker, reminded me of the man I had known.

The place did not yet smell of death, but a thick fug of unwashed clothes, putrefying food and stale tobacco hung in the air, suggesting that, towards the end, his personal habits had taken a dive. The hard, scrawny stubs of count-less roll-ups were strewn over the bedside table and the carpet. Bottles – wine, beer, whisky – were on the floor and, beyond them, a number of battered plastic-covered library books lay face down like small animals closing in to feed off the corpse. A pile of discarded clothes lay in the far corner of the room.

Upstairs, someone turned on a television and the distorted din of gunfire, screams and urgent American accents drowned out the sound of children playing football in the courtyard below. Through the window, stained brownish yellow by tobacco fumes, the sun shone high over the roofs of the neighbouring houses.

For the first time, I noticed, on a small table beneath the window, a brown envelope, bearing the words 'Mum and

Dad'. Beside it was a stack of notepads, which I recognized. I left the envelope and pushed the pads into my leather bag.

Soon the world would come crashing in, changing everything for ever. On some inexplicable impulse, I walked over to the bed. Kneeling, I laid my head on the pale, sad crater of his stomach, breathing in the musty, young male smell which had not yet faded from him. With the tip of my left index finger, I traced the trail of fine, dark hair that led from his navel downwards. Gently, I took him in my mouth. He was cold, hard and sweet. Eyes closed, I lay there for several seconds, tasting him, taking him in, remembering things past.

A few moments later, I stood up, slung the bag over my shoulder, and reached for the telephone.

Exercise
Construct a scene in which the following three items play a part: a bed, a letter and the sound of gunfire.

2

We are used to walkers and talkers around here. Shouters, self-exposers, drinkers on street corners. They are as much part of neighbourhood life as the vast turds (probably dog, although even that is not certain) to be found on our pavements. Most afternoons, the dusty, litter-strewn streets are positively singing with soliloquies. At the check-out counter of the dimly lit, lino-floored local supermarket, a queue of warbling, unsteady members of the local community stands waiting to be supplied with tobacco, cans of cheap lager, half-bottles of vodka. Outside, a man and a woman of indeterminate age sit drinking cider and staring, glassy-eyed, at the passers-by. Down the road, on the tiny patch of grass in front of the Pentecostal Church, a ginger-haired dosser lies sprawled, asleep. Beside him, gazing at the world with a gentle, martyred air is an ancient greyhound, ribs showing through its dull grey coat.

For those of us across the border, there is something reassuring about this hinterland of west London that is not quite Shepherd's Bush, that falls short of Hammersmith, that aspires hopelessly to Chiswick but never quite makes it. Other parts of the city may go up or down, develop or decline, but this little corner of urban mediocrity remains unchanged. Occasionally, like well-meaning members of an international body trying to grow crops in the desert, investors and property dealers have attempted to 'lift' the area with housing projects, offices, wine bars and shops selling antique pine. The area is given a name – 'Starch Green' or even 'Starch Green Village' – but soon, within six months or so, anonymity returns, the desert reasserts itself, the new buildings are vandalized and left empty, the shops and bars make way once more to the only enterprises which can survive here – betting shops, newsagent food-stores run by exhausted Asians and bargain emporia selling kitchenware from East Europe or cheap, garish plastic toys made in China.

Friends from other, less exciting parts of town occasionally wonder whether this is a suitable area in which to raise a child. The answer, so I used to think, was easy. From the earliest age, the young (my own sweet son, for example) are provided with a secret garden. They learn the inevitabilities of urban life: a car radio left overnight in a car without a burglar alarm *will* be stolen; a sapling newly planted in the park *will* be snapped off.

On even the shortest walk, they are provided with an ever-changing variety of street show and park theatre. One day it will be two elderly drunks brawling feebly under a battered oak in the park, the next a family exemplifying every kind of domestic dysfunction. An astonishing variety of physical impairments are on display while even those with a full complement of limbs, eyes and ears can behave in a startlingly entertaining manner – marching self-importantly down the middle of the road, directing traffic, compulsively collecting litter in a ten-yard area.

At first, briefly, our children are alarmed by this circus of everyday grotesques. By the time they reach five or six years old, they are merely curious and amused.

Look, Daddy, there's a man without any clothes smashing the car windows.

Look, Daddy, that man hasn't got a face.

What's that woman doing under that tree, Daddy?

All right, Dougie, don't stare. Keep walking.

So when, on an October afternoon touched with the first melancholy chill of approaching winter, a man emerged from Brandon Gardens, talking to himself, no one would have looked twice. While his clothes and a certain ascetic thoughtfulness might have set him apart from the nutters and soliloquizers who thronged the streets, there was something studiously anonymous about him. As he reached the High Street, he seemed to merge with the scenery.

An actor perhaps, learning his lines? A businessman rehearsing an address to the board? No, the scene he was reliving and enacting (I was reliving and enacting) was one created by his own imagination. It was from a work called *Insignificance*.

On the day that would change my life, my marriage, redefine my position within the community, and launch my career into a churning ocean of achievement and exposure, I took my usual twenty-minute walk to the West London Institute in excellent spirits. To the world at large, I would have appeared a man at ease with himself, in his forties, his light hair receding with dignity, a square-shouldered, confident walk in his brown corduroy teaching suit, something of a paunch, teeth perhaps rather more prominent than conventional good looks would demand, a certain artistic shagginess adhering to his person.

I made my way through the park, the territory of dogs and children. In this part of London, animal life is raffish and untamed, with dogs and their owners representing a sort of sub-species of their own which roam the territory, rending the air each morning and evening with growls, snarls and screams of rage or fear, canine or human (it is difficult to tell), and marking their territory by spectacular evacuations dumped everywhere but in the enclosures provided by the council for the purpose. In some parks, small dog-free zones have been established where, in a weird reversal, pensioners and mothers with prams sit behind a wire fence as if they were the penned animals and the rampaging beasts outside, the humans.

Yet, through sheer weight of numbers, the army of children holds sway in the parkland ecosystem. Here, mothers or minders sit with them during the week, slumped dull-eyed on benches, or resentfully pushing swings. At the weekends, middle-class fathers emerge briskly after breakfast to spend quality time, running, kicking balls with urgent, clumsy enthusiasm, all the while conveying important information about life and the world to infants bewildered by this brief overload of adult energy. When children become old enough to be bored by the company of their parents, they abandon the inner sanctums of play for the wider plains of parkland where, occasionally skidding on dogshit, they play football in small groups, mixing with children who have wandered alone through this part of London almost since they could walk. Sometimes after school, as on that October afternoon, games would coalesce so that eventually the whole park seems to become one vast football match, involving all ages, which can be joined or abandoned at leisure.

By the time I reached the High Street, I was striding with the purpose of the seriously employed. I took the steps to the Institute three at a time, nodding vaguely at the three smokers standing bleakly on the top step like people contemplating suicide. Shouldering the glass door, I entered the lobby to be enveloped in the institutional fug which pervaded every part of the building as if the doomed hopes of the students who had passed through here had left spores of

7

despair in the atmosphere that would soon contaminate this year's intake.

Perversely, because there was hardly a day when I did not feel compromised by the demands it made, I felt invigorated when I entered the building. Everything here – the stale, cabbagey smell, the sound of voices echoing down the stairs, the creaking, rumbling lift, the noticeboards bearing grimly cheerful, ill-designed posters opening up ever more avenues of self-improvement – reminded me of my own relative freedom, of my status as an independent spirit in this land of the tenured and salaried.

I entered the staff common room on the first floor where four of the regular teachers sat gloomily on the threadbare orange furniture. As I spooned instant coffee into a mug by the kettle, two of them (Pottery and Cinema Studies) glanced up, then resumed their conversation in low, discontented tones. With the exception of Anna Matthew (Mind and Body), with whom, some years back, I had dallied for a few brief and happy weeks, the regular staff viewed me with a certain antipathy, jealous perhaps of my reputation beyond the Institute. Taking some circulars from my pigeon-hole, I left the room to make my way to Seminar Room 4D.

I like to make something of an entrance when I meet my new class. On this occasion, I bustled in, exuding the distracted air of a man caught up in the world of the imagination. Without looking at anyone, I reached into my bag and pulled out a few pages of *Insignificance*. For a moment, I stared at the sheaf of paper abstractedly before realizing that I was not, in fact, holding notes for a class. Putting the pages away, I took out a blank pad, a pen and a finished copy of *Forever Young*, and laid them in a neat line before me.

After a sustained pause for contemplation, I looked up, the dazed smile of a startled dreamer upon my face.

'My name is Gregory Keays,' I said. 'And I am a writer.'

3

I like coming home. In the past, when my wife and I used to share a social life, our friends would proselytize on behalf of other, more obviously artistic parts of the capital but living here suits us both fine; recently it has become one of the few areas of agreement between us.

Our house, described in more than one press profile as a 'dream home', is set off by a teeming backdrop of urban life. To the west of us is a landscape of avenues and plane trees, houses with cats and security systems, a tennis club, a terrace of shops containing a wine bar, two estate agents and a delicatessen; to the east, the wasteland of the wild inner city, romping with misbehaviour, dancing to the thump of a million sound systems. Sometimes, turning into my road after one of my afternoon walks, my heart lifts, and I see 23 Brandon Gardens as a sort of cottage that is on the edge of a cliff, yet is safe and secure, overlooking a great sea thrashing with contained disorder.

Even in the gathering gloom after that first lesson of the new term at the Institute, there was something distinctive about the Keays residence – the way the house (there really is only one word for it) *nestled* at the end of a quiet cul-de-sac next to the park, exuding an elegant warmth with which inhabitants of other houses in the road occasionally and unsuccessfully tried to compete.

Often, I have heard my wife, Marigold, explain to a visiting journalist the importance of contrast between the interior and exterior. Outside, it is trim, draped in wisteria and creeping vine, a superior woodman's cottage which stands out, in this bleak urban landscape, like an illustration from a fairy-tale. Inside, another contrast: the décor is white and spacious and almost formal. The house's insulation from the world outside, combined with this severe lack of clutter is said, by my wife, to induce a state of calm and well-being in those who dwell in it although she has sensibly never expressed this view to interviewers when her husband or son has been in earshot.

That night, as I entered the dream house, the jangle of Marigold's stress-reducing Sri Lankan wind-chimes above the front door causing their usual knot of irritation in my stomach, a low thud, like a heartbeat, filled the faintly scented air and reminded me that some aspects of domestic life resisted design, retained their essential clutter.

Dg. Dg. Dg. Even in his choice of music, Doug had managed to impose his uncompromising seventeen-year-old persona on his surroundings.

I walked into the immaculate, spacious kitchen, poured myself a large whisky, then glanced at the note my wife had left that morning on the kitchen table while I was still in bed (like many creative people, I take time to 'get going').

1. Donovan's fur-balls
2. Speak Doug

Picking up the latest edition of the *Professional Writer*, I wandered into the living-room where I sat, leafing through it, on the expensive sofa Marigold had recently bought. Although I love my home, I sometimes feel out of place in Marigold's design scheme. I had, for example, never quite worked out how to sit on this vast item of furniture with any degree of comfort or decorum. The seat was just too long, the back just too short: any attempt to relax involved adopting the posture of a poleaxed boxer collapsed against the ropes.

Maintaining the spare, effortless charm of the dream house has, of course, required considerable effort and money. With each new profile or style feature, the décor will have been updated and upgraded. Paintings by yesterday's hot new artists will have been quietly traded in for today's hot new artist. The small concessions to everyday life (magazines on the impossibly low coffee-table, invitations on the mantel-piece) will have been ruthlessly culled. Something subtle and expensive will have been done to the floorboards, a new, attention-grabbing *feng shui* gewgaw will have been hung, or stuck, or floated somewhere. The few objects of decoration to be found amidst the arctic bleakness of the ground floor are regularly scrutinized to ensure that no object that was deemed desirable last year is now utterly unacceptable on environmental, religious or political grounds.

Then, of course, there was the bedroom. At some point, as the snoop of the moment lobbed soft and simpering questions to their celebrity interviewee, Marigold would refer to her favourite room – the place where she can retreat from the world to be simply Marigold Keays – private person, mother, and (a flash of the eyes, a suggestive softening of the lips) wife. The hacks would beg. They would implore. In their shriv-elled-up journalistic souls, they would know that no lifestyle fantasy is complete without the bedroom.

No cameras, Marigold would say. Just a quick look. It's probably an absolute *sty* at the moment.

It is, of course, a masterpiece of design. A few items of homely detritus carefully set off the minimalist tundra of the ground floor – a clumsily made ashtray, a bowl full of sea-shells, a Mother's Day card in fading crayon, a silver-framed photograph of Douglas aged three or four, standing beside me, staring out to sea on one of our Cornwall holidays. At the foot of the bed is a small, humble, expensive table on which sits the Buddha, hands outstretched, a small bowl of rice before him (which must be replenished every day). He gazes approv-ingly at the vast four-poster bed which speaks so eloquently of discreet, loving and entirely satisfying marital trysts that even journalists find themselves lost for words. Family, faith and a full marriage: the bedroom, I've always thought, was my wife's finest achievement.

The journalist goes no further. Thanks to a ruthless system of design apartheid, two rooms are safe both from my wife's attentions and from journalistic prying: the small cupboard-like bedroom of the designer's son Doug (teenagers!) and the top floor where her novelist-husband (of *Forever Young* fame) has his work-station.

I remembered the note, written in Marigold's busy, exasperated hand, and, as if on cue, Donovan and his fur-balls wandered into the sitting-room, gazed at me for a moment as if daring me to make a move, then stalked off contemptuously.

Cats, I could write the book.* It was soon after my wife had become involved in the *feng shui* scam, that Dougie, as he was then, expressed a desire for a pet. Perhaps because design was entering a softer phase, reacting against the hard-eyed ethic of the previous decade, Marigold acquiesced with surprisingly good grace, investing in a Persian kitten which our son named 'Percy'.

It was expensive and elegant. It added a touch exotic playfulness to the minimalist living-room. It was the sort of furry accessory which any suburban family might envy. When it reached the feline age of discretion, it was introduced, with some difficulty (Persian cats are among the stupidest of God's creatures) to the concept of the catflap. Eventually it learnt to go out, come in and go out – never to be be seen again.

Stolen? Probably. In this area, anything of pecuniary value, even if it has claws and teeth, is vulnerable. Lost? Equally possible, generations of cosseting and in-breeding had not ensured that Percy was irrevocably domesticated, beige in tooth and claw.

So there was grief, then reparation. Another Persian, lighter, fluffier and, on the semi-humorous grounds that it was likely to be more intelligent, female. At eight months, it

---

* Indeed, I might well have done so. Before my recent success, a proposal for an open-ended series of anthologies – *The Cat in Literature, The Dog in Literature, The Pig in Literature* and so on – was in my pending tray.

was found by the side of the road, dying beautifully like a tragic heroine. After a suitable period of mourning, we tried again, this time with a more proletarian and therefore street-wise ginger cat. Wrong: that too disappeared.

By now, Dougie, who was anyway reaching that age in a boy's life when confidence seems to drain out of the soles of his feet, was beginning to take responsibility for these deaths, as if they were yet more proof of his general unworthiness. The guilt spread to his parents. Rather than give in, thus confirming their son in his lack of self-esteem, we tried again. And again.

Six? Seven? I lost count of the casualty list. As one cat after another fled, or threw itself under the wheels of the first car that passed down the street, it became clear, to me at least, that in a sense Dougie was right. These were no accidents. One after another, the cats had been driven insane by the tidiness and mystical harmony of the house in which they had found themselves. They were topping themselves, responding to *feng shui* with *hara-kiri*.

Enter, in the nick of time, Donovan, a thin, scrappy thing of indeterminate hue which appeared through the cat-door one cold winter's night, demanding food and warmth. Grateful that at least one animal, however moth-eaten and socially inferior, had chosen us, we fed it, took it to the vet for a series of ruinously expensive injections, ignored its flea-ridden appearance. When Marigold claimed unconvincingly (the cat had no discernible sense of humour) that she had seen him gambolling across the lawn trying to catch the wind, like the Sixties hippy, he was named 'Donovan'. Presumably to avoid the dangers of positive *ch'i*, he took up residence first in my office, then, having been roughly ejected after confusing the box containing the first three chapters of my London novel *Mind the Gap* for a cat-litter, in the rankest outpost of this dream home, Doug's bedroom.

Although it would be an exaggeration to say that any form of significant teenager–cat bonding had taken place, a system of mutual tolerance was established. In the face of strict biological accuracy, he renamed Donovan 'Shagger.'

Speak Doug.

Draining my glass, I made my way upstairs, hesitated on the landing, drawn to the refuge of my office on the next floor, then turned reluctantly towards the door marked by a poster bearing a smiley-faced drug symbol, behind which skulked my son. The noise was louder now, the door seeming to push outwards with every beat. I knocked, an authoritative we-need-to-talk, four-strike rap.

After a few seconds, there was the sound of a bolt being drawn. The door was opened slightly. Even by his standards, my son's appearance was dispiriting. His cropped, curly hair seemed to be matted with some dark, dried gel. Since I had last seen him, his pale, watchful face had been invaded by pustules, which stood out among the wispy beginnings of a beard, like snowy mountain peaks in a forest. Between the torn mauve T-shirt, bearing some illegible and possibly obscene legend, and the sagging, baggy shorts a straggly, girlish waist could be seen. The bare feet at the end of his hairy, matchstick legs were encrusted with ancient dirt. Stale air wafted out from the room, seemingly propelled by the thump and noise of his music.

'Yeah?'

'Can you turn it down, Doug?'

'Eh?'

'*Down.* Turn it *down.*'

The face disappeared, the volume was marginally reduced.

'Are you all right?'

'Owi? How d'you mean owi?'

'I mean, work and things . . .'

'S'pose.'

'I've been down to the Institute. First lesson of term. Met the usual bunch of losers.' I paused but it was clear that my son was uninterested in exchanging small talk. 'I'll be in my office,' I said.

'Owi then.' He closed the door.

I climbed the stairs to the top floor. Normally, while reading, researching or working on non-fiction, I like to leave the door ajar, only enclosing myself in this book-lined capsule of literary endeavour when actually writing fiction, but this evening the world was too much with me, and I shut it firmly behind me.

It was Balzac who insisted that, now and then, the writer should subject himself to a *bain de foule*, but right now the bath I needed could only be provided by literature. I took off my corduroy jacket, laid it on the floor, and reached for a small pile of manuscript on the shelf beside the desk. Sometimes, after teaching at the Institute, I would raise my spirits by reading from a favourite work by Hardy, Ford, Greene or Heller, but tonight I felt in need of a more specific and personal validation.

'*Insignificance* by Gregory Keays.'

I spoke the title page of my novel out loud in the slightly hammy tone which writers tend to adopt when reading from their own work. Already, I felt reassured, more myself.

I glanced to my right where, on the wall beside Snowdon's famous portrait of Granta's 1983 Best of Young British Novelists, I had hung a mirror. When my wife first remarked upon this uncharacteristic act of home-making, I pointed out that, for a novelist engaged in reflection, it was logical and helpful to be able to turn now and then to his own reflected image. Her response was ungenerous.

Writer, teacher, family man: I dare to think that a photograph taken of me at this moment would have indicated a man on whom the conflicting demands of art and life had not taken too harsh a toll. While there was a certain fleshiness around the trunk, neck and face which was not evident in the startled, long-haired character to be seen in the second row of the Granta line-up, an easy humour now attended those watchful eyes – a hint of danger and energy which, to a civilian, might have seemed surprising and possibly inappropriate in a man in his late forties.

I breathed in, squared my shoulders and pursed my lips over

the slightly protruding front teeth which, in honesty, I must confess are not my best feature.

All things considered, it was not a terrible sight. I returned to *Insignificance*.

The Writer Speaks of . . . Marriage

The music at a wedding procession always reminds me of the music which leads soldiers into battle.

Heinrich Heine

O father, O mother, O wife, O brother, O friend, I have lived with you after appearances hitherto. Henceforward I am the truth's.

Ralph Waldo Emerson

The true artist will let his wife starve, his children go barefoot, his mother drudge for his living at seventy, sooner than work at anything but his art.

Bernard Shaw

Marriage is about roughage, bills, garbage disposal, and noise. There is something vulgar, almost absurd, in the notion of a Mrs Plato or a Mme Descartes, or of Wittgenstein on a honeymoon. Perhaps Louis Althusser was enacting a necessary axiom or lyrical proof, when on the morning of November 16, 1980, he throttled his wife.

George Steiner

It was a very wounding experience, but I got rid of it by writing about it.

V.S. Pritchett, of his first marriage

I believe that all those painters and writers who leave their wives have an idea at the back of their minds that their painting or writing will be the better for it, whereas they only go from bad to worse.

Patrick White

4

The class's second lesson was always a key moment. My students would begin to relax and reveal their true characters – the talkers, the sulkers, those who would trash anyone else's work, those without a negative critical bone in their bodies who would find good in the thinnest, most ill-written prose, the gradehounds looking to add that all-important suggestion of a successful inner life to their c.v., the twitchies looking to creative writing for some kind of value-added therapy, the few, the noble few, who want to be professional writers and change the face of contemporary literature.

They were opening out next door, too. Before we had even started the class, giggles and groans and murmured meditations, the sort of sounds one might hear through a motel wall on a Saturday night reached us from Anna Matthew's Mind and Body group. Year after year, I would joke to my students that this animalistic soundtrack, rising and falling like a ninety-minute sex act, served as a useful, if cruel, metaphor of the lot of the writer, for whom the real, pulsating world is always at one remove, beyond the thin wall of his creative self-consciousness. Quite often one of them would weaken, disappearing one week to join Anna's fluting, orgiastic chorus the following week.

As it happened, I preferred to winnow out the more fragile spirits before they could spread a miasma of amateurish sentimentality throughout the rest of the group. During the first lesson, I had, for the benefit of the more half-hearted, portrayed the literary life in all its foetid glory. For the let-it-bleed confessional brigade, I had sternly quoted the Flaubertian dictum that the less you feel a thing, the fitter you are to express it. For those dreaming of riches and the bestseller lists, I had evoked Gissing, starving in his garret. For the middle-aged mums turning to literature after half a lifetime of domestic duty, I dwelt, with gleefully frank vocabulary upon the intimate lives of writers – Rousseau exposing himself, Dreiser jerking off in public, Hemingway inspecting Fitzgerald's dick, the impotence of Kafka, the castration complex of James.

Sure enough, we had lost two of those who had been here the previous week. Now it was time for the rest of us to get to know one another.

'Here's what we are going to do this evening.' I flashed an encouraging smile around the table. 'Later on in the course, we shall devote each lesson to the work of two students. Their story or novel extract will have been copied and made available to the rest of the class the previous week for consideration by all of you. This week we shall be getting something of a sampler. We have, I hope, each brought a small contribution as an introduction to your own fictional world.' One or two of the politer students laughed ingratiatingly. 'But first, I'd like to hear what you've all been reading.'

This, by intention, was a surprise – I know from experience that advance warning sends most of my students to their A level reading lists or to the classics shelves of local book-shops. A certain restlessness was evident around the table, as if this divergence from schedule, from creative writing into literature, was in breach of Institute regulations. 'Don't try to impress,' I said. 'This is not a job interview. One of my own favourite authors, as it happens, is Elmore Leonard.'

'Oh yes, he's great.' One of two Roberts on the course, an enthusiastic, dapper type whom I had already identified as a would-be-thriller-writer. 'He's so, I dunno, authentic.'

I nodded eagerly, as if the idea of Leonard's authenticity had never previously occurred to me. 'Very authentic, yes. I've always liked his attitude to his work. He once said, "If it sounds like writing, I rewrite it." He never stops to think about what he is writing, whether a particular word is holy, because, as soon as he becomes self-conscious, he is essentially interrupting his character. A lot of our so-called "literary" writers could learn from that.'

(None of this, incidentally, is what I believe. I have read no more of Leonard than the occasional magazine interview and, although he has much to recommend him – he is old, American, and writes in a sub-genre which has never tempted me – I am allergic to his type of bang-bang fairy-tale with its cast of low-life grotesques, comic violence and obligatory irony. I abhor 'great reading entertainment', would rather watch a game show on TV than submit to a 'compulsive page-turner'; the idea that one day I might in a moment of carelessness actually write an 'unputdownable' novel myself sometimes keeps me awake at night.)

'Didn't he write *Get Shorty*?' Alan, one of two mature students on the course spoke up in a gruff Northern accent.

'Oh, that was a terrific flick.' The cut-glass accents of Serafina, clearly the year's uncritical enthusiast, cut in. 'I adore Danny de Vito.'

I allowed the conversation to drift pointlessly in the direction of Hollywood caper movies. It relaxed them, suggested (wrongly) that I was as happy to discuss middle-brow entertainments as to explore authentic literary work and, above all, took up time. When, eventually, we found ourselves discussing the work of Quentin Tarantino, I stirred myself and suggested mildly that the *cinéastes* could pursue the matter later in the pub. Were there any other literary enthusiasms to be declared?

'Is anyone here into Raymond Carver?' Jay, our one foreign student, good-looking in that sincere, coddled way of Americans, dropped the inevitable name to blank looks around the table. From him, I could expect a year of stories about car lots and trailer parks, trashy, tragic wives and defeated, self-pitying husbands with a fondness for whisky and violence. At least the stories would be short.

Slowly, the conversation moved forward. Lodge, Atwood, Byatt, Carey, McEwan, Boyd. There a pattern here: intelligent but not too demanding, the solid well-made story, a whiff of future Eng. Lit. exam syllabuses. As the class embarked upon a halting, uneasy ramble through the foothills of modern letters, mentioning the work of novelists I once regarded as rivals, I assessed the seven students with whom I was doomed to spend an evening a week for the next three terms. Two, I imagined, were on the course because it seemed a relatively painless way of getting grades: Jay, the American, and the second Robert, an unkempt, sleepy individual cut from the traditional student mould, bleary either from narcotic excess or (more likely) from some form of ghastly post-teen angst.

Serafina, I would guess, was a charming, willing girl who would make endless, ill-spelt notes. Privately educated, she had read nothing and would produce childish, optimistic sub-literate work that would test my generosity to the full, but she was so modest and sweet that she was impossible to dislike. Since last week, she had found a copy of *Forever Young* in her local library and was now obediently reading it. Once, when life was less complicated, I might at this point have been considering her as a potential student-mistress for that year – there was something perverse and seductive in her milky, dimpled complexion, her innocent, slightly overweight body – but the way she smiled back at me was so guileless that I felt a pang of guilt at even imagining her in a sexual context. She was corruptible, of course, but the rewards at the end of it all were unlikely to justify the tears, not to mention the dreary post-coital conversations. I was beyond all that. It made me feel like a pervert.

Alan from Macclesfield, bruised by a failed marriage and redundancy, was, I judged, entering education with a sort of despairing rage. Bev, the other mature student had, as we had already learnt at some length, produced and raised two children, and left her marriage; now she seemed to be fizzing with ill-directed post-menopausal zest.

None of them would be completely hopeless. Unread, too easily influenced by passing literary fashion as pronounced by the Sunday papers, each, with the possible exception of Serafina, would doubtless show enough talent when they read their stories to the group to allow a useful discussion to develop. Almost anyone can tell a story; it's finishing it, rewriting it, starting again and again, that tends to be the problem.

Then there was Peter Gibson. An absurdly tall and spindly figure with lank, long hair, he seemed at first to belong to the same school of surly student type as the second Robert. As the others chatted about their favourite writers, he listened in silence. When, out of no more than polite curiosity, I asked who his favourite writers were, he gave a slightly exasperated sigh.

'I'm not into the list-making thing,' he said. 'I read what I read.'

'We all read what we read.' A touch of impatience was in my voice. 'This course is about communicating what we know to fellow writers.'

'I communicate through my writing. That is what matters.'

Conveniently, a rare moment of silence had descended upon Mind and Body next door, so I allowed the leering arrogance of the boy, his pig-headed inability to enter into the spirit of the occasion, to hang in the air for a moment. Rather to my surprise, he blushed to the roots of his shaggy hair and, as if he were a schoolboy who had been rebuked by his teacher, pulled in his chair, made a thoughtful tent with his long fingers in front of his face, and began to speak, his eyes holding mine.

'I've been trying to come to terms with some of the more recently published French post-structuralists?' When he spoke, he terminated his sentences with an interrogatory rise of the voice, almost as if he were asking permission for his peculiar enthusiasm. 'Like everyone, I had read up on literary theory, but the new crowd of writers – *les néo-nullistes*, as they're called – have been looking beyond the primacy of the text to redefine the power relationship between reader and writer, taking the fictional project beyond narrative and character. In my own work, I'm looking to bring to bear the spare cerebral reductiveness of modern French writing but cross it with genuine emotional engagement?'

'Ah yes.' I shifted uneasily in my chair. Ever since I played with the form in my 1991 novel, *A/The/Until*, a ludic, experimental work which dispensed entirely with verbs, I have found that anything bearing the accursed prefix 'post' sets off alarm bells in my cranium (I am post-post). Yet the tone of Peter's little speech was so rapt and personal, as if he were confessing for the first time some profound and uncomfortable intimacy, that I felt temporarily disarmed. 'The dreaded *néo-nullistes*. Which ones in particular?'

'Labrun, Houellier-Masson, Geneviève Debru. I'm finding Tchaviev a bit of struggle.'

'Yes, not easy.' I made a note on my pad, then glanced at my watch. 'Perhaps at this point we should read our little fictions. Who would like to start?'

After the briefest of pauses, it was Robert – the neater of the two Roberts – who spoke. 'I'll go,' he said, taking some perfectly typed pages from a folder. 'It's a sort of murder thing.'

And so it was. Robert's unnecessarily brutal and hectically plotted set-piece, which told us rather more about his taste for violence than we wanted to know, was the first of the predictable readings. Scruffy Robert maundered on about his dad. Serafina introduced us, not for the last time, I feared, to the sun-dappled, Blytonesque setting of her childhood. Describing a man being fired, Alan revealed that his feeling for language had been fatally impaired by several years' exposure to the internal memo. Bev shared with us a conversation with a counsellor which may or may not have been an attempt at irony (confusingly, she herself was uncertain about the matter).

'And Peter.'

I smiled at the gangling youth, his chair pushed away from the table, his head sunk in his chest.

There was a stirring, a complicated untangling of spidery limbs. Peter reached for the folder in front of him and took out two sheets of paper and laid them on the table, with a careful flattening movement of both hands. Single-spaced, with no paragraphs, they looked unpromising and, as he stared down at the paper, Peter frowned almost as if he had brought the wrong story.

Frankly, I didn't warm to him. I had seen this kind of build-up before. The moody artist, dazed and in thrall to his muse, can play quite well at literary festivals where the audience is hungry for a glimpse of the tortured writer, but performed by an unpublished young pup in a seminar room, it tends to be less impressive. If he had been a poet, Peter might just have got away with it, but novelists, particularly would-be novelists, should be anonymous.

He looked up at me, those wary blue eyes between two dark curtains of hair holding mine, and I wondered briefly whether he had consumed some kind of banned substance. Since he seemed to be asking for permission to start, I encouraged him with a brisk little circular movement of the hand.

Peter's reading voice, when at last it came, was quiet and classless but with the hint of a northern accent, yet its very flatness conveyed a sort of stunned passion. He spoke so quietly that, even though, as if on cue, the hums and chants of Anna Matthew's Mind and Spirit class next door had died down (Peter had this odd magical effect on his surroundings), we had to strain to hear him.

The story he told was notable first of all for its simple, pared-down style, so free of embellishment or self-consciousness that, absurd as it may sound, it was almost as if we were getting the experience unmediated by prose, as if he had perfectly enacted Ford Madox Ford's requirement that the reader should be 'hypnotized into thinking he was living what he read'. It was a tale told by a three-year-old, a story of death – murder, probably – involving two adults, possibly his parents. Somehow, in 2000 words or so, he conveyed not just the event and its physical and emotional setting but also a sense of the years of blighted life stretching into adulthood that lay ahead of the narrator.*

When he finished, we sat in silence for a few seconds

* The story was later incorporated, with relatively minor shifting of narrative furniture, into the final section of *terpsichore 4:2*.

23

before, as it were, starting to breathe again. Then, impassive as ever, he returned the sheets to their folder and sat back.

'Fine,' I said. 'Comments, anyone?'

'Wow,' sighed Bev.

I looked round the table. 'Anything a little more critically developed than "Wow"?' I smiled at Bev, hoping that she wouldn't take my remark as a reproof. The fact was, her response was the only appropriate one but I tried, in the first lesson, to allow students to find their own reviewing voice. Encouragement, criticism, deconstruction from me could come later.

'That poor child,' said Serafina. 'I mean, I know it's a story and all that but it felt so real.'

'So were they his parents?' asked Scruffy Robert.

'Could be,' said Peter.

'You don't know?'

'I do.' Peter, mumbling into his chest, showed signs of losing interest. 'But I'm the writer. You're the reader. Ambiguity is central to my project.'

'I think she was his mum and he was her boyfriend,' said Bev.

'If it works for you,' said Peter with a private smile which I suspect I was not alone in finding unnecessary and irritating.

And so the discussion limped forward. Peter listened politely, contributing little. When eventually it tapered off, I announced that I would read a brief extract from my first novel *Forever Young*. I opened the book on chapter three, paused for a moment, then began. 'Jimi had never been to an orgy before. Be-ins, love-ins, sit-ins, lie-ins but never an actual orgy . . .'

Yes, I chose the scene in a squat in Eel Pie Island which has perhaps become one of *Forever Young*'s best-known set-pieces.* Normally it's an acceptable way to close the first seminar: comic, confidently written and frank enough both in its language and content to encourage my students towards

* 'One of the most outrageous sex scenes in contemporary English fiction.' *Books and Bookmen.*

an unbuttoned approach to their own work. On this occasion, though, the laughter seemed forced. After Peter's story, my prose sounded heavy-footed, my humour as crude and old-fashioned as the routine of an end-of-the-pier comedian, my characters no more than irritating shadows, like minor faults on a photograph, flitting across the incomparably more vivid and significant world which he had created. When I finished, there were polite murmurs of approval but I sensed that it had not quite 'caught' in the way it has on similar occasions in the past.

Later, walking home, having discussed with Serafina and Bev their lack of a typewriter or word processor, I passed a wine bar on King Street. There, holding on to a glass as if it were a lifeline, was Peter Gibson. I hesitated. He looked up. Our eyes met. I gave a little wave and hurried on.

Top Ten Start-Up Rituals of the Great Writers

1. Malcolm Lowry would rise early and go for a swim. His wife was only allowed to stir in the house when she heard the animal-like noises that he would make once he had entered his trance-like state of creation.
2. John Galsworthy installed his wife in the room next door to his study and required her to play the piano quietly.
3. Somerset Maugham would read *Candide* so that 'I have in the back of my mind the touchstone of that lucidity, grace and wit.'
4. Jack London wrote for twenty hours a day and rigged up a device attached to his alarm-clock that would drop a weight upon his head to wake him up.
5. Ernest Hemingway sharpened twenty pencils.
6. Virginia Woolf wrote a little sketch every morning to amuse herself. 'They might be islands of light – islands in the stream I am trying to convey.'
7. John Steinbeck wrote warm-up exercises on the left-hand side of his notebook.
8. Alan Garner likes to watch a black-and-white B-movie, preferably starring Ronald Reagan, with the sound turned down.

9. Isabel Allende starts every new book on 8 January and places the collected works of Pablo Neruda under her computer 'with the hope they will inspire me by osmosis'.

10. Toni Morrison gets up before dawn, lights a candle and walks around the house. If she waits until sunrise, when it's too late to light the candle, she knows she will be unable to write that day.

5

Insignificance was in trouble.

I found myself reluctant to leave my bed in the morning, indulging in an ever-more protracted series of displacement activities, spending hours fiddling with chapter heads, fonts, spelling checks or, most painfully of all, word counts. An awful staleness now seemed to emanate from the pitifully small manuscript which, it appeared to me in my state of writerly paranoia, begged, demanded, to be put out of its misery by premature retirement to that rest-home for uncompleted projects, a filing-cabinet drawer mockingly marked 'Work in progress'. It became agony to reread the few words I had completed, every word and phrase seeming flat and dull and tetchy from over-use. Sometimes, as a sort of dazed, masochistic boredom tightened its grip towards the middle of the morning, I would kill a few moments comparing a paragraph of my writing to that of some past student who had shown such exemplary lack of talent that I had kept the work to point up some common failure among inexperienced writers. Was one really so much better than the other? Read blind, would it be immediately clear to a reader that one was by a writer once publicly recognized as one of the Best of Young British Novelists, snapped by Snowdon, while the other was by a receptionist with brief and soon-to-be-dashed dreams of writing a successful historical romance?

Worst of all, a sure sign of danger ahead, I took to reading pages from my own earlier work, from *Forever Young, Accidents of Trust, Mind the Gap, Adultery in Hampstead, A/The/Until, Tell Me the Truth about Love, about Love, Giving It Large, Cenotaph*, even my tawdry attempt at 1980s populism *Glitter*. It seemed clear to me that, where there had once been personality, there was now derivativeness, where there had been wit, there was cynicism, where the words had jumped off the page with impudent joy and bounce and swagger, they now dragged their feet wearily onwards, emitting a susurration of exhausted dullness and defeat. Suddenly, my prose was an old man's snore, slack, toothless, wet-lipped, waiting for that moment of painful, yet blessed closure.

Even my writing workouts were becoming heavy-footed. I would stare out of the window and haltingly record the progress of activity in the park – the enraged young mother pushing a pram, her older child lagging five yards behind her, the old woman whose face seemed to be imploding, eaten up by some wasting disease, the dog-fights, the drunks on a bench, the footballers at lunch-time, the teenage dodgies wandering about in shifty manner in their puffa jackets. I lifted them from life, teeming and urgent and secret, and laid them carefully on the page, stone-dead. Words. Worthless, empty words. Who needed them?

At the back of my mind, I heard the mocking echoes of Peter Gibson's story – direct, easy, full of feeling expressed in unfussy, confident prose. It seemed to me even then that Peter was me – the younger, confident me that me I had lost.

I took the familiar, radical decision. I was too close to the work. I was becoming stale. There was a project, with a real contract and a real deadline, that demanded my attention, *The Book of Literary Lists*. Maybe, while researching and compiling charts and surveys revealing the habits, working methods and domestic arrangements of the great writers, I would be infected by their industry and dedication and fall back in love with my novel.

So, at the end of another arid and agonized day of noncreation, I placed *Insignificance* in the 'Work in Progress' drawer, vowing with a weary solemnity that this was not *adieu* but *au revoir*.

It was a Friday evening. Soon after I had taken my notes for *The Book of Literary Lists* and laid them in neat piles across my desk for the next day's work, I made my way downstairs. There, to my surprise, was my wife. She was in the kitchen, cooking, or rather unwrapping an expensive pre-prepared meal that she had bought from a shop in Chiswick specializing in food for the busy professional couple. In my memory, I see her wearing an apron but this must be husbandly fantasy. She was, as far as I remember, in an elegant little purple dress of *haut* bohemian style. At forty-two, Marigold has the slight, confident figure of a woman whose sensuality would radiate from sackcloth and this simple, priestly and faintly perverse garb caused me a familiar pang of lust. Seeing my wife in the kitchen tended to do that to me, even then and even after everything we had been through.

She glanced up as I stood in the kitchen doorway and, sensing what was going through my mind, pursed her lips. 'I thought we might eat together,' she said, fussing with fake competence over a salad. 'As a family.'

'Mm. Treat,' I said.

Ever since Doug had taken to eating his meals upstairs alone, Marigold and I had been dining separately. When she was not with clients, my wife would partake of some fashionable, nutritious cold snack in the kitchen early in the evening, sometimes even standing up at the kitchen table, as if to ensure a hasty conclusion should I choose this moment to appear after my day's work. With a few muttered words of acknowledgement, she would take her glass of wine to the living-room where she would read some modish book of spiritual guidance and personal fulfilment while I prepared my more traditional cooked meal in the kitchen.

In truth, we had little to talk about now that our one common project of the past seventeen years was hiding from the world. Each of us, I suppose, had come to the conclusion that this rota system afforded us one of the comforts of long-term marriage – the ease of company without the effort of conversation.

I took a bottle of Blanc de Blancs from the fridge, opened it and gave Marigold a glass. She mumbled thanks.

'Can I help?' I said, sitting at the kitchen table and opening a copy of *Interiors* magazine. It was an old joke of our marriage, a distant echo from earlier, happier days, and briefly Marigold's face softened. 'That'll be the day,' she said.

There had been a time, before she moved among professionally arty types for whom an aesthetic sensibility delivered a financial and social pay-off, when the simplicity and purity of the creative life had appealed to Marigold. By a cruel paradox, it was my success shortly after we had married which alerted her to the fact that artistic integrity and worldly success could live together – a short step from her current position where the first could not in any real sense exist without the second. When *Forever Young* was causing a small but gratifyingly significant flutter in the literary world, I ran with a crowd of aspiring writers and even dared to entertain my friends at the flat we then shared. Although Marigold tolerated them, I occasionally discerned even then a certain impatience when my less successful, unpublished friends indulged in the traditional literary activity of complaining about publishers and agents. Occasionally, after they left, she would wonder out loud if I should not be raising my sights and ask whether, since I was now among the cream of the country's writing talents, I should not be inviting some of the Granta Best of Young British crowd to our evenings. Although I doubt that she had ever heard of Cyril Connolly (she has never been a great reader), Marigold would certainly have agreed that 'failure is infectious . . . and unless a writer is quite ruthless with these amiable footlers, they will drag him down with them.'

In those days, the telephone seemed to ring all day. Editors. Producers. Journalists. I was young by the standards of the book world. My promise had been confirmed by my presence on the Granta list. I was hot. When Martin or Salman were not available to deliver a quote on the literary issue of the week, literary editors would turn to Gregory Keays. This was the cultural life which my wife understood: visible, profitable, social. The romance of the garret soon faded.

As if in sympathy with my change of fortune, she abandoned dreams of becoming an artist and, after a brief flirtation with the idea of running a gallery, discovered a talent for interior design, for the moneyed minimalism in vogue during the Eighties. Briefly, a matter of eighteen months at the most, we were the enviable metropolitan family unit of her dreams: the novelist, the designer and their quiet, angelic baby son.

Money became a problem: not the lack of it, but the balance of distribution. My second novel, *Accidents of Trust*, was mired in technical difficulty. As my confidence became eroded, so did my position in *le tout Londres littéraire*. Marigold worked harder to sustain our desirable family unit and may even, at that point, have been proud that her entrepreneurial efforts were helping to support a true writer. She was now a freelance designer and, with an unerring instinct for a trend, had sensed a cultural shift from overt consumerism towards the gentler form of self-obsession afforded by spiritual growth. Before virtually anyone else, she moved into the area of *feng shui* décor.

Now, when the telephone rang, it was for her. I was no longer an acclaimed novelist but merely a husband who wrote. She bought this house. She decorated it in her own fashion after only the most cursory consultation with me. The adorable infant Douglas became the playful child Dougie. As Marigold acquired the sheen of a public person, I, with a sort of self-lacerating miserliness, became ragged and pale and distracted – a living, shuffling breach of my wife's house style. To appease her, I took up the offer of a monthly column in *The Professional Writer*, then began to work part-time at the Institute. Yet the miserable trickle of revenue that these forays into the world of salaried employment provided somehow seemed to irritate her more than if I were earning nothing at all. There is, we quickly discovered, little comparison between the earnings of a top *feng shui* designer and those of even a compromised writer. Marigold did not need to point out (although now and then she did) that a month's part-time consultancy for a large firm responding to the pitiful New-Age yearnings of their employees was worth two years' fiction writing. She used to leave bank statements on the kitchen table.

Money was always the problem: when it was there, when it was not.

I looked up to see that my wife was no longer fussing over the food but was staring at me as I gazed sightlessly at the table.

'Sorry to interrupt,' she said.

Self-mocking, I blinked owlishly and shook my head. 'Working. You know how it is.'

'Ah, yes. I forgot.'

'Graham Greene used to say that so much of a novelist's writing takes place in the unconscious that, in those depths, the first word is written before the first word appears on paper.'

'Or doesn't.' Marigold smiled to herself as she inexpertly peeled an avocado.

'As it happens, I'm working on my literary list project. The stuff's pouring out.'

'What happened to the novel?'

'Back burner. If it's so important to bring in some money –' I spoke bitterly, allowing the full tragedy of the writer's life to enter my voice. 'I'll do some paid work for a while.'

'Maybe you could take on work where you can combine that productive staring into space with being paid. The caretaker at my office does it all day.'

I paused, refusing to take the bait. 'It's a different quality of staring.'

'Maybe he's writing a novel, too. Most people seem to be writing novels these days.'

'Mind novels. Perfect in every way except that they never get written down.'

My wife looked up, seemed to be about to say something, then smiled, almost sympathetically. 'I see,' she said.

Sometimes, having these conversations, I felt like an actor in a drawing-room comedy whose run had gone on for too long. The badinage concealed too much unexpressed tension. The jokes were imitation jokes, whose life had been drained out of them years ago. We enacted intimacy out of habit and fear of the alternative. Yet now, looking at her, I noticed something different about Marigold, something forgiving, almost mellow, which I found discomfiting.

'So you won't have to worry about my not earning for a while,' I said, pushing it a bit. 'I'll be doing a literary version of your caretaker's work. Those who can, write. Those who can't, draw up lists about writers.'

'Don't blame it on us.' She spoke quietly. 'It's your decision to put the novel aside. Don't you dare let yourself off the hook by playing the domestic martyr. As far as I'm concerned, you can stare into space for as long as you like.' She took two dishes, walked past me out of the kitchen. I heard her lay them on the glass table next door. She returned and stood before me. 'We each have our own lives to live.'

'Where were you today?'

As she walked back to the oven, I noticed something languid about the way she moved, a lascivious swing of the hips. The wifely concern for my work, her preparation of a meal: there was something wrong and out of kilter about it all.

'Working.' She held my gaze and smiled shamelessly. It seemed to me that there was more colour in her cheeks than usual, that her lips were full. Her voice, throaty and sensual with a sort of jazzy catch in it, brought back distant memories of afternoons in bed or late-night conversations as we lay, glowing, intertwined and breathless. It was the voice of a well-fucked woman. As if reading my thoughts, she muttered, 'I had a good Friday.'

'Good? In what way?'

'Don't pretend you're interested, Gregory. Go and tell Doug we're having lamb. It's his favourite.'

'Is there any point?'

'Try.'

I stood up and walked slowly upstairs. I knocked on my son's door. The volume lowered slightly and I shouted my message. He replied that he would be down later. Maybe. By the time I had returned to the sitting-room, my wife was at the table, holding her wine-glass with both hands, her narrow shoulders hunched forward as if she were cold or wanted to be held by someone. She looked pretty and sad and lonely, flanked by two empty chairs, the dishes and food laid out before her.

'It's just you and me,' I said.

'Oh, goody,' she said

We both laughed, recognizing in that instant what we had become. I picked up my knife and fork and cut into the artichoke hearts before me. I glanced out of the window and caught our ghostly reflections in the glass. It was a shame that there was no photographer or profile-writer there right now to catch our domestic scene: the celebrated designer and her novelist husband, dining together in their dream home.

Affirmation

Today I shall study my scars. In them, I shall read the story of my life. Every moment of hurt will be a paragraph, every dysfunctional relationship a page. From the ugliness of loss and pain and injustice will emerge the beauty of creation.

6

Soon there was jealousy in class. It was noticed that, while I betrayed symptoms of boredom or impatience enduring the prosaic, overheated efforts of Bev or Alan or one of the Roberts, I lingered over Peter Gibson's work, allowing it ten or fifteen minutes more than the informally allotted period for discussion. Even when Peter was not the direct focus of attention, I would frequently and unashamedly use his prose as a touchstone against which lesser efforts could be judged. I could see that this irritated the others but ignored the martyred sighs, tapping pencils and rolling eyes. It was important, I always felt, to introduce my students not only to the technicalities of writing but also to the tests of character which are part of the literary life – disappointment, hopelessness, despair, a grinding envy of one's peers. Mine is a holistic course.

It was said, after the tragedy, that there was something obsessive and personal in my response to Peter Gibson. Nothing could be further from the truth. If I spent more time socially with him, took him to readings and launches, it was, at that early stage, merely because he was the only member of that year's intake upon whom such experiences would not be wasted. I had resolved at an early stage in my career as a creative writing teacher that to be seen too often in public with one of my students would be unhelpful to my public image. I am a writer, not a teacher taking his charges on an outing.

From the start, I could see that Peter was not one of Connolly's 'amiable footlers'. The apparent shyness belied by every swaggering syllable of his prose; the way he sat apart from the other students, contributing occasionally, but tellingly, to the discussion; the notes he made in a small book, his hand-writing neat and microscopic, always at the most unlikely moments, as if a separate, more significant lesson was taking place in his head: these things suggested to me, from the start, that he was more a colleague, a fellow toiler in the vineyard of literature, than a pupil. His talent deserved nurturing.

He was usually first out of the seminar room at the end of the evening but, on the Thursday of the third week, I asked him to stay behind. When the others had gone, I told him that I had been contacted by South Eastern Arts who were sponsoring a collection of short stories which might be of interest. Ignoring his marked lack of enthusiasm, I suggested that we might discuss the matter more comfortably at a local wine bar. He hesitated, as if even drinking with his tutor represented a small but significant compromise, then gracelessly nodded his agreement.

I chose Glaisters, a bright, hangar-like wine bar frequented by young professionals, not a place I would normally visit but one which had the advantage of being avoided by students. As we entered, we were buffeted by the sound of fake, end-of-day merriment, by office workers clucking with gossip and excitement like battery hens at feeding time, the din punctuated occasionally by the plaintive, insistent call of mobile telephones. Glancing back as I pushed through various dark suits, I noticed that Peter seemed to be almost cowering, shoulders hunched, his hair falling girlishly across his face. I found us a table and, when a young, harassed-looking waitress appeared, he surprised me by asking for a whisky. I ordered him a double.

'It may be of no interest, this idea of mine,' I said easily when our drinks arrived. 'It's a sponsored collection for unpublished writers under thirty. With a following wind and a friendly word from your tutor, one of your stories might make the cut.' I hesitated, perhaps half-expecting a muttered word of curiosity or even gratitude from my student, but Peter was looking around the room as if, at any moment, the Chardonnay set would recognize us as outsiders and turn upon us. 'No promises,' I added, 'but I know the editor.'

'I'm not unpublished,' Peter mumbled eventually. 'When I was doing A levels, my English teacher sent something of mine to a Sunday paper that was doing some kind of competition. It won and got published. "Playground". Embarrassing stuff.'

'You kept quiet about that.' Although still smiling, I was irritated. I remembered the competition and even read the first paragraph or two of the winner out of professional curiosity. It was, I recalled now, an astonishingly confident work for an eighteen-year-old. Yet he had failed to mention it in his application to the Institute.

'I told you. It was crap.'

'It was published.'

'So they say. I never saw it. I wanted to withdraw it but the school wouldn't let me. Still, it made me £250 – not forgetting lunch with a publisher.'

'Lucky old you. Which publisher was it?'

'Never found out.' Peter shrugged. 'I declined.'

'Wasn't that a bit unwise? You want to be a writer. It was a step on the ladder.'

'The ladder.' Peter Gibson laughed, an odd, unattractive snickering sound, and I found myself feeling uneasy in his presence, almost as if he were my tutor, rather than the other way round. He reached into the canvas shoulder-bag he always carried, took out a tin of tobacco and rolled a thin, white, Martin-like stick. He lit up, coughed unhealthily. 'Yesterday. It's what I do now that matters,' he said.

'Purity. The Garret. You'll forgive me, Peter, but it's pure romantic tosh. If you're serious about being a professional writer, you will at some point have to tread that fine line between the muse and the bank manager.'

'I'm not interested in that game.' He spoke haughtily, as if publishers were already pestering him with offers and, truth to tell, it was not such a fanciful notion. He had looks; he had talent. These days, editors were even more youth-struck than when Granta's Best of Young British Novelists were heirs to the kingdom. 'In fact, I can hardly bear to read that story now. It's sullied.'

I laughed. 'By readers?'

'It was . . . premature.' He seemed irritated now. 'It's like a creative writing class. The story loses something when other people have had their fingers all over it. The purity's gone, the tension. I can hardly bear to read it again. The performance, the phoney compliments, the tedious *critiques* –' He spoke the word with real venom. 'It feels unnatural, all this exposing work to the light before it's ready. It's like strangling puppies.'

'I see.'

He looked at me and, for a moment, dabs of colour appeared on his cheek. 'I didn't mean to be offensive. Obviously your comments are helpful.'

I smiled. 'I don't entirely disagree. When I get home after class, I need to read a few pages by one of the masters simply to wash the bad prose out of my system. All those redundant adverbs and ghastly, effortful, earthbound descriptions. It feels contagious. I often think that the business of making public and communal what can essentially only work when it is private and solitary destroys more than it creates.'

'So why do you do it?'

'Because, now and then, I find that I'm teaching a real writer. A natural.'

Peter looked away quickly and stared at a nearby table where two women in their thirties sat on opposite sides of the table, each conversing animatedly into neat, dark telephones. He seemed to have regretted saying as much as he had.

'When I'm dealing with someone of talent, I can help them,' I said. 'Not to write fiction but to spot the traps in the path ahead, maybe provide a few shortcuts. It's not the most noble activity for the creative artist but then I suppose we all have to make compromises.'

The whisky seemed to have mellowed Peter. Returning his attention to me, he pushed his hair back out of his eyes and, holding a handful of dark locks, placed his elbow on the table. I noticed for the first time a hint of red, eczema or psoriasis around the roots. 'Tell me about compromises,' he said.

I caught the eye of the waitress. As I ordered us both another drink, I noticed her glancing with clear erotic interest in the direction of Peter whose hirsute and wild looks did, it was true, stand out against the backdrop of office drones all around us. He seemed oblivious to her interest.

'I suppose, when I set out in this business, I felt like you. A writer writes. He doesn't spend his essence on teaching unpublished mediocrities, or interviewing published nonentities. Every working moment away from the desk is time and effort lost to literature. Now –' I sighed. 'Put it like this. There are perhaps ten or fifteen writers of serious fiction in the country who earn enough from their work not to be obliged to scrap and scrub around the dustier corners of the literary scene to survive. The rest review. They toss off TV scripts, write biographies, sidle into advertising agencies where, in exchange for some ludicrous sum of money, they write copy extolling tampons or tyres or a private water company. Some even remove their brains, don the writing equivalent of nappies and write kiddie-fiction.'

Peter stirred. 'I'm not doing that. I'd rather work in a pub. Write in the day, pull pints in the evening.'

'I'm lucky enough to have been able to resist most of these diversions. Reviewing, someone said, is a form of failure – you hurt people for things you have failed to achieve yourself. Insecure as a writer, you bolster your own self-importance by demeaning or over-praising professional colleagues. I've seen the way critics work – they're as vindictive and scheming as anything you would find on a City trading floor. Television drains a novelist of his voice as surely as does journalism. Biography? As Martin said, it allows mediocre, Second XI types to feel and act superior to the knights of the First XI. It simultaneously negates and aggrandizes its practitioners. To become even the smallest part of the cynical, over-excited, coke-fuelled world of the professional advertiser is such a shameless prostitution of the word as to render meaningless all authentic literary acts of love that may occur after the infection takes hold. There are always those who argue, in all apparent sincerity, that telling tales for "kids" is serious artistic work but, having had the misfortune to attend, in a professional capacity, a children's book festival, I have concluded that authors working in this area, good-hearted and amiable as they may well be, invariably suffer from the writing equivalent of maternal brain-fag. I could have fol-

lowed that route – when my son was five, I published something called *The Lonely Giant** before deciding that I was
exploiting his childhood in an unacceptable way. The
Institute and my regular column for the *Professional Writer*
are enough for me.'

'*Professional Writer*?'

The waitress returned. 'Another whisky,' she trilled, making another unsuccessful attempt to catch Peter's eye as she
placed his glass before him. 'And a wine.'

'Yes, it's not perfect but, in my own way, I have managed to
retain a *cordon sanitaire* around my purely artistic endea-
vours by taking journeywork that does not require me to dip
into the well of creativity. I meet writers and interview them.
Not the kind of writers that you or I would read but purveyors
of entertainment for the masses. I provide writing and publishing tips for my readers – none of whom, it goes without
saying, are professional writers. I deal in a harmless dream
world.'

'Is it really that harmless?'

'That's not my problem. the *Professional Writer*, with its
interviews, its plot and characterization tips, its breathless
reports of deals and alliances in the sunny, charmed world of
authorhood exists to feed the fantasies of the great and ever-
growing army of would-be – that is, won't-be – writers, the
Not Yet Published.'

Peter laughed, and there was something arrogant and
collusive about him now.

'We shouldn't mock the Not Yet Published,' I said. 'They
are all around us. Taxi drivers, TV presenters, secretaries,
lawyers, comedians, accountants, computer programmers,
receptionists, bellhops, politicians, even journalists. The
book that they will one day write may differ in seriousness
and content but they all share the dream. One day, one day,
the words will flow.'

'Poor bastards.'

* 'A sure-fire winner for the reluctant reader.' *School Librarian.*

39

'In the meantime, the *Professional Writer* provides the monthly illusion that they are serving some secret, non-executive apprenticeship, they are breathing in the writerly air. The success of those knights of the First XI will scatter gold-dust on their dreams.'

Peter Gibson was looking at me with more interest now. 'And that pays enough to keep you going?'

'Yes.' I elected not to mention that I had recently completed the annual humiliation of filling out a tax form. In addition to the £12,500 paid by the Institute and a little over £4,000 from my magazine work, the few pence accruing from royalties was only slightly in excess of appearance fees and readings. 'My wife works.'

'That must help.'

'It does, yes.' I sensed that it was time to change the subject. 'Funnily enough there's a party tomorrow night. A reading of new authors in a pub in west London. Maybe you'd like to keep me company.'

'You're not trying to corrupt me.'

I laughed. 'Not at all. I'm showing you the way of the world. You can make up your own mind.'

And, to my surprise, he accepted the invitation.

Exercise

All serious writers need to 'play themselves in' with what is technically known as writing workouts, a period of approximately forty-five minutes in which words are committed to paper without hesitation, head-scratching, throat-clearing, introspection or indeed thought of any kind.

Sometimes the result is occasionally no more than a higher form of gibberish – often a confession or outburst of domestically-directed anger too intimate for the public gaze – but quite often a paragraph of such natural grace and unforced clarity bursts forth, a gift of encouragement from the Muse, that you will be able to incorporate it later into a work in progress. Several of the more striking passages in this work, for instance, have emerged during these free-association sessions.

Put aside a notebook for your writing workouts. Relax and stretch the sinews of your talent with no thought for the race ahead. If your daily exercise has quality, that is simply a bonus; it is the activity, not the result, that is important.

7

Three days a week, Miguela, a timid Venezualan with no recognizable English would keep the dream house clean, avoiding Doug's room and my own eyrie as if they were no-go areas run by bandits in an otherwise orderly country. On Wednesdays the garden was tended by Ned, a stooped, defeated former lawyer who, after some horrific mid-life freak-out, now lived a tranquil, and probably tranquillized, life as a handyman. Occasionally, I would hear my wife communicating in schoolgirl Spanish with Miguela or in New-Age gobbledegook with Ned but neither servant seemed to acknowledge my role in the household: when, blearily patrolling the house during a creative break, I encountered one of them, I would be granted no more than a cursory simper or a dazed nod. It was as if I were the visitor, they were part of a private security force keeping Marigold's fiefdom in order.

I was doing a lot of patrolling these days. My wife was having an affair. I felt more marginal than ever. On those rare occasions when, apart from Doug in his pulsating lair, the house was empty, I would attempt to confirm my suspicions, delving in the backs of underwear drawers for notes or cards, checking the contents of waste-paper baskets for a tell-tale hotel receipt, but the flawlessly designed police state that was our house admitted no sign of moral untidiness. The key evidence, of course, would be contained in Marigold's diary or in itemized telephone bills or in our various bank statements but all such documents she kept at her office. At times like this, I regretted my decision (taken shortly after Martin had revealed in an interview that he was physically unable to open a brown envelope) to cede to my wife control of all financial matters concerning house, family and civilian life.

My wife was having an affair. But the search for proof was not only pointless; it was humiliating. It scoured the soul. Soon, I elected to accept her ever more frequent absences, to abjure the husband's natural right to ask snippy, resentful questions, catch the sinner in a lie, play the age-old guilt game. Writers should not have to endure such things. I took to mooning about the house like one whose hurt was beyond words.

But there was no escaping the fact. My wife was having an affair. The evidence was there before me. She kept adultery time, becoming unavailable during weekday afternoons, attending mysterious meetings beyond the reach of telephones in the early evenings, a routine which suggested that her lover was as married as she was – more, probably. For some reason, I imagined him as being slightly younger than her, one of those smooth, well-maintained designer types who work out and wear expensive after-shave lotion. I imagined them lying in bed, after sex, in some hotel or flat across London. He would talk about his young children. She would refer to the grumpy, scuffed writer she had left at home. A mood, somewhere between regret and self-congratulation, would hang in the air over their naked bodies. It was so sad, this life of theirs (hands would roam, bodies would stir), yet they would have this moment, they would have each other.

My wife was having an affair. When she was with me, she seemed happier, more at ease with herself. She cooked meals and hummed as she went about the domestic chores which she had once loathed. Sometimes an insulting, knowing smile would play upon her lips. She would indulge me, ask about my work, feigning interest in the erotic habits of Marcel Proust or the number of great writers who had married prostitutes or whatever arcane statistic I had discovered that day for *The Book of Literary Lists*. Physically she seemed changed, energized. Even her hair had taken on a new life, losing its pre-menopausal dryness and acquiring a heartbreaking natural bounce and sheen which, in my agony, I assumed was the result of some intimate organic process – a regular infusion of health-giving liquid, supplied by her lover, a general gingering up of the hormones.

My wife was having an affair. She was getting it. She was getting it regular.

Not that we were able to discuss any of this. For some time, we had, like many couples locked together in a long-term relationship, lived in a state of armed neutrality. The smallest hand-grenade from me could so easily provoke an exaggerated nuclear response. Territories left ignored for years might be overrun, frontiers could be shifted. Lethal weapons of marital destruction might be deployed. Once that first unprovoked act of aggression had taken place, there was no knowing where it would all end. Marigold had the weaponry. She had the fire-power to destroy me.

Some seven or eight years after we had married, between those two great landmarks, the publication of *Forever Young* and the birth of my son, I had an affair with a junior publicist at my publishers. Since she is now a senior marketing executive, married with a string of children, I shall call her 'Sarah'. It was at the time when I was the young novelist of the moment, invited around the country. Sarah was my minder, charged with arranging my routine, buying my train tickets, booking me in to hotels, ensuring that the many and various foul-ups which can occur on an author tour were kept to a minimum. Thrown together, travelling the country, book celebrity and the attractive younger woman in nurturing, wifely role: no doubt it happens all the time.

My only surprise and disappointment was that Sarah held out until the Excelsior, Lincoln, by which time I was in a state of near combustion – the combination of interviews, public attention and the caring, almost ever-present attentions of my publicist having (any author will confirm this) a powerful eroticizing effect. Even if Sarah had been a dumpy, doe-eyed little nobody, I would have wanted her; the fact that she was slim, with showy long blonde hair, that she had read all the right books and made no secret of her independence made her irresistible. Every night our dinner-time conversations were less to do with the world of books and more with our private lives: my marital frustrations (cue the clouded, distant, tragic look of the misunderstood male artist), her restless search for a man worthy of her. Soon there were late-night drinks, silences heavy with the great unasked question, a certain amount of lengthy leave-taking outside hotel bedroom doors. Until the Excelsior, Lincoln.

Poor innocent fool that I was, I believed my nights 'on the road' with Sarah had some sort of significance. I took her excessive competence in bed – almost nurse-like in its brisk, open efficiency – as a reflection of her feelings for me. The marked diminution in her daily attention to my authorly needs (insisting that I carry my own train tickets and the like) I read as a mark of the new relaxed intimacy that had developed between us. Too late I understood the nature of the romantic search to which she had so plaintively referred in our pre-coital candlelit moments, naïvely misreading the various hints she left me.

One morning, we were lying in bed together, enjoying a few quiet moments before setting off for a mid-morning local radio interview. She was reading the proof of a new novelist she would be promoting later in the year, while I caught up with Martin's ambition novel. I remarked, with casual joviality, that the book was crucially misnamed that a more accurate title would be *Failure*. 'You should have seen the first draft,' Sarah casually remarked, without looking up.

'You read an earlier draft?'

'Yup.'

'What – the editor showed you?'

She smiled significantly.

'*Martin* showed you?' I may have allowed the incredulity in my voice to show. 'I mean, I didn't even know you knew Martin.'

'Oh, I know him.' She glanced up briefly. 'In fact, we had a bit of a thing for a while.'

'A thing? You had a thing for Martin?'

'A thing *with* Martin. I was sure I had mentioned that.'

'No. I think I would have remembered.'

It was at a point in my career when I was still interested in the work of the small man, before his achievements, his precious *success*, had begun to irritate me. We were part of the same élite, covering the same general territory. In spite of his apparent arrogance and coolness, I felt that we were attuned to one another, writer to writer. I am man enough to admit that, at that particular moment in my career, I found a certain piquancy in sharing a bed with a woman who had once shared a bed with Martin.

In a spirit of good humour, I asked Sarah whether her former lover's erotic habits were like his prose – the hectic, self-absorbed preening, the stuttering, tough-guy swagger, the effortful cleverness that went round and round in circles before finally disappearing up itself. My curiosity may have seemed inappropriately eager because at this point Sarah laid down her book, and with much swishing of the famous mane, walked across the room (she must have been about three inches taller than Martin, incidentally), put on her silk dressing-gown and sat down on a chair on the far side of the room, looking somewhat affronted.

'Let me get this straight. Are you seriously asking me what Martin Amis was like in bed?'

'Of course not, don't be disgusting. But as a writer, I – Well, come to think of it, yes, I am.'

'Have you any idea how creepy that is?'

'As a *writer* –' I spoke with cool authority, hoping vainly to remind her that, even in these moments of relative intimacy, I was the author, she was the facilitator of interviews. 'As a writer, I happen to take an interest in human behaviour. What would be prurience for ordinary people is the bread and butter of my artistic existence. There is, actually, a direct connection between male desire and the act of creation – what

45

William Gass once described as "the blood-congested genital drive which energizes every great style".'

Sarah sat in her chair, tucking her legs up under her as if to deny me even the sight of a bare ankle. 'In my experience, the blood-congested genital drive of writers is remarkably similar to that of any other man.'

'In your experience? Since when were you the big expert on the writing life?'

'We'll be late for the interview.' She stood up and walked briskly to the en suite bathroom, closing the door behind her.

There were two more days of my tour, one more night, during which we made love in a perfunctory fashion that was almost marital. Sarah resisted my suggestion that I should spend a night at her flat in Fulham before I returned home.

Years later, at this painful moment when Marigold seemed to have joined the adultery merry-go-round, I suppose I can admit that I had been hoping for an arrangement with Sarah – nothing long-term or involving emotional commitment, but a mutually advantageous liaison. I was successful, she was pretty, we were both moving in the same world. Lunches, I thought. The occasional afternoon in a flat which I imagined as small, tidy, book-lined with crisp clean sheets on the bed, family photographs on the mantelpiece, a battered teddy-bear on a corner seat. But, after our return, she became evasive, failed to return my calls, avoided accompanying me on the few signings and talks that still remained for me, sending a plump, owlish assistant in her place. When, finally, I cornered her at a literary gathering and muttered something sensitively ambiguous about our unfinished business, she smiled coldly.

'Darling, it was nice, our thing. But it was just one of those . . . adventures that happen.'

'*Adventures*?'

'Look, to tell the truth, I've become a bit involved, OK? It was all great fun but . . . let's just leave it, shall we?' She squeezed my arm and walked away through a throng of guests.

Today, I can tell them a mile off, the Sarahs *de nos jours* –

the looks, the sparkling, ambitious eyes that fasten on their prey, the brittle, apparently brilliant conversation propelled by casual reference to the books, the films, the people of the moment. Theirs is a trainspotting approach to seduction: motivated by nothing as crude as snobbery or social climbing, they are excited by success and by writing. They sense that proximity, (extreme proximity) to a man who, at that moment, is culturally fashionable will do them good. Somehow, during those nights when they are together (always more than a crude and vulgar one-night stand but invariably less than a month), the distinction of their lover will rub off on them. Together, they will meet other revered literary figures, their liaison flattering each of them in different but entirely satisfactory ways. He will gain credibility and the sense that he is behaving badly in the time-honoured manner of authors. She will gather opinion, phrases, anecdotes, contacts that will serve her well, both socially and professionally, long after the affair has run its course.

A bit of a thing for a while. Sarah's description for whatever acts of sleaziness had once briefly occurred between her and Martin was characteristic: not exactly name-dropping but a casual establishment of erotic credentials. Now I can see that, for those few days, my promise and reputation were being confirmed – Sarah's instinct in matters of literary fashion was sharp enough to be almost a defining act of credibility. If she slept with you, your career was in good shape. One day, in bed or at dinner with someone else, your name might come up in conversation. Didn't you know? (The tone would be neither boastful nor particularly tender.) We had a bit of a thing for a while.

All would have been fine were it not for my inclusion, two years after our little adventure, on the list of the Best of Young British Novelists, beside the names of Martin and other ageing literary youngsters. That momentary revival in my public visibility prompted my former paramour to mention my name, in the context of the thing we once had, rather too often. The adultery grapevine, a highly effective communication network among young professional women, ensured that Marigold, by then a successful young designer, heard of the affair.

There have been others since then, more serious relationships in which love (a dirty word in adultery circles) was even mentioned, but Sarah has come to represent something lost in our marriage. A bond which neither of Marigold nor I knew existed snapped, never to be repaired. From then on, we lived in a world of half-truths and compromise. This was the common state of the long-term married, I had once believed. It was the normal, controlled misbehaviour of contemporary man and woman. I was wrong. Eventually it was no longer background; it permeated everything. We had lost something precious. I had thrown it away.

After Sarah, infidelity became a habit – a sort of escape, a way of reassuring myself that I was not yet finished. And because my marriage had survived that first post-affair hurricane, I came to believe that it would survive others; maybe, in some admittedly cynical and superficial way, minor and regular acts of betrayal helped to keep it alive.

What I thought was an escape from unhappiness turned out to be an essential part of it. All affairs, I discovered, are marked from their first night with a sense of the disappointment that lies ahead, like a black cross on a condemned tree. The one thing which propels normal, legitimate love is denied them: hope. However good and true and different it may be, it will eventually be just another affair. Only the manner and timing of its end are uncertain. So each new adventure provided its own version of essentially the same story: the fake excitement of secrecy, the sense of putting one over the rest of the world, of stealing love and pleasure out of the normal framework of time and situation. But the unhappiness was there, from the first glance. From the passing flights of fancy, like my brief fling with Anna Matthew of Mind and Body, to the semi-serious two-year affair with the wife of a BBC producer that, a year or so after its demise, was to provide rich comic material for my campus novel *Adultery in Hampstead*. Wives, authors, publicists, arts journalists, really quite a considerable number of my students, even some girls who had nothing whatsoever to do with writing: however cool and contemporary the arrangement, however sincere the vows of non-involvement, the choice was a limited one: cynical-unhappy, with its casual, well-organized exchange of sexual release, or romantic-unhappy, a fairy-story from the Land of If-Only in which no one ever lived happily ever after.

What were they for? All those words and promises, those dinners in deserted Italian restaurants which only survive as regular safe houses for the adultery community, those glasses of wine beside the bed, those glances at bedside alarm clocks, that careful washing away of traces in endless bathrooms, that awkward dressing in the middle of the night, those farewells – sad, loving, matter-of-fact, angry, some to a figure in a dressing-gown on a doorstep, some to a bed, some to a back – those endless arrangements and dates and times and furtive calls. What was the point of them all?

They were not for sex, that was for sure. The heat that had existed between Marigold and me was never discovered with her substitutes and understudies. Although my lovers were usually in their twenties or early thirties, it was not their youth that I craved. As it happens, I have always preferred the older body – the warm paperiness of the skin, the various smiles and swells of the flesh which give it character. Frequently, as an affair wore on, I found myself fantasizing about my wife in order to stoke up enthusiasm for my lover, which I dare say is unusual. No, the problem, had more to do with experience. Women of my age, I discovered after a couple of unhappy experiments, knew too much. They had heard all the lines. Cynicism was in their soul. There was something in their laughter – fruity and amused – which I found off-putting. For them, it was all some sort of game, and where was the fun in that?

Looking back now, I think that adultery was a form of fiction. With every new affair (the term's inadequate, being both too romantic and too seedy, but it's truer than 'relationship'), a new narrative developed, a new voice, a new hero. That was perhaps the excitement. Meeting, sex, and then, suddenly, somewhere around chapter two or three, it was just as they say in the best writing circles – *the characters took over*. They started to go their own way, individual yet symbiotic, mysteriously and subtly different every time.

The plot thickened, then thinned, then faded away all together. My lovers usually made the first move for the door; I preferred it like that and made it happen in the various cruel ways that men learn early in their lives. Being abandoned was like finally giving up on a novel that had initially been thrilling but had eventually become torture to write: the agony was soon swept aside by a vast surge of relief. I had reclaimed my life, my future.

This is a creative primer, not the memoirs of an adulterer. The fact is that while each of the six (seven if you include a brief, intense week spent with the wife of a Welsh opera singer at a writers' conference in Derbyshire) prolonged romantic events that have occurred during my marriage contained different emotional and erotic dynamics, none of them individually has any bearing on this story. I was unfaithful, severally and serially, from 1984 onwards. I never stopped loving my wife. Marigold and I reached a stage when the adulterer's symphony – the click of a telephone as, somewhere in the house, the extension is being put down, the casual tearing of incriminating notes, the easy, unchallenged excuses, the single late-night ring – provided an easy-listening backing track of normality to our marriage.

Now I found myself wondering whether Marigold had started playing the same game out of retaliation or loneliness or frustration. It was difficult to imagine her as a cheat. Infidelity was too childish for her, too trivial and selfish. It occurred to me that, at the very moment when I was the one taking control of my life, expressing my needs in a controlled and orderly fashion with regular, furtive trips to the Agency, she was regressing, or maybe enacting some tawdry act of revenge for those past years of hurt. 'See?' She was saying. 'See how it feels?'

I did see, and it hurt. I felt sorry for us both, for the young couple we had once been. Over the years, we had let something vital slip through our fingers, something which part of us would long for and regret losing, whatever happened, for the rest of our lives.

My wife was having an affair. One day I noticed that, on one of the low glass tables, a small silver-framed photograph had made a reappearance after years in some bottom drawer. Marigold and me, in front of our old Saab, leaving our wedding reception for the airport. I seem to be drunk – even when I'm not drunk, I seem to be drunk in photographs – and she's waving a happy, short-arm, little-girl wave. We look like children, so full of hope, so buoyed up by optimism and plans and the good wishes of the world.

Was my wife now trying to tell me something? Was it an absurd thought that her fling was no more than a way to catch my attention, to shock our stale and flagging marriage back into some kind of life? Or was it simply that small domestic framed photographs, replete with loss and incipient tragedy, were absolutely the thing this season among *feng shui* designers? It seemed unwise to ask.

The Writer Speaks of . . . Success

'Success improves the character of a man, it does not always improve the character of an author.'

W. Somerset Maugham

'It's no use. I find it impossible to work with security staring me in the face.'

Sherwood Anderson

'A writer must refuse to allow himself to be transformed into an institution.'

Jean-Paul Sartre

'The deepest desire of any writer is anonymity, not to be pointed out in the street.'

Ted Hughes

'Every success is an eventual failure.'

Graham Greene

'It is very easy to fall off the tightrope that writers walk; no one is there to catch you. That shame and secrecy about failure is worse than the thing itself.'

Maggie Gee

8

So, for a while, we ran with the literary crowd. Two or three times a week, Peter Gibson and I would go out on the town to readings, launches, *vernissages*, debates – to whatever excuse for a party was being held that particular night. We hung out in clubs and bookshops and restaurants and galleries and the smoky upstairs rooms of pubs. We drank the free drinks, grazed upon the small, damp items of food, listened to the low-grade gossip, watched the process of chat and contact without which no book of significance can be published.

To be sure, this was not the world of the big-timers. We were among the B-list literati – the sad-sack reviewers whose eyes betrayed a lifetime of disappointment, the books page totties, the twitching agents and book publishers forever combing the scene for the new, the young, the seducible, the corruptible. As we went, I provided Peter with a running guide to the topography of this ill-appointed landscape. Here was the alcoholic editor still living off a reputation gained two decades ago. There was the randily persistent poet touting his ageing charms and faded literary reputation about the room in search of his conquest for the night. Here was the career critic as careful with his friendships as with the phrases invariably included in his reviews to ensure that all-important appearance of his name on the back of the paperback. There was the blowsy literary agent whose availability over the years had provided her with a peerless network of influential men who had once spent the night with her.

These occasions were essentially about barter, I explained to Peter as we stood on the stairs of one of London's swankier bookshops gazing down at the literary herd gathered for an annual party. To survive and flourish, you had to bring to the party some kind of currency: new work, youth, contacts, gossip about which author was discontented with which agent, who had delivered which hot new literary property.

My student smiled in a tolerant, almost regal way. Unlike the female students I had introduced to the book world in the past (functions such as this being as good a way as any of shifting a relationship from the educational to the social and eventually to the sexual), Peter appeared to have no interest in mixing with the influential or the semi-famous, but stood back and observed, like one who knew that soon enough the throng would be making its way to him. Even his inappropriate garb, faded, denim and torn, imbued him with a certain careless dignity.

'And what is your barter?' he asked me.

I considered for a moment. 'My next book. A knowledge of the scene. Maybe an interview in *Professional Writer.*' I smiled significantly. 'The inside track on a promising new talent.'

Ignoring my last remark, Peter murmured, 'None of them seem much interested in the books that are all around them.'

'It's not about books, this world. It's about introductions, favours, positioning yourself for the right product, the right job. Very few of the conversations down there will be about words on the page. Books are merely the product, the focus of a deal.'

'They don't read?'

'They all read the same books of the moment. They want to know the secret, to catch a hint from today's success of what will "work" tomorrow. Mention the name of an author who is out of fashion and you'll be regarded as deeply suspect. You reveal yourself as a real reader, a lurker in dusty libraries and second-hand bookshops, some sort of ghastly literary enthusiast.'

Peter was looking at me, that irritatingly knowing smile on his face. 'Yet here we are, playing the game. You seem completely at home.'

I sensed a coolness to him now, as if he had suddenly recognized that I had not brought him here out of teacherly generosity, but that he was part of yet another deal. It was true that, over the past few weeks, I had been gratified to see how, soon after I had offered him up, the sharks were circling, sniffing eagerly at his unsullied promise and his lanky beauty. I had smiled as they were rebuffed. He wanted to be the real writer, he had explained. He was not a journalist. They smelt talent, or rather they sensed a look, a personality, who might be promoted.

'At least at this party we're among fellow authors. It's not just what is known as "the trade".'

We watched the room for a while. It was one of the few parties during the autumn to which only the grandest or most reclusive of authors would decline an invitation. Guests circulated one another warily, assessing who was here, who had slipped from the invitation list, who was talking to whom, who sought them out for conversation, who avoided them or passed by with a glazed, desultory nod of acknowledgement. Sometimes, dancing attendance upon the more august luminaries, you might see a young journalist or editor or even a favoured critic, enacting the traditional symbiotic relationship of age and beauty, youth and celebrity, ambition and experience. Over the eager, gossipy throng, there seemed to hang the polite, edgy, anxious question with which authors all over the world greet one another. *What are you working on?*

At the centre of the room, the veteran novelist Francis Speight, a beaky, grey-haired man, was holding forth to a small, respectful entourage. Most of us who had read his work knew that Speight was nowhere near the top order of writers but, over the past three decades or so, the sheer, bullying volume of his output, the persistence with which he appeared at the right conferences, on the right TV discussion programmes, had established him as a sort of literary eminence. Now, as he talked and talked, he seemed to gaze over the heads of his listeners with a rapt and distant look as if seeing a well-deserved knighthood approaching him across the room.

'Observing the fair field of folk?'

I turned to see, leaning against the banister in the manner of a Hollywood star making her entrance, the assiduously ambitious literary journalist Tony Watson. He smiled briefly at me and then gazed at Peter with a degree of interest that would have seemed erotic to the few people in this room who did not know that he was married, with a mistress in the BBC and that this queeny air was merely one of his many affectations. 'Yak yak yak.' He pouted in the direction of Speight. 'If they ever give grants to encourage novelists to stop writing, Francis will get my vote.' He extended a hand downwards. 'Tony Watson.'

After I had introduced him to Peter, Watson, without any obvious encouragement, began talking languidly about himself.

Now in his early forties, with the fleshy, pampered look of a man who has not broken out of a stroll since he left school, Tony Watson had first made his reputation as something of a young Turk, gleefully dismantling work by novelists whose reputations had outlived their talent. Then in his midtwenties, he had sensed that a new generation of readers was tired of the old critical proprieties, of the widely accepted rule that critics should politely avert their gaze from the declining powers of respected older writers. A new brutality was in the air, a lust for blood. Tony Watson became a Lord High Executioner of the new establishment, a sneering, clever boy who, while trashing the work of others, never failed to point up his own precocious learning and vocabulary and knowledge, not only of what he called 'the canon' but of other, newly fashionable traditions from South America or Eastern Europe. Watson tore through reputations, bringing to his judgements a tough-guy swagger, a feline contempt, the compulsively fascinating spectacle of a young prodigy giving his distinguished elders a thorough duffing up from which many of their careers would never quite recover. The almost palpable distaste for civilized values and sagging flesh, now the norm in certain quarters, was then startlingly new. To a world used to the 'underdog's snarl' that Gilbert Pinfold had once identified in literary journalists, this leering sense of his own intrinsic superiority was shockingly entertaining. How *dare* he? they asked at first. The *nerve* of this little pipsqueak. But soon, as he became more powerful, they watched him with fear and anticipation. Whom would he destroy next?

His reputation and influence grew. A collection of essays was published, followed by a rather good, if surprisingly sentimental, account of his life-were-ever-so-'ard childhood which gave the town of Walsall a brief, surprising literary distinction. Then, unwisely, he introduced a new element into his magisterial *tours d'horizon*: during his regular reports on the state of contemporary British fiction which he had found to be, if not clinically dead, then in intensive care, he would confide his own creative problems, invoking the names of Ozick or Conrad, Gaddis or James. Could it be true? We longed for it to be true. At last, during the course of an essay on the decline of the political novel for the *London Review of Books*, he declared himself. Tony Watson was writing a novel.

We waited. A collection of criticism appeared, followed by a TV history of the English novel which saw Tony striding, windblown, across the Yorkshire moors, loitering camply in the East End of London and, less successfully, sporting a helmet with a lamp down a Nottinghamshire mine. He was as confident as ever, yet that generalized, infuriated disappointment which had once been his trademark seemed somehow to have abated. When reviewing new novels, he no longer reacted to their shortcomings as if they were insults specifically and personally directed at him. His references to the work of established novelists sometimes revealed a note of genuine, if haughty, respect that suggested that his secret agonies as a novelist had blunted the edge of his rage. A certain gravitas, plump, self-important and prematurely middle-aged, took hold of his prose. He married a plain but well-regarded Oxford medievalist. Children were produced, followed by the inevitable features and diary columns extolling the joys and travails of the writer-parent. Today Tony, a reviewer for the *Observer* and, in his more essayistic moments, for the *New York Review of Books*, had arrived at the position for which he had clearly always been destined, at the very heart of the literary establishment for which he had, fifteen busy years ago, professed such contempt.

I had not been attending to Watson's halting conversation with my student until I heard the great critic mention the title of my first novel. 'Mm?' I shook my head briefly. 'Sorry, I was mid-scene.'

Tony linked an arm through mine as if we were literary compadres. 'I was just saying to Peter that what the scene needs these days is the sort of wit and intelligence that one found in a certain *Forever Young*.'

'The world has moved on.'

'There's always a place for laughter.' He turned back to Peter. 'Such a precious gift, that of a comic novelist. When I reviewed Gregory's novel for the *New Statesman*, I mentioned Firbank, Leacock and Peter de Vries. Some people thought I was –' He lifted his hands in a faggoty two-fingered clawing motion '– "damning with faint praise" but I'm of the school that there's nothing quite so serious as humour. Look at Martin. Suddenly he has taken to describing himself as a comic novelist – although, frankly, one has never exactly turned to Monsieur Amis for a belly-laugh.'

'Tony also described me as belonging to the hopeless English male tradition. All fingers and thumbs and premature ejaculation. "Keays offers us the unsavoury face of the clubbable Englishman, who disguises a fear of engagement, of passion, of women, of life under a cloak of facetiousness.'"

Tony Watson laughed gaily. 'I meant your character, not you, dear boy,' he said. 'And I never expected you to learn it off by heart.'

'What are you working on these days, Tony?'

'Oh, nothing much.' Watson glanced over my left shoulder to ensure that no one of more use to him than me was in social range. 'FatherLand's shaping up well.'

'Surely that title has been used for a novel.'

Watson grimaced with mock-irritation. 'It's not a novel, silly. It's an anthology. Some rather remarkable new writing about fatherhood, as it happens.'

It was my turn to smile. This was better than I had expected. Yet another celebration of drooling dads, blubbing over childbirth, gruffly coming to terms with their new domesticated status as they changed nappies, using some mewling infant as a means to investigate, with tearful honesty, their own sensitivity. 'What a very original idea,' I said, as seriously as I could manage.

'Got any sprogs yourself?' he asked.

'Just the one. A teenager.'

Watson, who had been studying a group of fellow guests across the room, betrayed a flicker of interest. 'We haven't done the teenage thing. Most of my gang are rather too young. And I started a little late.'

'I'm not really a domestic writer. I favour the large canvas these days.'

Watson glanced at Peter and, for the briefest instance, I thought that he was about to deploy the stiletto with some pointless reference to my children's work *The Lonely Giant* which I had unwisely discussed with him during the heady moments of completion, but he merely said, 'We're not talking domestic. We're exploring the new memoirism. It would need to be toe-curlingly frank.'

It occurred to me that a spot of media visibility might not do my career too much harm at this point. My bracingly clear-eyed perspective on family matters would doubtless shine beside the lachrymose self-adoration of my fellow contributors. There was the small question of whether Doug would like his young life served up, however elegantly and wittily, in memoirist mode but then I realized, with a certain relief, that to imagine him reading anything, let alone a book of new writing about fatherhood, was absurd. 'Sounds possible,' I said. 'How much?'

'Five hundred pounds. And fifty for the kid.'

'The kid?'

'Yeah, that's the other thing. We're getting a sort of *vérité*-ish child's eye view at the end of each piece – the kid bites back kind of thing. So your boy would be interviewed about you. We'd do a little 150-word tailpiece.'

'Ah.'

Watson must have noticed some sort of change of expression on my face because he muttered to Peter, '*So* difficult these writers.'

'No. It just sounds a tad exploitative,' I said carefully. 'I've always been careful not to use my family for professional purposes. You'll remember what David Lodge once said about the wonderful material you can't write about without hurting somebody –'

A faintly irritating smirk had settled on Watson's face. He turned to Peter and muttered with camp confidentiality, 'I've always thought that Gregory was doing more social and literary good these days than the rest of us put together. Teaching would-be scribblers and compiling books about writers' tricks and habits that save the rest of us having to read all those endless biographies that appear on the market.'

I had heard enough. 'So how's the old novel coming on?' I asked amiably. 'We're dying to read that, after all those reports from the front line.'

Watson looked away with a sort of twitch of pain. 'I've temporarily put it aside. Lot of essays. Had to earn a living. I think about it every day.'

'They say words on the page are the thing,' I said, turning the knife. 'Are you still stuck in Chapter Three?'

Watson seemed to have spotted an acquaintance in the room below us. With an exaggerated wave and a muttered 'Excuse me', he moved purposefully down the stairs. Ahead of him, as if by magic, a way cleared through the partygoers, revealing that he was walking, too briskly to change direction, towards nothing more welcoming than the fiction shelves. He reached them, stood, frozen in a moment of unavoidable social shame, facing away from the other guests like a child who had been told to stand in a corner. Slowly, he turned. At the end of that convenient path between guests, I smiled and raised my glass to him. Blushing, he plunged into the nearest group of partygoers.

'Poor Tony,' I said. 'He'll be trapped in Chapter Three until the end of his days.'

Peter Gibson sipped at his wine. 'Shame about *Father-Land*,' he said. 'I would have liked to read about your son.'

Top Five Fastest Novelists
1. Jack Kerouac wrote *The Subterraneans* in three days.
2. Georges Simenon allowed himself six days to write a Maigret novel.
3. Walter Scott finished two Waverley novels in three weeks.
4. Ernest Hemingway, D.H. Lawrence and Evelyn Waugh each completed a novel in six weeks.
5. Anthony Burgess wrote five novels in a year.

9

Doug was out. Doug was on the binge. The day after the bookshop party, I had been working on *Literary Lists* when, late in the morning, the telephone rang. Unusually, it was for my son. Even more unusually, the voice that asked for him was that of an adult – brisk, businesslike, on the move, the sort of voice that could be closing a drugs deal, selling a car or transferring stock options. I went downstairs, banged on his door. There was no reply. I pushed it open. A brief, stomach-heaving glance into the room revealed that Doug was not there. Taking my time, I returned to my office.

'He appears not to be at home.' I cranked up my accent to indicate a generalized disapproval. 'Can I say who –?'

'Nah. Chiz.' The oaf hung up.

I stared for a moment at a list on which I had been working revealing the surprising number of great writers whose parents had died during their childhood, but found myself unable to concentrate. I realized that, of late, the normal throb of life from Doug's room had been less evident. It had been several days since I had actually seen my son. I rang Marigold's number.

'Doug appears not to be at home.'

'Doug?' For a moment, she seemed to have forgotten her son.

'Someone rang for him but he's not here.'

'Oh sugar.' My wife sighed, as if a disappearing son reported by an inadequate spouse was all she needed on this busy morning.

'I wouldn't have bothered you, only the man on the telephone sounded a bit dodgy. Did you see him last night?'

'No, I was . . . caught up in a meeting. You?'

'Launch party.'

'Of course.'

There was a moment of brief, embarrassed silence. 'He probably met up with some friends,' I said eventually. 'You know, teenagers.'

'Teenagers are doing things – taking exams, getting part-time jobs, going round the world. The nearest thing Doug gets to action is going to the corner shop for a packet of cigarettes.' She sighed. 'I have something this evening which I just can't cancel. Can't you deal with this for a change?'

'He's our son, Marigold.'

There was another pause and I imagined her glancing at her Vogue diary, reprioritizing as we spoke. 'I'll try to get home early.'

'If it doesn't disrupt your plans.'

'What does that mean, exactly?'

'Just that I can manage if you're too busy.'

'If only you had talked to him,' she muttered, almost to herself, before hanging up.

I gazed at the notes about death and authorhood but somehow the fussy statistics recording real pain and loss made my own life seem dreary and pointless. Instead, I found myself thinking about Peter Gibson, his ambition, the clear-eyed way he saw the literary scene, the mysterious hold he exerted on those who met him. How much older was he than my own son? Three years, maybe four? Had he spent his adolescence locked away in a room? Had he been allergic to the outside world? Had his parents let him down? Had he too been sucked into a whirlpool of impotent domestic blame? I compared the way he focused upon his work, ignoring the very distractions of the youth culture which invariably snagged Doug, kept him locked away in his room, paralysed by computer games, sexual fantasy and music that seemed to have been recorded in a torture chamber.

My son was not exactly a recluse but he had, undeniably, during the eleven months since leaving school, developed a powerful attraction to staying within the four walls of his own small room. The first indication that he was withdrawing from conventional family life had been when he took to piling his plate with food at meal-times and withdrawing wordlessly to eat it upstairs. We had never been a family for solemn, communal eating – the everyday bonding over food which other families manage so effortlessly had always been beyond us – and, by the time we recognized that a pattern was developing, it was too late to change it. Weakly, with only the merest hint of adult sarcasm, we would ask him now and then whether he would be gracing us with his presence at dinner. His response was a silent, cold-eyed, neo-psychopathic stare which invited all sorts of interpretations, most of them negative, fearful and, above all, guilt-ridden.

These days he emerged only rarely, with rat-like scuttles to the fridge or the lavatory which were timed with precision for moments when neither parent was likely to be around. At dead of night, we could sometimes hear his door open, the clink of plates being left on the floor, a sloppy, bare-footed trudge to the laundry basket where he would occasionally leave congealing T-shirts or undergarments stiff with dirt. Only Donovan, to whose scratches at the carpet outside his door Doug was preternaturally alert, was allowed regular access to his tiny, scummy world.

We had enrolled him at a ruinously expensive cramming establishment but, after he had failed to appear for any lessons during the final month of term, we had shelved any thoughts of his acquiring further academic qualifications. Doug was sorting himself out, regrouping. It was, if not normal, the sort of thing which parents of teenagers became used to. In the early days of his decline, I used to enter his room to find him lying, blank-eyed on his bed. He told me that he was thinking, that he was all right, that the best thing his mum and dad could do was leave him alone. So we did.

Occasionally, Marigold and I would discuss whether such behaviour qualified as a genuine and serious breakdown, whether we should call in some kind of roving shrink, but these exchanges invariably degenerated into bickering over which of us was responsible (personally, behaviourally, genetically) for our son's behaviour. In the end, we had tried to put his way of life down to teenage blues, to a phase from which some time soon he would emerge, smiling sheepishly, Douglas once more.

At moments of rare openness between us, we would talk about the way he used to be, before the world in which he moved was reduced to a tiny room of noise, smell and wank mags, before even his name had become contracted. For the first three years of his life, the odd formality of Douglas – a favourite among the Camerons down the centuries and

63

distinguished in that thin-lipped, disapproving way which is the special province of the Scottish upper-middle-class – had suited him. A solemn, watchful baby, he had seemed to sense that his parents were successful people whose lives had been disrupted enough by the very fact of his birth, that they had time to make up, careers to pursue.

Even when Marigold weaned him onto the bottle rather too early in my view (claiming discomfort but I wasn't taken in; she has always been vain about her figure), Douglas was accommodating.

At the age of four or five, the hopeful years, Douglas became Dougie. Smiling Dougie. Running Dougie. Dougie, the very apple of his parents' eyes. Then, quite early, at eleven or twelve, the openness and optimism faded. The laughter died or, rather, grew conditional and guarded. His face became closed, watchful. His sweet and natural accent, neither posh nor proletarian, gave way to a lazy, street grunt. He told us that he wasn't Dougie any more, refused even to answer to the name. He was Doug. As in thug, or drug; as in glug-glug-glug.

He left school, enrolled at the crammer, then went into his decline. By that stage, the diminished, lethargic creature which we had brought into the world was hardly recognizable to us as Douglas, Dougie, or even Doug. It seemed only a matter of time before he became Dg, D-, or simply nothing at all – a blank where there had once been communication.

It occurred to me now that perhaps it was a good sign that he had spent the night out, that he had been on the binge. Maybe that's what you did at seventeen. One minute you were hanging out on street corners, chewing gum, skimming the curb with skateboards, communicating in monosyllables, returning later than promised, dirty, sweaty, wiping your nose with your forearm, swigging at a coke, in training to be a grown-up.

Then, quite suddenly, you understood: you were no longer part of this sad, suburban, little scene, with its kickabouts in the playground, its shandy-and-grope youngster-parties at the tennis-club, its mums with baby-seats in the back of their saloon cars, its worried, nagging fathers. You had rejected it; it had rejected you. A couple of years ago, you had been popular, a kid with a future, controllable, cute. You had an open smile. Adults talked to you. Then, almost overnight, you had become invisible, neither truly child nor truly adult. Words left you. The smile left you. Girls suddenly seemed to belong to a different universe – one of chat and friendship and laughter where only older boys had a place. You entered a twilight zone where no one, not even your parents – especially your parents – liked you, where no one, except the other guys, understood you. Your looks went. You became gawky, uncoordinated, your body looked like it was put together late on a Friday afternoon shift on the human being production line, when the raw materials of muscle, hair and decent skin were running short and you were thrown together just to get you out of the childhood factory before the weekend. You spent hours in front of the mirror trying to make sense of what was happening to you. Deserted by language, you developed a strange system of grunts, squawks and facial tics. Girls mocked you for this, parents raged at it; your secret language became more obscure. Purr, you'd say. Egg. Ractic. Odded. Grout.

Shit, man, where did you go from there? You went to the pub. You hung out with the lads. You got it down you. You chatted. Owi, then? Yeah, owi, chiz. You changed your style. No more baggies now. Certainly no more baseball caps turned the wrong way round. Something was beginning to happen.

Now, suddenly, people were aware of you. They paid attention but it was not your cuteness, your kiddiness, that drew their eyes to you. It was something much better. It was almost like fear. Soon you found that the world was on its guard against you and your new male danger. Policemen stopped you on the street. Shopkeepers watched your every move. Kids, adults, stepped aside as they saw you approaching. Curtains twitched when you stopped to chat with your mates ('Those boys are out there again, dear'). But the girls started to notice you, too. It was time to find your own world, a place where you could be yourself without a secret language, without the approval or disapproval of other generations. You go out. You don't go home. You binge. Maybe it was all natural.

Downstairs, the front door slammed. I closed my eyes, relieved. Talk to him. That's what I should do. Talk to him, caring yet authoritative, a father.

By the time I had reached the kitchen, Doug was at the sink, gulping back a full glass of water. I stood at the door for a moment. 'Well?'

He refilled the glass from the tap and drank it down. Chucking the glass in the sink, he walked to a sideboard, took out a chocolate biscuit, crammed it in his mouth, wiped his face with the back of his hand.

'And?' I tried again. 'Would it be too much to ask where you've been since yesterday – all night and all today?'

'Would it be *miew miew miew miew*?' My son's face contorted in a grimace, his head wobbling wildly as he imitated, with crazed exaggeration, my precise, concerned-parent tones.

Although I was angry enough to ignore the signs, it occurred to me that this behaviour was unusual for Doug. He had never been a slammer, a strider, a mocker; stealth and evasion were more his style. It was not that he was afraid of confrontation with his parents, more that he was wearily dismissive of them, of the entire lame adult world.

'Don't be rude,' I said. 'We were worried.'

'Oh yeah, right.' His voice was loud as if he was having to shout down some argument in his head. 'Worried, yeah, great, right. Thanks, Daddy.'

'Both of us were worried. Unfortunately, your mother had an urgent meeting.'

He exhaled, a noise of profound, knowing disgust. I noticed for the first time that his face was pale and gaunt, apart from a flash of red where someone or something had grazed his cheekbone, breaking the skin. A smut of dirt on his chin reminded me, with a faint stab of pain, of the child he had been not so long ago. There was something odd about his eyes; his pupils were dark and dilated as if he had been staring for too long into a bright light.

'There was a call for you this morning,' I said calmly.

'Big wow.'

'It was a man. He sounded –' I sensed from the way that Doug was staring at me that I was venturing into dangerous territory. 'Well, to tell the truth, he sounded a bit sinister.'

'To tell the *twoooth*.' Doug parodied my prissiness with another grimace, the muscles in his neck extruding with contempt. 'You mean, he didn't sound like a designer or a nice little writer.'

'Who was he, Doug?'

'Mind you own fuckin' business.' The shoulders hunched and he seemed to shiver and I knew, with the certainty of a parent, that he was afraid. He looked up suddenly and, seeing the concern on my face, recovered his anger. 'Just back the fuck off, right? Leave me alone.'

'Don't shout at me.'

'Shout?' he shouted. 'What you talking, what you fucking talking about, do what, shout?'

'Calm down. Douglas.'

'Want to go to my room, owi.' There was a crack in the voice, as if tears were not far away.

'In a moment. You owe me an explanation about what's going on.'

'Owe? You what? What exactly do I owe you for, *Daddy*?'

I laughed uneasily.

'No, go on then,' he said. 'Tell me what I fuckin' owe you for?'

'Your education, your food.' I faltered. Put like that, it didn't seem much. How to sum up the years of worry, of occasional pride and more frequent disappointment, the general sense of displacement and loss of equilibrium that, effortlessly, guiltlessly, he had introduced into our lives from the moment he was born until now? 'General life,' I said feebly.

'Yeah, right, thanks for nothing. Life. Just what I fuckin' needed. Life. Like I really asked to be born, didn't I? You think you're God or something –'

'We try to help you.'

'Then get out of my fuckin' face.' His dark, staring eyes filled with tears. 'Leave me alone. You don't own me. You don't understand anything about me. All you care about is your lame careers. I leave you alone, you leave me alone, right.'

I hesitated, lost for words.

'Here comes the big daddy sigh,' he sneered. 'Big tragic fuckin' daddy sigh. Let's all feel sorry for him and his sad little loser life.'

Rage welled up inside me. For years, I had been able to dismiss these moments of childish contempt as nothing more than a tantrum. But the snotty nose, the tiny red, enraged face, the screams of rage, the flailing little hands and hopeless kicking feet had gone. Now he had words – not many words, it was true, but enough words to hurt. So why should I hold back? I was a parent, not some kind of punchbag for a spoilt adolescent. He was old enough to understand that I hurt, too. I had feelings. Or at least, if he didn't understand, he should be made to. It was part of growing up, part of the education for which I was responsible.

I stepped forward, grabbed my son by the chest of his T-shirt, pulled him towards me so that, for a second or two his dark, unfocused eyes were inches from mine, then pushed him back, my fist striking his bony chest. He sprawled on the kitchen floor where he lay, looking up at me, openly afraid. We stared at each other idiotically for several long seconds before Doug's customary sullen expression returned. 'What you going to do now, Daddy? Give me a good kicking? Would that make you feel better?'

'I'm not a loser.' Suddenly I was aware that I had behaved precisely as my son had hoped, that he, lying there on the kitchen floor, was the victor of this round. 'I'm –' Somehow the word 'sorry' froze in my throat. 'I'm really disappointed by the way you've behaved.'

He stood up, rubbed his chest. 'You tore my fuckin' T-shirt,' he said. Then, muttering 'Thanks for the chat, Dad,' he brushed past me and made his way, with long, angry strides, back to his bedroom.

I waited for the beat, the sound of Doug defiantly in residence, but there was just silence.

Let's all feel sorry for Daddy. At that moment, as I returned to my study, pausing briefly outside Doug's door, I'll admit that I was overcome by an uncharacteristic spasm of self-pity. This, then, was where being a parent led – screams in the kitchen, a punch to the scrawny chest of your grown child, blazing eyes, hurt, hatred. An end to the illusion that parenthood, like neighbourhood or brotherhood, involved some sense of belonging, of unity. Maybe it was a phase; perhaps all fathers and sons reach a moment in their lives when they square up to one another.

At my desk, I stared at the empty screen. What did we expect, we wrinklies, we groans? A prize? An end-of-term certificate for being good mummies and daddies? At this point, when sweetness faded, when the going got rough, it suited us to think of ourselves as social heroes, nurturing the next generation, from nappies to now, bringing them through their moments of ill health and fear and insecurity and loneliness, coaxing them into bed for half their young lives and out of bed for the rest, preparing the next generation but, of course, this great assumed nobility was a lie. Doug was right. We were in it for ourselves. A chapter in *The Book of Literary Lists*, unavoidably entitled 'The Pramless Hall', assembled modern male heterosexual novelists who had not only declined to play the fatherhood game but who actively disliked the company of children. Naipaul, Larkin, Greene, Roth, Richard Ford: the list went on and on. It worried me. Cyril Connolly's argument that 'children dissipate the longing for immortality which is the compensation of the childless writer's work' seemed altogether too facile, one kind of fertility neatly precluding another. Ford was nearer the mark when he owned up that it was the responsibility, the lack of freedom, which had kept him childless. He went further: 'I don't like kids much. I always saw children as little hobbles around my ankle.' Little hobbles! That was more like it. So he deals with teen crisis in neat, controllable fiction form with the central relationship between Frank Bascombe and his son in *Independence Day,* as tortured and unconvincing as that between the Swede and his rebellious daughter in *American Pastoral.* Compare these recalcitrant, rebellious teenagers with the real thing and you begin to see the attraction of the work over the life. The fictional versions argue – they discuss, they rage with articulacy. What would Roth or Ford do with Doug and his squeaks and grunts and 'owi then's'? No wonder they run from the churning, unexpressed agony of real parenthood into fiction. 'Paternity would confine me within those ordinary ways of living,' said Flaubert.

Yeah, right, Gus. Like we really believe that.

The Relative Position of Writers in the 'Risk Factor Listing' of the Association of Motor Insurers

1. Accountants, loss adjusters, doctors, solicitors, civil servants. Computer programmers.
2. Business people not obliged to travel for their work. Manual workers (skilled). Nurses, shop workers, teachers.
3. Business people obliged to travel for their work. Housewives. Night-shift workers. MPs. Members of the police. Professional sportsmen and women.
4. TV or film actors. TV presenters, newscasters and weather operatives. Journalists. Taxi-drivers. Advertisers and those working in a general media capacity. Academics.
5. Comedians. Pop stars and anyone involved in the pop business. *Writers (book and general).* Stuntpersons.

10

Under the circumstances, it was perhaps not surprising that, over the next few weeks, I chose to spend rather more time on the literary circuit than usual. My wife was seeking solace in another man's arms. My son was either roaming the streets or locked away in his room where he spent much of his time talking on a mobile telephone which he seemed mysteriously to have acquired. On the rare occasions when I encountered either of them around the house, few words were exchanged.

So Peter Gibson became my escape from the unhappy family unit in which I had suddenly found myself. Often, when we met, I would unburden the cares of the family man/ writer with an openness which I had not experienced since the days, now over three years ago, when I was last involved with a non-professional lover. Of course, Peter was slightly younger than most of the girls I had seen over the years and, unlike them, had not made that moral compromise in his own life which makes for a sympathetic listener, but he somehow seemed attuned to my inner torment. He explained Doug to me. He understood my unhappiness with Marigold. While he was evasive about his own parents, I formed a picture of them as poor, simple good-hearted folk, buffeted by life and confused by their brilliant dreamer of a son in a way which reflected in an almost uncanny fashion the blindness of my own family to my writerly needs and rhythms. When I pointed out this similarity in our situations – both practitioners of the inky trade, both outsiders some-what at sea in domestic life – he reacted with a surprise and awkwardness which I put down to natural modesty.

I was due to spend a day at the Gloucester Festival, a new event scheduled neatly between Edinburgh and Cheltenham, in order to interview Brian McWilliam, a celebrity-criminal whose career path – from robbery with violence to perfor-mance artist and now to author, was the kind of success story which appealed to readers of the *Professional Writer*. It would be amusing, I thought, to introduce Peter to the fantasy world of the literary festival and I suggested that he should join me for the weekend. He accepted my invitation, almost with enthusiasm.

Yet, when I picked him up at Hammersmith Broadway that Saturday morning, he seemed oddly distracted, behaving almost as if I had tricked him into this expedition. I suggested that he place his bulging canvas shoulder-bag on the back seat but he kept it with him, holding the strap throughout the entire journey. I made a joke about the new school of muggers who loomed out of the White City flats to help themselves to bags and briefcases on the passenger seats of cars waiting at traffic lights, but he merely gazed at the passing cityscape. What the hell? Writers are not well known for their talent for small talk. As the road widened and the traffic thinned on the outskirts of London, I switched on a classical music channel and we made our way west without speaking.

We were staying at a village pub about five miles from Gloucester, a King's Arms sort of place, all beams and history and fake Tudor lettering on the outside and fire doors, cheap patterned carpets and the smell of stale cigarette smoke within. My room was tiny, essentially a double-bed and a TV, causing me a brief pang of nostalgia for the days when such a venue would be the setting for some happy, furtive tryst.

I had agreed to meet Peter for dinner in the 'carvery', a grim little room behind the saloon bar, but I was on my second gin and tonic when he turned up, looking, if anything, more rumpled than he had when we arrived. He had, he told me, been asking at reception for a writing desk to be put in his room.

'Writing desk?' I said. 'There won't be much time for writing.'

Peter opened the plastic menu and stared at its predictable contents as if trying to work out a complicated equation. 'I may not make it tomorrow,' he said eventually.

'Make it?'

'To the festival. I've got . . . work to do.'

I laughed. 'Give yourself a break. You might learn something at the festival.'

'I don't want to hear those other voices,' he said sharply.

'They're writers.'

'Exactly.' Peter placed the tips of his fingers to his temples as if even now, in this very carvery, his brain was being assaulted by alien presences. 'I'm going to finish. It's all that matters. Sorry.'

'Surely the story can wait a day or so.'

He looked up, and there was a smile on his face that was almost goofy in its radiance. 'It's not a story,' he said. 'I've been meaning to tell you but, as you always say, if you give it away through talk, then you don't give it away through writing.'

'That wasn't me. It was Ted Hughes.'

'It's a novel.'

'Yes. A novel. Of course.' I imagine a look of undisguised weariness might have flickered across my face at this point, but fortunately the moment of awkwardness was broken by a skinny youth in a stained black waistcoat who had appeared to take our order. I watched my guest as he discussed with the waiter the various unpalatable examples of plain English food on offer tonight. Yes, a novel. I really might have guessed it. All my pupils were writing a novel. Sometimes the novel existed only in an embryonic, theoretical form, as yet unsullied by articulated prose. Often the novel was merely pulling on its boots for the long march ahead. Inevitably, though, the novel would have to be discussed at some length. There have been times when it has seemed to me that I have spent half my life listening to would-be novelists unburdening the plot, the characters, the voice, the towering ideas contained in their own glorious, never-to-be-completed fictions.

When the waiter had gone, I braced myself for the inevitable flood of authorial confidences, but a sulky pout had returned to Peter's face.

'I shouldn't have mentioned it,' he said. 'I just needed to explain why I had to work tomorrow.'

'You were working on a novel, all the time you were producing stories for class?'

He shrugged. 'They were old stuff. Cannon fodder.'

'How very flattering for the rest of us,' I said with more than a hint of impatience. 'Did it occur to you that you may have been wasting the class's time?'

'Oh, come on.' The colour had risen in Peter's as he fixed me with those strange sky-blue eyes. 'You must know better than anyone that, as soon as a work is laid out on the slab for a post-mortem in class, it's already a stiff.'

'There may be a modicum of truth in what you say,' I replied coolly, realizing as he spoke that he had identified the essential paradox of learning how to write. The talkers in class, the critics with their firm grasp of theory, the swots and grade-hounds, might win marks and the admiration of their peers but they would never produce work of quality. The writers kept quiet. 'It had better be good.'

'It is.'

Our food arrived. Without waiting for me to start. Peter began to eat, spearing the whitebait, neatly tidying it with his knife, then, like a competent, slightly bored conjurer, raising it to the double curtain of hair which obscured all of his face but the thin nose and the strangely predatory mouth. I was annoyed by this last-minute rejection. Although, on the whole, I like the company of young people, there were times when their rapt self-preoccupation, the way they concealed their own egocentric concerns behind the cloak of moral probity, was unendurable. I remembered, for some odd reason, a female student for whom I had plans of a personal nature who had waited until we were at the coffee stage of a rather expensive meal in Chelsea before announcing, with a fine show of bashfulness, that she had decided that our relationship was becoming 'inappropriate'. I was married; it was a sisterhood thing. Oh, for fuck's sake. The rage I had felt then (the knowledge that by the time this youthful primness had been eroded by the compromises of maturity, it would be too late for me) was with me now. Who did they think they were, these prissy little purists?

Peter glanced up and, as if sensing the direction of my thoughts, smiled in a manner that was both apologetic and inexplicably confiding. In spite of myself, I felt a lurch of envy for my own pupil. Of course, he could finish his novel. Did he have to earn a living? Was he trapped in a domestic nightmare? How easy it must be to attend to the call of the muse when everything – money, family support, education, a reason to live – is accorded to you as part of the unchallenged rights of youth. And how typical of the man that he would agree to accompany me to a festival, then queenily withdraw the privilege of his company at the last moment on the grounds that he had to write. Big fucking deal. Did it not occur to him for a moment that I would far rather be working on *Insignificance* than be obliged to interview some half-witted criminal with a publishing contract, compile pointless statistics about other writers, or indeed teach a group of students with ideas above their talent?

'I'll pay for the room, of course,' he said, his mouth full of small fish.

'Don't you even want to see Martin? Maybe I could introduce you – we used to know each other, you know.'

'You've told me. But I was never that much of a fan, to tell the truth.'

'Nor me,' I said quickly. 'He's massively overrated, we all know that. But he's interesting as a cultural indicator.'

Peter laid down his knife and fork and ran his fingers through his dark, uncombed hair. 'You can tell me about it tomorrow night.'

'Yes, of course. So why are you here?'

He looked away. At the bar, a middle-aged couple sat engaged in lugubrious conversation with the barman. From the look of the woman – teased and lacquered hair, heavy jewellery, high heels – this was their weekly night out. 'See the world,' he said. 'A bit of an adventure.'

He turned back to me. I held his eyes. If this was mockery, I would make him regret it. 'It would be even more of an adventure if you came along tomorrow,' I said quietly.

Peter shook his head slowly. 'I make my own adventure,' he said.

It was not only for personal reasons that I was disappointed by Peter's last-minute loss of nerve. Over the previous weeks, we had been engaged in a bantering, yet profoundly serious debate about the literary life in a modern age. To my argument that the contemporary writer should be seen moving in the right circles, accept commissions which may represent a small artistic compromise but which kept visible his name, his authorial *persona* as Mailer has it, Peter would respond with a bewildered purity, an insistence that a serious artist had responsibility only and exclusively to his work. Among several books I had leant him had been Janet Hobhouse's *The Furies* and he had taken to quoting from the descriptions of the character Jack, a novelist said to have been based on Philip Roth: 'the monkish habits of his solitude, the grim, even depressive minimalism of his life . . . his stony separateness and self-sufficiency'.

A literary festival would test Peter's precious 'stony separateness'. By its very nature – a bookish little world, cut off from vulgar everyday concerns – a festival provided a fantasy version of the writer's life. Here every novelist, biographer and poet was a success, every career a soaring parabola of prizes and sales and profound, revealed truths. Here every member of the audience adored the printed word, asked intelligent, sensitive questions of the author before queuing for a signed copy of his book with the quiet devoutness of a communicant. Here, in every bar, the talk was not of sex, TV or football but books, books, books. At a festival, even the readers are the cream of the crop and what Brian Aldiss once described as the inbuilt class structure of reading – author, publisher, bookseller, reader – was seen at its most orderly and harmonious.

I had learnt down the years how to gain the most benefit from these events. I would don my cream linen suit – well-cut enough to represent a healthy royalty account, baggy enough to speak of hours of distracted endeavour at the writing table – swoop down, attend one or two of the more significant readings, conduct an interview if necessary, and spend the rest of my time hanging out at the bars and parties where writers and their entourages gathered. I was well known on this circuit, if not by members of the literary aristocracy, who affected not to recognize me, then by writers on their way up or on their way down, and by the various functionaries from the world of publishing or journalism who made up the numbers. No novelist is truly at home anywhere, even at home (especially at home), but at gatherings like the Gloucester Festival, I felt among my own kind. I was sorry that Peter had been too absorbed in his own project to see me in this context; it might have reminded him that it is not obligatory for a serious writer to lurk moodily in the cave of his imagination like a pious and dreary hermit.

I drove into the centre of Gloucester, deployed my complimentary parking ticket and entered the cavernous lobby of the town hall to collect my press pass, which I pocketed. A party was taking place in a room adjoining the main assembly room where many of the readings would take place. I flashed my pass in the direction of the girl sitting behind a desk. On these occasions, I preferred not to identify myself with news-hounds and profile-mongers but to move among my peers and literary compadres as a fiction writer, confident in the knowledge that, while some of my income is earned from journey-work, the heft and texture of my prose sets me apart from mere journalists as surely as do the occasional visits to Grub Street by Updike, Naipaul, Rushdie or even Martin. I like to think that, in every sentence created by a true writer, the mark of the novelist is identifiable in even the roughest company.

'Name?' The girl was looking up at me with an impertinent

smile. 'It's a writers' party. There's a press reception this evening.'

'I know it's a writers' party,' I said more testily than I had intended. 'Gregory Keays.'

'Yes?' She frowned and turned the page of invitees. 'You don't appear to be on the list, Mr Keays. It's really for people appearing this year. If you'd like to come to the press party, you'd be most welcome.'

'That's impossible. I need to see Brian McWilliam. I agreed to meet him here.'

'Brian?' Her face lit up. 'Maybe I should put you down as his guest.'

I sighed, reflecting, not for the first time, on the many and various humiliations meted out to the professional author. 'Yes,' I said icily. 'That might be a solution to our problem.'

'Thank you, Mr Keays. Enjoy the party,' she trilled.

I made my way into the room and looked around. It was an A-list gathering, all right. There were travel-writers and political writers, celebrity novelists and novelist celebrities, science writers, eco-writers, confessional memoirists of every sort and description, nature writers, self-consciously kitted out in safari jackets and desert boots, the heroes of the new school of journalistic, recognition fiction assiduously working the room in their leather jackets and tattoos and look-at-me haircuts, bossy veterans of the literary scene, holding forth to any one who happened to be passing. Amid the gatherings of twos and threes (few had the confidence to stand alone, observing, doing a writer's job, as I was), eager, clotted little knots of partygoers could be seen. At the centre of each of these groups top-of-the-bill types preached the gospel of success to the faithful congregations of publicists, agents, publishers, lovers and general hangers-on without whom they went nowhere. Now that writing genres had been definitively blurred – memoir/novels, novels/travel books, travel books/self-help manuals, self-help manuals/ novels – the only division in the literary world that mattered was between the truly famous and the would-be, wanna-be, going-to-be famous. When Cynthia Ozick wrote that 'the economy of writing always operates to a feudal logic: the aristocracy blocks out all the rest. There is, so to speak, no middle class,' she might have been gazing upon a gathering such as this.

I collected a glass of champagne from a passing tray, biding my time. One or two of those in my vicinity held my gaze for an instant but, after a momentary reference to some internal filofax of the useful and famous, looked away quickly. I have, it seems, one of those presences which does not snag in the memory – a writer's face, if you like. Ten years previously, I might have been hurt or offended by this invisibility, by the fact that I can meet someone whom I had met the previous week without their showing a flicker of recognition but by now I had accepted this as the fate of the serious novelist: to be anonymous, to be everyman, the universal, unremembered face in the crowd is central to our art. In fact, every time I was cut dead by a fellow novelist, I would congratulate myself that in a very real sense, I was the truer, more honestly anonymous writer. I felt sorry for those authors braying greetings at one another at these absurd social events, the bookish luminaries towards whom all heads turned as they enter a room. Famous, they wore what Updike calls 'the mask that eats into the face'; as writers, they had lost something important. I checked out the largest group and made my way towards it. Almost obscured by several layers of female admirers, who seemed to be swaying and craning towards him, was my interviewee, Brian 'Pussy' McWilliam.

He was a short, lean man, probably in his late fifties, with the taut, tanned skin, broad shoulders and flat stomach of a man who took trouble to keep himself in trim. It was easy to see why producers and picture editors loved to use McWilliam: in those coarse, even features, in that large head adorned by aggressively luxuriant grey hair, the personality of a perversely seductive bully was eloquently expressed. The success of his second career as a wrong-'un turned wordsmith had been as much due to his beautiful, brutal looks, captured for style supplements in a variety of shadowy scowls, as his famously violent and body-strewn past.

I hovered on the outer circle of his audience. He was, as he might say, giving it a touch of the verbals. Gangsters, actors, tarts, villains, dodgy politicos, geezers who were a bit handy with their fists; his line, perfected over many interviews and one-man shows, was that, while he may have been a bit naughty in the past – he'd be the first to hold his hand up that he wasn't exactly a choirboy, no way – it was all part of the give-and-take, rough-and-tumble of private business conducted between colleagues in the same line of work. All right, so maybe the line of work wasn't legal in the strict sense of the word, but he had his code. No civilians. Nothing personal. Nothing nasty. Business only.

'He was a bit silly, see.' McWilliam's piercing blue eyes fixed a long-haired girl, who seemed to give a shudder of appalled desire. 'He did a few things that, at the end of the day, in my book, were well out of order. Not on. I had to give him a bit of a smack. What we call a reminder.'

I was amused by this performance, with its hint of brutality, safely distant and vague, its stagy, loaded euphemisms.

'Mr McWilliam.' I edged my way forward through his fans.

He turned his gaze on me, narrowing his eyes, irritated at the interruption.

'I'm Gregory Keays. I believe we're talking later.'

'Yeah? The girl at the publisher's did lay on a few chats. Which one are you?'

'A magazine called the *Professional Writer*.'

He gave a little bark of laughter. 'That rules me out then. I can hardly write my own name.'

'I'm sure our readers will be very interested by that,' I said smoothly. 'You have a lot of fans out there who take the magazine.'

McWilliam shrugged. 'Want to do it here? Then you can fill in the bits from my talk this afternoon. It's basically the same old crap.'

'We'll need some privacy. Just thirty minutes or so.'

'How much do you people pay?'

I raised a laconic eyebrow. 'The idea is that it helps the book.'

'Are you getting paid?' He looked around his admirers and seemed to be enjoying the situation.

'Yes, but I haven't got a book to sell.'

'Seems all wrong to me. Giving away my material to some geezer I've never met writing for a magazine I've never heard of.'

From just behind him, a woman in her late twenties whom I recognized from her statuesque, *faux*-aristocratic bearing and trim, auburn hair as Tara Winstanley, one of the more fashionable of the new generation of book editors, laid a well-manicured hand upon his arm. 'Actually, Brian it would really help,' she said quietly.

McWilliam glanced at her, a sharp, cold look, and, to my surprise, she blushed and looked away. He looked across to me. 'The *Professional Writer*, do me a favour,' he muttered mutinously, then shrugged. 'Two-thirty at my gaffe. The Brobury. Ask for the Tower Suite.'

'Fine.' I turned to go.

'And what do you write then, Mr Professional Writer?' he asked, in humorous mode once more.

'I write novels.'

'Yeah?'

'*Forever Young*? I was on the Granta list of Best of Young British Novelists.'

'Oooo.' He made the sarcastic, high-pitched, girly noise that had become a contemporary form of mockery. The women around him laughed adoringly.

No. I didn't warm to Mr Brian McWilliam.

Exercise

You are a small spider hanging from a microphone in the main venue of a major literary festival. Over the period of a weekend, you benefit at close hand from the advice, analysis and public reminiscences of many of the greatest writers of our time. Use the conventions of magical realism to explore in a short story how this experience metamorphoses your life.

I I

There are interviews and interviews. With Julian or Jeanette, A.S. or A.N., even with Martin himself, I would invest a serious amount of time and consideration. Having researched in the archives at the *Professional Writer* to ascertain areas of special interest and/or sensitivity, I would make a telephone call to the interviewee outlining the general area of discussion. There would probably be a lunch of some kind, an off-the-record sort of event, at which I would establish a writer-to-writer bond of trust and understanding. After an in-depth taped discussion about authorly life and craft, methods of working, ways of relaxation, rate of wordage per day and so on, we might enjoy a 'warming down' process – perhaps a trip to the Tate (A.S.) or a couple of frames of snooker (Martin). A copy of the proposed interview would be sent to the subject, followed up by some friendly honing and elaboration over the telephone or, in certain circumstances, a drink at their place.

As it happens, I have yet to put this action plan into effect. The authors favoured by readers of the *Professional Writer* (which has nothing approaching an archive in its poky two-room office in Battersea) are those who require the minimum amount of preparation and input: a riffle through the press hand-out, a 30-minute chat (*What gave you the idea for . . .? How did you research the . . .? What writing routine do you . . .?*), an hour or so to write up the piece. Light and shade, atmosphere, scene-setting, meditations upon the nature of the artistic life; these have no place in the *Professional Writer*. Tips, how to write the book, find a publisher and get famous are essentially the only items on its editorial agenda.

So Jeanette and A.S. and A.N. and Martin, writers who

clearly belong to a different galaxy of the imagination, are of less interest than the newcomers and flukes. Firm believers in the great literary lottery, our readers pore gormlessly over an interview with the 22-year-old geek whose first novel has made him six figures, the mediocre actress whose career has been resurrected by a winsome, anorexic memoir, the journalist who has cracked some winning formula, the crim who's the toast of literary festivals, and they take heart. It could be them.

Out of deference to this fantasy, the magazine's resident columnist-at-large will neither impose his own views nor allow any expression of the natural superiority and scepticism a long-term professional writer and novelist may justifiably have for the flash-in-the-pan *arriviste*. I am a camera, yes, but a camera directed from a flattering angle in a kindly light.

Brian McWilliam was a *Professional Writer* kind of writer – that is, no writer at all. A small-time hood from Peckham, he had finessed a media career out of a past of violence, theft and general unpleasantness which had eventually landed him in Wormwood Scrubs doing a seven-year stretch for robbery with violence. He had always been known as something of an anecdotalist in his circle and while 'on the in' as he liked to put it, he had come up with the clever and timely idea of exploiting his vulgar charisma and violent, low-life past.

A few weeks after his emergence from the Scrubs in the late 1980s, he approached a minor showbiz agent called Barry Storm who, without too much difficulty, found him work on the burgeoning club circuit. McWilliam had a knack of falling on his feet, to which his underworld nickname 'Pussy' paid partial reference (he was also relentlessly lustful and had more than once been accused of over-enthusiasm in pressing his attentions on younger female fans), and his brand of raw, hard-eyed humour was what the clubs wanted at that moment. After the saucy but safe radicalism of the stand-up gang – the middle-class boys with fake cockney accents, the career lesbians – audiences discovered a taste for the street, for tales of death and hard drugs and sex taken fast and on the hoof. The bully-boy tactics of the Eighties had brought out the nation's incipient sado-masochism, teased up its weakness for voyeurism and violence.

So Pussy McWilliam relived his past or at least relived a past buffed up and polished for public consumption. With his trademark dark suit, his shiny black shoes, his slicked-back hair, his hands which stretched and flexed and danced like glove puppets stripped down to bare knuckle and fingers, he faced up to his pampered audiences and introduced them to real crime, where real blood was shed, where no one had time for relationships or concern for the Third World, where everything was available at a price and everyone was on the take. And, just when the punters were becoming uncomfortable with their own complicity in Pussy's heartlessness, he would take the edge off his stories with a leavening of humour and sympathy, leaving them with a cleansing aftertaste of remorse.

His act was too hard for a TV series of his own but on the chat shows, for which he perfected a cleverly sanitized version, McWilliam became a regular fixture. When some law and order debate was briefly in the public eye, producers and news editors would know where to turn for a flip, witty, salt-of-the-earth quote to close their reports.

Attitudes changed. Those critics who had once railed against the amoral, value-free world which McWilliam glorified and glamorized began to seem increasingly priggish and out of touch with the new spirit of the age. Pussy, it began to be argued, was dealing in a form of post-modernist irony, rough yet surprisingly sophisticated. His was essentially a moral act. The very fact that incidents of casual greed and lust could be recounted with a laugh and a joke provided the inevitable 'powerful indictment' of contemporary mores. New subtleties were found in the manner he told his stories. Resonances, variously described as 'Hogarthian', 'Dickensian' or 'Runyonesque', were revealed by anxious, admiring critics.

Inevitably, Pussy McWilliam caught the eye of a publisher. When an editorial director from one of the more respectable houses took him, accompanied by Barry Storm, to lunch at the Caprice and suggested he write a book, he had, according to rumour, been reluctant, possibly aware that, without the charming delivery, the sinister dancing hands, his true nature would be exposed in cold, revealing prose. The editor had explained (so I imagine) that he was not looking for a mere smack-and-tell memoir but something which appealed to the new hunger for pain and confession. If Pussy expressed a certain lack of enthusiasm for the idea of sitting down in front of a desk hour after hour to work over appropriately sensitive fancy prose, the editor will have casually remarked that these days fancy prose came cheap – it was for sale on every corner. Pussy would provide the chat, the experience, the persona; the publishers would do the rest.

A year later, *Sorted* by Brian McWilliam was published and soared to the top of the bestsellers list on an irresistible air current of profiles and author publicity. McWilliam (the feline nickname was quietly phased out at this stage) became the rough geezer *du jour*. Gloucester was proud to have landed him, as was the *Professional Writer*.

He was not in his room at the Brobury at the time we had agreed. Or, to be strictly accurate, he was not responding to his telephone. I had been waiting in the lobby of the hotel for a little over fifteen minutes when Tara Winstanley, the editor I had seen in the VIP tent, skipped down the stairs. Her normally well-groomed hair seemed in some disorder and there was a decorous, maidenly blush to her cheeks. As she passed me, she raised her eyebrows in an oddly eloquent gesture of exasperation, either at herself or at her client. McWilliam, I imagined, was not quite as easy and amiable as he liked to pretend.

Two minutes later, he rang down to Reception to enquire if I were waiting. Not in the best of moods, I made my way upstairs to his second-floor room.

'Greg.' He appeared, barefoot, at the door and, with a casually imperious gesture of invitation, turned back into the darkened room.

'Gregory,' I said, following.

'Yeah, sorry about the delay, Greg.' He drew the curtains. 'I crashed out – power nap, you know.'

As the lineaments of the spacious room became clearer, I found myself staring at the wrecked, dishevelled bedclothes on the four-poster bed. Attached to the headboard were a gleaming pair of designer handcuffs.

Seeing the direction of my eyes, McWilliam looked slightly embarrassed. 'Something came up,' he said with an unattractive smirk. 'I got interrupted.'

I walked over to the low, glass table by the window, opened my bag, took out a notebook and my tape machine. Frankly, I was in a state of some irritation, and it was not merely the fact had I been kept waiting while an ageing thug had indulged in tiresome sado-masochistic games with one of London's more attractive new editors that annoyed me. There was a sense of territory being violated. This man, this criminal (alleged criminal; many of the deeds to which he laid claim had never been tried in court nor been confirmed by an independent third party) had, on the basis of one book, which he had not even written himself, marched into the literary world, commandeered our bestseller list, colonized our festivals, and was now taking the cream of our womenfolk, manacling them to hotel beds and casually having his way with them at the very moment when a writer (a real writer, who over the years has sacrificed company, sex, career in order to enter the heart of creative darkness) waited downstairs until he had achieved his tawdry little moment of satisfaction. It seemed all wrong. Tara Winstanley was precisely the kind of publishing woman who, when I was around, exuded literary snobbery, admiring precisely the right books and the right authors, was contemptuous of those caught still admiring last season's successes. Yet, a matter of minutes ago, she had been in this room skipping out of her designer clothes for an ageing, sub-literate Neanderthal whose reading was doubtless limited to a headline over a pair of breasts in the tabloid press.

'Nice girl, Tara.' As if reading my mind, McWilliam looked from the far side of the bed where he had been vaguely straightening out the bed linen rumpled and drenched by his lunch-time activities.

'Yes, she has an excellent reputation.'

McWilliam chuckled. 'I bet she has.' He adjusted his crotch vulgarly. 'What is it with these book women, Greg? I swear, I've done rock gigs and comedy festivals, even party conferences, but the only place that I know, I just *know*, I'll get lucky is at these book festival jobs.' He gave up on the bed, wandered over to where I sat and slumped wearily on to the chair opposite me. 'I'm surprised you blokes get any work done at all.'

'We manage somehow.'

He considered me for a moment, perhaps noticing for the first time that I was not in the best of humours. 'Family man, are you?'

I nodded. 'Wife and a son.'

'Lucky fella. Never managed that. Couldn't get the hang of the old marriage thing. Just –' he glanced blearily in the direction of the bed, '– this.'

'Yeah, well. Different strokes.' I reached for the tape machine, then hesitated, unable to resist my own curiosity. 'Have you known her long?'

'Tara?' McWilliam looked surprised. 'I only met her this morning. Swanned up to me and said that she would be looking after me from now on. She was right and all.' He gazed back at the bed, almost regretfully. 'It's a good idea before you go on stage. Relaxes you. If it's a rough gig, I sometimes just stand there, looking at the audience. You know what I'm thinking? You sad bastards. An hour ago I was up to my oysters in posh crumpet. Nothing can hurt me after that. It's a self-esteem thing.'

I smiled. This, I supposed, was the legendary McWilliam

charm, the man-to-man act which had hooked so many of the more gullible journalists. 'How does it work?' I asked, genuinely curious. 'D'you just ask?'

McWilliam stood up, walked to the head of the bed and released the silver handcuffs with a click. 'I let them see the old two-hand bracelet,' he said. 'Maybe I'll just let them slip out of my pocket when we're alone, in the back of a cab or something. It's like, whoops. Sometimes, just now and then, the girl ignores them. More often you see the old eyes widen slightly. The posher they are, the better they like it.'

'Why?'

'I often wonder myself. Some sort of guilt thing maybe. A need to be punished by Daddy.'

'Real life. You're the outside world. Makes a change from books.'

'Could be, Greg. Could be.' He was staring at me. 'Maybe it helps that I'm just me, on my own. I don't have those family demons.'

I thought of Marigold, her hand on my chest, her face turned away in an angry grimace of orgasm. I thought of Doug's locked door. 'Tell me where the idea for *Sorted* came from,' I asked.

McWilliam held up his arms in a sort of helpless shrug. 'Straight up, Greg. You're going to have to help me here. Fact is, I don't do this writing thing. I'm a manager, a supervisor. I've got one person working on my journalism, someone else on book work. I just took on a very good lad to look after my *Pussy Power with Brian McWilliam* website. It's a corporation and I'm the MD.'

'Ah. That's not really what our readers want to hear. We're in the dream business.'

'Tell you what, I'll give the basic gen. You put in all the crap about the writing, yeah?' He leant forward and switched on the tape machine. 'Even when I was a nipper, back in Miss Beckwith's class in Lambeth, I used to enjoy the old story-writing lark. Like all the other kids, I used to bunk off school, do a spot of thievin', a bit of breakin' and enterin' – we had to earn our own pocket money in them days – but, you know, I'd always be there for those English lessons. I think I had talent, I do. But, course, when I left school, I had to pursue my career and that was it for the old words. Until I found myself with a bit of time on my hands. I lived in the Shepherd's Bush area at the time. Wormwood Scrubs, to be precise . . .'

So it went. I hardly had to ask him any questions. The fraudulence in which writers indulge while revealing their working methods came naturally to him. Writing was always there with him, see? Inside of him, like down in his gut – even when he wasn't writing. On the out, when he decided to retire from his former way of life, he took to doing these performances, shows – but writing was always the dream. In fact, bottom line, straight from the shoulder, writing saved him. If it wasn't for the old words, for getting it down on paper, he'd like as not be back in the Scrubs.

I smiled as I switched off the machine. For the ten minutes or so of the interview, I had found myself warming to him. In a world of pretension, directness had much to recommend it. Even his lies had a sort of rough integrity to them. 'D'you want to see a transcript before I file my copy?'

'Transcript? Nah, I trust you, Greg.' He stood up and wandered across the room and picked up his socks from the floor. 'Coming to my gig this afternoon, then?'

'There's someone I hoped to catch who's on in the big tent at the same time as you – he's sort of a friend. Martin Amis.'

'Oh yeah. Used to like his stuff. *Money*, wasn't it? With that fat slob, Self?'

'Yes. I'll come to your talk if you think it would help the piece.'

'Nah, it's all bollocks. You stick with the real writers, Greg.' Tying up his shoe laces, he said casually, 'You're in trouble, aren't you?'

'Trouble?'

'Something's going on. In your life. I can tell.'

'You know writers. Being fucked up goes with the territory.'

He stared at me, not for a moment buying the line I was giving him.

'Let me know if I can help. Maybe you can come on board, help me with the old books. I think we're quite similar you and me. I've got an instinct for these things.' He reached into his top pocket and gave me a card. 'Bear it in mind, Greg.'

'Gregory.'

He laughed. 'Whatever.'

Top Five Peculiar Erotic Habits of the Great Writers

1. Theodore Dreiser was so erotically charged that he was known to masturbate publicly in a room full of writers.
2. Jean-Jacques Rousseau used to 'expose myself to women from afar in the condition in which I would like to be in their company'.
3. Marcel Proust liked to watch live rats being beaten and pierced with hatpins.
4. Gustave Flaubert used to visit a brothel with friends, choose the ugliest girl and make love to her in front of the others without removing his cigar from his mouth.
5. Gabriele D'Annunzio liked to sleep on a pillow stuffed with the locks of a hundred mistresses.

12

Family man. Was it really that obvious? As I made my way through the streets of Gloucester back to the festival, did I emanate the proud, stubborn weariness of a veteran foot-soldier in the matrimonial army? Was there something in the slope of my shoulders that spoke of years of being tugged earthwards by the small arms of a child?

I had felt uneasy and out of place all day. Now I remembered why. This weekend my wife would be with her lover. They would be luxuriating in the extra hours together in bed that my absence afforded, sad but proud that they had salvaged this at least from the wreckage of their domestic lives, this Saturday afternoon of sex and talk and laughter.

I thought of Doug in his noisome, pullulating cave, of my wife and her busy, cold career, and experienced a familiar stab of guilt that the demands of literature had taken such a toll on the lives of those I loved. 'The life stuff, the living, gets skimped,' Martin says, as if, in a neat, throwaway phrase, the blood-soaked battlefield that we leave behind us can be explained and justified. I knew, with a certainty beyond comprehension, that I would lose my wife and son, was losing them right now, maybe had lost them already. And I knew, with equal certainty, that there was no going back. I had always been a family man and a family man I would remain until the end of my days.

How did this happen? When had the closed, exclusive club that was Marigold and me become part of a great, untidy domestic unit? Long before Douglas arrived, certainly. It occurred to me now that, as soon as I had begun to love the woman who was to become my wife, I had also fallen in love with the idea of family which she represented, the unruly tribe of cousins, nephews and uncles who were so much part of her life.

When we first met, at a party held by a mutual acquaintance, she was at art college, a would-be illustrator who had yet to discover her talent for interior design and I was passing time in an office before I discovered, shortly after turning twenty-six, that grown-up work was not for me. We had both blundered about in the shallows of emotional engagement and were ready for the big plunge.

She stood out in that clamorous, edgy gathering of people caught uneasily between student hedonism and the first mortgage. There was, at first glance, something of the little girl lost about her – not only in her physical slightness but in the resolutely plain way she dressed and the way she stood on the edge of things, looking on and listening like someone who was trying, unsuccessfully, to enter into the spirit of things. I talked to her and was immediately attracted by the studious way she discussed her work, her innate modesty, her refusal to flirt. Only later did I realize that she had been as attracted to me as I had to her.

I asked her out. We dined in a cheap French restaurant in Soho. On the way back to the car, I put an arm around her narrow shoulders, she leant against me and – what exactly happened? It's hard to describe. A sort of electric charge, a jolt of attraction that was so unlike anything either of us had experienced that we both actually gasped, then laughed at the sheer force of what we felt. We kissed on that pavement in Greek Street; it was not a grinding, tonguey grope but a moment of sheer, awe-struck longing. I felt (forgive the cliché) complete. It was not the time for games-playing, for dating etiquette. We went home, up the stairs to my flat and straight to bed, hardly talking, as if nothing in our relationship could move forward until we were properly a couple. It was a perfect night. She, who had slept with only two other men, was as shameless and knowing as a courtesan; I, a virgin until I was twenty-one, was a mighty Casanova. We awoke late the next morning face to face on a devastated bed. Eyes wide, her face close to mine, she said, 'Blimey' and her breath was as sweet as honey. I knew at that point that I wanted her to be my wife although it would be another three weeks before I had the courage to propose. We made love again.

And her family was part of that perfection. I liked the idea that she was a Cameron, part of an ancient and moderately distinguished Lanarkshire family which she liked to describe, with mock exasperation, as 'the clan'. I loved to hear stories of how they all gathered in the chilly Georgian family house outside Edinburgh at the slightest excuse – not just at Christmas and at significant funerals and weddings but at Easter and on anniversaries or obscure church festivals the significance of which had long been forgotten.

It's an odd fact that, apart from the sex, the incidents I remember best about my early weeks and months with Marigold occurred at Dean House where her parents Gordon and Dorothy Cameron lived. I suppose that all over the world there are seasonal gatherings at which, through rows and misunderstandings, in spite of divorce, death and unhappy children, the great unexpressed bond of blood kinship is renewed, but it was new to me. In fact, coming from a family that had never quite acquired the knack of intimacy, I found it a kind of miracle.

Intimacy is perhaps too strong a word. The social atmosphere at Dean House where we spent every Christmas was as bracing as the temperature in the house (even when there was snow on the ground, Cameron liked to keep the antique oil central heating just slightly too low for comfort, as if discouraging his guests from making themselves too much at home). Marigold's older sister and brother rarely seemed to meet between family occasions and behaved towards one another with a polite antipathy, as if each of them was waiting for the other to apologize for some ancient slight. As for Marigold, she would, as soon as she entered Dean House, become the pampered, wilful youngest daughter, lightening the atmosphere with her life and optimism, teasing her father indulgently. I never loved her more than when I saw her in the context of her odd, stultified family.

Not that I got on badly with her parents. Old man Cameron must have been in his early sixties at the time I first met him, yet he had already taken on the *persona* of a gruff, cantankerous, put-upon paterfamilias, an act which he imbued with an element of self-mockery which fooled no one. His wife Dorothy had planned to be an actress before meeting Gordon, ten years her senior and already qualified as a barrister; they married when she was nineteen. Still a beautiful woman, she expressed a loving but restless impatience with her family, simultaneously bickering and playing up to her husband, muttering semi-humorous com-plaints about his selfishness to anyone who would listen. When, year after year, he repeated the same joke or anecdote from the courts, she would groan or cast her eyes to the ceiling. 'Don't encourage him,' she would tell the family if they laughed.

When I arrived at Dean House that first Christmas after I had met Marigold, I was confused by this ménage. There had been perhaps fifteen or sixteen people there, including non-family members who on these occasions gravitated for various reasons to the Cameron household. There was a resentful and monosyllabic old nanny who had looked after all three Cameron children, a couple of rather gauche male cousins and Hugo, an old golfing partner of Gordon's whose wife had died. The group was so big and unfocused that one could wander from one group gathered in the hall where an ancient black and white television had been installed for the children, to the library where Gordon and Dorothy sat in state on either side of large log fire or to the kitchen where some pre-or post-meal business was taking place. Children, neat in tartan and buckled shoes, ran up and down the stairs. Inevitably, there were games – charades, hunt-the-thimble, something called 'spoons' which involved much scrabbling about under tables and furniture and which was later banned after a niece's head was gashed open in the scrimmage.

At one point, on my first Christmas Day at Dean House, one of Marigold's nephews, Henry, a boy of around nine, whispered in her ear. She smiled and nodded. 'The farmer wants a dog,' the child (now a law student) called out.

The family, with the exception of Mr and Mrs Cameron who looked on from their thrones on each side of the fireplace, formed a circle around Henry in the middle of the hall and I found myself holding hands with Marigold and one of the cousins. We moved around, singing.

'The farmer wants a wife, the farmer wants a wife, ee-aye, ee-aye, the farmer wants a wife.'

The movement stopped. Smiling yet solemn, Henry chose his younger sister Zoe who joined him in the centre of the circle.

'The wife wants a child, the wife wants a child, ee-aye, ee-aye, the wife wants a child.'

94

Zoe chose Marigold.

'The child wants a dog, the child wants a dog, ee-aye, ee-aye, the child wants a dog.'

Marigold chose her niece Lucy.

'The dog wants a bone, the dog wants a bone, ee-aye, ee-aye, the dog wants a bone.'

At first, Lucy chose her mother. Laughter. Marigold whispered in her ear, pointed at me. I was chosen. I was the bone.

'On your hands and knees,' cried my wife-to be. I crouched in the centre of the circle. It closed on me and suddenly hands, big hands and tiny hands, were plucking at my back, my legs, my head.

'We all pick the bone, we all pick the bone, ee-aye, ee-aye, we all pick the bone.'

Head down, eyes closed, protesting dutifully in mock horror, I endured the initiation ceremony, a bone picked with a curious mixture of warmth and roughness with a hint of threat. When, finally, I stood up, flushed and dishevelled, they all applauded. I was a Cameron.

And so, oddly, I have remained. Married, a father, published, celebrity husband, through the ups, the downs and the strange wrong turnings of my life, Dean House has remained at the centre of it all. Another generation of children now run up and down the stairs.

New members of the family – boyfriends, girlfriends, one husband thus far – have been absorbed into the group, fresh bones to be picked. The house has not grown warmer. Gordon and Dorothy sat in their chairs, bickering. Yet, for all the changes that were occurring in all our lives, the atmosphere on those occasions at that house remained the same.

It was not that there was anything transcendently caring or unusual about the extended Cameron family; individually, we were as lost and bemused in our lives as anyone, but somehow, together, we were less ourselves – beneath the determined triviality of conversations, there was a serious-ness. The family took over and briefly, over a period of two days or so, our individual concerns and worries and ambitions went into a sort of natural, unforced remission.

Douglas loved Dean House. When he was small, he basked in the attention of the older children. Later, even after he turned in upon himself, soon after his eleventh birthday, he would revert to his happier, more childish self for the few days that we were there. Now, in his surly teens, he would somehow manage to talk in halting tones to his grandfather, telling this gruff, apparently unsympathetic old man more about his life in a few hours than he told us in the course of a year.

'It's all about children,' Dorothy Cameron said to me as I sat beside her one Christmas afternoon. 'In the end, they're all that matters, aren't they?'

I elected to borrow my own child's favourite word. 'Maybe.'

'You're a good father, Gregory,' she said, glancing towards her daughter, my wife. 'You mustn't forget that.'

At first, I thought she was mocking me. But she wasn't.

The Writer Speaks of . . . Children

I don't know what Scrope Davies meant by telling you I liked children. I abominate the sight of them so much that I have always had the greatest respect for the character of Herod.

Lord Byron

Children dissipate the longing for immortality which is the compensation of the childless writer's work. But it is not only a question of children or no children, there is a moment when the cult of home and happiness becomes harmful and domestic happiness one of those escapes from talent which we have deplored, for it replaces the necessary unhappiness without which writers perish.

Cyril Connolly

If I could not have children . . . I would be dead . . . My writing a hollow and failing substitute for real life, real feeling.

Sylvia Plath

> Until I grew up I thought I hated everybody, but when I grew up I realized it was just children I didn't like.
>
> *Philip Larkin*

> As a father, I was angered by the way that he [V.S. Naipaul] actively disliked children, because any parent has an animal awareness of that hostility. It made me protective. I also saw that the man who disliked children and doesn't have any of his own is probably himself childish, and sees other children as a threat.
>
> *Paul Theroux*

> Even if my marriage is falling apart and my children are unhappy and my spouse is unhappy, there is still a part of me that says, 'God! This is fascinating!'
>
> *Jane Smiley*

13

I was at the press bar when I first caught sight of Martin. He was at a corner table, chatting with self-conscious casualness to a group of his acolytes, including Tony Watson, an old pal who traditionally played the John the Baptist role on these occasions. Casually, I positioned myself at a nearby table and opened a novel in proof form, which I had brought with me in my shoulder-bag. Martin, I noticed, was looking demoralizingly well, if anything younger than when I had last seen him, his hair teased expensively so that what, in others, would seem like male pattern baldness was merely a distinguished thinning, a hint of patal sheen showing through as if to remind the world of the massive cerebral cortex it contained. His clothes might have been designed for the *Esquire* famous-novelist collection – loose, creased, elegantly dishevelled, autumnal beige and brown. Above all, I noticed his tan. It was neither the pinkish, embarrassed hue of an Englishman just back from his holidays nor the leathery countenance of some sub-Hemingway literary cowboy. Martin had been blessed with *exactly* the right amount of sun; he wore the burnished sheen of accomplishment, as if success itself had ripened him to achieve this perfect, bronzed, mature result.

For many years now, I have indulged this small fantasy that, at one of these events, Martin will look up, see me, narrowing those eyes in the way that he does, and call me over. '*Forever Young*, wasn't it?' he would say. 'Shit, I always meant to tell you what a difference that book made to my life. Put it there, kid.' And we would shake hands in a moment of pure bonding, writer to writer. To this effect, I have favoured events where he is speaking, taken to hanging out where he hangs out, emerging from doors as he is passing them, appearing around corners, generally popping up and making myself available for discussion. Now I found myself glancing across the room occasionally, hoping to catch Tony's eye and be drawn into the group but, unlike the last occasion when we met, he was too busy gazing at his hero, or engaging in eager banter, to notice me.

As you might have gathered, we have something of a history, Martin and me. Even before we became directly involved with one another, appearing on the same list and in the same photographs, we had been part of each other's lives, since his first novel had appeared at precisely the moment when I was first considering a career as a writer. Jejune and puppyishly anxious to please as it was, Martin's teenage masturbation novel gave the illusion of blowing off the library dust from fiction, of clearing its stale, mannered, middle-aged fug. He proved that you could be young yet serious, write about frustration and seediness without being tawdry. Of course, a few of us, not blessed with Martin's family connections, were working in similar directions in our bedsits and student digs, but it was he who lit the way.

Our paths diverged. I, like Waugh and Greene, Boyd and Le Carré, taught briefly in a private school, while never taking my eye off my ultimate literary ambition. Martin used the springboard of privilege to work in the kind of books-page jobs (high-profile, low-effort, part-time) reserved for the sons and daughters of the book establishment while assiduously acquiring a reputation as 'the voice of a generation'. If already there was something of the sleight of hand to his writing, an emotional evasiveness, a willingness to sacrifice an awkward, angular truth to the slick, attention-grabbing phrase, what could one expect? A boy to whom everything had been given without struggle – position, reputation, money, sex – could hardly be expected to understand about the despair and striving and loss the rest of us already knew so well. A chance comment in an interview at the time, in which he conceded that he would sacrifice any psychological or realistic truth for a phrase, or a paragraph that had a 'spin' on it, sounded less like a boast than a confession.

In 1982, my novel *Forever Young* was published. A couple of the lazier critics deployed the term 'Amisian' to describe the jazzy, demotic verve of its prose, the gamy whiff of corruption and curdled desire that attended its crafty, satirical intent. One reviewer, admittedly only in the *Sunday Express*, noted sneeringly that my work 'belonged in a junior class of the school of Amis-*fils*'. I was no more than mildly offended. We all – Martin, Julian, Graham, William, Ian, myself – were drawing water at the same narrow well of contemporary experience; under slightly different circumstances some of Martin's better work might easily have been described as 'Keaysian' or even (a term I tried to coin in a piece written under another name) 'Gregorian'. As for the jibe from the *Express* hack (last spotted, doing romance round-ups for a supermarket magazine!), I recognized that, in my first novel, I may have been slightly rawer than Martin but I was also, essentially, truer. I was a writer; he was a flashy bystander, recording changes in the passing scene.

My problem with Martin became more serious and personal when, with eighteen other young luminaries, we were ranked together on the now-legendary Best of Young British Novelists, selected by *Granta* magazine in 1983. We only met once during the publicity campaign, at the group photocall, after which a brutal bifurcation occurred, Martin and a couple of others heading off for the national TV shows, the rest of us being distributed among assorted man-and-a-dog local radio stations. All the same, it seemed to me that, in that instant when we had shaken hands in the photographic studio, a very real moment of recognition and bonding had taken place – that we had both understood that, whatever the differences between us in trivial matters of reputation and fame, we were, in a real, creative sense, in this together, part of the same team, working on the same great writerly project.

Yet the next time we met, in 1984 at a publishing launch party, he affected not to recognize me. Three months later, I attended one of his readings only for it to happen again. Since then, we have been introduced no fewer than eight times; each time, he afforded me the same distant, crooked smile, as if I were a reader, a fan, some fucking punter who had plucked up courage to ask him to sign a copy of one of his novels. It was childish behaviour, graceless, an affront to the muse we shared.

The growing respect accorded to his work, his carefully nurtured reputation, began to impinge upon my own writing. It seemed that every time I turned a corner, the trim figure of our man was already there, kicking up dust, a dot on the horizon. I would be wrestling with the complex polyphony of *Accidents of Trust* when his dual narrator novel appeared. I would be stoking the satirical fire of *Adultery in Hampstead*, only for it to be doused by the appearance of his eighties novel. I would be caught up in my urban alienation novel *Mind the Gap* when, almost to the second, his own crude working of the same theme, goosed up with modish apocalyptic concerns, arrived to squat plumply and snugly on the front tables of bookshops.

Nuclear awareness, the end of the world, the new physics, historic guilt, the family: it began to seem as if he were in possession of some kind of bug which tapped into my creative consciousness, so that, just as I considered a new theme for my fiction, a work from Martin, covering the same ground would appear, gleaming and complete, in the bookshops.

The pre-emptive theft of my inner musings was most evident in the interviews he would occasionally give. At the very point when a thought, a cultural theory, a neat aphoristic insight was making its way from the unconscious into the articulating part of my brain, it would appear, perfectly and conclusively expressed, in his latest press or TV profile. I became a connoisseur of Martinisms, collecting those smart, sardonic, carefully rehearsed throwaway lines in which he encapsulated the very things that I had been just about to say. I would serve them up to my pupils at the Institute, even taking a sort of proprietorial pride in the eagerness with which the would-be writers noted them down.

'I don't think writers need more than two or three subjects.'

'Every writer thinks he's in the foreground of breakdown and collapse.'

'There are no rules for the novel.'

'I think you don't want to know too much about what's going on out there. You walk through it but you don't go looking for it and then it will have your imprint on it.'

'To be any good you have to think you're the best of your generation.'

'At no point in history has the writer spent so much time telling everyone what he's saying.'

'Just as you find out something about someone when they laugh – when they really laugh – you find out a lot by seeing them in a sexual situation.'

'The definition of a writer is he or she who is happiest alone.'

'Someone watches over us when we write. Mother. Teacher. Shakespeare. God.'

Mother. Teacher. Shakespeare. God. And Martin. Over the years he became more than merely a shrewd writer with an eye to cultural fashion and an ear for the catchy, bouncy phrase. He was a living emblem of what we could, what we should be. He was Everywriter. Physically, he seemed to grow. With every unsmiling photograph, his drawling, easy authority was more in evidence.

Even the lineaments of his personal life contributed to the myth. It was not enough that, while the rest of us were making our first tentative steps into sexual experience, he was reported to be engaged on a priapic romp through the most famous and brilliant beauties of our own and of the previous generation; his high erotic strike rate, far from draining creative endeavour, was said by those in the know to have contributed to the confident, randy swagger of his prose. It was not enough for him to belong to smart snooker and tennis clubs while the rest of us made do with pubs and wine bars; his partners and competitors had to be high-profile types, Hitch and Fent, Julian and Clive, guys who, even as they served and potted, added to his credibility. It was not enough for him merely to succumb to the travails and satisfactions of domestic life; he had to be a famously, fashionably doting Daddy. It was not enough for marital happiness to seep away in the normal, time-honoured fashion; he had to have a glamorous writer-lover, a showy divorce, a camp and perfect soap opera from which everyone somehow emerged happier, more fulfilled, better looking. It was not enough to have sired an illegitimate child in his late teens; no, father and daughter had to discover one another twenty years later. Of course, she was not a sad runt of loser living a life of anonymity but good-looking, balanced, and doing rather well at Oxford. How could we doubt it? She was a daughter of Everywriter.

Those who do not understand the ways of the novelist may be surprised that I came to see a direct and unavoidable connection between Martin's precious worldly success, his effortless accumulation of money, and my own inability to complete my second, third, fourth, fifth, sixth (if you include *Glitter*, written under the *nom de plume* Ivana Schuyler), seventh, eighth, ninth and tenth novels, and for the fact that the stories in my collection *Tell Me the Truth About Love, About Love* remained more minimal and fragmentary than would have been acceptable even to the master, Raymond Carver. This account is not about failure ('An author with a grievance is of all God's creatures the most tedious,' Max Beerbohm once said) but, in the interests of truth, it must be noted that, by annexing and colonizing my creative life, one man has come to represent the futility of everything I have attempted to write. Mother, teacher, Shakespeare, God: they were all by my elbow as I forged forward. But, when I hit the inevitable quagmire on page 70 or 80, in Chapter Five or Six, it was Martin's voice that I heard whispering sardonically in my ear that just possibly my time might be better spent on *The Write Stuff: A Resource Book for Creative Writing Teachers*, in collecting authorly affirmations or in angrily fulfilling a much-delayed contract for *Ride the Magic Dragon: A Kids' Guide to Story-Writing*. Although it has turned out that all but a few of my uncompleted works were not dead but sleeping, there have been dark moments over the past decade or so, crises lasting months or years, during which Martin's achievements have seemed entirely responsible for my lack of them.

It was, perhaps, a perverse comfort that, as his career developed from young promise to middle-aged establishment figure, one failure, at the very epicentre of his writing life, became increasingly evident. At a moment when his life seemed to be falling apart, with the loss of wife, children, teeth, agent, friends (Martin's mid-life crisis was, it goes without saying, more dramatic and garish and yet more lucrative than anyone else's), he admitted, in that weary mid-Atlantic drawl, so indistinct that many of the brilliant things he says seem to come at you twice – once when you catch its general drift, then again when you realize how perfectly, wittily and adeptly it has been expressed – he confessed to an interviewer that he guessed he was never going to be regarded as a chronicler of the human heart.

Of *course*. A chronicler of the human heart was precisely what he had increasingly longed to be. No one, not even Martin, could build a literary reputation entirely on being cool. Families happen. Children happen. Life happens. The witty, elegant skimmer over the surface needs eventually to acquire some depth. He cranked up his subject matter, from the personal and sexual to the universal and apocalyptic but it wasn't (he knew, we knew) enough. Thoughtful and interesting as his meditations on such major league tear jerkers as the Holocaust or the death of the planet may have been, he, the author, little Martin, had remained at the end of it all the same disapproving, sneering figure observing wittily, brilliantly and coldly, from the outside. In his next work, the long awaited literary envy novel (what kind of subject was that for a grown-up writer?), he tried again, this time playing the fatherhood card, the flinty-male-heart-melting-with-parental-love card, the little-kiddies-in-danger card.

Nope. Yet again it didn't work. You laid the novel down, awe-struck, impressed, dry-eyed.

Now, in Gloucester, it was time for Martin's gig. With his courtiers in attendance, he made his way out of the bar. I put away the novel I had been pretending to read and, before taking my seat in the hall, I visited the gents' lavatory, where something faintly discomfiting occurred.

I was standing at a urinal when the door opened behind me and, as if I were dreaming, the small, distinguished figure of Martin was suddenly there, beside me, fishing in his underpants not more than two feet away from me. We stood, sharing that moment of forced intimacy when two men are shoulder to shoulder with their penises hanging out in a public place. It occurred to me that I might break the silence in an easy male manner (but instead of the usual banalities, I would have had to say something more literary and informed, like, 'What on earth possessed you, in the London novel, to equate black holes in space with an act of inverse sexuality performed with Nicola Six?' He would have explained that he was attempting to put a spin on a banal, everyday act, to give it universal resonance, and in reply I probably would have joked, 'Every day? You filthy bastard, Martin' and we would both have laughed in a blokeish though literary way, buttoned ourselves up, washed our hands and left) but, when I glanced at him, he was staring ahead, chewing gum, like a boxer before a fight. I remembered that he was about to appear on stage and decided that it was possibly a touch insensitive to probe him about his work at what was, in any event, quite a vulnerable moment, that he might even have thought it slightly creepy that some guy wanted to talk about sodomy and Nicola at a urinal. A great, manly, lagerish stream issued from him. I tried to relax myself. I thought of things to distract me, listed the names of the novels I have failed to finish. Nothing happened. I had dried up. Martin had done it to me again. I stood there, in an agony of self-consciousness, feeling like an intruder, the sort of person who goes to the gents and stands there, dick exposed, for the sheer hell of it, like someone who gets a thrill from visiting a brothel and not going to bed with any of the girls. Without so much as a glance in my direction, he finished, put himself away with that little backward thrust of the buttocks that men do and walked out.

Now I peed, my shoulders slumped in despair. There had been nothing actively hostile in his behaviour over the past few seconds, and yet it had not been entirely normal, as if the usual business between men – a nod of acknowledgement, maybe a few casual words – was something he, as a successful writer, had outgrown. Compared to other novelists I had seen at festivals, he seemed to have acquired that kind of transparent outer shell that celebrities have to protect them from the world of nosy civilians. It occurred to me that here was a direct connection between his easy, confident assumption of the role of the public writer and his utter inability to inject feeling or warmth into his novel. 'The best seeing is done by the hunted and the hunter, the vulnerable and the hungry,' says Updike. 'The "successful" writer acquires a film over his eyes. His eyes get fat. Self-importance is a thickened, occluding form of self-consciousness.' Briefly, as I washed my hands, then dried them on paper tissue, I sympathized with Martin for his fat eyes, his palpable lack of writerly vulnerability and hunger.

I walked into the big adjoining hall and took a seat near the back (it was, of course, packed and the audience was younger, more female, attractive and somehow more *open* than any other audiences at that festival) and listened as Tony Watson effected a smooth, empty, ingratiating introduction, laden with the many critical clichés that had appeared in countless profiles and reviews over the years but sugared with a simpering intimacy. Legs crossed, emanating a languor that was within a scintilla of being outright boredom, the novelist sat on a chair in a semi-sprawl, staring over the heads of his audience as if he had become so used to being surrounded by people who listened to his every jewelled word, admired his tan, his clothes, his perfect hair, that they no longer existed for him. After several long minutes of waffle (the more Tony struggled to gain a purchase on his talent, the more it slipped through his fingers), during which the audience grew restless in a way that was almost sexual, Martin was invited to take the stand. He stood up, his lack of stature oddly adding to his air of distinction, laid some rough-looking papers on the lectern, and cleared his throat.

I've heard the intro. The sleepy drawl, delivered at a volume which, like his novels, demands his audience to sit up and make an effort. He'll throw in some faintly contentious but always interesting idea – about humour, or sex, or science, or writing – as if it had just occurred to him as he was speaking. Now as he chatted to us, like a tennis champ warming up before a big game with some effortlessly flashy shots, I looked around the marquee, taking in the guy's constituency.

Several of the other middling-to-major literary performers were here, some in the row of VIP seats at the front, others sitting a touch self-consciously among the members of the public. This was unusual: it is an unspoken rule that only for a friend or a higher member of the literary aristocracy (some revered international figure, or perhaps a Nobel Prize winner) does a writer turn out for these talks. Like getting a book signed by a fellow author, a ghastly solecism in writerly circles, sitting respectfully as some rival reads his work, talks about his life, dilates weightily upon his views of the novel, is simply not done. I thought of Cheever's likening of the crazed rivalry between novelists to that of sopranos. To see one lording it over an adoring public is worse, far worse, than experiencing the ecstatic reviews for his book. It eats into the soul.

He seemed to be talking about some kind of family holiday. Martin, the family man, with the boys, the baby, the loving rigmarole of domestic life. I had to smile. *So* transparent, this fresh pitch for sympathy. I could just about take the version of him put about in the male glossies (the tennis, the pool, the darts) but the Dad thing had never come alive as a drama for him – not as domestic comedy, nor as mid-life tragedy. It remained dead on the page, even when he shamelessly flashed an anecdotal family photo album as he was doing now. Please, Martin, I murmured. Give us a break.

A woman in her twenties, of the type often found at festivals (has read all the right contemporary novels, is work-ing on something right now but she can't tell you about it) half-turned to me with undisguised irritation before turning back to listen, lips slightly parted, eyes shining. As she crossed her legs, revealing the elegant, intelligent limbs in an unfeasibly short skirt (this was a *literary* festival, for Christ's sake), it occurred to me, with sickening clarity, that she was participating in this event with an enthusiasm that was more erotic than intellectual. There were other women, I now saw – young, attractive, apparently normal – who were looking at their hero with the same rapt, yearning, opened-out expression.

I shouldn't have been surprised – at the launch of one of the classier novelists, you will find more beautiful women than at a fashion show – yet I was. This was a man who, although he had acquired a reputation as something of a rabbit in the past – having his way with an entire generation of dark-eyed, talented media beauties as if he were representing a vast army of his male peers (which in a way he was) – was now post-first marriage, post-dental rethink, post-mid-life collapse, post-virtually everything that was youthful and dynamic. He seemed to have come to terms with his age: he had talked about retiring from writing, causing a spasm of joy in the hearts of the rest of us; he had taken to referring, in an almost avuncular way, to the 'young guys' moving up to take his place. He was showing signs of acting his age, but the junior, female division of his army of fans still behaved as if he were still there, rooting and rutting among the female intelligentsia. Who knows? Maybe (this was a thought that made me swear out loud, causing another twitch of distracted irritation from the woman in front of me) he was.

He's a good reader. That lazy, corrupted voice, that has had just too much of everything, ambled its way into a short story. Within a few paragraphs, it was clear that this was a most unMartinian piece – no tough-guy side-of-the-mouth narration, no sleeve-tucking, look-at-me-Mom narrative tricks, not even any swearing.

Something else strange: Martin had joined the memoir gang, the novelists who have lost their confidence in fiction and who now reach into the murk of their own tawdry pasts in order to give their work the fake prurient charge of a *True Confessions* shocker. Traditionally, wives, lovers, friends and children have been ruthlessly served up in fiction – 'discretion is not, unfortunately, for novelists,' as Roth says – but they have usually at least been transformed a bit, cooked by the process of fictionalization so that they are not entirely recognizable. Now they came at us, raw, with novelists managing to have it both ways, conveying the tang of reality while reserving for themselves the right to change a few facts, traduce the occasional character for the sake of their art.

Yet, in spite of myself, I was soon absorbed in the story, forgetting the other novelists, the audience, even the girl with the legs, allowing the rhythm of the words to draw me into its imaginative universe of holidays, kids squabbling in the back of the car, Dad wearily tolerant, sweet, wise words spoken by small mouths, turning dark in its final passage, the events casting a shadow forward to less sunny days. It was a small story but it had a touch of the universal to it.

Applause. That familiar, awkward, social smile from the author. He sat down to submit himself to the usual dreary questions from Tony Watson but, after that story, his heart wasn't in explanation of writing methods. Nor was the audience listening; the power of the story we had just heard was still resonating in our brains. It was then that, with a lurch of the stomach, I realized what had happened.

Just when it seemed that he was caught, that his limitations were at last about to be revealed, he had jumped free once again, just as he had done so many times over the past quarter of a century. He had become a chronicler of the human heart.

Fuck. Fucking Martin had done it again.

Affirmation
Today I am a sailor crossing the mighty swell of an ocean. My guide? The stars.

14

There was little noise beyond a respectful, church-like buzz as the audience made its way out of the hall. They had liked him. They had been impressed. They had responded to the sheer humanity of the man. In a few minutes' time, after the spell had worn off, they would become engaged in eager discussion with fellow admirers of the small man as to what this new direction in his career meant.

I was not immediately inclined to hurry back to the village pub to deconstruct with my student the cultural significance of Martin's discovery that he had a heart. I wandered the streets of Gloucester, past knots of festival visitors, jostled by people emerging from pubs at closing time. I felt unusually disconsolate. Although writers like to believe that we are united in a brotherhood of creative toil, there are moments of vulnerability when the triumph of a contemporary can be hard to endure. Normally, the brief spasm of pain occurs privately, while reading a review or even, with a growing sense of admiring despair, the book itself, but tonight's victory had been achieved in a public context, to laughter and applause, before the moist adoration of girls in unfeasibly short skirts. The humiliation of the rest of us felt almost personal.

Martin, the good father. I had seen it all now. In past interviews, he had identified with such icy precision the domestic failings of the creative artist that it had been easy to visualize him at home as a distracted, tetchy figure, a short-fused domestic bully (I'm a *writer*, for Christ's sake, he would scream at wife or children), a snarling family tyrant who had clung obstinately to scruffy bachelor habits, smoking roll-ups in the nursery, leaving skid-marks on the bath-towels, destroying carefully planned dinner parties with his leery boredom, preferring to play snooker with Will or Julian or some Keith Talent type in a smoky dive in Notting Hill rather than kick a ball about in Dogshit Park with the kids. Yet here he was, having it all, doing it all, triumphant after another surprise flanking movement, battered by separation and decay, the doting dad.

So smooth, so tanned, so fucking happy. At some time after the pubs had closed, I found myself sitting on a park bench somewhere in the centre of the town, the ghostly shadows of a playground before me, like dinosaurs frozen in an urban landscape. I saw myself, a pasty, middle-aged man, running to fat, a slumped, exhausted figure, hands sunk deep in the pockets of his raincoat. Then I thought of Martin, on a beach in some swanky East Coast resort in America, amusing and being amused by his children and their friends, giving to them and, in the gentle, sneaky manner of writers, taking from them.

In this area at least, we were different. I have chosen not to pilfer the family album for fraudulent authenticity, cheap smiles and easy tears. The emotional striptease, revealing the novelist in all his touching bony nakedness, his pale, abnormally sensitive skin flayed by experience, will never be part of my work. It is a cheat, a short cut to the reader's heart, which owes more to a magazine agony column than to the art of fiction. Frankly, I was surprised that Martin could stoop that low.

Then again, precisely what kind of material would have been available to me? The beach scenes of my memory were not sun-dappled and full of infant laughter and those odd, yet strangely perceptive things that kids say. They were damp, grey, regretful and oddly silent.

I thought of the holidays spent every year camping on the north coast of Cornwall since Douglas had been two, a time caught for me in the silver-framed photograph on Marigold's dressing-table showing an English beach scene, low tide, the sea a dark line on the horizon, a windblown family of three apparently oblivious to all but themselves. Marigold and I sat in front of a rock, me skinny with an absurd haircut, she an almost unrecognizably plump and motherly figure. I was smiling, she had her arms outstretched towards the small, spindly figure of our son, running towards her, straight-limbed, his silken hair streaming behind him, his eyes closed, his mouth open in what seemed to be a cry of joy and belonging.

At first we had all been in one tent, but the sea air seemed to carry an aphrodisiac quality for both Marigold and for me and restrained, secretive love-making had never been to our taste. When Dougie was seven, we bought him a small tent of his own. The treat of independence quickly wore off yet, with a determination to this day I find slightly shocking, he was sent to bed early every evening – it's grown-up time now, Dougie – so that his parents could grapple angrily in the darkness like animals, wild and free, mating in the savannah.

It was at about that time that Dougie lost his taste for the company of his peers, drifting away from the groups of other children on the beach to his parents who would play with him in a dutiful, quality-time fashion. The other children seemed to sense that he was different from them in some mysterious but not terribly interesting way. On occasions, I noticed other larger families, real families, noisy groups with Gran and Grandpa and a pram and a picnic basket, people who had grasped the concept of family and holidays, darting glances at our self-contained little group of three, as if they knew that we were frauds, imposters in the land of normal mums and dads and kids.

Even before Dougie became Doug, that open smile caught in the photograph had faltered, faded and finally disappeared. On the long drive down to the west coast, he would be silent on the back seat, either staring out of the window or playing listlessly with the computer game of the moment. Sometimes, when I looked in the rear-view mirror, I would find myself staring into the clear, unhappy eyes of my son, as if it had finally dawned on him that he had drawn a duff card in life's lottery, that his family was not as others were, that each of the three of us was as lost and lonely as the others.

There were voices behind me, a man and a woman, loud and cheerful and I looked up from my bench to see a couple, arms wrapped around each other, approaching. Seeing me, they stopped chatting and seemed to hurry on as if I had reminded them of something they would prefer right now not to know about. I stood up and walked slowly to where I had left my car.

It was about half past twelve by the time I reached the hotel but, in the half-lit bar, two men and woman were sitting like sculptures moulded to their stools. They glanced at me as I entered, stared at me for a moment before resuming their conversation in low, bored voices.

I needed to talk, too. The intimacy and emotional charge of Martin's story, then remembering Cornwall and the chill, damp nights when my wife and I had fucked like strangers, as if we were fucking for our very lives, had made me feel restless. Unlocking my room, I sat on the double bed which occupied most of the room and, after a moment's hesitation, picked up the telephone and dialled home. To my surprise, Marigold answered. As soon as I heard her voice, I knew that calling at this hour had been a mistake.

'It's me,' I said. 'I just rang to see how everything was.'

'Now? Have you any idea what time it is?'

'Sorry.'

There was a pause, and, as I imagined my wife arranging herself in bed, turning over, pulling the duvet over a naked shoulder, I felt a pang of nostalgic lust. 'What's the problem, Gregory?'

'Problem?' I sighed. There were times when the mere sound of my wife's voice, with its distant echo of disappointment and impatience, deflated me. 'No particular problem. I was just thinking of Cornwall.'

'*Cornwall?*'

'The tent. You and me. Those nights.' I closed my eyes and there before me was my young wife, crouching over me, like some bird of prey on its victim. For her, I had ceased to be me on those occasions, so caught up was she in her own erotic project. I was not Gregory, not her husband, but just a man, the man, Man. Her need was so awesome that when she made love, riding me, grinding me downwards so that my back pressed against the hard earth, it was as if she were trying to expunge something, to destroy it for ever. *Pah! Agh!* She came with an urgency which must have been heard across the campsite. Or maybe, it occurred to me now, it was *Puh! Ugh!* – there was a sort of loathing, disgust even, in that moment of final abandon.

'It made me sad,' I said.

Marigold yawned. 'It was all a long time ago.'

'Are you alone?'

She laughed. 'Yes. Unfortunately.'

'There's no need to be gratuitously unkind.'

'Don't ask, then. Gregory, I'm tired. Was there anything else?'

'How's Doug?'

'Out.'

'I'm worried about him. He seems so alienated. Lost.'

'I've told you.' Another yawn, or maybe a sigh. 'You should talk to him.'

Lately, it had been easier to communicate with Marigold over the telephone than in person, when the sight of me seemed to irritate her inordinately – as disembodied voices down a wire, we became oddly more ourselves – but not tonight.

'Have you been drinking, Gregory?'

'No. I went to listen to Martin.'

'Martin who?'

'Doesn't matter. I'm sorry I woke you.'

I hung up. Then I stood, heeled off my shoes and walked in my socks to the door, pocketing my keys as I went. I padded down the corridor and knocked on Peter Gibson's door. Hearing from within a sort of distracted grunt, I entered.

He was writing. In the far corner of the room, he sat, crouched over a pad, illuminated by a single light, a lamp on the desk, wearing a baggy, faded T-shirt and boxer shorts. To judge by the heavy, foetid atmosphere in the room and the unmade bed, he had not been out all day.

After a few seconds, he turned and smiled blearily as if, far from there being anything unusual in this visit from his tutor in the dead of night, he had been expecting it.

'Still at it?' I stood uneasily in the middle of the room.

Peter ran a hand through his lank, dark hair. Even against the light, there was a glitter to his eyes, an animation which seemed new. 'Yeah,' he said finally. 'How was it?'

'It was all right. Did the interview. The guy's a fraud but an amusing one.' Remembering McWilliam and his wrecked bed, I glanced at dishevelled blankets on Peter's bed. 'You had a kip then.'

'Yeah. Slept a bit this afternoon.'

'Sensible. Very few decent novelists can work in the afternoon. That's why they all have affairs. Fills up those empty hours before the evening shift.'

'Right.' He smiled.

I gazed at the figure bathed in light in the corner of the room, the long hair falling forward, the pale neck and painfully bony shoulder-blade. As if in a dream, I moved across the room. Standing behind Peter's chair, I laid a hand on the bare flesh of Peter's shoulder. 'Then I saw Martin,' I said as casually as I could manage.

'Yeah? What was he like?'

'Fucking brilliant.'

'Bad luck.'

We both laughed. I strengthened my grip on his shoulder. Peter turned and, with a moan that banished in a trice what was left of ambiguity, threw an arm around my waist and buried his face in my stomach. I hesitated, shocked, and lifted my right hand to disengage, to push the boy away. But when it fell, it landed gently on the scruff of his neck. I tightened my grip on his hair, turned his head upwards and towards me and, with a deep groan that seemed to come from someone else altogether, I kissed him.

Twenty-Five Great Authors Who Lost a Parent in the First Ten Years of Their Lives

Charles Baudelaire	Somerset Maugham
Charlotte Brontë	Friedrich Nietzsche
Emily Brontë	Sylvia Plath
George Byron	Edgar Allan Poe
Albert Camus	Jean-Jacques Rousseau
Elias Canetti	Jean-Paul Sartre
Samuel Taylor Coleridge	Henri Stendhal
Joseph Conrad	August Strindberg
René Descartes	Jonathan Swift
John Donne	William Thackeray
Fyodor Dostoyevsky	Leo Tolstoy
Joseph Heller	William Wordsworth
John Keats	

15

Whether erotic contentment stimulates or deters the creative impulse is, I discovered while researching the 'Love and Work' chapter for *Literary Lists*, a matter of some dispute among the great writers. On the one hand there is Browning, who wrote precisely one poem during the first three years of marriage to Elizabeth Barrett; on the other, George Eliot who was only able to write fiction when she found contentment with George Lewes. Balzac permitted himself sex but not ejaculation ('I lost a book this morning,' he wailed to his friend Latouche after a moment of carelessness) while Larkin, in a letter to J. B. Sutton, confessed that 'this letting-in of a second person spells death to perception and the desire to express', recommending the contemplation of 'glittering loneliness' for the writer. As Kipling has it, 'Few lips would be moved to song if they would find a sufficiency of kissing.'

I align myself with those for whom the letting in of a second person meant a great releasing of artistic expression: it was precisely at the moment when I first found happiness with Marigold Cameron that I began to write fiction with any degree of passion and confidence. It was as if we had discovered a new form of loving, both grander and more intimate than anything we had experienced or even heard about before. This was not just sex – sex didn't begin to cover it – but sex was where it started. Sometimes the lurch of physical yearning occurred before my conscious, sentient being had realized I had seen her. I would be aware of the sharp scrotal tingle of need, look up, and there she would be walking towards me down a street, hair, hips swinging wantonly, smiling in the knowledge of what we were both thinking. It was a sensation I had never known before. I never will again, I suppose.

The miracle (today it seems to me more of a miracle than ever) was that she wanted me as much, possibly even more, as I wanted her. When at last we were alone and I could touch her, indecorously plunge my hand between her legs like the fat boy groping in the sweet jar, I would find her drenched with need. This small, neat, controlled person who, minutes before, had been conversing so earnestly about minimalism or Warhol or the latest Conran shop was now a writhing, gasping, trembling, ravening entity of desire, all mouth and cunt and eager groping fingers.

We didn't wait. We couldn't wait. Against back street walls, on park benches, in bushes, on the deck of a ferry, in a train carriage, on the top floor of a night bus, but, most frequently of all, crammed, crouching, laughing in countless lavatory cubicles across the south of England. No word was necessary on these occasions; just a look, a nod. She would go first. I would follow seconds later, a light finger tapping on the locked door and soon we would be home, garments flying, limbs at impossible angles, straddling basins, grasping pipes, crouching over toilets, in our own gymnastic display of lust.

Sometimes we would be caught, emerging, aglow and triumphant, or, at some other time, an alert stranger might catch a look between us and, understanding in that instant that we were in thrall to an almost comically all-consuming youthful need, would look away quickly like a voyeur caught in the act, as if the mere expression on our faces was too intimate and naked for public gaze.

We talked about it, proud of the quality and quantity of our sex, smugly comparing the sharp, dangerous pleasures we enjoyed in the secret world we had invented to those experienced by other couples or on screen. For a while, during those first months, we went out of our way to court danger and discovery, as if this experience were too overwhelming to be kept to ourselves, too intense not to be on unofficial but open display.

It grew stronger. Fucking was no longer enough. We did it all, the cuffs and restraints and smacks, the power games, the bathroom stuff, the jerk-off races. We chafed at the limits of human erotic geography that excluded enticing inner territories (spleen, lungs, large intestine) from our probing and licking and penetrating. Sex boutiques were our toy shops,

Soho strip joints our cabaret. When we weren't doing it, we talked about it, fascinating one another with the differences between male and female sensation and fantasy and pleasure. At one point, we discussed sharing a lover, and even set up an informal audition over dinner for one of her friends, a slim, dark-haired type who was between boyfriends and thought to be open to experimentation, before deciding with a wordless glance early in the evening that each of us was simply too good to share.

Meanwhile we were developing what they call a relationship, acquiring a social circle, moving in together, attending young-people dinner-parties, becoming acquainted with one another's families, getting married. It was as if we were living parallel lives, one adult, responsible and socialized, the other childish, wilful, indulgent and pleasurable.

We saw our friends change as they became habituated to one another, dulled by a world of mortgages and children and disappointment. Yet, when Marigold became pregnant, the dance became if anything, more feverish. There was something ineffably arousing about this beautiful, swelling creature that still – morning, noon and night – wanted to fuck and suck and play games. Douglas arrived, the fruit not of Mr and Mrs Keays, citizens of this parish, but of their glorious lower, lust-driven natures. It had been a difficult birth and for a while Marigold's body was too tired and battered for our parallel life to be restored. Then, one night, as our baby slept, my wife knelt on the bed, peeled off her nightdress and, with a crazy, hilarious formality, presented me with the gift of her beautiful, dazzling, blue-veined, shiny-nippled breasts. I was the happiest man alive.

And so it remained. That intimacy was our constant. Through my brief moment in the sun during the early 1980s, through the financial pressures of young marriage, through the infant years of Douglas Keays. We were no longer part of the exhibition game, of course – the years of alfresco gropes and cubicle sex were over – but our bedroom became a refuge which even our son (we took to locking the door) could not penetrate. If there were times when one of us felt irresponsible, or even adolescent, in our pursuit of pleasure, we did not risk breaking the spell by confiding these thoughts to the other.

Seven years into our marriage and we were still making love every day – at night or in the morning when we awoke or, most often of all, during Douglas's sleep time during the afternoon. Lying in bed beside my beautiful naked wife while, beyond the closed curtains, the world went about its important, trivial business, I would feel absurdly blessed.

Of course, the parallel lives never do remain entirely separate; they influence and infect one another without ever quite meeting. Sometimes the effect can be benign: there were occasions – social, professional or domestic – when a glance or a touch could remind us of another reality, purer, simpler, uncompromised by words, than that with which we were both obliged to deal during our adult, clothed lives. It kept us sane, put things in perspective.

There came a time, though, when the influence seeped the other way, when even the honest lust we felt for one another was complicated by our lives as grown-ups outside the bedroom door. It was a time when I was at work on *Accidents of Trust*, yet mired in the agonies of a Chapter Five from which I would never emerge. The calls from publishers, literary editors, fellow authors, radio producers, no longer came in. Now when the telephone rang, it was from some wealthy idiot wanting London's hot new designer to energize their flat with *ch'i* and ceramic waterfalls and correctly positioned lavatories. Briefly, Marigold had persuaded herself that what appeared to be a decline in my career was, in fact, a function of integrity, a literary seriousness that precluded accepting the jobs and compromises that lesser, more successful novelists were prepared to accept, but, in those days when achievement was weighed in pounds and dollars, this was an unfashionable position and my wife could be anything but unfashionable. She became the head of the household.

The love-making, that had always contained rage in its

tenderness, safety in its danger, changed, and our shared separateness gave way to something more rivalrous and muscular. The balance of power shifted. I would catch a look in Marigold's eyes that belonged to her other life, irritated, determined and cold. Sometimes it seemed that we were no longer making love but wrestling for supremacy, looking for weakness, waiting for a moment when, with a pelvic twitch or a cunning shift of body weight, we could achieve a submission.

Her will was stronger than mine, her grip almost masculine in its power. What had for so long been fluid and sinuous was now angular and stubborn; the melting flesh became sinew and bone, elbows and knees. At first, I put the change down to my wife's new enthusiasm for the modish business of pumping iron, bicycling and rowing at the local gym but, no, it was more than a mere question of physique. An element of resentment was there, as if my way of making love had become something imposed upon her, an obligation she was no longer prepared to accept. Why should she need to be touched and caressed into readiness when, in a vulgar, male way, I was ready within seconds? And look at it, that absurd, quivering thing of mine: what once had been a shared instrument of pleasure, a link of flesh between us, she now treated with the rough lack of respect or affection accorded a weapon raised in anger against womankind, a baton representing generations of oafish patriarchal repression.

Our refuge, our sacred bed, suddenly seemed to become little more the site for a hand-to-hand-skirmish in the gender war. The new, assertive Marigold found something insultingly passive in the very geography and physics of male-female intimacy. Was it fair that I should enter her, as if she were some kind of receptacle? Where did it reside, my right to sexual completion within seconds if I so wished (although I never did) if not in the traditional male-female hegemony? Why, in fact, should she be obliged to lie beneath me like some beast of burden upon which the squire of the bedroom had elected to take a ride? She became active, aggressive, often treating my body as if it were no more sentient than one of the toys with which we used to play. I (it) was there for her pleasure. She rarely looked at me now, but fucked with a grim, abstract determination. The more advanced her desire, the further she slipped from me.

Was it normal? I wondered. Was this the intimate expression of a great general change in the balance of power between men and women? Perhaps, all over the western world, wives had begun acting in bed like men, using their husbands as little more than sexual aids to be taken up, used, and pushed away. Now and then I attempted to assert myself, to make love in a more active, masterful, manly way, but if I was not rejected (she was either in the mood or not in the mood – there was no middle way), a bizarre sort of tussle would develop which, under any other circumstances, would be funny but which now made me feel like the archetypal male abuser, the marital rapist. Invariably, after a certain amount of push and shove, I would submit. We never talked about this, perhaps because each of us, in our different ways, felt ashamed by the way we behaved.

In the end, sexual superiority was no longer an option. Why should the person who, in every other area was less potent and active, assume a position of power in the bedroom?

When I made my move, Marigold would push me back impatiently and take control. When she straddled me, face turned away, one hand pressing down upon my chest or even my neck as if to prevent me from escaping, the other working away at herself like a housemaid trying to remove a stubborn stain, I would lie still, undulating obediently. When she came with an angry gasp and a wince (even her orgasms were resentful now), I followed a few steps behind, apologetically, insignificantly, in sex as in life.

Within minutes of disengagement, she would turn her back on me and quickly fall asleep.

16

It would be convenient and tidy-minded to gloss over the events of that night in Peter's room, to treat what happened between us as an act of bonding, a passing moment when the spiritual communication between teacher and pupil, writer and writer, found a brief physical manifestation.

Convenient, tidy-minded, but untrue.

I awoke the next morning to find myself in a tangle of

sheets, my face buried in the unkempt dark mass of Peter's hair, my hand resting on his waist. The window had remained closed and the air in the room was thick with the stale, sickly memory of the night's activity. I pulled him gently towards me; sleepily, he rolled over, lying against me. I lowered the duvet and gazed at his lean body, so pale that it seemed to glow in the light that penetrated the curtains. I had thought that desire would pass but now, breathless and aroused, I knew it would not.

I am not gay. Apart from the few isolated incidents at public school, which I subsequently regarded as functions of loneliness and the adolescent need for tactile comfort, I have remained steadfastly and unfashionably heterosexual. It is true that, over recent years, I have caught myself daydreaming of those days, specifically of a younger boy for whom a passing *tendresse* found less innocent expression in my bed on my very last night at school, but then the writer's imagination is an intrepid traveller; 'all great novels, all true novels, are bisexual,' as Milan Kundera has said. In reality, I have many gay friends, whom I have accompanied to their favoured clubs and leather bars, without the thought of upgrading our relationship ever arising. While I have read the cream of male homosexual fiction, from Gide to White, from Baldwin to Hollinghurst – indeed have taken an interest in the arcane practices they describe – I have studied them with a cool, artistic inquisitiveness, untouched by the slightest breath of carnality.

Yet, of course, one is curious. The options available, the etiquette involved in resolving who does what to whom, the physical equality, the brute simplicity of it all. With a woman, however brief and inglorious the encounter, the ghost of Relationship, of Future, of Hope hovers over the bed. A power struggle is being enacted. Homosexual man has resolved this difficulty, affording primacy to desire and desire only. Or at least so one gathers from the extensive literature available on the subject.

Much of this natural writerly curiosity was satisfied during my night with Peter Gibson. I discovered that, with the right man, there is no 'After you, Cecil; no no, after you, Claud'. There was no edgy negotiation around the giving and taking of pleasure. With the right man, it is all giving and all taking, all consumed and all-consuming. Far from being overcome by shyness and lack of experience, we let instinct lead us. We became our bodies, beyond words and thoughts and manners, glorying in the unaccustomed touch of man's flesh under hands and lips. Lacking women's scented softness which even during her earth-mother, hairy armpit phase Marigold retained (as if the female has a sort of natural soap gland), physical love with Peter felt feral and natural. Possibly, on any other night, one or both of us might have recoiled from what we were doing to one another but we were each in a state of extreme vulnerability, Peter from his writing, me from my life.

For a few moments we lay there in silence. Peter's head was turned away from me but I sensed that he too was awake. There was a tension to his body, as if he feared that, when I remembered what had happened last night, I would leap from the bed in girlish horror and embarrassment. Truth to tell, there was no danger of that. We had made love three times before falling into fitful, satiated sleep and each time we had found each other seemed better and more natural than the last. I ran my hand down the long, shallow channel of his backbone, coming to rest between his damp, angular but-tocks. He squeezed my fingers twice, flirtatiously.

'Good morning,' he mumbled sleepily, and I was discon-certed by something new and faggoty in his voice. Or maybe it had always been there, a bat-squeak inaudible to the hetero-sexual ear, and it was only now that I could hear it. He turned towards me and smiled randily. That moment of open day-light intimacy alarmed me briefly; as if he knew that I needed to be converted once more, he pulled me closer, slithered down the bed and took me in his mouth, rolling my softness around his palate like an expert wine-taster. I stared ahead of me and found myself gazing at the stack of foolscap writing pads on the desk where he had been writing the previous day. I counted twelve of them.

'Have you finished?'

He murmured something unintelligible into my crotch.

'You don't want to hurry it. So many novels lose themselves in the final quarter when the author is hurrying for the finishing line. I always think Greene has that problem.'

He held my balls and gave them a gentle but slightly irritated twist. 'Shut the fuck up, teach,' he said, then began to work on me in earnest.

I took a handful of his hair and pulled him off me, his lips making a comical sucking noise as they slipped off me. I knelt over him and gathered up his long, spidery legs as if we were engaged in an erotic wheelbarrow race. He looked up at me, smiling, more open and happy than I had ever seen. I laughed, at the absurdity of it all, at the release and freedom. I guided myself into him and made love to him, not with the savage, flailing need of last night, but slowly, contemplatively, teasing him by holding off as long as possible, almost as if he were a girl.

Later, we lay in each other's arms, a smell entirely unlike anything I have known after sex with a woman – a scent of pure, honest, unsullied desire – clinging to both of us.

'Would you like to read my novel?' he whispered.

'Of course.' I ran my fingers down his rib cage.

He turned and touched my face. 'Was this the plan?' he asked. 'Was it what this weekend was all about?'

'How do you mean?'

'To get your student in the sack?'

'No.' I shook my head, shocked by the implication. 'I was as surprised as you were.'

'You are?'

'I'm not like that. I've never – I mean, I don't . . . do this.'

'Nor am I.' He sat up and kissed me. 'Nor was I.'

It was then that I began to feel distantly, obscurely alarmed.

17

I had heard the novel, or at least I felt as if I had heard it. On
our way back to London, my pupil, apparently liberated in
some strange way by the events of the previous night, gabbled
and bubbled and laughed like a child on the last day of term.
At first, this garrulousness – jokes, snatches of songs, zany
biographies created for our fellow drivers as we drove past
them on the M40 – amused me. Then he turned to the subject
of his novel. He outlined the narrative, dilated upon its
themes and characters, described scenes with such vividness
and fluency that the text might have been there written on
the road before us.

Banbury. Oxford. Thame. Hearing a bad novel recited can
be a trial, but hearing a good one, written by a boy of twenty,
can be worse. Hypnotized by his words, I found myself
forgetting where I was, almost letting go of my natural tutorly
scepticism and being drawn into the strange alternative
reality Peter was creating. He had reached that point in a
work when, suddenly, the long uphill trudge becomes a
joyous downward romp towards completion. Nothing could
stop him now; every disparate element of the novel had fused
into perfect coherence. He could talk about it for hour upon
hour if allowed, because it was there, an established thing,
which conversation could no longer destroy.

Aylesbury. Princes Risborough. Slough. On and on he went.
I thought at the time that it was lack of sleep and the delayed
trauma of what had happened the previous night which made
me unusually susceptible to Peter's narrative. Now I know

that my first instinct was correct: there was something undeniably powerful, original and strange to this work.

I felt sick. I found myself hoping that Peter was revealing a hidden talent as a performer, that the written version would turn out to be a faint and blurred shadow of what I was hearing. I willed him to be quiet but, when I glanced across at him, he misinterpreted my look and smiled back at me with an open, bashful affection which made me shudder. I longed to be back home in my loft, surrounded my own novels, working quietly on some interesting literary list or statistic ('Great Writers Who Have Discovered They Are Homosexual in Middle Age', perhaps) but I was unable to escape from Peter's voice, his story.

He directed me though west London to the block of flats off Hammersmith Broadway where he lived. I parked in what at first glance I took to be some sort of scrapyard but turned out to be a car park for those who inhabited the flats. Weary, irritated by the prolonged, brilliant threnody of egotism to which I had been subjected, I left the car's engine running.

'Sorry, I seem to have run on a bit.' Peter smiled confidingly.

'No problem. It was all very interesting,' I said, gripping the steering-wheel with both hands.

'Shall we take the urine-soaked lift to my little hovel?' he asked in the gently mocking voice he seemed to have acquired since last night.

'I had better get back.' I smiled briefly, coldly. 'Real life awaits me.'

Peter laid a hand on my thigh. 'You mean last night wasn't real life?'

'You know it wasn't.'

'It felt real enough to me.'

I glanced across and saw, for the first time, how different he was today. There was an openness, colour in the cheeks, an alertness to those startling blue eyes. Mysteriously, his teeth seemed less grey than they had been yesterday; his hair, no longer lank and dull, had a sort of glow to it. Memories of last night caught me unawares. I felt constricted and uneasy. Peter whispered my name, looked around him to see that the coast was clear and, with a sluttish knowingness, leant across and unzipped me. Before I could protest, he lowered his head. He took me in his mouth, his right hand holding me, his left reaching between my legs as if somehow he wanted to take all of me into his mouth and consume me just as he had quietly consumed my knowledge, my experience, my life as a writer, for the novel he had secretly been writing. In that moment of unnerving expertise, as I sat, helpless, eyes closed, in thrall to his ministrations, it occurred to me that overnight he had become the teacher, I the pupil. In spite of the longing I felt, I resented his precociousness, remembering details of his novel – how easy, authoritative, convincing and full of incident it seemed beside the stuttering, empty uncertainties of *Insignificance*, or *Mind the Gap* or even *Adultery in Hampstead*.

I opened my eyes and checked that no passers-by were approaching. It was not, heaven knows, that I had engaged in a semi-public act of sex, alert yet lustful, but there was something sharper and sweeter and more dangerous to what was happening and I didn't like it at all. As if sensing the direction of my thoughts, Peter moved and nuzzled me against his cheek, like a child with a toy. 'Come with me in the lift to paradise,' he whispered.

'No.' With as much dignity as I could muster, I pushed him away from me. 'I don't think that's a good idea.' I zipped myself, did up my belt and looked pointedly at my watch. There was something smug and triumphalist in Peter which made me distrust his new flirtatiousness. I hated him right then – hated his assumption that, limping and sweaty with need, I would follow him to the pigsty where he lived, hated his power over me, hated his youth and his golden future. He had lured me onwards, tricked me with his fake unworldliness, until he was almost – *almost* – in control.

He sat up and stared ahead, sulky and affronted, his lips wet and swollen like those of a porn starlet resting between takes. 'I'm sorry if I embarrassed you,' he said.

'We shouldn't go too fast.'

'You didn't think that last night.'

'I'm not supposed to get involved with my students. I could get fired.'

'Fired.' There was real contempt in his voice.

'I'm not saying we can't see each other. Just that . . . well, I'm sure you understand.'

'No blow-jobs in the car park.' His voice was thin and venomous. 'No bunk-ups on the tenth floor because someone might see us. What will it be then – the next Gloucester Festival?'

'I'm a married man. I have a teenage son. I'm –' I sighed, suddenly irritated by this conversation. 'I'm straight, Peter.'

He looked across at me and I, with a lurch of alarm, I noticed there were tears in his eyes. 'Please come upstairs,' he whispered. 'You needn't stay long.'

A knot of rage tightened in the pit of my stomach. I was not unused to this kind of scene but somehow enacting it with another man seemed absurd and humiliating. I cursed myself for the writerly vulnerability which had drawn me to my student's bedroom the previous night, yet another false move in my life for which Martin had been indirectly responsible.

'I'll see you in class on Thursday,' I said. 'Maybe you could bring some of the novel to read.'

He swore, not at me but to himself, like a man who had suddenly forgotten something. He opened the passenger door and, half falling out of it, loped away towards the cavernous entrance to the tower block. I leant across, pulled the door shut, jammed the car into gear and drove off without giving him another look.

> **Top Five Early Starters Among Modern Writers**
> 1. John Updike knew he wanted to be a writer as soon as he saw his mother at a typewriter.
> 2. George Orwell wrote his first poem at four and knew from the age of five that he would be a writer and had completed a verse play by the age of fourteen.
> 3. Norman Mailer wrote his first novel at seven.
> 4. Evelyn Waugh was also writing stories at seven.
> 5. Gore Vidal had published five novels by the age of twenty-five.

18

My son was stirring into life in a manner that made me uneasy. We had had become used to his reclusiveness; now that he was leaving his room, he became less recognizable, more mysterious, than ever.

When he went out, he never explained where he was going but the evidence on his return – dark, dilated pupils, violent mood swings and long, gulped drinks of water at the kitchen sink – suggested that, while at large he had given himself some sort of narcotic treat. There was a new bearish confidence to him now, as he crashed about the house; he talked rarely and, when he did, he spoke in a loud, belligerent voice. No longer shifty, he sometimes stared me straight in the eye as if waiting for the moment when he could gain violent revenge for the excess of parental zeal that had led to my pushing him to the floor in the kitchen.

One morning he startled me by barging into my room as I tussled with a section of *Literary Lists* for which I had gathered material but had not at that moment conveyed into finished form. The way that he stared down at the blank page in front of me made my stomach lurch with rage.

'Have you any idea how annoying that is?' I asked.

'Wha? *Wha?*' It was the impatient squawk of a young crow demanding food from a parent.

I sighed. 'Doug, I'm working. I know it doesn't mean much to you, but it's important to me. It may not look much –' I waved wearily at the sheet in front of me '– but it involves thinking.'

My son stared out of the window.

'You wouldn't do it to Mum,' I said.

'Wha?'

'Burst into her office without knocking.'

'She's got a secretary an' all. It's a bit different, ennit.'

I looked at my son – unshaven, barefoot, in a torn and faded T-shirt, long baggy shorts over his thin, yet oddly hairy legs. I sensed that he wanted to say more, perhaps dispense some casual act of adolescent cruelty, but that something was holding him back.

'Just because I don't make as much money as Mum, it doesn't mean that what I do is meaningless.'

For a brief, telling moment, my son glanced down at the blank pad in front of me, then smiled, almost sympathetically.

'Writing's all about the blank page,' I spoke quickly before he could say anything. 'Sometimes it can be worth a hundred pages. Graham Greene said –'

'Who's he then?'

'Never mind.'

For a moment he stood in silence. There was nothing that put Doug more quickly on the defensive than any suggestion that he and I might have something in common, that I could talk to him as a fellow adult. In the past, the mildest attempt to engage in a normal, neutral discussion of subject of interest to me would send him scurrying back to his room, as if mere conversation with me risked some form of subtle contamination.

'It's ridiculous,' he said suddenly, and I knew that we had reached the reason for his visit. 'I just have no money, ever, right? I go out, right, and I try to have a normal life, right, and

I'm with these people and, I dunno, I just have to sit there, like holding on to this half-pint like I'm some sort of kid. It's just totally ridiculous.'

Although I knew that the impulse behind this outburst (quite a peroration by Doug's standards) was entirely mercenary, I none the less found it oddly moving. I saw my son, down the pub with his mates, trying on adulthood like an ill-fitting suit, grunting and laughing and going 'owi, owi' in a clumsy attempt to join the lager culture. Although most of his friends were middle-class cockneys like him, none of them seemed quite so full of dull despair as my son. They had part-time jobs; one of them even had a girlfriend, a sulky, wordless blonde girl with a chewing-gum habit. I sensed that none of them was quite so alienated from the two people who had brought him into the world as he was.

'You've got pocket money. Twenty quid a week's not bad, considering everything's paid for you.' Already, I felt wearied by this argument. Not only was I venturing into treacherous territory, hardly being a financial success story myself, but somehow the whole business of money seemed so marginal. I longed for Doug to be able to go out with his friends and buy his round, I loathed playing the part of the skinflint parent, yet I knew that merely handing over cash would add to the harm that, somehow, Marigold and I seemed to have inflicted on him. 'If you worked, it would be easier to justify.'

'What's the difference between me reading a few magazines and you sitting at your desk?' A closed angry look crossed Doug's face and I knew I had lost him. 'Why's one such a waste of time while the other's really hard work? If I decided that I was this writer geezer and spent all day picking my nose and doing nothing, would you be really proud of me and give me loads of pocket money?'

'I happen to be a professional writer.'

'Oh yeah, right.' He seemed to be about to say something.

'And I teach once a week. I do interviews. I don't like it but I do it.' I waved at the shelves along the wall of one side of the office where I kept carefully labelled box-files containing my various uncompleted projects. 'There are very few days when I do absolutely nothing.'

Doug laughed nastily and nodded in the direction of the virgin page before me.

'Owi, so all this sitting about and thinking makes you feel tired, right. That's why you have to go out most evenings. And Mum's the same. You leave me and fucking Donovan here on our fuckin' tod, right?'

Not entirely happy as to the direction the conversation was going, I reached for a copy of D'Israeli's *Curiosities of Literature* as if to look something up.

'You know what? I feel tired, just like you do.'

'There's no need to shout, Doug.'

'So I wanna go out, right. But I can't, 'cos I got no fuckin' dosh, have I.'

I laid down D'Israeli. 'I'll speak to your mother,' I said.

'Owi, you want me to get money?' Doug was standing his ground. 'I can, you know. There's ways. You won't like 'em but I can do it. No problem.'

I looked up at him and suddenly felt that my son was stronger than me. He had delivered the ultimate teenage threat. Pay up or see what happens.

'I have to work,' I said weakly.

'Owi, suit yourself.' He left chirpily, slamming the door to my office behind him.

After Doug's pocket money was increased to £30 a week, an odd self-consciousness descended on the house. Where normally we would pull against each other, a family that was not quite a family, parents who did almost anything to avoid parenting, a child cocooned in his room and longing to fly free, now we seemed to become aware of our reliance upon one another, boats frozen in the same lake, together yet apart.

It must have been a quiet time in the world of *feng shui* design. Marigold would visit the office briefly during the morning, returning home to potter unconvincingly about the garden, sometimes directing towards Ned the gardener what were not so much instructions as gentle indications of what might possibly be done, subject to karma, astrological appropriateness and general vibrations. She took to making fussy vegetarian meals which she insisted Doug and I should share. Some evenings we would sit in the kitchen, making stilted conversation like a dysfunctional family whose rehabilitation into normal life was being recorded by a hidden camera.

Doug's presence at these occasions, and other small concessions to civilization ('Owi?' he would say, encountering me during the day) seemed to be only partly the result of his pay-rise. There was a sort of kinship in his attitude to me these days. We were both lost, both spiritually alone. We both spent much of the day doing nothing in particular and worrying about it.

'How's the old blank page going, then?' he asked me one evening as we picked at some highly-coloured Buddhist thing Marigold had prepared.

'I've discovered a rather intriguing connection between the writing life and sewing-machines.'

Marigold looked from me to Doug as if this new level of communication was not entirely welcome. 'Sewing-machines,' she smiled thinly. 'Riveting.'

'Nice one, Mum.'

'Oh.' Marigold laughed, genuinely this time. 'A pun.'

'Actually it is rather interesting,' I continued, taking encouragement from this unusual outbreak of good humour. 'There was George Gissing who gave Nell Harrison, the young prostitute who became his wife, a machine. Samuel Butler became involved with Lucie Dumas, a whore from Islington, and again the sewing-machine was an essential part of their relationship. So much so that, after her death, Butler would keep a kettleholder she had made pinned up above his mantelpiece. Arnold Bennett was so impressed by this story that he asked his wife to sew next door to the room where he was writing, but unfortunately he was disturbed by the sound of the needle against the thimble.'

'Fascinating,' said my wife.

'What's with all these prostitutes?' asked Doug.

Glancing at Marigold, who is uncomfortable with any discussion of a vaguely sexual nature in front of our son, I said, 'Funnily enough, writers do have something of a *faiblesse* in that regard. I've recently been compiling a list of eminent literary figures who lost their virginity to a prostitute. Byron, Hugo, Flaubert, Joyce, Maugham. When he was in Africa, Graham Greene was said to have received consignments of condoms from London in batches of a thousand.'

'Thank you, Gregory. I think we've heard enough now.'

'Five hundred words a day, then off he would go. Apparently he liked doing it in churches.'

My wife sighed.

'Behind the altar.'

She laid down her knife and fork.

'With his god-daughter.'

'Grow up, Gregory.' At last she spoke but with more weariness than anger. 'You're showing off and it's very silly.'

It was that word 'silly' which doused the conversation. Silliness was the enemy for Marigold: it covered everything from gossip to jokes to irreverence towards the role of toilets in *feng shui*. Above all, it covered all references to sex. Even my good-hearted attempts, when we were alone and talking to one another, to remind her that there had been a time in our lives when we had thought, talked and done little else but varying forms of silliness, failed to move her.

'Anyway.' My wife picked at the salad and I could tell from the casual tone in her voice that a small conversational hand-grenade would soon be on its way. 'I've always thought that people who end up paying for it are particularly sad, requiring some sort of *agency* to find women for them.'

I looked across the table and she stared back and briefly. We both forgot that Doug was there. I must have blushed at her careful deployment of the word 'agency' because she laughed angrily. 'Or maybe they're just writers,' she said.

19

There are times in the life of a writer when mere written words are no longer enough. The inner turmoil is such that brisk, externalizing action is needed. Some set off on a perilous solitary journey; others go scuba-diving or plunge down a pot-hole. Doubtless, Martin plays a couple of vigorous sets with Fent or Hitch or another of his brilliant pals.

None of these things work for me quite as well as Bayswater and the Agency.

Until three years ago, I had been in the habit of turning in these moments of crisis (decision, indecision, exhaustion from over-production or under-production) to the lover of the moment. There would be a brief call to her office or library or classroom. She would have learnt quickly enough that a writerly cry for help brooks no delay. Moments later, we would be falling upon one another, escaping into the one act, so simple yet so complex, so pure yet so unutterably filthy, with which humans have, since time immemorial, consoled themselves at moments of stress, conflict and pain. The Novotel, Hammersmith, was a favourite meeting place.

That, at least, was the fantasy. In fact, only one of my lovers, a witchy mature student with long dark hair and a taste for various subtle forms of masochism truly understood that the entire point of these occasions was their cold, infuriated anonymity. The others would, after a few moments of half-hearted role-playing, descend into motherly mode, expressing concern, offering wine or back massages, talking and talking and talking as if it were not words that had caused the problem in the first place. Sometimes they would even suggest that it would 'nicer' if we met at their place. It is in the nature of the artistic life that what D. H. Lawrence called 'the dark side of the moon' is rarely understood.

I discovered the Agency by blessed accident. A young and indigent Polish student at the Institute had tearfully revealed to the Institute's Student Counsellor Mike Summers that she was paying for her tuition fees in Design Technology by selling her body once or twice a week on a part-time basis. Chatting with Mike in the staff room, I learnt the existence of several organizations which, under the guise of friendship or penpal agencies, provided the services of foreign students who needed to supplement their incomes. The Agency was not the one used by the compromised Pole, but might well have been. Some time after the fuss had died down, I made further enquiries.

An ordinary civilian, failing to understand the affinity between those who give themselves to art and those who give themselves on a double bed in Bayswater, might regard my visits to the Agency as tawdry and humiliating but to my fellow writers there will be no mystery. It was Flaubert who pointed out that within a house of sin are found precisely the elements that appeal to the novelist: 'lechery, frustration, negation of human relationships, physical frenzy, the clink of gold'.

Not that I have ever been attracted to the traditional 'brothel', the time-honoured 'prostitute'. The Agency exists in the moral grey area between love and commerce; to put it in literary terms, the questions that provide key subtexts for the average date (Will I get sex? What is in this for me? How much money will it cost me, or make me?) become, gloriously and unavoidably, the thrust of the main narrative. Its setting, a three-storey house in a small square off Lancaster Gate, is dignified, understated and Georgian. Its administrator, Annabel Beauchamp, is in her early forties, a greying blonde with a comfortable figure and the air of a woman whose racy past had given way to a passion for cooking and gardening. By some cunning piece of design, the rooms at the Agency, as neat and welcoming as a girl-bachelor flat, are so organized that male visitors are never in danger of encountering one another while furtively making their way up or down the stairs. All in all, the establishment provides a perfect illusion of normality, shot through with the merest hint of the forbidden.

There were, admittedly, complications in my arrangements with the Agency. The small influx of funds from Marigold's business earmarked 'living expenses' restricted me to a monthly visit. Then, despite not being by nature a pluralist in amatory matters, I have had to come to terms with the notion that, either I must sacrifice my need for spontaneous expression or on occasions 'make do' when my girlfriend Pia is unavailable. Charming and good-looking as Annabel's girls were, Pia and I had come to understand each other so well that, in the end, I took to making reservations. At first, planning weeks in advance in Annabel's study made me feel bourgeois and trammelled, like a businessman booking his next check-up at a clinic, but the indiscriminate, any-girl-will-do promiscuity of the alternative was worse.

Gloucester, Martin, Peter, marital and parental unrest at home: suddenly, four days after my weekend away, I knew that I was unable to wait the fortnight until my next appointment with Pia. I needed reassurance – soft, female reassurance, a reminder of my essential manliness. After a morning spent listing redhead writers, I picked up the telephone and dialled the number of the Agency. I was so agitated that I almost, but not quite, forgot to introduce myself by my *nom de boudoir*.

'Tim.' There was the merest hint of surprise and disapproval in Annabel's voice. She ran an establishment where certain proprieties were observed. For regular visitors to cast their diary aside and ring, breathless and on the hoof in search of immediate romance was regarded as a breach of etiquette. 'Are you changing your appointment?'

'Is Pia there?'

'Pia?' Cruelly, she hesitated long enough for the sickening possibility to occur to me that Pia had left, returned to Macedonia or whatever miserable part of East Europe she belonged. 'Pia's at work, Tim. She's got exams after Christmas. I'll see if I can find Svetna for you. You know her, don't you?'

'Yes.' I remembered a trim, hard-eyed Serbian with brisk, knowing hands. 'I've met Svetna, but I really would prefer Pia.'

'Tim, I told you –'

'I'll pay double.'

Annabel sighed and pretended to check in her diary. 'I can make no promises,' she said. 'Be here in an hour and I'll see what I can do.'

'Would a credit card be all right?'

Annabel laughed. It seemed she had overcome her misgivings. 'It will do very nicely, Tim,' she said.

Gasping my thanks, I hung up.

An hour. I considered killing some time in a pub, calming myself with alcohol, but then I realized that calm was not what I needed, that the company of ordinary, non-writing people with their dull, inane chatter would take the edge off me. I wanted edge. Edge was part of the deal, part of being a writer. I drove east, parked in a side street and waited, my breath shallow and feverish, my entire being abuzz with anticipation.

'Tim.' When, after an interminable 45 minutes, Annabel Beauchamp opened the front door to me, she was actually wearing an apron. 'Sorry I can't touch you.' She held up two plumpish hands on which there seemed to be traces of flour. 'I've been baking.'

'Right.' I smiled, playing the game. 'Very nice too.'

'Hope so.' She went ahead of me through the hall, her hands held out comically from her sides, like a penguin. I followed her into the kitchen. 'Help yourself to some Chardonnay.' She nodded in the direction of an opened bottle on a sideboard. 'Glasses are in the cupboard.'

139

On every visit to the Agency, I would be startled by its proprietor's brilliant façade of ordinariness. To a non-expert eye, she could pass as the wife of an estate agent, living in one of the smarter suburbs of west London. With that comfortable figure, going but not quite gone, the short blonde hair around a pretty, mature, carefully tended face, she belonged to the Volvo brigade – hubby, dinner-parties, part-time job, kids, a carefully controlled affair with someone who posed no social or emotional threat (a tennis coach, a small-time actor). Only those attuned to such things, fellow misfits and hooligans, would discern the direct, predatory eyes ever alert for sexual weakness or opportunity, eyes which, at some time or other, had seen virtually every indignity man and woman inflicted upon one another in the name of pleasure. If she had any private life, I assumed, from the flash frost which descends on her features at the merest hint of flirtation, that it was of the sapphic variety.

'Now, don't sit down, Tim,' she said, taking up a position behind a breadboard on which there was an unsavoury lump of dough. For a moment, I thought she would ask me to help her in some kitchen chore, to be a love and peel those potatoes for her, but now, as she briskly grated some turnip-like object, I sensed a certain displeasure. 'Don't make a habit of this, Tim.' Without looking up, she spoke quietly, a reproving schoolteacher disappointed by a normally reliable pupil. 'We're not officially open and Pia has her exams to think of. It was only because she likes you that she agreed to come over.'

I wanted to believe her – my more innocent nature *did* believe her – but I was not in the mood to be patronized and lectured by an up-market madame. I smiled, resting my eyes upon her busy right hand so that she knew that I was not taken in for one moment by this housewifely charade. 'Some plastic,' I said, taking a card out of my wallet and laying it on the kitchen table.

Annabel darted a beady glance in its direction. 'I can't deal with that now. Leave it here and you can sign on the way out.'

She wiped her brow with the back of her hand in a manner which reminded of my wife. 'Why don't you watch some TV in the sitting-room? I'll tell you when Pia arrives.'

I made my way to the small, tidy sitting-room next door and switched on the television. On some loud and vulgar confession show, a row of plump, unlovely disgruntled women with their menfolk in unconvincing drag were shouting and pointing at one another while an audience whooped and hollered in almost ecstatic disapproval. 'LOSE THAT COCKTAIL DRESS OR LOSE ME!' read a banner in one corner of the screen. I turned down the sound and watched the freak show in silence.

Annabel had done a good job with this room; it had the air, relaxed yet slightly impersonal, of some sort of waiting-room or, at best, the lounge bar in a second-rate club. Just the right number of just the right magazines, all this month's, lay on the low table in the middle of the room. The sofa and two chairs were comfortable and elegant enough to grace any normal middle-class home. The Victorian reproductions on the wall cleverly combined respectability with an unmistakable, repressed, pent-up longing. The Lady of Shallot. Ophelia. Love Locked Out. Only the absence of photographs, invitations or other indicators of family life gave any clue that those who sat in this room were within minutes of the most intimate relief.

Catching a glimpse of myself in a small framed mirror on the wall to the right of me, I looked away. Then, irritated by my own furtiveness, I stared myself in the eye. A man in a room. Love Let In. I looked all right: there was something taut and drawn up and ready about me. The figure that I sometimes saw in the reflection of shop windows during my afternoon walks (dishevelled, lost, so anonymous as to be almost invisible) had given way to someone firm, purposeful, strong – a man about to fulfil the erotic purpose which was his right and duty. On an impulse, I reached for my wallet and took out the Snowdon shot of Granta's Best of Young British Novelists which I like to keep with me. It seemed to me now that, to the perceptive viewer, I had already been showing signs of being out of place in that august gathering. Never good-looking in the traditional sense, I had acquired in my mid-thirties the first traces of a general spread and slackening of muscle tone which unhappiness and lack of exercise would later exacerbate. My front teeth had begun to obtrude as if they had had enough of my mouth and were making a break for freedom, and I was smiling for the photograph, innocently unaware that any serious writer should scowl when cameras appear. Beside the faces of those around me (Salman's sleepy eagle, Martin's sneering bad boy, Julian's head prefect, Graham's bank-clerk intellectual) I cut a jovial, goofy figure, like someone who had blundered into the shoot from a nearby rugby club dinner.

I wondered how, after all my adventures, I had ended up here. Once I had thought that I was cutting down on the time, the lying and excess emotion demanded by an affair, but now I knew that a different form of economy was at work. 'A sexual act leaves no memory. There are no sexual madeleines,' D. M. Thomas has written. Nothing, in my experience could be further from the truth.

It was not the social or conversational hinterland of the women of my past which had remained with me – not what they said, or believed, or what made us laugh together. It was the moments of true, inescapable nakedness and erotic self-exposure which, to this day, startled me with their vivid immediacy: the moment when Anna returning to her flat from the Institute slowly raised the skirt of her dark suit to reveal that she was knickerless and ready; the way that Caitlin would turn her head away from me and whisper, as if talking to a child, 'Push, push'; the tears that, for reasons she could never explain, filled Maria's eyes when we made love; the almost clownish blush that suffused Ruth's face seconds before, chewing her lip like a child with a maths problem, she came; the sighs, the words, the looks, the shameful little secret desires and tricks and peculiarities which, unique as a fingerprint, express more truly and eloquently a woman's character than any words. For me, it was *only* the sexual act which left a memory – sharp, erotic and discomfiting. The rest (jokes, conversations, rows, even names, sometimes) was faded and indistinct.

At the Agency, the extraneous life of conversation and feeling had no place. Once, in the early days of my arrangement with Pia, I had asked her if for women, past acts of sex remained as snared in the memory as they do for men. Vaguely puzzled, she replied in her harsh cockneyed East European accent that 'A man's a man. Some good, some bad, most are in the boring medium. It is not interesting.' Verbal communication now played little part in our dealings.

I was already afraid of the way I was heading, of this segregation of the sexual from everything else within my life. Where would it end? In furtive, tottering visits to massage parlours in Mayfair? In, after some kind of traumatic Cheeveresque realignment, a desperate search for relief with hard-eyed rent boys on heaths and in public lavatories?

There was a knock on the door. 'She's here,' Annabel called out. 'You know the way.'

I knew the way.

The shoes were wrong. It was the first thing I noticed when I entered her room, having knocked twice (my only and last concession to the intimate hierarchy in which we were both involved) to find her sitting on the bed. Great, clumsy, platform-soled things utterly at odds with the impression of lightness which I require. The skirt was too short: it was almost tarty.

She looked up, dark moon eyes in a pinched, pale face peering, reluctant, almost resentful. It took my breath away. I felt a knot of anger within me. Then I remembered that my visit had been unannounced, that moments ago she had been living her life rather than playing a part in mine. If she was breaking the rules now, then so was I.

'Wash your face.' When I spoke, my voice was husky, more imperious than I had intended.

She shrugged, stood up and walked in a casual, slatternly way to a wash-basin. I closed my eyes briefly, hating that lazy amble, wondering why so consummate an actress in bed betrayed herself so obviously, swinging her arse in lazy invitation, when out of it. She washed her face, carefully with soap, rinsed and dried it. With both hands on the basin, she looked at me in the mirror.

'Better,' I said and nodded in the direction of the bed.

She gave a sort of sigh and seemed, briefly, to be about to say something. Then, thinking better of it, she turned and wandered towards the bed, kicking off her absurd shoes and reaching back to unzip her dress. As if I were not there, she undressed, folded her clothes on the chair like a well brought-up child, then lay on the bed, staring at the ceiling.

I asked her to look at me. Slowly, she turned and gazed at me, one eye hidden in the dark profusion of her hair. It might be the tilt of the chin, or the hint of downward curl to the thin lips, or maybe something in those dark eyes. Whatever it was, the likeness took my breath away every time I saw her.

No, we don't converse any more. In the early days, when I had discovered her, we used to share a few pleasantries but her hard, Eastern European accent and the banal, obscene vocabulary she employed fatally undermined our fiction with faulty dialogue. I talk now and then. She listens.

So, moments later, lying together on a double bed in Bayswater, my body pale and bloated beside hers, I talked about Cheltenham and McWilliam and Martin as I caressed her hair, her face, her breasts, allowing my hand to work its way slowly downwards, murmuring all the while. Did I mention Peter? Of course not. Like writing fiction, making love requires the maintenance of a deft balance between passionate commitment and cool, controlling distance. I reached between her legs and, to my surprise, an involuntary gasp escaped her lips, followed by a few muttered, angry words in her native language. She had not been working for her exam when the call had come but had been in bed with some oikish young lover. I felt the knot of pain and anger tighten within me. I lifted a shoulder and she turned over, her eyes closed, her face against the pillow. Above her, I massaged her narrow shoulders, her muscular back, running my hand over the sweet curve of her buttocks, reminiscing about the times we had had, our feelings for one another, about the past, words only dying when, arching her back, she lifted herself to my lips, moving at last, unable to resist the tide of her own pleasure. Soon, too soon, I felt her shudder beneath me and slowly relax, until she lay still, breathing heavily.

I lay my head in the small of her back, feeling her cold sweat against my cheek. There seemed to be tears in my eyes.

'Marigold,' I whispered. 'My Marigold.'

Top Five Literary Brothel-Creepers

1. Victor Hugo was such a legendary user of brothels that the day of his state funeral was, according to the Goncourt diaries, 'celebrated by wholesale copulation, a priapic orgy, with all the prostitutes on holiday from their brothels, coupling with all and sundry on the lawns of the Champs-Elysées'. As a mark of respect to their greatest client, Paris prostitutes wore black crepe underwear.

2. Gustave Flaubert confessed to Hugo in 1853, 'It is perhaps a perverse taste, but I like prostitution . . . a glance into its depths makes one giddy and teaches one all manner of things. It fills you with such sadness! And makes you dream so of love!'

3. Samuel Butler picked up a 21-year-old French whore, Lucie Dumas, at the Angel pub in Islington. For the next twenty years, he and his friend, the biographer Henry Festing Jones, visited her once a week (Butler on Wednesday afternoons, Festing Jones on Thursday afternoons), paying her £1 a visit, on the understanding that she gave up all other clients.

4. Theodore Dreiser sometimes took three whores in a day and still could not resist pawing women and brushing against them in crowded places.

5. Joseph Heller boasted: 'Brothels are in my work and in my life as well.'

20

I was back on course. The printed-out manuscript for *Literary Lists* to which I added pages every day was growing and taking on the life of a real, to-be-published work beside my desk. My wife was spending more time away from the house than was strictly normal or healthy but would occasionally permit me a few moments of cool, unengaged conversation. I suggested that it might be a good moment to attempt to re-establish relations with local friends, fellow parents, with whom, perhaps as a result of our isolation from one another, we had lost contact, but somehow we seemed to have lost the facility for the informal neighbourly dinner party. There had been a time when I had worried that my only social contact was with other writers or literary journalists, that I was cutting myself off from the stuff of real life, but now I saw that any material to be gained from the anxious, ambitious lawyers, BBC producers and marketing types of Brandon Gardens and environs was of little interest to the writer of serious fiction. Who, seriously, would want to read about these people as they grew old, worried about their children, gained ulcers, had career crises and became ever more self-parodically dull and middle-aged?

On my daily walks these days, I headed away from the rackety front line, preferring the comfortable certainties to be found to the west. I took refuge in its rows of dignified semi-detached houses discreetly shaded by plane trees, its terraces of small shops, its ballet schools and estate cars and tennis clubs and piano practice after school, its precious Neighbourhood Watch schemes. There was crime here, but it was ordered and professional, committed by outsiders, qualitatively different from the east's crime wave, which was a scummy stream of misbehaviour washing down every street, lapping at the doors, removing anything not chained or locked away. There, some low-grade crim might break into a house to discover, for no particular reason, that he was not just a burglar, but also a rapist, maybe even a murderer. Out west, a certain etiquette applied. Radios might be removed overnight but only from BMWs and in a carefully defined area; bespoke break-ins would occur where a single top-of-the-range item would be neatly extracted in a manner which made the victims feel perversely proud at the implied compliment to their good taste.

I needed rules, suburban order. My walks were brief, briskly taken escapes from a harsh working schedule, my deadline for *The Book of Literary lists* recently having taken on a new urgency. I attended to my family. I courted my wife and once even attempted, albeit half-heartedly, to revive our sexual relationship. I screened my calls.

For the first few days after Gloucester, Peter Gibson had been persistent, ringing five or six times every day, sometimes through the night, and leaving short messages on my office line. Not for the first time in my life, I was glad that, at Marigold's insistence, the number to the family line, as she called it, was ex-directory.

At first, he was circumspect and succinct. His work was progressing well. He needed to discuss further matters raised at Gloucester. Would it be possible for me to return his short story *Mise en Abîme*? Then, after the first few days, he simply asked me to call him. His voice, never exactly manly, seemed thinner and more defeated than I remembered. Occasionally piano music could be heard in the background, some abstract, modern thing that sounded like a depressive child let loose on a Steinway.

My wife, attuned to the language of the unanswered telephone call, was suspicious and made jaunty, barbed comments implying that, as had happened in the past, I was having difficulty in extricating myself from an affair. I ensured that, once when she paid one of her rare visits to my office, I played back Peter's message. A student, I explained. He was having a creative crisis.

'He sounds terrible,' she said. 'Shouldn't you call him?'

'Nah. He's a writer. He's got to learn it goes with the territory. I'll call him soon.'

She looked at me in a manner which suggested that she was not entirely taken in, but said nothing.

One day, I received a letter from him – or, rather, a one-line message, written in his neat, cramped hand on the back of a filing card.

'"The trick is to love somebody. If you love one person, you see everyone differently." James Baldwin.'

I added the quote to my database, made a note that I should attempt to find the source, and threw the card away.

The fact is, and was, that I was not James Baldwin, nor André Gide, nor E. M. Forster, nor Edmund White, nor even John Cheever. I was Gregory Keays, a straight and straightforward novelist. I had not suffered any significant sea-change in my sexual orientation. Reassured by Pia, I had returned to my daily life untroubled by memories of Peter or what had happened between us. I did not find myself gazing wistfully at the muscular bottoms of cyclists as they sped by in their lycra shorts. My nights were not disturbed by restless dreams of smooth-skinned boys or rough, priapic lorry-drivers. The incident, or series of incidents, that had occurred between us that night were more psychological than physiological, originating in an odd coincidence of one man's vulnerability and another's need for comfort. That was it. No regrets, but also no post-event analyses and, above all, no fumbling repeats.

If Peter had discovered what Baldwin had described as 'the trick of love', he was alone. It was harsh, but I had concluded that the best way to convey that reality was not to engage in stuttered explanation but to re-establish our teacher-pupil relationship by dint of a sensible cooling-off period. My first two lessons post-Gloucester I cancelled, claiming that I was ill. When I returned on the third week, Peter was not there.

It was almost five weeks after I had last seen him, when I received a brief message from him, delivered in a melodramatic whisper.

'I'm finished.'

In my innocence, I assumed he was referring to his novel.

The Canon of Self-Slaughter: The Top Twenty Most Celebrated Literary Suicides

John Berryman 1914–72	Jumped (height)
Thomas Chatterton 1752–70	Poisoning
Hart Crane 1899–1932	Drowning
Romain Gary 1914–87	Poisoning
Nikolai Gogol 1809–52	Starvation
Ernest Hemingway 1899–1961	Shooting
Randall Jarrell 1914–65	Jumped (car)
Arthur Koestler 1905–83	Poisoning
Jerzy Kosinski 1933–91	Asphyxiation
Primo Levi 1919–87	Jumped (height)
Malcolm Lowry 1909–57	Poisoning
Vladimir Mayakovsky 1893–1930	Shooting
Yukio Mishima 1925–63	Disembowelling
Cesare Pavese 1908–50	Poisoning
Sylvia Plath 1932–63	Gassing
Delmore Schwartz 1913–66	Poisoning
Anne Sexton 1928–74	Asphyxiation
Simone Weil 1909–43	Starvation
Virginia Woolf 1882–1941	Drowning
Stefan Zweig 1881–1942	Poisoning

21

There was nothing I could have done. I remain convinced of that.

Throughout the night of 27 November, the telephone rang again and again in my office. I had fallen asleep, the muffled tintinnabulation from behind the closed door becoming no more than a distant alarm bell in my dreams, when Marigold awoke me.

'You've got to do something, Gregory,' she said, sounding oddly wakeful. 'Something's going on.'

'I'll take the phone off the hook.'

'It could be serious.'

'It's work. They're calling my work number.'

Marigold gave a quiet, disbelieving laugh, the wife who knew too much, and at that moment the telephone rang again.

Grumbling, I got out of bed, put on my dressing-gown and went upstairs.

The green light on the answering machine revealed that there had been fifty-three messages over the previous two hours. I pressed 'Play'.

'Gregory.' Peter's voice sounded faint and despairing. A long silence followed during which I could hear his breathing. Then, 'Please, Gregory.'

The next one was more or less the same. On the third, he was crying.

Shit. I thought for a moment, then dialled his number. He picked up, apparently before it had rung.

'Peter, it's Gregory.'

He snuffled hopelessly into the receiver.

'You must stop doing this.' I spoke as coolly as I could, although I found myself shaking. 'I shall come round to your flat tomorrow and we shall discuss your work and your novel and agents who might be able to place it for you. I am of course concerned for you but I must ask you not to disrupt my private life in this way.'

'Pri – *private*?' He seemed to be having difficulty speaking.

I tried another approach. 'This is what writers go through when they have finished a novel. Martin uses the phrase "scoured out". He says one is so scoured out when emerging from a novel that one can hardly tie one's shoelace. What this is telling me is that you are the true article – a novelist.'

'You are so –' There was a curious wheezing noise which might have been laughter or a sob, '– *so* full of shit.'

'I realize that we have issues.' I hesitated, choosing my

words carefully. Not for the first time it occurred to me that, as a responsible tutor, I should refer Peter Gibson to the Institute's pastoral care office, but that I was holding back, aware that my position would be seriously compromised should he reveal the events which had taken place in Gloucester. I had been given unofficial warnings in the past about the dangers of establishing intimate relations with any of my charges. Although even my worst enemy would have difficulty believing that I had seduced a male student, the fact that I had apparently ignored his later cry for help would not look good were anything to happen to him. 'I shall visit you tomorrow and together we'll resolve these problems, all right?'

He muttered something, querulous and unintelligible, about my being late, which I took to be a reference to my less than perfect time-keeping.

'I won't be late.'

There was a snuffling noise which might have been laughter or a sob.

'I promise,' I said in a tone of gentle finality, and hung up.

I deleted the messages on the answering machine and was about to unplug the telephone before I thought better of it. Whatever Peter's problem, our conversation seemed to have calmed him down. I was sure that my promise to visit him the following day would preclude the need for further nuisance calls. As a tutor and friend, I had demonstrably behaved in as sympathetic and helpful a manner as could be expected, calming him and reassuring him in the small hours of the morning.

I returned to my bed.

'The student,' I said to my wife. 'He seems to be having some sort of creative crack-up. I'll go over tomorrow.' Even to myself, my voice sounded odd and brittle.

In a gesture so uncharacteristic that it made me start, Marigold laid a hand on my arm. 'You're trembling,' she said.

'Winter.'

After a few minutes, I heard the rise and fall of her breathing. I lay awake, thinking of Peter, remembering our night, until the sparrows stirred and started singing in the tree outside our window. At last, I slept.

I was woken by the sound of the telephone beside the bed. I glanced at the alarm clock beside the bed. It was past eight. My wife, I could hear, was having a bath.

'Gregory Keays.' I tried to sound alert.

'Gregory, it's Mike Summers. Sorry to bother you so early but there might be a problem with one of your students – a boy called Gibson?'

I slumped down on the bed, as Summers, the Institute's Student Counsellor, explained that he had been called at home by Serafina. She had been worried about Peter who had telephoned her that night. Was I aware of any problems in that area?

I told him that I had spoken to Peter during the night, that he seemed to be caught up in some sort of work crisis. I would go over to his flat as soon as I had finished breakfast.

As I say, there was nothing more that I could have done.

Top Five Literary Veterans
1. Lord Tennyson lost his virginity at forty-one.
2. Leo Tolstoy learnt to ride a bicycle at sixty-seven.
3. Theodore Fontaine wrote ten novels between the ages of seventy-six and eighty-four.
4. Thomas Hardy boasted of having sex at eighty-four.
5. Anthony Trollope wrote eight and half books between the ages of sixty-three and his death at sixty-seven.

22

Under normal circumstances, life is kept at a distance by the act of writing. The more you create an imaginative world, the more frivolous and irrelevant reality seems. So, over the years, the business of everyday existence for professional novelists is increasingly at one remove: what had been a fine, barely discernible spider's web during the writing of *Forever Young* became more opaque and gauze-like during my comedic domestic phase with *Mind the Gap* and *Adultery in Hampstead*. By the time I was tussling with *A/The/Until*, *Tell Me the Truth About Love*, *About Love*, *Cenotaph* and *Insignificance*, a sheet (a blanket) surrounded my inner consciousness. Today, nothing in the daily newspapers truly engages me: war, famine, crime, rape, the abduction of children are little more a than busy backdrop to the enthralling deals and spats and ever-changing realignments of the literary world.

Under normal circumstances, this holding back from experience acts like an anaesthetic, dulling the pain of marital unhappiness, easing the guilt of inadequate parenthood, deleting all but the faintest shade of self-loathing that followed acts of infidelity or a visit to the Agency. I regarded incidents and feelings coolly, across a frontier, as if my real, physical life were just another narrative, to be shaped and cut, ordered and dramatized, edited and resolved at some later stage.

But these, I discovered, were not normal circumstances.

At first, the events following Peter Gibson's suicide passed like the unedited rushes of a film in which I had played relatively minor part: the arrival, first of the police, then the ambulance, after I had discovered the body; the discussions and sorrowful announcements at the Institute, a couple of oddly barbed interviews with a policeman named Beckwith, the carefully composed note of condolence to Mr and Mrs Gibson. Throughout it all, I was treated by my wife and my son with uncharacteristic gentleness and sympathy, as if somehow they sensed that what I was experiencing was more than the understandable guilt of a tutor whose most promising student had just taken his own life.

Yet I found sleep difficult, normal conversation impossible. I would walk for miles every day, my mind full of words and memories: that long, unblinking gaze when I turned to him during the first lesson; the little irritated frown of concentration that crossed his face when another pupil discussed his work, talking about his novel in the car back from Gloucester; his voice, his clear blue eyes, the hollow in his back. Even now, I feel sick to think of him.

So, during those unhappy days, when I was more exposed to public gaze than any writer likes to be, except around the time of publication, I took refuge in work. At first, I returned to *Insignificance*, hoping (it may sound cynical but such is the writerly soul) that the emotional turmoil of the past few days would jump-start the novel back into life, but every time I sat down to write, my thoughts turned back to Peter. *The Book of Literary Lists*, and its reduction of the writing life to facts, figures and charts, depressed me still further.

In the end, one task extricated me from this state of funk – a task that was to prove as cathartic as it was painful, which would lead me through the darkest tunnel eventually into a dazzling light.

Soon after I had returned to the house in a state of shock after Peter's death, I realized that, in a moment of distracted misery, I had taken from his flat the project upon which he had been working. At first uncertain what to do with these notepads, I had placed them in my 'Work in Progress' file drawer, where I traditionally kept unfinished manuscripts. Unable to work the next day. I had, on an impulse of mournful curiosity, opened the drawer and extracted the first of the pads.

I started to read. Three hours later, I was still reading.

What Peter Gibson had written was not a novel to change lives, although it did admittedly change mine. The later claim, made on a radio arts show, that it was 'the most life-affirming evocation of youthful sensibility since *The Catcher in the Rye*' simultaneously exaggerated and underrated its importance. Yet I was utterly absorbed. Work by students or friends is invariably difficult to read with pleasure – voices and memories from the real world draining the life from the pages – but these pages were so bright and so confident that, within moments of embarking, I had become oblivious to the fact that behind every syllable and thought was not just a student or a friend but a former lover.

Such was the work's authenticity of tone, its masterly creation of atmosphere and effortless stylistic elegance, so superior was it to anything that Peter had produced in class, that I briefly imagined that, in his later state of mental delusion, he had solemnly copied out some lesser known masterpiece and lightly updated it.

But no. Even if the self-conscious stammerings and mannered flourishes of his class work were nowhere to be found here, a distinguished, resonant echo of them was unmistakable and, besides, the setting and tone of the novel were too precisely of the moment to have been lifted from the past. Reading it a second time the following day (the original manuscript was slightly longer than it is today), I heard my pupil's voice in every word.

He had been playing us along with his stories: what he had offered week after week were the chippings and shavings off this magnificent construct. Perhaps I should have been hurt, but then I have always been a writer first, a teacher second. Any sense of pique or even jealousy soon gave way to the simple heartfelt admiration of one creative artist for another. I felt closer to Peter than ever before – closer even than I had felt during the night in Gloucester when we made love.

It was, I imagine, that very closeness, aligned perhaps with a sense that our relationship was what is vulgarly known as 'unfinished business', which helps explain what happened next. In one of those responses that the creative artist can no more explain than understand, I began to jot notes in the margin of the first chapter, to rearrange material.

Soon I was scribbling extra paragraphs, using (significantly, I see now) my blue writing pen rather than my green editorial biro. At some point I must have glanced at the absurd, passionate tangle of words, his and mine, the growing confusion of paper through which something utterly ordered was emerging, switched on my computer and started writing, from the first page of chapter one, leaving, as is my wont, the typing of the title page to last. Soon the tips of my fingers were numb, my forearms were aching.

How did I feel? Like an impotent man making love for the first time in years. The words flowed – Peter's words, my words, suddenly the division between us seemed meaningless. It is a short opening section, as is now well known, and no more than four hours later, it was complete.

What had begun as a sort of grief therapy, a way of distracting myself from the churning confusion of my life, quickly became an obsession. I would be awoken at five or six in the morning by thoughts of the day's writing, the plot pulling me in. For the first time since writing the final chapters of *Forever Young*, I would work for an hour before breakfast, go downstairs to consume in rapt silence the cardboard-and-cowshit breakfast cereal my wife inflicts on her family in the name of Buddha (there's a connection between active bowels and spiritual validity that I have never had the energy to question or resist) before returning, almost at a jog, to my desk. There were days when I simply forgot to shave; the telephone, an old friend in less productive times, was ignored.

I would emerge from my study, after ten or eleven hours work, smelly, unshaven, blinking, so caught up in the imaginative universe I was creating that I felt like an alien in the actual world.

I was creating? Yes, I. Quite early in the enterprise, it became quite clear to me that, for all its brilliance, Peter's work was not so much a novel as a research document, a collection of notes. It has been said that, just now and then in a novelist's life, a fiction descends upon him, like an act of grace, as if it had been there, ready and fully-formed, simply waiting for him to pick up his pen. Here, it seemed to me, was my act of grace, my reward for years of agony, humiliation and non-completion. I had, during the brief time when I had known him, provided Peter Gibson with the benefit of my frequently dispiriting experience of the inky trade. Now, in the mysterious way of things, he was giving back to me, not only on his own posthumous behalf but on behalf of the hundreds of would-be writers for whom I have toiled down the years. If Peter had lived, he might have been able to transmute the words on these notepads into a mature work of fiction but he had not. I was proud to take up the task on his behalf, subsuming the raw material he had hewn out of the rockface of youthful experience into my own work. If, as the testament of writers from Tolstoy to Greene quoted in my *Muse of Fire* confirms, the true writer needs to be both creator and editor, I had, at last, managed to establish that inner equilibrium.

It felt good. The prose had the optimistic swagger of *Forever Young*. There was a depth and subtlety of characterization which I felt I had not achieved since the early (only) chapters of *Accidents of Trust*. I have always striven for a gritty social authenticity in my fiction but, apart from the stories of my foray into dirty realism *Tell Me the Truth About Love, About Love*, I had never managed the moving painterly detail of everyday lives that I was achieving here. In the short stream-of-consciousness sections of the text there were echoes of my uncompleted prose poem *Vermilion*. Its thematic sub-structure developed many of the ideas I had been exploring in *Insignificance* but whereas that work, I can now admit, was so ideas-led that any kind of plot was like a drowning child caught in a rip tide of theory and internal musing, the new novel's galloping narrative carried ideas on a breathtaking joyride of forward movement. As for the disappointment that was to be expressed by the less generous critics (the merest, self-serving trill of reservation, in most cases) that some of the mordant wit of *Forever Young* had given way to a plainer, gloomier vision, that is easily explained. Humour darkens with the years, sometimes becoming indecipherable from tragedy. It is a process that might have been traced through *Accidents, Adultery, Gap, Lies, Insignificance,* not to mention many of my shorter works had any of them been

completed and published. The fact that they had not sub-
tracted in no way from the real, experiential journey that lay
behind them.

I would be the last to play down the influence of the late
Peter Gibson upon my work. As I alchemized the rough ore of
his research, reordering, compressing, honing, expanding,
bringing life to the dry, arid path of his narrative with my
own dashes of colour, or sometimes simply following that
path by directly transcribing his handwritten work on to my
computer ('copying' would be a harsh but not entirely in-
accurate description), I became aware of a new energy, a sense
of direction that I had all but forgotten was within my gift.
Innocent, guileless, unaware of the traps and obstacles that
litter the path of the long-distance writer, Peter Gibson had,
as I had so long ago, reached that winning-post, that moment
when the novelist, muscles aching, brain fuzzy with exhaustion, can write 'The End' and sink to the floor. As I reran that
race, making it an incomparably more lively and sophisticated event than it had previously been, the fact that my
predecessor had achieved closure (before achieving closure in
a different and more tragic sense) offered me a beacon towards
which I moved with the speed and directness of an arrow.
Some might say Peter's contribution, his general marking out
of a track, was a minor contribution to the final work that saw
publication; not me. I had been a writer for whom completion
had become the most daunting and intractable aspect of my
work. Simply by finishing what he had started, my student
was nothing less than an inspiration to me.

No wonder that, even in the excitement surrounding the
acceptance of the novel, I insisted upon a full-page dedicatory
note, stating simply and eloquently, 'To Peter Gibson, 1976–
1998. With gratitude and admiration'. Somehow it seemed
the least I could do.

The title, incidentally, was entirely mine. Noting musical
imagery throughout the novel, I played around with the term
'terpsichore'. A list of titles, including such clonkers as
Terpsichore of Life, Not Yet the Terpsichore and *The*

Terpsichore of Angels was drawn up. Finally, and in a semi-humorous reference to modish modernity which I was sure Peter would have appreciated, I arrived at the title which now denotes a significant landmark in late twentieth-century literature.

terpsichore 4:2.

We were on our way.

The Writer Speaks of . . . Self-criticism

Everything that is written merely to please the author is worthless.

Blaise Pascal

Read over your compositions and wherever you meet with a passage which you think is particularly fine, strike it out.

Samuel Johnson

In a writer, there must always be two people – the writer and the critic. And, if one works at night, with a cigarette in one's mouth, although the work of creation goes on briskly, the critic is for the most part in abeyance, and this is very dangerous.'

Leo Tolstoy

A tale from which pieces have been raked out is like a fire that has been poked. One does not know that the operation has been performed, but every one feels the effect.

Rudyard Kipling

It is in order to shine sooner that authors refuse to re-write. Despicable. Begin again.

Albert Camus

When it comes easily, throw it away. It can't be any good.

V. S. Naipaul

23

I was distracted. I see now that, as I worked a shift of nine or ten hours, events beyond the study door were changing in ways which would have a profound effect upon my life. 'When you're writing a book,' Alan Sillitoe has pointed out, 'you're 2,000 feet underground with your little miner's lamp, picking away at a seam. The atom bomb can drop for all you care. And worse, your children can go to analysts. You're just quarrying away to produce another book. "Why did I do that? To alleviate the pain of the world that would kill me if I didn't."'

My child was not going to analysts, but he was spending more time away from the house. Marigold and I had given up speculating as to where he went, even though he now sometimes stayed away for up to two days. We were both busy – me with my novel, Marigold with her decoration and her lover – and, separately, we may have reached the conclusion that for Doug to be involved any project, however odd and nefarious, was preferable to the life of solitude, gloom and masturbation that he had previously been leading.

One morning, my wife left the window and door of his room open, allowing the stale acrid smell of adolescence to waft through the house, reminding me inescapably of the last time I had seen Peter. It was at about this time that I found thoughts of my son and memories of my student had become weirdly conflated: I heard Doug's booming, adolescent voice behind the words I was transcribing, imagined Peter returning to the house to crash about the kitchen, pale, hostile, but alive.

Soon Marigold was making brave little sorties into Doug's room to empty an ashtray or waste-paper basket, to remove a few coffee cups in which mould was gathering. Once, emerging from my loft to replenish my supply of coffee, I found her on her knees in Doug's room, talking to herself with a sort of dazed disapproval as she lifted a grey sheet to peer under the bed. My wife's neat, girlish arse has never lost its power to move me and the sight of it there, taut against designer jeans, evoked in me a startlingly powerful feeling of tender, melancholic lust. I knelt down to pick up a stray cigarette carton and laid a hand between her buttocks. 'Nice butt,' I said, quoting a private catchphrase from happier times.

'This is just too revolting for words,' she muttered, surprising me by not moving away.

'Couldn't you let Miguela do it?'

'Certainly not. What would she think of us?'

'She's from Venezuela. I'm sure she's seen worse on the *barrios* of Caracas.'

In reply, Marigold raised the sheet slightly.

I winced. 'Yes, well. Maybe not.'

Sighing, my wife sat back on her haunches. 'I remember when he used to smell so sweet. I'd hold him to me before he went to bed just to get that pure scent of childhood. He was all warm and soft and –' she laughed, '– pyjamay.'

'You wouldn't want to do that now.' I stood up, leaving my hand on her neck but, oddly, it felt more uncomfortably intimate there and, after a decent interval, I withdrew it.

'This is a man's job, Gregory.' She smoothed down the sheet. 'There are some things that a mother shouldn't see.'

Something in that self-mocking primness reminded me of the old days. I looked down at my wife, as she knelt at my feet. It was worth a try.

'When Georges Simenon took a break from writing, he would visit his wife as she worked with a secretary in her study,' I said. '"What d'you want?" she would ask. "You," he would say. And they'd go to the bedroom. Afterwards, he would return to work, refreshed and energized.'

'Was Simenon the one who wrote three novels in a month?'

'I could write three novels in a month under the right circumstances.'

'Clear this out and I might see my way to accommodating you.'

I glanced into the room. It might be argued that it is as

much part of the writerly experience to delve among the porn magazines and tissues stiff with dried semen of a teenage son as it is to sit in an opium den in Saigon or hang out among the lowlifes of west London, yet somehow I doubted whether Graham Greene or Martin would be asked to do such a thing. 'I'm under a lot of pressure,' I said feebly.

Marigold stood up, once more her irritated, wifely self. 'Bloody men,' she muttered, and what once had been a humorous refrain now seemed filled with despair and boredom. She pushed past, a breast brushing my arm, and made her way down the stairs.

Nice butt. Bloody men. I might just see my way to accommodating you. The days when we would tumble into bed, day or night, and laugh at the idiot insistency of our desires, seemed so close and yet so far away. There was a time when my wife could sense when I was retreating into the melancholy interior of my authorly soul, when she would follow me and bring me back to her and to the world, holding me in her arms, talking and talking, making love to me with slow, soothing, pastoral sway. Sometimes she would hold me close to her and bury her face in my hair. 'My writer,' she would breathe, and this whispered confidence, this secret that we shared, would make me strong.

That evening Marigold and I spent time together, talking. We sat in the bright sitting-room, with its perfect décor and appropriate room-temperature, glasses of chilled white wine in our hands, and attempted, with only a slight sense of strain, to make the best of what we had.

Over the years, the territory covered by our conversation had become more circumscribed. Once we had talked about sex: when we were not fucking, we were talking about fucking. Then we had enjoyed comparing notes about our burgeoning careers. For years, Douglas provided common ground until he too became a source of conflict, even embarrassment.

This process of disengagement was reflected in our social life. The small set of youngish couples within which we

moved dispersed as we hit our thirties, becoming too successful or not successful enough, too married or not married
enough, for us to feel entirely at ease with them. For ten
years or so, we found common cause with disparate group of
men and women whose children were the same age as
Dougie. The anxieties of parenthood were so all-absorbing
that a sort of weird comradeship developed and vast intellectual, political and social differences were forgotten in our
devotion to our great common project. But when our children
reached the age of eleven or twelve, changing schools, shifting up (or, in Doug's case, down) a gear, these fellow foot-
soldiers became the enemy. The competitiveness which we
now realized had always been there became ugly and explicit.
Parents whose children were skipping up the straight and
narrow, passing exams, making new friends, joining teams,
developing ambition or a social conscience became boastful
or patronizing and lowered their voices sympathetically
when asking about Doug and his less glorious progress.
Those of us with children whose only A's were in angst,
anorexia, anger and acne grew silent, weary of social gatherings where we would field enquiries with effortful optimism.
He's *very* absorbed in the new music. He's becoming something of a *silent intellectual*. Of course, he has always been
something of a loner.

Burdened by our disappointment, our resentful conviction
that not all of this sadness and failure was our fault, that some
responsibility must lie with them, our children drifted away
from the friendships which had once seemed so sincere. Or
perhaps the friendships had never been sincere at all and, just
as Mummy and Daddy were tolerating, for the sake of the
children, the company of cheery, dull, sincere, tennis-playing
fools with whom they had nothing in common, so the
children, out of deference to their parents, had hung out
obediently with their happier contemporaries, those accountants, producers and managers of the future.

I had lost touch with the community of family some time
ago but Marigold, who was more attuned to the neighbour-

hood gossip, occasionally and cruelly kept me up to speed on the progress of our son's former friends. Gareth had been accepted for Oxford. Simon was appearing in TV advertisements. Leonora was doing marvels in Africa during her gap year. It is sometimes said that, over those first eighteen years of life, a kind of perverse justice prevails – that the gilded, carefree childhood of the blessed ones degenerates into a messy and turbulent adolescence while for the asthmatic, thumb-sucking no-hopers of the early years, an unexpected brilliance and grace arrived with puberty – but, for those of us in the parental B-stream, the idea was a cruel illusion: the children who had softened the teacher's eye during the first year at primary school were now marching, proud, lithe-limbed and clear-eyed, towards adulthood; those whose names were never quite remembered on parents' evenings were crouched in their rooms, growing spotty, hating the world and masturbating.

Some of the losers, of course, acquired a sort of notoriety. A boy in the class above Doug had taken an overdose in Goa; the class thickie had impregnated a fourteen-year-old; someone else from the school was in a youth detention centre after a series of break-ins. When these titbits reached us, we shook our heads, offered commiserations, our hearts singing with joy and relief: our son may have been sulky, miserable, reclusive and emotionally repressed, but he was not a criminal.

So it was a desultory, uneasy conversation that Marigold and I had that evening as we sat, facing one another in Marigold's new Aeron chairs, like mature models in an advertisement for an upmarket estate agents. Something had happened which had seemed to change the atmosphere between us. It might have been that the sudden surge in my creative output had given me more confidence; those few moments when my hand had rested comfortably on my wife's rump may have evoked some sad memory of ancient need. Most likely of all, we had, while staring into Doug's room, his presence fading as surely as the sour smell which drifted through the house and out of the window, suddenly caught sight of the fearful loneliness of middle age before us. Our son was going. Soon we would be on our own.

We spoke of local matters. At this moment when the next generation was preparing to move away, several of their parents, as if enacting some grim Darwinian precept, were cracking up, keeling over, sometimes even dying. Some sort of brain seizure had struck down one mother who was found one evening, stretched out cold in the kitchen, last night's washing-up half-completed. A traditional squash-court heart attack had taken out one of the more active fathers. Others had merely been winged by time's sniper bullet with tumours, clots, shadows or turns.

'Apparently John Potter's not too well.' My wife sipped at her wine. 'They found something on a lung.'

'John? Poor chap.' It had been some time since I had last seen Potter, who was younger than me but whose years in a solicitor's office had imbued him with an air of gentle decline. He used to seek me out at neighbourhood parties or parents' evenings and talk about the novels (usually some good-hearted middlebrow tome by John Mortimer or Elizabeth Jane Howard) that he had been reading. 'He once told me that he had always wanted to be a writer,' I said. 'It was his great fantasy.'

'A writer, John? Are you sure?'

'He swore me to secrecy. When the children left home, he said, he was going to take early retirement and write a legal thriller. Is it serious, the lung thing?'

'They're not operating.' My wife sighed, then sipped at her wine. 'We promise ourselves these little treats for when we have the time to reclaim our lives. Then suddenly it's too late.'

'I doubt he would have written it. Very few people have the energy to start writing after the age of fifty. The nerve goes.'

'Well, I'm not waiting for my treat.' She looked up and, for the briefest of moments, I saw in that small, alert, determined figure, the art student with whom I had fallen in love over a quarter of a century ago. I wanted to reach out and touch her hand but sensed it was not the moment.

'When I've finished the novel, maybe we could take a holiday,' I said. 'Go somewhere unusual.'

Marigold laughed briefly, sadly. 'When I finish the novel. That will be written on your gravestone.'

For a moment, our eyes locked. At that uncharacteristic moment of frankness, when thoughts of Doug and the dying solicitor were fading, when it was just her and me, a little couple in a big world, we might have stepped back from going too far – opened another bottle of wine, switched on the television – but our defences were down. Inept, abandoned parents, socially isolated, we turned back to each other and discovered that the person we once thought we had understood, had somehow slipped away. Love for another man had made my wife a stranger. What she had thought was a fling (a treat) had become something more complex and difficult. These days, when she returned home late at night, there was no longer the smell of smoke and alcohol and public places upon her, but – the sure sign of an affair entering a dangerously domestic phase – a faint, intimate whiff of soap. I imagined her in a bath after an evening of love, contemplating the home to which she was about to return as she washed him out of her.

'I remember when you started writing.' Marigold spoke quietly, as if responding to my thoughts. 'You would make notes about everything, every evening, sitting in that very chair. School, the other parents, changes to the house, me, you, the things that Douglas said and did during the day. D'you remember?'

I nodded.

'It seemed the way it should be,' she said. 'Writing was life. It took it all – words and colours and smells and experience – and gave it all shape and relevance. It marked it in time. I admired the way you were holding the moment, scrutinizing and treasuring it – the way you were somehow managing to live twice over.'

'I'm not sure you admired it that much. You said that *Forever Young* was "jolly". You might just as well have called it "chucklesome" or "a rib-tickler".'

It was a familiar charge, to which Marigold normally replied that she had meant I could do more serious work (the remark hung over me for the next fifteen years), but this evening she had something else on her mind and would not be diverted.

'Something happened.' She closed her eyes, frowning, and for a moment I thought she was going to cry. 'I could feel it but there was nothing I could do. After all the fuss died down after the Granta thing, you went back to work on *Adultery in Hampstead* –'

'*Accidents of Trust.*'

'Whatever. And a sort of film came over your eyes. Suddenly everything that surrounded you seemed to become too idiotic and domestic to qualify as material for your novels. In fact, you appeared to want to keep us at a distance from your precious work, in case the triviality of our lives somehow contaminated it. We lost you. Day by day, you drifted further away from us. Nothing could reach you – not company, nor Dougie, nor, in the end, me, us. You went through the motions of being a husband and father but you were just playing the part, to keep us quiet.'

Martin's remark about the life stuff, the living, getting skimped in a writer's life occurred to me but I thought it wiser not share it at this point. 'Perhaps I drifted away because I was married to someone who was no longer interested in my work, who gets the name of my novels wrong, who calls them "whatever".'

My wife stared at me coldly. 'Do you want to discuss your body of work?'

I shrugged, and looked out of the window. 'Whatever.'

'I was just thinking about the way you sneered at poor John Potter and his desire to write a book. It occurred to me that maybe *you* were the one who had it wrong all these years. Those of us who have been blundering onwards – John, me,

Doug, the rest – living our lives, making mistakes, hurting and being hurt – maybe we were the ones on the dangerous edge of things. Maybe the novelist, hiding away in his imaginary world, isn't this heroic figure after all. He's actually running away from life and engagement.'

'The writer as coward.' I disliked the direction the conversation had taken but right now seemed an unsuitable moment to leave the room. 'It's a thought, I suppose.'

'Those who can do. Those who can't, sit at home and write about it.'

'John Updike says –'

'Fuck John Updike. Fuck all of you sad writers, huddling in your little bunkers, blubbing about the agony of being an artist while the rest of us – all the people you sneer at from your study – are keeping the show going. I don't care what John Updike says. What do *you* say? How do you feel about all those years spent writing novels which you never actually finished.'

'Art is struggle.' I said, startled by my wife's uncharacteristic bluntness. 'Not only for the artists but for the artist's family. I'm sorry but that's the way it is.'

A familiar feeling of fraudulence assailed me. I was acting the part of a father: after all these years, it was a role I had yet to master. Lately, I had found myself assailed by memories from the early years of my marriage. The ante-natal class in a brightly lit hospital room where Marigold, so serious and intent, learnt how to breathe properly while I self-consciously followed along, an ironic fellow passenger. The birth when, as if sensing my ambivalence and feeling of apartness, the nurses shouldered me aside as my wife, torn apart by the child she was bearing, held my hand, then pushed it away, stared at me, red-faced and infuriated, then, muscles straining, turned away as if the very last face she needed to see at that moment was that of the man who had brought this agony on her. The visits from in-laws, the colic, the night hours spent pacing back and forth, a tiny bundle of distressed wakefulness tense against one shoulder, the never-ending flow of body fluids that were suddenly at the centre of our daily existence. As Dougie stood and walked and talked and became a person, we would go on family holidays, a perfect, sunny, idealized version of which remained in the photograph albums on my wife's desk.

Were we, in those moments, a real, happy family or even then were we all, even Dougie, playing the part? The holidays went on but with each one, there was more unease, awkwardness. The single child buggy on the back seat. The cheap, tasteless meals (plaice, chips and bright green peas) were consumed in silence, the small figure of Dougie less and less able to turn the engine of action, laughter, rows and jokes that propelled family life. As if our failure as parents had infected his childishness with an awful, adult self-consciousness, he became less able to mix with other children. We would watch him, trailing along after them, absorbed in his own world, ignored, and we would hate those other children, with their ease with one another, their laughing playfulness, their brothers and sisters, the cute things they said, joyously related by their perfect parents. The photographs told their own story: no more unforced sunny smiles were to be found from, say, 1990 onwards. There was a rehearsed holiday jauntiness to the expressions on the faces of Marigold and me. Dougie was looking away, pulling a face or, most frequently of all, was obscured by an adult shoulder or a deck-chair, or another bigger, bolder, happier child.

We worried. What had we done to give our only child this instinct for sorrow? We wondered silently what freak of genetics had filtered out our talent – Marigold's looks and athleticism, my more verbal imagination, our shared (though different) social skills – from our son. Should we have read to him more, exposed him to classical music, visited art galleries and the Science Museum on a Saturday afternoon? If, every year, we had taken him to children's concerts at the Festival Hall, or the more responsible kind of pantomime, would he have become more outgoing? Would the habit of screaming 'He's behind you!' with hundreds of other children have subtly shaded over the years, into confident every-day articulacy? If it was the growing distance between his mother and father that chilled his tiny heart, then why were his contemporaries, many of whose parents were divorced, or living in a permanent state of open hostility, not affected? Perhaps in that one unhappy area, that of vulnerability to the disappointment of others, he had succeeded beyond his peers.

Now, Marigold seemed to have resolved the question of responsibility. I was to blame. It was all the fault of writing. 'I gather from Doug that you hit him the other day,' she said suddenly.

'Hit? Hardly.' Even to me, my laughter sounded forced, unconvincing. 'It was a . . . minor scuffle.'

We sat in silence for a few seconds. Further explanation seemed to be required. 'There comes a moment when they have to take responsibility, when they can't just go on taking.' I paused, startled by this image of our children as a group, a herd, moving through suburbia, exacting some kind of retribution on their exhausted parents. 'I just lost it. I felt so . . . insulted by his indifference. He's in our house, filling his angry little face with our food from our fridge. That teenage sarcasm –' I shook my head, remembering the con-temptuous mockery in Doug's voice. 'It's lethal.'

The cat, Donovan, wandered into the sitting-room and sat at Marigold's feet, gazing up at her, eyes half-closed.

'He calls you Psycho.' My wife smiled sadly. 'Psycho Dad.'

'And I was always so big on non-violence.'

'He remembers that, too.'

I ached with a sense of my own hypocrisy. When Dougie was small and was first discovering that he had a talent for being bullied, I had been full of stern, liberal admonitions. Don't get drawn in, Dougie. Rise above it, don't play them at their own game. Nothing gets solved by hurting people, Dougie. Hitting isn't strong or clever, it's weak. The really brave person just walks away from it. You'll be the winner in the end, Dougie. And ten years later, I was slamming him to the floor in our own kitchen. Psycho Dad. I wanted to explain all this to my wife but I sat, abject, silent.

'He feels he has lost you and he's angry about it,' Marigold said eventually, her eyes on the cat at her feet.

'That's absurd. I'm here every day. I see more of him than most fathers – more of him than you do.'

'You're not here. You haven't been for years.' She looked up at me. 'You used to be so close, you two. I was so proud of you. My men.'

'Don't.'

'You were such a good father. Even my parents admitted that. You'd spend hours making some Lego castle or writing songs together or going to the park with a football. All those silly jokes you used to make about my cooking or pretending to be asleep at your desk when he walked in. Once you told him that some naughty children stop growing and become smaller and smaller. It was why you had to be very careful walking about the house – the smallest crumb might be a naughty child.'

'No wonder he's so fucked up.'

'He loved you. He still does. It was why he tried to join in the football games in the park, why he used to bring those stories back from school. He knew he had me but he felt, he just knew, that you were slipping away from him. He couldn't understand it. What had once been so natural and fun seemed to become a duty to you, yet another domestic chore. Even when you were playing with him, you weren't there.'

'Of course I was.'

'No. You were putting in the hours before returning to the world that really mattered to you – the one made of words. Good grief, you'd been *fun*, Gregory – it's hard to believe now, but people used to enjoy bringing their children round here. Those silly camping holidays in Cornwall – I used to look forward to them for months. So did Dougie. Then they too became an interruption, something to be endured.'

'It goes with the territory,' I said weakly.

'So then our social life dried up. I gave up inviting my

colleagues around because you made it so obvious you were bored by them that I became embarrassed. Other couples, parents, took to avoiding us as if our unhappiness were contagious. You used to get your writer friends over but that ended too. I suppose you decided that domestic life and parenthood was no longer quite the image you wanted.'

'Nonsense. Parenthood's hot at the moment.'

'It wasn't then. Not in the Eighties.'

'I suppose not.'

'You know, even Dougie's little friends picked it up in the end. The grumpy dad in the background. He took to visiting them at their houses. Then, even that stopped.'

After several minutes' internal debate, Donovan hopped on to my wife's lap, an act of almost unprecedented affection which seemed at that point like yet another small betrayal.

'He blamed himself.' Marigold's voice was bleak and defeated. 'He decided that it was his fault that he was losing you, that you were drifting away from us. He was on his own. I was busy with my career. Sometimes it must have seemed that the weight of the family rested on his skinny little shoulders. If only he could be like the other children – chatty and confident, popular at school, good at football or tennis – it would keep us together. But he couldn't do it. The more he tried, the less he succeeded. He saw you withdrawing day by day and he sensed that it was your disappointment with him and with family life that was the cause. Then, when he was about twelve or thirteen and had just changed schools, he looked at us and saw failure, his failure – a cold non-family, three lonely people. And he gave up. He went into his room and just . . . gave up.' She stroked Donovan, smoothing down his fur. 'So when you talk about taking responsibility, you miss the point. It's exactly what he is doing. He's taking our unhappiness and anger and sense of disappointment and making them his.'

'He told you all this?'

'Of course not. But he tells me more than you think.'

'It hasn't been easy for any of us.'

'The suffering artist.' My wife invested the words with sudden, biting venom. 'We were the ones who paid the price. We could do nothing while all the warmth and humour and life that you once had leaked away into your fiction.' She paused, tellingly. 'Or at least so one assumes.'

'That was unnecessary.'

'To tell the truth, it wouldn't have made any difference if you had written one of the great masterpieces of the twentieth century. The effect on us would have been the same.'

I sat in silence, like a child being admonished.

'You made your choice, didn't you. On the one hand, a child and a wife; on the other hand, a book, a story. Maybe you'd make the same decision again.'

'A surprising number of novelists remain childless.'

'But you didn't. So what would it be – book or child?'

I raised my eyes and said nothing.

'I see.'

'But after this one it will be different.'

'You mean you'll actually finish it?'

'It's going well. I think it might win prizes. When it's out there, I'll do some reviewing, a bit of telly. I'll lighten up. We'll spend more time together.'

'It's too late, Gregory. You've lost your son and now you've lost me.'

'I think you'll see me differently when the new book comes out. It will be like the old days, the *Forever Young* days. Maybe I'll get on to the list of Granta's Best Middle-Aged Novelists.'

Marigold didn't smile. 'It's too late,' she said.

Affirmation

Writing is my companion. I can talk to it through the darkest hours. One day, it will talk to me.

24

For reasons that seemed insignificant at the time, Peter Gibson's funeral had been delayed. I had proposed that I might deliver a few eloquent, heartfelt words at the ceremony but the family, no doubt overcome by the gravity of the event, had told Mike Summers that they wished the occasion to be private. So, in a brief respite from *terpsichore 4:2*, I elected to write a note of condolence to his parents.

A non-writer might assume that the professional word-smith would find letter-writing an easy task. The opposite, of course, is the case. For one who weighs every phrase, who holds it up to the light before deploying it, the casual informality of a 'quick note' is particularly difficult to achieve. How often, reading the letters of the greats, does one sense that a phrase seems too *written*, too well turned, to be entirely natural, like a man in immaculate morning dress at a pub? Yet, on the other hand, too relaxed and chummy a tone in my letter to Mr and Mrs Gibson might also seem inappropriate, even patronizing. I am not ashamed to confess that the letter took me a full three hours to complete. For the true writer, nothing requires more effort than apparently effortless prose.

Dear Mr and Mrs Gibson
Words are never adequate on these occasions but I wanted to add my small voice to the tributes you will have been receiving for Peter, whose tragic death has affected us all, staff and students alike, at the West London Institute, where I am Senior Tutor in Creative Writing.

Peter was a remarkable student – perhaps as promising a young writer as it has been my pleasure with whom to work during my ten years here. Although his talent had yet to achieve the full flower of maturity, the work that he had produced under my guidance already revealed a sure, lyrical touch and a clear-eyed honesty which indicated that here was 'the real thing'.

Under these circumstances, I have conceived the notion that a suitable tribute to his career at the Institute might be a small memorial volume consisting of some of the work he contributed to my class. I would be happy to put together this little book and would very much appreciate the chance to discuss it with you at some future point. I am frequently attending writers' conferences and literary festivals in the Midlands and hope you would not regard it as an intrusion on my part if I rang to make an appointment with your good selves.

In the mean time, my thoughts and condolences are with you as, like Wordsworth with Thomas Chatterton, I contemplate, with fondness and grief, that *'marvellous boy,/ The sleepless soul that perished in his pride.'*

Yours ever

Gregory Keays

Having transcribed my handwritten letter on to the personal notes file on my computer, I dispatched it with many a thought of the way it would be received in Wolverhampton. Working on my novel, I had naturally felt close to the good folk who had brought Peter into the world and nurtured him as best they could. Although I had yet to meet them, and Peter had rarely spoken of his home life, I established a writerly contact with them which, dare I say it, was as valid and true in its way as any so-called 'real' acquaintance.

I had somehow imagined Peter to have been raised on some bleak and devastated estate, but the address that Mike Summers had given me, Clematis Crescent in Meadowfield, gave me pause. Then I remembered that the developers of thirty years ago liked to give their most blighted projects an air of fake pastoralism with names plucked from the kiddy fiction of yesteryear. Just as today's headlines – 'Riot in Bluebell Village', 'Tinkly Stream Rocked by Crackhouse Bust', 'Gangbang on Sunnybrook Farm' – mock the delusions

175

of yesterday's pot-head idealists, I had no doubt that Clematis Crescent would be a tangle of concrete and weed, while the hilariously named Meadowfield (abutting Forest Wood, perhaps, near Borough Town, adjoined by Stream River) would be as vernal as the local rubbish tip.

In my writerly eye, I had seen Peter's childhood with crystal clarity. He would have been a quiet, studious, awkward boy, a worry to his mother and father. While his peers were going out, kicking balls about, joining gangs, engaging stickily with gum-chewing, hard-eyed members of the opposite sex, growing towards a doomed, deprived adulthood in the accepted proletarian way, he would have stayed at home, growing inwards rather than outwards, acquiring words and thoughts through his reading but rarely expressing them. The blare of a television, the smell of frying, Dad sitting dead-eyed on a threadbare sofa, perhaps a can of lager in his hand, Mum ironing angrily nearby, Peter reading. Through the din, the unhappiness and disappointment, he would be consuming books as if his life depended on it. There would be regular family events, moments when Peter would have felt like a changeling, a freak within the Gibson household. Chortling, dewlapped aunts would make clumsy jokes at his expense, uncles would ruffle his hair and ask him what team he supported, cousins would dart looks of undisguised suspicion and antipathy in his direction. As he grew older, he will have taken to speaking up now and then, expressing awkward yet oddly irrefutable views in the flat, confident monotone in which he was later to read his stories in class. When members of the family gathered, wary and jealous of the son whom Ted and Doreen (as I imagined Peter's parents being called) had, against all the odds, brought into the world, they would attempt to silence him with the usual jeers ('Ooh, 'ark at Einstein down there!' 'Swallowed the dictionary, have we?' 'Bloody hell, talk about more brains than sense!'), and he would turn those clear, unblinking eyes on them, casting a chill on the entire party ('If looks could kill!' 'Ullo, he's gone into a brown study' 'What you lookin' at, sonny boy?') Later, after the guests had gone, his mother would sit slumped in the room strewn with plates and glasses, gazing blankly at the screen, her eyes watery. His father, blundering around the flat looking for his cigarettes, would swipe Peter across the back of the head ('Ow, what was that for?' 'You know, you bloody little snob, I've a mind to take you outside and show you what happens to sons who show their parents up.' 'I didn't.' *Thwack!* 'Don't answer back, you bloody little yahoo. Why can't you be normal like all the other lads?' 'I am normal.')

But he wouldn't be normal. He couldn't be. He was a writer.

Meeting them now would be a difficult encounter. I imagined them, sitting there in a room smelling faintly of yesterday's cigarettes. In one corner, on an absurdly large TV, a game-show would soundlessly mock the drab, banal misery of their world. Now and then, as I spoke my tribute to Peter with quiet, moving conviction, their eyes would not be on me but on the fake, tinselled gaiety being enacted on the screen, as if that was their world, not this searing insight into a universe of art, of pain and death. They would be suspicious at first: more words. They had always known that all those words would do Peter harm and they had been right. And yet, when I finished, my words (eloquent, spare, yet bearing an emotional charge) will have reached them. For a few seconds, we would be united, the great social and intellectual gulf between us forgotten as we each of us remembered our own differing versions of Peter Gibson. The moment would pass. Dad might raise the question of clearing Peter's flat; we would discuss what needed to be done in a manly way, while Mum, wet-faced, went to the kitchen to put the kettle on. I would, as sensitively as I could manage, turn to my own practical matters, I would make to leave. There would be heartfelt shakings of the hand, muttered thanks for my journey, an awkward embrace from Mum, perhaps. After I had left, they would turn up the TV and watch without another word.

As it turned out, Meadowfield was not a slum, but a neat,

suburban overflow from the main conurbation nearby. Nor were Mr and Mrs Gibson (Ted and Doreen turned out to be Bob and Sally) quite as I had imagined. When, after a couple of weeks, I had not been granted the courtesy of an acknowledgement to my letter, I wrote again, inventing a literary conference in Wolverhampton – a nice touch, which made me smile as I wrote it – that I was due to attend. Would it be convenient if I called by to introduce myself and discuss Peter's memorial volume?

The following day, I received a call from Bob Gibson. He had a distinctive sing-song voice, the sort of mannered, self-conscious Englishness which, in happier times, would probably have been replete with 'heigh-ho's' and 'cheery-bye's'. There was a careful politeness evident which suggested that grief had almost, but not quite, broken down his sense of good form and I felt a passing stab of guilt as I pressed my case, mentioning the amount of time and effort I was putting to Peter's commemorative volume. Etiquette reasserted itself, and I was in.

Driving north two days later, I gave some thought to the etiquette of post-suicide introductions – specifically, how best to convey respect, concern, polite affection and deep, sincere regret in those all-important first few seconds. A mere handshake was too buttoned-up to be acceptable, a hug too aggressively heartfelt. I considered the shake-hug which has become popular in media circles (grasp of the hand, eye contact, inward tug, embrace, all in one fluid movement) but rejected it on the grounds that it was too frankly emotional to play in Wolverhampton. The gesture I finally arrived at, after some rehearsal in a lavatory cubicle at a service station, involved a moment of attractively shy hesitation, followed by a spreading of the hands in mute, eloquent despair, then a lunge forward for a firm (possibly two-handed) handshake, eye contact maintained throughout, a sorrowful smile playing about the lips.

I reached the neat dreariness of Meadowfield rather early and pulled the car into the side, switched off the engine, rolled down the window and, for five minutes or so, watched the little community where my pupil had once lived go about its business.

It was strangely quiet here, the voices of children, a barking dog, the sound of a distant piano seeming muted, sleepy. I thought of the great chroniclers of middle-class urban life (Cheever, Updike, the Alices Macdermott, Munro and Hoffman) and wondered what private hells and heavens they would read into the scene – the fathers who drank too much and lusted after secretaries, the mothers engaged in quiet, unhappy affairs, the children glimpsing scenes through half-closed doors, hearing the tail-end of urgent, illicit telephone calls, catching suburbia as they grew older, like a disease – but somehow Meadowfield resisted such overheated imaginings. On a small, perfectly square lawn across the road, a white cat lay stretched in the sun. Down the pavement, a dark-haired woman walked with two young children, going home at an easy child's pace, pointing at the cat, talking. I could see why Peter had to leave, why he had invented a childhood so alien and odd. This was no place for a writer.

The Gibsons lived in the heart of Meadowfield down one of the many roads that led to nowhere. As I drew up behind a silver saloon car of middle-management style, I noticed, standing at the window, a tall, white-shirted, balding man with a trim moustache, staring from the gloom in a vaguely proprietorial way.

I had not forgotten the need for a wordlessly eloquent self-introduction but, irritatingly, Bob Gibson threw me off my rhythm by briskly opening the front door as I walked up the path and firmly extending a hand. I moved into my prepared routine but, even as I danced back, waving my hands expressively, I realized that the impression might have seemed more effete than mournful. Looking mildly startled, Bob held his position until my hand finally made contact with his and then, with a cursory nod, turned back into the house.

I followed him through a dark hall, where a small pile of bills and bank statements lay unopened on the hall table, and into a sitting-room. A faint smell of pizza hung in the air. 'Sorry about the mess.' He waved a hand in the direction of a dining-room table covered in files and notepads and what looked like history books, 'The daughter's doing her mocks. She's decided she wants to work downstairs since –' He sat carefully on the sofa, gesturing towards an armchair, '– since this term.' He smiled, almost daring me to connect his daughter's insecurity to their recent family tragedy. 'Sally's just getting us tea. She'll be through in a minute,' he said.

It seemed sensible to delay my carefully planned address until both parents were present, so I filled in the slightly awkward moments during which the reason of my visit remained unclear with easy, fictional chatter concerning my meeting at a writer's conference in Wolverhampton to discuss the status of the contemporary novel, the implications of global interconnectedness on traditional linear narratives, the changing public role of the author. I can talk easily and interestingly around these topics and, as I spoke, I studied Peter's father. Now that he was seated, I saw that there was something slack and defeated about him, like a man of military yearnings who had failed his medical and ended up in the Catering Corps. In his tidy beige trousers, white short-sleeve shirt and rubber-soled shoes, he dressed with the unconvincing vulgarity of a golfer. Only in his expressionless eyes, and the slight sag to his shoulders was there any indication of the effects of recent events.

'I didn't know there were any writers in Wolverhampton,' he was muttering when his wife entered bearing a tray. 'Ah, Sally,' he said, standing up, clearly relieved that any further exploration of the town's literary wealth was unnecessary.

Tall, dressed in a modestly becoming cardigan and skirt, her grey hair mysteriously giving her a manner that was both distinguished and yet almost almost wanton, Mrs Gibson was an even greater surprise to me than her husband. She put the tray on a small table in front of the sofa and smiled.

'The teacher,' she said, shaking my hand as easily as if I were a dinner-party guest.

'Writing's my main job,' I said. Then, aware that my response might have seemed over-hasty, I added quickly. 'But, of course, teaching is a great love of mine.'

'Writing was important to Peter, too. He told us he was going to a class although, I must confess that he never actually mentioned you by name.'

'The best teachers are invisible,' I said. 'For us, it's the kids who count.'

Her eyes fixed on mine, wary yet naked, and, in that instant I saw Peter, his face beside me on the pillow.

'Take a pew,' Mr Gibson said, waving a hand in the direction of a neat, small armchair. Mrs Gibson sat down beside her husband on the sofa, taking a closer position to him than is entirely normal in couples who have been married for some twenty or so years.

I allowed a moment of silence. Then, looking from one parent to the other with a sort of rapt sincerity, I said quietly, 'I'm just so sorry about what happened.'

There was a barely perceptible intake of breath from Mrs Gibson, as if, for a few seconds, she had forgotten why I was there.

'You're very kind,' she said. 'I'm sure there was nothing anyone could do.'

'He was an exceptional student.' I paused, gathering myself and my thoughts. 'Almost all of those I teach are not in love with writing – they long for something different, the life of the writer. They think there's this magic process that will somehow make their lives whole, give the triviality and mess of their suffering a shape, a public, artistic validity. But Peter had come to terms with this strange non-thing called "writing".'

Mr and Mrs Gibson were looking at me with what I took to be curiosity.

'He had discovered the sacred vocation beyond the millions of demons whirling suggestively around, between him and his work, beyond the fear of feeling piddling and foolish,' I continued. 'He had realized that he must cut through, beat on regardless to soar above the petty, the niggling and the nagging. He had discovered that, no matter how much you finally achieve, the pursuit has its own innate dignity.' I sat back, momentarily overcome by emotion.*

Bob Gibson seemed moved, too. Sitting, unnaturally calm, at one end of the sofa, he looked past me as if seeing someone he knew passing the window. When he chewed at his top lip in the way that men with moustaches do, I was aware of a certain tremble, a quiver of the chin. After a few seconds of silence, during which I became aware of the sound of a guitar being strummed from somewhere upstairs in the house, he looked back at me, his eyes unmistakably damp.

'Bollocks,' he said.

I smiled calmly. 'Perhaps it would only make sense to a writer.'

'We've always encouraged him to write,' said Mrs Gibson. 'From primary school, he has always had good reports for English. Some lovely work. A real imagination. Peter has a truly original talent.' She smiled as if reading the reports for the first time. 'We clung to that, didn't we, Bob. We thought that, if he can only believe in his stories, then one day, eventually, he'll believe in himself.'

'Confidence is everything, isn't it?' said Bob Gibson. 'It's the great gift we all want to give to our children. And the more we push it on them, the less confident they feel.'

Sensing parental guilt, perhaps some sort of need for absolution, I pointed out that he had reached university.

'Three Counties University,' said Bob. 'A tarted-up poly. They had courses like Leisure Studies and Tourism.'

Mrs Gibson stirred nervously beside him. 'We were disappointed but we didn't let on. We didn't want to undermine him.'

'We left that to him.' A humourless smile crossed Bob Gibson's face, revealing a row of even white teeth.

'He was a depressive,' his wife said suddenly. 'During his

* A fuller version of this argument can be found in Elizabeth Smart's 'On the Side of the Angels', *Journals, Volume II*, 1994.

teens, we tried everything. Therapy. Pills. There was even talk of some kind of shock treatment. We thought it was teenage blues. But somehow we always knew it was more serious than that.'

'Had he ever –?' I winced, unwilling to articulate the hated word. 'I mean, was this the first attempt?'

Bob nodded. 'Whatever he tried, he did to the best of his ability. Even that.'

'All he wanted to do was write.' Sally Gibson was clearly anxious to change the subject. 'That was why he dropped out of Media Studies. We explained that he had the rest of his life for that sort of thing, a degree would give him options – he'd have a breathing space in which to decide what to do with his life, but no, he said, it would give him nothing. He didn't want a career, a structure to his life. When I told him he needed some kind of qualification before he was too old, he said you didn't need a certificate to be eligible to write well.'

'Age is just a number,' said Bob Gibson softly. 'It doesn't matter. It's just a number, Dad.'

'We did encourage him with his writing. We bought him a computer – a laptop. He kept it here and worked on it over the weekends. He said it would only get nicked in London.'

'Tap tap tap.' Bob sighed. 'Great bloody company he was.'

'He was a writer,' I said kindly, as my mind took in this surprising and somewhat alarming item of news. 'It's what we do.'

There was another silence of respect for Mr and Mrs Gibson's tap-tap-tapping writer son.

'As you know, one of the reasons I wanted to meet you was to discuss my tribute to Peter.'

Bob Gibson looked at me sharply. '*Your* tribute?'

'The Institute's tribute. But I would put it together. I feel I owe it to Peter.' I smiled, as if remembering their son. 'He was such a very promising writer that I wanted to produce a little booklet – nothing lavish – containing some of his best work. Something I know his fellow students would like to keep and so would I.'

'I suppose that would be nice.' Mrs Gibson glanced at her husband who appeared to have drifted off. She squeezed his hand with an intimacy which I was beginning to find grating in a couple of their age. 'Don't you think, Bob?'

'It would be all right, I suppose,' Mr Gibson muttered.

'I'd be very happy to clear material with you before it's included.'

'And the Institute would pay?' he asked.

'If they didn't, I would.'

'That's very kind of you, Mr Keays.'

'Gregory, please.' Briefly lost in reminiscence, I pulled myself together. 'Would he have printed out the material he wrote on the computer?'

Both parents looked surprised. 'No,' said Bob. 'I always assumed they were just notes.'

'Sometimes a writer's notes can contain his best work. If I could just borrow the laptop –'

'I don't know.' Sally Gibson spoke to me but gazed at her husband. 'It feels like an invasion.'

I allowed a couple of beats before making my move.

'You're right,' I said decisively. 'Maybe the idea of publication itself is an invasion. Some writers believe that merely to be read is a compromise of their . . . their soul, if you like. Perhaps I should drop the idea of a tribute volume altogether.'

Bob Gibson twitched into life. 'Compromise their soul? He wasn't that daft, Peter. Of course he wanted readers.'

I allowed the inconsistency of their position to sink in. 'I'd only borrow it for a week or so.'

Sally Gibson stood up. 'I'll fetch it for you,' she said.

When she returned, bearing a small grey laptop, she remained standing. Clearly our meeting was over. With promises to be in touch soon with details of Peter's memorial volume, I was soon on my way.

There had been something about Meadowfield that gave me the creeps. Its neatness, its secrets, its smug sense of unchallenged domestic security. The smell of normal family life in the Gibson household seemed to cling to my clothes, reminding me uncomfortably of the days when I used to collect Dougie from birthday parties. In the houses of his friends, I had always been aware of the warmth and noise and the backchat of adults and children, a sense of connection with normal, everyday life which was somehow lacking at home. I found myself wondering now how it was that the Gibsons, with their oddball son, managed to achieve that ease and intimacy while Marigold and I, with our oddball son, had merely conjured up a chilly wasteland of hostility and non-communication. I took small, heartless comfort in the fact that, for all their smug family happiness, the folk from Meadowfield had produced a young suicide while we, for all our many failings, were merely having to deal with normal adolescent dysfunction.

I was driving towards Wolverhampton, Peter's laptop on the seat beside me. I pulled into a lay-by and switched it on. There were, I was relieved to see, only two documents: one consisting of notes, the other letters to one Mary Kydd, who seemed to be a student at Keele. I reached into the pocket of the case. There were three letters, still in their envelopes, addressed in a girlish hand to Peter at his home. I glanced through the letters – gossipy accounts of student life with occasional questions about Peter's writing. In the third envelope, I found a photograph: a dark, slightly plump young girl stood on the steps of a redbrick building.

Mary Kydd. Not a girlfriend, I judged, but a friend, maybe even a fellow writer.

> **Top Five Health Tips from the Great Writers**
>
> 1. John Keats advised, 'Whenever I feel myself growing vapour-ish, I rouse myself, wash and put on a clean shirt brush my hair and clothes, tie my shoestrings neatly and in fact adonize as if I were going out – then all clean and comfortable I sit down to write.'
> 2. Frederick Nietzsche believed that writing brought its own health. 'When my creative energy flowed most freely, my muscular activity was always greatest,' he wrote. 'I might often have been seen dancing; I used to walk through the hills for seven or eight hours on end without a hint of fatigue. I slept well, laughed a good deal – I was perfectly vigorous and patient.'
> 3. T. S. Eliot could only write when anaemic.
> 4. A. E. Housman needed to be 'rather out of health' to work at his best.
> 5. Georges Simenon would insist on a full medical before he started writing a novel. If he was interrupted by ill health, he abandoned the novel.

25

As a creative artist, one is confronted by a fundamental, practical dilemma. Your life, the backdrop to your work: will it be a teeming, ever-changing, turbulent carnival of movement, drama and heartache, the colourful mix of which will seep into your writing, so that rivals will not only want to write like you but will long to be like you? Will you move around the world, pounding the streets of Hanoi, Budapest and Quito, the invisible outsider, alert to adventure, a spy, a buccaneer, a visitor of brothels, engaging fleetingly and regretfully with exotic lovers unable to cure you of your rambling cowboy writer ways? Or perhaps the adventure will be a more intimate one, a riotous progress in and out of bedrooms, an assault course of love and infidelity, of ecstasy and pain, bewildered children scattered behind you like broken, discarded toys, the garish confusion of your life contrasting intriguingly with the neatly paginated order of your writing and incidentally providing perfect material for wary but intrigued interviewers and profile-writers.

This, the ramblers' course, is *de rigueur* among the new generation. Contemplation, the book-lined study, is out. Tears, intemperance, drugs, emotional hooliganism of one kind or another are touted in the public prints as if they were guarantees of artistic authenticity. He kicked in the door of his publisher; she left her husband after six weeks of marriage; they must be serious writers, talent and emotional incontinence being but different sides of the same coin.

Then there are the stickers, the stayers, those who have followed the Flaubertian dictum that all the colours and dimensions in a writer's life should be saved for his work: a house, a desk, regular meals, a 'dull life, so calm and flat' whose very lack of colour brings a pent-up vibrancy to the page.

Each path contains a trap. By his nature, the rambler is self-destructive. The very stimulants which propel the early work will, over time, fry the brain cells. The life may become more important than the work. For the sticker, the peril is more insidious. Healthy, hard-working, punctilious and dutiful, he might suddenly find that the dreariness of his daily existence has seeped into his work, that there is nothing to fill the page but a stale, fiddling introversion.

And, over both the rambler and sticker, there hangs one terrifying, unavoidable question: what happens to the novelist who either devotes himself to screwing up his life, to boozing, cheating, and doing damage or, taking the alternative route, who locks himself away, cultivating dullness, making words his only pleasure in an unpleasured world – what happens if he does all this and, at the end of it all, the words are crap? Too late he will discover that he has taken the wrong road, that, however much and for however many years he had rambled or stuck, he might just as well have lived the blameless, contented life of a civilian. After all the effort and sacrifice to himself and others, he has achieved nothing of literary worth.

I shall be frank. There have been times when I have wondered whether, by taking the sticker's path – dutiful father, supportive husband, member of the tennis club, to all appearances as dull a suburbanite as you would ever dread to meet – I had not wilfully starved myself of material. Every week I would read in the newspapers of my peers, blundering onwards, drugged, lustful, gloriously incapable of living the grown-up life of a citizen: far from disqualifying them from the ranks of the serious, their crazed egotism and rampant immaturity were widely perceived as a sort of artistic qualification. Not only were they having a better time than me, they were building their public reputations, garnering a rich harvest of raw experience.

What did I have? The page. The screen. The study. The home, the family. Before, in a rare moment of self-centredness, I ejected my son from his loft, I had worked where he now slept in a small, dark room but a thin wall away from the bathroom. Often (in this at least my family were regular and healthy), I would find myself writing fiction to the accompaniment of bowel music from the adjoining room. With every dribble and grunt and fart and splash, with every rumble of the toilet roll and watery explosion from the cistern, I would become angrier and less able to write. It was as if my family's easy evacuations were mocking the ever-increasing agony of my own artistic *blocage*. In my desperation to write something – anything – I included in *Adultery in Hampstead* a climactic turd-centred comic set-piece in the manner of early Kingsley Amis or Anthony Burgess. It may seem ludicrous but today I see there was a sort of integrity to the way that I transformed the most banal of domestic occurrences into material for fiction. McEwan had murder, Rushdie had the birth of India, Martin had eighties greed; I had my family's daily dump.

At my lowest point, it even occurred to me that, since

Forever Young, a historical novel in which, as even my harshest critics conceded, I had attempted to address an entire society,* my writerly horizons had, with every uncompleted work, contracted daily: from the world at large, to a particular social group, to the small field representing my own domestic experience, to the page or the screen on which I was writing. Now, researching *The Book of Literary Lists*, I was that pitiably limited creature, a writer writing about writing. What next? A writer writing about a writer writing? The sheer futility of the enterprise assailed me every morning when I sat down at my desk.

Now all that was past. There had been something about the events in that Gloucester hotel, followed by the death of Peter Gibson and my collaborative work on *terpsichore 4:2* that shifted me, definitively and for ever, away from the ranks of the home boys, the stickers. Suddenly the demands of my wife and son which for years had distracted me from my work seemed distant and, heartless as it may seem, less significant than the writerly events occurring within and around my novel. I became a rambler.

The notes on Peter's computer were frankly disappointing. Of course, even the great writers will indulge in gibberish in their private notes or prose workouts, but these observations – banal events from a dusty, sexless private life, freighted with absurd, mythic significance – exposed the eggshell fragility of his undoubted artistic promise. I managed to quarry a few incidents from his accounts of childhood with a view to deploying them as moments of colour to the early chapters of *terpsichore 4:2*, then edited a few of the less abject efforts into a first draft of his memorial volume, which I had decided to entitle *The Marvellous Boy: Peter Gibson 1976– 1998*.

Some might think it was a small betrayal to have included embarrassingly slight jottings in the tribute to go out under Peter's name while his more serious work was to be found in

---

* 'BE-IN AND NOTHINGNESS' was the headline in the *New Statesman*.

my own novel, but somehow these notes seemed more appropriately personal, more genuinely Peter, than the material which, as I worked over it hour after hour, was feeling less and less like a joint project and increasingly like the flowering of my own talent after a long period of hibernation.

Yet, of course, the creative process is always open to misinterpretation. What I saw as a cross-generational fusion between master and pupil – a harvesting, if you like, of seeds of learning I had planted within Peter, others might regard as little short of plagiarism. At the best of times, the line between writing and editing is blurred and only those versed in the history of literary collaboration – Beaumont and Fletcher, Conrad and Ford, Eliot and Pound, would truly understand that my transcribing raw material from handwritten form on to my computer was as true an act of creation as the more traditional method of writing.

In order to forestall a sterile, distracting debate about the 'integrity' of the text, I elected not to make the original draft notes available to prying eyes, brushing the footprints behind me as I made my long journey by the simple, if brutal, expedient of destroying the manuscript when I had finished with it.

Every day, when I took my daily walk towards Acton, Chiswick or Bishop's Park, a few pages of Peter's handwritten work would be in my pocket. Every day, they would be left in one of the many recycling bins which the local councils made available to citizens. Every day, I returned, purged of debt to my former pupil. Every day, in a very real sense, the work became more mine and less his.

Another confession. There were times, during the days after my return from Meadowfield, when I found myself examining my late student's notes for information of a private, non-literary nature. The girl Mary Kydd, it seemed clear, was more a literary confidante than a lover: references to her in Peter's *carnets* were invariably in the context of something he had read which he planned to show her.

My response to this relationship was interestingly confused. Although, at heart, I wished Peter to be like me, a heterosexual male who, at a moment of supreme emotional and creative vulnerability, had sought comfort or understanding or something in the arms of a man, I was aware of the faintest spasm of jealousy within me.

What were Peter's desires when he was writing his novel? Did he yearn for this Mary Kydd person? Novelists caught up in creative fervour do not, my research for *Literary Lists* suggested, seek out erotic relief or, if they do, it tends to be of the most fleeting, emotionally disengaged kind. What then of those who were writing notes for a novel?

I began to wonder about Mary, and how much she knew about my former lover.

The Writer Speaks of . . . Self-love

I think most artists find that when they're writing something, they become sexually excited. But it would be a waste of time to engage in a full-dress – or undress – sexual act with somebody at that moment. So they often go into the bathroom to masturbate when they write. Our sexual energy has been aroused, now we come, now we're able to concentrate on the other aspect of this energy, which is the creative aspect.

Anthony Burgess

No less than the great Flaubert used to pull his pollywogger right at his desk, with insouciant aplomb, wipe the viscous semen on his velveteen smoking jacket, and go blithely and resolutely on with his masterpiece about the sappily romantic Emma.

Frederick Exley

I cannot write any kind of story unless there is at least one character in it for whom I have physical desire.

Tennessee Williams

One can no more think of making fiction without onanism, or selfishness (ask our wives), than of the sea without waves.

John Fowles

I have never successfully masturbated to Updike's writing, though I have to certain remembered scenes in Iris Murdoch; but someone I know says that she achieved a number of quality orgasms from *Couples* when she first read it at age thirteen.

Nicholson Baker

How do I like to write? With a soft pencil and a hard dick – not the other way round.

Hanif Kureishi

26

Four days after my visit to Bob and Sally in Meadowfield, I made a call to Brian McWilliam and requested a meeting. He behaved as if he had been expecting my call. We agreed to meet at a pub called the Queen Bess near Shepherd's Bush Green. The next evening, I rambled east once more.

Although I was in a direct, cut-to-the-chase frame of mind, I took the scenic route, making my way down the streets with their bullying, confident imperial names (Adelaide Grove, Bloemfontein Road, Kaffirbash Crescent), between the blocks of flats which, like bad giant imitations of prisons, had outside walkways where young mothers stood, smoking and talking, the air humming with the discordant electronic clamour of TV and music, trash American movies and jungle beat. Occasionally, raised voices, a crash of crockery, the universal anthem of domestic pain cut the evening air before subsiding into angry, hopeless mutters. Between the buildings, small boys kicked a football to and fro, bored, uncompetitive, seemingly mesmerized by the smack of slack, scuffed leather on tarmac and brick. The newspapers called this area 'Murder Mile' but somehow the Shepherd's Bush mortality rate, while being astonishingly high, hardly registered on the consciousness of those outside the small, self-harming circle in which it took place. These were dealers, drug dukes enacting their own little bloody border disputes. There was something almost clean about death in Murder Mile: a club, early hours of the morning, bang, a bullet to the head, maybe two heads, maybe three. No messy woundings. Life or death. Civilians excluded.

Going east to meet Brian McWilliam, I was no longer impersonating Gregory Keays, the middle-class novelist with a great future behind him, the suburban scribbler getting by on the chilly outer fringes of the literary scene. I was the writer as man of action, a hoodlum of prose, a fast-track fictioneer whose life was as near the dangerous edge of things as it was possible to be without toppling off. The division between life and work? There was no division. Suddenly I was my own material.

In a spirit of doomed optimism, many of the pubs in this area had been redecorated with lights and cheap ersatz sophistication, renamed with fake wit, the Prince of Wales becoming the Rat and Carrot, the White Hart being transformed into the Gargling Weasel. There were big windows, TV screens, computer games, brightly coloured carpets, unchanging 'menus of the day' offering steak and mushroom pie, chicken niblets, scampi and French fries, ham 'n' cheese quiche. Only the clientèle had not been upgraded. Instead of laughing, attractive young folk bundling in and out, chatting and flirting over margaritas and spritzers, the men and women here sat slumped at tables nursing their pints, ashtrays brimming with butt-ends and discarded chewing-gum. They looked as if they had been there for a decade, as if the pub had been changed around them without their noticing, as if nothing – no exciting new techno-entertainment, louder music or bigger TV screen – could shake them from their grim, defeated self-absorption.

The Queen Bess had resisted the trend towards modernization. It was not just free of music and noise and colour and youth; it was pretty much free of customers. By the time I arrived at around ten, the drinking rush hour seemed to have passed the place by. A couple of ancients sat at the bar, looking as if they had been there so long that they had become part of the fixtures and fittings. A middle-aged man and a younger woman – on some grim little adulterous tryst, to judge by the way they both glanced up as I entered the bar – were in the darkest corner. At a table in the middle of the room, McWilliam sat in the company of a thin Asian girl who at first glance seemed like a child wearing the tight dress and make-up of an adult woman for a primary school play. Wearing pressed designer jeans, a black silk shirt and double-breasted jacket, McWilliam looked like a successful retired footballer or bookmaker.

'Greg, the writer.' He extended a hand across the table. 'The very man.'

'Good to see you, again.'

'Mine's a large Scotch, dash of water.'

I looked at the girl, awaiting an introduction. 'Can I get your friend something?' I asked eventually.

McWilliam glanced over at her as if he had momentarily forgotten she was there. 'Get her a coke, Greg,' he said. 'Otherwise she might get a bit out of hand.' He squeezed her thin, bare leg and, briefly, the girl seemed to shrink from him. 'Coca?' he said loudly.

'Coca,' she mumbled.

I returned with the drinks. McWilliam had folded his camelhair coat over the chair next to his and seemed disinclined to move it. 'How's the book going?' I asked, pulling up another chair.

'Search me.' McWilliam looked around the pub, suddenly bored. 'I've done my thing. It's down to the publishers. I'm on my new project these days.' He frowned stagily. 'Come to think of it, Greg, you might be the very fellow I'm looking for.'

'I'm a bit committed at the moment, time-wise.'

'It's not a fucking writing gig. I've got a writer, haven't I. It was more in the nature of a consultancy.'

Frankly, the last thing I needed was to be pulled into some iffy scheme being developed by a small-time media lowlife but, for any freelance, there's something strangely attractive about the word 'consultancy'.

Smiling, as if he could read my mind, he pulled his chair in and lowered his voice. 'Ever worked in the film business, Greg?' he asked.

'There was talk of an option in *Forever Young*.'

'None of that bollocks.' McWilliam's hand had returned to the girl's leg and he was absent-mindedly caressing her inner thigh under her skimpy dress. I noticed the adulterers staring at him with undisguised disapproval. 'This is a low-budget, fast turnaround money product. All you'd have to do is turn up for a few meets and come up with some titles. It'll be a cash-in-hand job.'

'Titles?'

'Me and a few business associates are interested in funding a series of remakes of classics. *Women in Love*, *Hard Times*, *Tender Is the Night*.'

I smiled with relief. 'So you've really caught the literature bug.'

'Yeah, right, whatever. The thing is these films would basically be your average naughty pictures – graphic but tasteful. We'd have all these fancy titles from books and that – give them a bit of respectability and wit. So instead of your regular bestiality number – *Debby Does Donkeys* or whatever – you'd call it *Animal Farm*.'

I laughed at what I assumed was a joke. 'But *Animal Farm* is a political satire about totalitarianism.'

'Not any more it ain't. There's no copyright in titles. This way we get a bit of credibility with a touch of the old irony. Porn's really big now as long as you dress it up as something a bit more respectable. Trouble is, we don't know the book stuff. We got *Black Beauty* and *Lady with a Lapdog*. One of the lads came up with *The Iron Man* by Longfellow.'

'Hughes.'

'Hughes?' McWilliam thought for a moment. 'Nah, Longfellow's better.' He turned to the Asian girl. 'Ku here's one of our stars.' He winked at me. '*Little Women*.'

The girl smiled uncertainly.

'Have you acted before?' I asked.

'She doesn't speak English.' McWilliam smiled. 'We communicate in other ways. You're a very good fuck, aren't you, Ku?'

The girl looked confused.

'Isn't she a bit –?' I hesitated. 'I mean, she looks as if she should be at school.'

'Nah. They all look like this, Koreans. Then one day, whoomph, they've gone. They're good for nothing after nineteen.'

'I'll think about this proposal,' I said, changing the subject. 'But I need a bit of unofficial advice on a personal job. I need a consultant, too.'

More defensive now, McWilliam swigged at his whisky. 'What kind of advice would that be then?'

I lowered my voice. 'By personal, I mean . . . wet.'

'Wet?' He laughed. 'What the fuck you on about, Greg?'

'A wet job.'

'A woman? You're hitting on me for a woman? What is this?'

'Harm. I'm looking for a bit of harm. To a third person.'

'Like, a smack? Someone to be slapped around? Greg, it's really not something I –'

'I can pay.'

'Wet job.' McWilliam shook his head, then drained his drink. 'You've been watching too many American movies, my son.' He stood up, reaching for his overcoat which he slipped on with a comically business-like, shrugging movement. 'Let's go somewhere else,' he said.

We made our way out of the pub, followed uncertainly by Ku. Outside, McWilliam turned to her, as if suddenly remembering she was there. 'Home.'

'Hom?' Disconcertingly, her voice was that of a little girl.

'Home. Mummy. Daddy. Telly. Fuck off.'

A look of disappointment crossed Ku's face. Then she walked off, disconsolately.

'Sweet girl.' McWilliam winked. 'But none too bright, between you and me.'

He turned and began to walk briskly towards the Green, his hands sunk deep into his pockets.

'I hope I didn't do you out of a date,' I said, catching him up after a few strides.

'No, problem. Greg.' McWilliam spoke without turning towards me. 'I'll call in later. Ku's open all hours, if you know what I mean.'

'Ah.'

We walked in silence for a while. 'How's the family, Greg?' McWilliam asked suddenly in a tone that suggested that he had more than small talk on his mind.

'Good.'

'That nipper of yours all right, is he?'

Had I mentioned Doug when we had met in Gloucester? It seemed unlikely. McWilliam glanced across at me, his eyes catching the street lights.

'Teenagers,' I said. 'You know how it is.'

'Tell me about it.' The lights changed and he swung into Ladbroke Grove.

'Wife working, is she?'

'Yeah. An interior designer. *Feng shui*.' I realized, with a pinch of conscience, that I had spoken the words with a sneery oriental authenticity. *Fung Sheway*. I was relieved when McWilliam didn't laugh.

'Oh yeah?' he said. 'She should have a go at my gaff. It's a fucking tip. One of my girlfriends told me it was because my *feng shui* was all to bollocks.'

'She's a bit booked up, but I could mention it.'

He looked across. 'You're talking shit. I warned you about that.'

I smiled, irritated at having been wrong-footed once more.

'You're like me,' he said. 'You like to compartmentalize things. Relationships. Sex. Business. Fun. We've got tidy minds, you and me. They're all in little boxes, aren't they? We only feel safe if we can keep them apart. That's how we keep control of our lives, how we avoid confusion and mess.'

It had not in fact occurred to me that a media criminal with a history of violence and deception was, in any sense, 'like' a professional writer and family man, but, at this moment, it seemed wise to play along. 'Maybe,' I said.

'Yeah. Right. Fucking maybe is right.'

We turned into a dark street behind the Green, then into an alleyway. After a few yards, we stopped by a heavy, panelled door with a small brass plate bearing the legend 'Jesters'. It was a club whose name I vaguely recalled. It was said to be a favourite hang-out for dope-peddlers, footballers, tabloid models and the new breed of lad-novelists. While I had no objection to frequenting the dive *du jour* – being seen in the company of Brian McWilliam, indeed, would do my image nothing but good – this was an occasion when publicity would be something of a complication.

He stood by the door, rang a bell and nodded imperiously in the direction of a camera lens. He pushed his way in.

At the end of a narrow corridor, we found ourselves in a small, dark room, with battered furniture. The only source of light came from behind the bar where a man in his sixties, with the thinning, slicked-back hair of an ageing Ted and an aggressive paunch, glanced in our direction and raised his eyebrows in weary welcome, before returning his attention to a TV screen in the corner on which a football game was being played. There were two other men in the room, also gazing at the screen but without particular interest. No exotic black men, no young girls with their legs on, no media types on the slum. If this was the Notting Hill high life, they could keep it.

'My usual, please, Greg.' McWilliam spoke without looking at me, made his way to the darkest corner and slumped into a leather armchair.

I ordered two double whiskies from the barman and went over to join him.

'Cosy place,' I said.

'Fucking fleapit, but it does. They only have one member-ship rule here. No fucking journos.'

I winced facetiously.

'All right then, so it's not about the book, you don't want drugs, and it's personal. Tell me what you want from me, Greg the writer.'

I glanced over my shoulder to ensure that the fat barman was out of earshot.

'I was wondering if you could advise me about removing someone from the scene, keeping them quiet for a while.'

'What, cause them a bit of grief, discourage them.'

'Grief, yes. Harm.'

'And you'd pay.'

'I'd pay.'

'I told you in Gloucester. I don't do things. I can point you in the right direction, maybe make a couple of calls. I'm a delegater – in the supervising business.'

'Of course.'

'Who is it then. Some bastard author who got up your nose? A dodgy critic?'

I took out the photograph and handed it to him.

'Oh Gregory, behave.' He looked up, a vulpine smile on his lips. 'You serious?'

'Bit of discouragement,' I said. 'A bit of quiet.'

'What – a holiday ticket abroad, is it? Do my friend a favour and make yourself scarce for a few months, darling?'

'No. A bit more . . . definitive than that.' Seeing that McWilliam was having difficulty catching my drift, I searched in my mind for a useful term from one of my fictional manuals. 'I need closure,' I said.

He looked down at the photograph again, and ran a well-manicured thumb over Mary's smiling face.

'For this, Greg, me old son, I might just come out of retirement.

27

Something strange and unusual happened that night. I fucked my wife. I had been out in the real world, arranging, supervising, sorting out problems. I had been a man, and now I came home to do the manly thing.

I returned to the house after midnight. There was no sound from Doug's bedroom, a single light shone in the hall. I climbed the stairs, weary but purposeful, like a good citizen returning from a long day's work. I went to my study, as is my custom, with a view to jotting down some notes for tomorrow's writing, but suddenly the world of invention seemed too insubstantial to detain me. I undressed, went to the bathroom, washed my face, and entered the bedroom.

Over the past two years, Buddha had been stealthily colonizing this room. First there was a small picture on Marigold's dressing-table. Then a prayer hung on the wall where a perfectly harmless watercolour had once been. Now the place was a shrine: harmony chimes hung over the bed (Buddha is a stranger to irony), a scented candle glowed on a bedside table; at the foot of the bed sat a model of the plump godhead himself, with the bowl of fresh rice which my wife, murmuring devotional gobbledegook, would replenish when she returned from work.

It was a still, warm night and, under the eyes of the fat boy, my wife lay, naked, on her side. These days she slept well – as if, after years of being alert to the slightest sound coming from Doug's bedroom, she was now capable of sleeping through anything. I settled on my side of the bed in my usual position, on the edge, facing away from her. I felt wakeful and, after a few moments, turned to look at her as she slept. For maybe five minutes, I stared at her back, the heavy dark hair on the pillow; there was an air of peace around her at night which was rarely evident during the daytime. Unlike most of her contemporaries, whom motherhood had gently transformed into a sweet, comfortable and shapeless middle age, Marigold had kept her figure; indeed she seemed to have become more compact, more herself, over the years. It was not just that she had taken to working out at the gym, but that something within her would not succumb to the ageing process. Oddly, she seemed more single now than she had been, over two decades ago, when we had met during her years as a striving artist.

I stretched out my right arm, hesitated, briefly fearful of her reaction, then laid my hand lightly on her shoulder. She muttered sleepily but the shoulder, which once would have shrugged me off with practised ease, remained still. I ran my index finger down the valley between her shoulder and collarbone, down her backbone before holding her right buttock, easily, like a ten-pin bowler.

She stirred. 'Gregory?' she said and, briefly, I was reminded that I was not the only one with the right to touch her up in the middle of the night.

I chose to ignore the note of soft admonition in her voice, slightly increasing the pressure of my hand. She said, more loudly, 'No, please.' I took my hand away, then placed it with gentle firmness over her mouth. She tensed and seemed about to speak but I held her still, my fingers tingling with her disapproval. To my astonishment, she relaxed. After a few moments of lying like this, an erotic parody of coercion, my hand meandered downwards, lingering over her right breast, across her stomach, before finally coming to rest between her legs.

She twisted her head. 'It's too late,' she said.

'Not that late.' My left arm sidled under her body, pulling her more closely to me.

'I don't mean the time. Life. It's too late in life. It's gone.'

But it was not gone. 'Oh, shit,' she whispered, turning over to face me. Her eyes were closed and she was frowning, irritated.

At any other time, I would have taken what was on offer, stolen, like a thief, in and out, before the alarm was raised. But right now, that was not what I wanted.

I crouched over her and, briefly, found myself staring into her eyes, which were wide with surprise or anger or maybe even alarm. I stared back. I was like him, McWilliam had said. I was not going to cower or flinch before that infuriated gaze. I placed my hand on her forehead and, like a policeman at the scene of a murder, stroked her eyes shut. Her own hands were clasped together frumpily on her stomach. I took her wrists, one in each hand, and held them down against the bed close to her hips. Then I headed south.

It had been a long, long time since I had last been down here rooting about in the sweet undergrowth but for years of my life it had seemed I had spent much of my happiest waking hours there. While all else changes, that does not. I felt as if I were home again.

Briefly and unconvincingly, my wife tried to free her arms, muttering words of protest, but she was mine now, it was the young Marigold I was making love to. After a few seconds she moved herself to me, her thighs quivering. When I freed her hands so that I could gather her up and feast on her more deeply, she merely laid them on my head like a priest blessing a communicant. She had never been a noisy lover but now I heard a prayer of need coming from her, occasionally punctuated by an involuntary gasp. As she pressed my head downwards, the fingers of her right hand twitching as if she were making love to herself through me, I paused.

202

'Turn over,' I said.

I knew my woman. I worked at her for a few seconds before her back arched. She buried her face in the pillow, clawing, muffling her moans, her whole body shuddering for what seemed like minutes but must have been around thirty seconds. Then, suddenly, she relaxed and was limp and slack, and self-contained once more. The established etiquette on these occasions had dictated that I should now make love to her slack, unresponding body until I too had come to rest, but I tugged her shoulder. Sullenly she turned to face me, eyes closed, embarrassed now, indifferent. I lifted her legs, just as I had once lifted Peter Gibson's, and, thinking of him, made love to her in a lordly, leisurely way, a man taking his pleasure from his wife. She winced. She sighed. At one point, she clicked her teeth in a put-upon housewifely way. Unperturbed, I finished casually and moved to my side of the bed.

After a few seconds, she briskly pulled the duvet over herself, flicking one side of it my direction. Even before she spoke, I knew I was in trouble.

'So what was all that about?' There was the merest hint of post-coital languor in her voice.

'I'm working hard. I desired you. I wanted it.'

'It. You wanted *it*. So you took *it*.'

Already I felt my husbandly strength ebbing away. 'Don't go political on me, Marigold.' I said. 'Not now.'

'Good grief, it's not *political* to prefer not to be mauled around in the middle of the night by a man who happens to be feeling pleased with himself and thinks he deserves some kind of treat. I'm not a box of chocolates, you know.'

I said nothing.

'Why *are* you feeling so pleased with yourself, by the way?'

'The novel's going well.'

'Congratulations.'

'And it's been a long time.'

'Huh. You could say.'

'I'm not talking about the writing.'

'Ah.' She pulled the duvet around her shoulders. 'Speak for yourself,' she said, almost to herself.

There was something in her voice which caught my attention, a sort of smugness. 'Are you in love with him?' My voice hung in the dark for a few seconds.

'What's it to you?'

'You're my wife. You matter to me.'

'You don't really want to know, so don't ask.'

Didn't I? Marigold moved in a world of sharply dressed high achievers who treasured personal happiness and self-expression above all else. I had always known that nothing could have been more natural than that she should choose to express herself in the most traditional and direct way. I could hardly blame her. Besides, given what she knew of me and my past, she could respond to my pea-shooter of reproach with a battery of howitzers and hand-grenades.

'We need to talk about Doug,' she said.

For once, I was not going to allow the hulking, guilt-laden presence of our son into the marital bed. 'It's not too late, M,' I said, using the nickname of our early years together.

'I think he's getting himself into trouble.'

I reached out a hand and laid it on the valley of her waist.

'Let's not do this to each other.' I tried to pull her towards me.

She moved away with an angry twitch of her hips, letting my hand fall.

She half-turned. 'See?' she said, almost laughing. 'See how it feels.'

'That was the past.'

'You reap what you sow,' she sighed. 'I'm going to sleep now.'

She huddled under the duvet as if finally to shut me out. For the millionth time in our marriage, I found myself staring at her dark hair on the pillow, the angry jut of her small shoulder, listening to the rise and fall of her breath.

A COMPARISON OF THE EARLY MORTALITY OF GREAT
POETS AND GREAT NOVELISTS

Shortest Living Great Poets (in reverse Age-of-Death Order)

Thomas Chatterton	18
Rupert Brooke	23
John Keats	26
Christopher Marlowe	29
James Elroy Flecker	29
Percy Bysshe Shelley	30
Sylvia Plath	30
Wilfred Owen	32
François Villon	33
Hart Crane	34
Average:	28.4

Shortest Living Great Novelists (in reverse Age-of-Death Order)

Stephen Crane	29
Katherine Mansfield	35
Thomas Wolfe	38
Jack London	40
Edgar Allan Poe	40
Franz Kafka	41
Jane Austen	41
Guy de Maupassant	43
Robert Louis Stevenson	44
F. Scott Fitzgerald	44
Average:	39.50

28

If, as Auden said, a writer's autobiography is his capital, I have been dealt a duff hand. My parents, still living, a couple of perky pensioners in Leicester, provided my childhood with neither the acts of mindless abuse and neglect nor the background of domestic dysfunction that offers a rich seam of material for the writer in later life. They fucked me up, my Mum and Dad, simply by not fucking me up. I forged wearily onwards to a normal marriage, normal parenthood, normal suburban life. Once I attempted to invest the creative capital accruing from early infidelities into the comic novel *Adultery in Hampstead*, but even I could see that the creative dividends were negligible, that scenes and insights intended as a frothy light-hearted sideways glance at gender misunderstanding emerged merely as sour misogyny.

Now, at the very moment when a hint of the truly dramatic was entering my life, the narrative took a wrong turn once more. An inspector called.

The arrival of a policeman is rarely good news in any serious work. Half in and half out of daily life, he brings with him an oppressive, distracting sense of more exciting events happening elsewhere. When serious novelists, in a moment of desperation, allow the heavy tread of law enforcement to enter their work, it invariably loses what tension and interest it ever had. The moment that Martin, floundering about in mid-career, actually elected to narrate the American novella through 'a police' had me punching the air with joy and relief.

Yet here he was, my policeman, cluttering up a narrative that had been going so promisingly with his investigation, his suspects, his routine lines of enquiry, changing my life for ever. Beckwith.

When he appeared one morning on the doorstep of 23 Brandon Gardens, I was absorbed in the closing scenes of *terpsichore 4:2*. Feverishly anticipating the moment when the agony of parturition would be over, I had quite forgotten about McWilliam, Mr and Mrs Gibson, about Mary Kydd, even Peter himself.

Until Beckwith.

Living near the wild frontier, I have had dealings over the years with the local police as, with an air of exhausted defeat, they followed up that day's act of theft, vandalism or street violence. A few were hard-eyed opportunists, indiscernible in manner and moral character from the villains they were allegedly pursuing, but most were the traditional dogged, sincere, pencil-licking plods.

Beckwith was different. With wispy light hair prematurely receding from his pale, fleshy features, he had the look of a man who spends too much time in front of a computer screen. His voice – 'Mr Gregory Keays? I wonder if you could spare a few moments on the matter of your late student, Peter Gibson' – was flat and suburban but there was something about the way he looked about him as I showed him into the hall, not so much intelligence as a sort of contemporary brightness, which put me on my guard. I imagined him to be the sort of policeman who would see crime in terms of productivity and turnover, who was but a short semantic step from describing criminals as 'customers'. Somewhere about his neat be-suited person, or in his guy-next-door black briefcase, there would be various small items of communication technology (phone, pager, electronic notebook) to remind him of the day's agenda, of where and who he was.

I showed him into the sitting-room. He admired a small figurine Marigold had recently imported from Papua New Guinea before casually taking a seat in front of the window. As I served him coffee, he chatted in a dutiful, non-specific way. He had heard of my wife, of course, but – not much of a bookworm, to be honest – had not had the pleasure of reading my novels. *Forever Young*, was it? I mentioned that I was caught up in the final stages of a new work but Beckwith failed to pick up the hint. He seemed casually, unnervingly well-informed about my life.

After a couple of minutes, he sat forward in his armchair, put his hands together in a thoughtful, self-important manner, and said, 'There has been a development which we wanted to share with you. Concerning Peter.'

'Yes?' My tone indicated only mild curiosity. Briefly, when the policeman had introduced himself, it had occurred to me that his visit concerned Mary Kydd, that perhaps, in his enthusiasm, Brian McWilliam had misinterpreted my request for help, but Beckwith's manner was too informal for that. Besides, old Pussy was nothing if not a professional in these matters.

'We ran certain tests on the body of Peter Gibson.' Beckwith sat back so that it was difficult to see the expression on his face against the light outside. 'It appears that he may not have been quite as solitary as we had previously thought.'

'Solitary? Peter was always something of a loner but he had friends. Several of the pupils in his class –'

'Between you and me, Mr Keays, we're not talking socially here.' Beckwith gave a sort of wince of apology at having interrupted me. 'It was more a matter of . . . a lover.'

'Yes?' My dignified, man-of-the-world manner conveyed, I hoped, a touch of disapproval that such matters should be deemed worthy of police investigation.

'According to our forensic department, there are indications that Peter had, in the hours before his death, some intimate contact with another person.'

'He had sex, you mean.'

'There were traces of another person's DNA on his – well, on his penis. Our people say that he had not had full, completed sex but something definitely of that nature had occured. There was a matter of saliva.'

'Ah.'

For a moment we sat in Marigold's immaculate room like two actors on a stage who had forgotten their lines. I looked out of the window, seeing not the street outside but that last scene in Peter's unlovely flat, my head bowed over his thin, white body, his poor, cold cock in my mouth. I felt proprietorial, angry that the innocent corpse of my student had been pored over by some dirty-minded geek in a white coat. I was defensive of myself, too. It had been a moment of purity, of silent, wordless tribute. Why the hell should I not say goodbye to my lover in that way? I was a writer, for Christ's sake.

I returned my attention to Beckwith, suddenly aware that I was breathing more deeply than was entirely normal.

'We may not tell his parents.' The policeman's dull,

cybernetic tone of voice was unchanged. 'I thought I would tell you because, as his teacher, you might be able to shed light on the matter.'

'Does it change anything?'

'It may just cast a different light on his death.'

'He was ringing me all night,' I said. 'My wife can be a witness to that. And, if he died in the early hours of the morning, no one can have seen him that day.'

'Precisely.'

'You're not suggesting murder.'

'No. There were no marks of violence on his body, no dabs around the flat. Apart from yours, of course.'

My mind ran over the implications of what I was hearing. 'So you just want to know if he had a girlfriend.'

'It was the DNA of a male person, sir.'

'Ah. I see.'

'Did he mention any sort of romantic involvement to you? Were there any rumours among the other students of clubs, gay bars, that sort of thing?'

I laughed sharply and more loudly than I had intended. 'Gay bars? You have no idea what he was like, do you? He wrote. He hardly went out at all.'

'Maybe he had some sort of guilty secret which caused him to top – to tip himself over the edge.'

I sighed and shook my head at the absurdity of this line of investigations. 'It wasn't sex. I can tell you that.'

'Yes, well.' Beckwith glanced at his watch. 'It was just a thought. Maybe I'll have to have a word with the parents, after all. If there were any of his fellow students in whom he might have confided, it would be useful to have their names at some point.'

I thought for a moment. Then I knew what I had to do.

'I think I can help you,' I said.

29

It was late morning. A pale, chilly sun lit the discreet mews in Kensington where Marigold led her professional life. On the few occasions when I had visited her, I had understood why my wife spent so many hours at her office, why a small cloud of irritation seemed to descend on her when she returned home. Here was order, money; here the sheer, enraging disorder of the commoner type of urban crime had no place. In the past, I had suggested that we might actually move into this area but Marigold had resisted, pointing out the cost of property, arguing that Dougie needed parks in which to play. In my more insecure moments, I had sensed that somehow she suspected that I would bring the disorder with me, that a little scummy trail of badness would follow me from Shepherd's Bush to Kensington.

As usual, there was an air of calm in the ground-floor reception; as usual, Marigold's personal assistant Tania, a viciously neat woman in her mid-thirties, looked up as I entered as if a scrap of litter had blown in from the pavement, before adopting a starchy, House of Correction smile.

'Is she in?' I asked.

'She's doing her correspondence.' Tania made the activity sound like a religious devotion. 'She won't be long.'

I took a seat, impatiently flicking through a copy of *Interiors* as, in a professional undertone, the receptionist rang through to announce the unusual, unscheduled, unwelcome visit of the boss's wife. I imagined Marigold's little frown of annoyance at this intrusion of the personal into her working day.

She kept me waiting more than five minutes, at the end of which any mild sense of nervousness of the ordeal before me had evaporated in the glow of my impatience. Now of all times, she had elected to play one of the little games with which the long-term married will be familiar.

'Hi.'

Marigold's office was on the first floor, directly above reception, allowing her to descend the stairs and lean over the banisters in a girlish, informal welcome. Her unrecognizably warm and friendly disposition vanished as soon as we were alone in her office. For some abstruse *feng shui*-related reason, there was no desk here, no paper nor even a telephone. The large, light spacious room had a group of low chairs near the window. In the wall beside where my wife sat, a minute intercom and a discreet computer screen were set into the wall. Oddly, the effect was of temporariness, of the sense that the boss was using the place while her real office was being refurbished.

'Well?' She waved in the direction of one of the chairs as if I were some kind of junior employee.

I sat down slowly. 'Not that well, as it happens,' I said. 'Can we talk?'

'What else were we going to do?'

I nodded in the direction of the intercom. 'That's not switched on, is it? This is very . . . personal.'

Impatiently, she turned and pressed a button on the wall. 'I've got a lunch.'

'We had a call from the police today. It was about Peter Gibson's death.'

'Now? Isn't it a bit late in the day for that?'

'They did some tests on Peter's body. They found traces of a quasi-sexual contact which they found interesting.'

My wife was giving me her full attention now. 'I should think so. It changes everything, doesn't it?'

'No.'

'But if he had a lover there, she must have been party to what he did.'

'He.'

'I never knew he was that way inclined – but then I never do know about your pupils.' Marigold smiled coolly, as if she were winding up a meeting. 'It must be upsetting for you but I can't quite see why we can't discuss it tonight.'

'It was me.'

My wife sat very still, as if waiting for the punch-line of a joke. 'You,' she said eventually.

'The DNA was mine. I've told the police that I'll take a test but there's no need. I've told them all they need to know.'

'*You*? You had sex with Peter Gibson on the day he died?' She laughed dryly. 'I've heard everything now.'

'Not sex. I said it was quasi-sexual. When I found him, I –' Hesitating, I glanced at my wife and was rewarded by her expression of appalled incredulity. 'When I found the body, I said goodbye in a somewhat personal oral manner.'

My wife shuddered. 'But why?'

I raised my eyebrows a couple of times. It was a gesture she remembered from our past, a touch of self-parodic raffishness, the erotic hooligan caught bang to rights, half-ashamed and half-proud of his offence, and it told her all she needed to know.

'You're not going to tell me you were lovers, you and this young man.'

I nodded. 'We were lovers. Or rather, it was only love in the vulgar sense of the word. I was helping him with his work and then, somewhat unexpectedly, the help became more personal, less tutorial.'

The colour had drained from Marigold's face. 'Somewhat unexpectedly? You made love to a man.' She gave a little gasp. 'And then you made love to me.'

'Don't worry, it was safe. I was his first lover.'

'Where?'

'At the Gloucester Festival. And –' I hesitated. Then, perversely anxious to avoid giving the impression that this had been a brief drunken fling, I added a fuller (falser) detail. 'Later we'd meet at his flat occasionally. He was needy. It seemed such a small thing, really. Such an easy way to help.'

Marigold sat back in her chair and crossed her legs. My eyes flickered downward, remembering last night.

'I don't believe you,' she said.

I imitated the guilty slump of the rumbled adulterer but, even to me, it seemed unconvincing. 'I realize it must be something of a shock.'

'A *shock*. Good grief.'

'I don't quite understand it myself, to tell the truth. It was an aberration.'

'I mean it, Gregory. I don't believe you. I know you too well. You've got the morals of a skunk. You'd do pretty much anything to advance your career. But you don't like men.'

'That's probably what Mrs Cheever thought.'

'Who's Mrs Cheever?'

I sighed wearily. Normally a wifely confirmation of my red-blooded heterosexuality would have been welcome but right now a touch of hurt and confusion seemed more appropriate. I stood up. 'A policeman called Beckwith might call you. I wanted to break it to you myself.'

'Have there been other men?'

'No. And there won't be. It wasn't about sex. It was something else.'

'How often? With the boy, how often?'

'Not that often. Five. Maybe six.'

'You're lying.' She gazed at me evenly, as if she could hardly summon enough interest to be curious as to my motives. 'I'm not sure what your game is but I know you're lying.'

I stood up and made my way to the door. 'You've got your lunch. I'm sorry you've taken it this way.'

'You are not a homosexual,' she said.

I closed the door quickly and walked down the stairs. Tania looked up at me from her desk. She seemed almost interested in me.

Top Eight Most Married Great Writers	
Six wives:	Norman Mailer
Five wives:	Henry Miller
	Saul Bellow
	John Osborne
Four wives:	John Middleton Murry
	Bertrand Russell
	Ernest Hemingway
	Sherwood Anderson
Four husbands:	Mary McCarthy

30

I was completing my novel, a strange and heady experience, the joy of which I had all but forgotten. My deft and complex *pas de deux* with the shade of Peter Gibson, transcribing, reshaping, ordering, editing, often creating several paragraphs of new material, was reaching its hectic and triumphant final chorus. I was now working so fast that, for therapeutic as well as practical reasons, I took my walks to the local recycling bins two or three times a day. With every cathartic shedding of the handwritten sheets, I felt more liberated, more myself. As I reached Peter's last pad, I longed for that final discarding with which he would truly be lain to rest and *terpsichore 4:2* would unequivocally be mine.

Wrung out yet exultant, I found myself acting in a manner that was more direct (more shameless) than was entirely normal for me. Several days had passed since Beckwith had visited me. I had rung him to discover whether a DNA sample would be required of me but, to my alarm, he had replied in the distracted manner of one who had moved on to more lively and appetizing cases. For the first time, it occurred to me that the details of my relationship with Peter might not be leaked to the press. Normally, in our age of tabloid morality, the police can be relied upon to enact this small act of bad faith, but I was not a TV personality or a politician. I was a novelist, a grey, negligible creature who, in the ecology of celebrity, hardly registered as a life form. An event that might have seemed noteworthy, sensational even, in the literary world was, it appeared, not even worth a casual call to the local paper, a £50 tip-off to a metropolitan diarist.

Only the more unworldly reader will be surprised that, at this point, I actually wanted to be publicly 'named and shamed'. For the fact is that, in those few seconds after Beckwith had revealed his discovery, horror had quickly given way to the realization that, suddenly and fortuitously, the last piece of the jigsaw had fallen into place.

terpsichore 4:2 was clearly a work of startling originality; in a more serious age, that would have been enough. Yet today, the written word, the art itself, is but a minor part of the entire confection. There are more important matters to consider. Has the author had a problem with drugs? Are his parents famous? Was he abused as a child? Is he known to have been to bed with anyone interesting? Has he been attacked in print by a wife, child or by himself? Does he hit people at parties? Where, in others words, is the peg?

Now I had my peg. I had transgressed against generally acceptable behaviour in several interesting areas. I had betrayed trust. I had loved in a way that had proved fatal. My defence (I'm a writer, for Christ's sake) would, with a bit of luck, enrage the bourgeois sensibilities of the middlebrow tabloids, instigate a tetchy debate about the artist and society, the muse and family, the sexual crisis of the middle-aged man, the unacceptable face of contemporary this, that and the other. My novel, surely, would now be launched on a churning swell of controversy, propelled into public consciousness on an irresistible current of outrage.

I waited. A week, ten days. The novel was reaching its conclusion. Nothing had appeared in the press. I took action.

From a telephone box off the Askew Road, I called a scandal magazine that battened on tales of misdeeds in the media village. It was an anonymous call, from a friend of Peter Gibson's who had been horrified by the police cover-up of the activities of Gregory Keays. A call to a local detective officer by the name of Beckwith would reveal more.

It worked. A paragraph appeared. One of the tabloids took the bait. Beckwith was obliged to provide details. Columnists picked over the bones of the story. As if by magic, my public persona, moribund for so long that it might generally have been assumed that it had passed away, twitched, then came to life. The calls started coming in.

There were other distractions during those strange, hazy days during which I struggled to complete my work.

Marigold had closed down on me. When we had experienced crises in the past, she had expressed wifely rage, disappointment, sarcasm and alienation in the various approved and accepted ways. I was usually obliged to sleep in shame and banishment on a mattress in my study. On this occasion, I had expelled myself, preferring to sleep with my work than with my disgruntled spouse. She avoided me, stepping past me in the corridors as if I were a stranger, vacating rooms as I entered. For two nights running, she stayed out – taking advantage of the situation, I assumed, to enjoy some guilt-free quality time with her lover.

None of this would necessarily have alarmed me – I had a novel to finish, the calm of marital freeze was not unwelcome – were it not for Doug. He seemed to have disappeared. When, during one of our rare exchanges, I had suggested to Marigold that we should inform the police, she told me that she knew he was safe, that he was staying with friends. He had been so devastated when he had read about me in the newspapers that he had decided to stay away.

One night I worked late, then took a walk around the area to clear my head. It was around 2 a.m. I had walked a long way, into Acton, occasionally doubling back and checking that no over-enthusiastic reporter was following me. I was alone. I found a recycling bin that not even I, who had become such an expert in this area, had previously found. Glancing around me, I reached into my shirt and removed a newspaper within which was contained the last of Peter Gibson's notepads. I held it in my hand for a few moments, then posted it, with a sudden, decisive movement through the flap.

I walked slowly home, feeling suddenly lonely without my collaborator. From now on, there was only one person to take the blame or the credit. At last, *terpsichore 4:2* was mine.

I awoke late the next morning and, for an hour or so, lay on my mattress, staring ahead of me. On the desk was the neat, completed shining manuscript. Its white pages caught the sun. It looked like a holy item of worship, some sort of grail. I felt wearily triumphant, a victorious marathon runner who has just breasted the tape and now lies, breathless and dehydrated, beyond the finishing line.

I went downstairs. The house was deserted. My son had not been seen for weeks now, my wife had apparently spent the night out with her lover. Today, none of that seemed to matter. I was free, full of the novelist's sweet sadness of completion. Soon my child (my literary child) would be taking its first halting steps in the world but, for these few moments, it was fully formed yet still part of me.

I took breakfast slowly, then went upstairs, leafed through *terpsichore 4:2* one more time. It read well. It was good work. Perhaps, like V. S. Naipaul, I could say that it was major. I was content, ready to face the day. I switched on the answering-machine that had been accumulating messages for me over the past week.

Some were from journalists. A couple were from the editor of the *Professional Writer*. Then there were a few surprises.

'It's Fay, darling – your agent just in case you had forgotten. Just ringing to say how frightfully sorry I was to hear about that ghastly business with your student. It's a youth thing, you know – I had a cousin who hanged himself. All very sad. But Gregory, life must go on and, if there is a teensy silver lining to this horrid cloud in your life, it's that literary London has been beating a path to my door to ask about you and what you've been up to. Dare I ask about a novel, the novel – any novel? Or novella. Or even a short story, if you must. There are various journalistic, anthology thingies you might like to consider – you could do them in your sleep, darling, and I think we're talking reasonable amounts of money. I know how you feel about such things. In other words, it's a touch of the old *carpe diems*, darling. Give me a buzz when you have a moment. Love to, er . . . everyone.'

'Brian here. We need to talk about business. The commission we discussed has been completed and there's another proposal for you which I hope you might find of interest. Call me on my mobile – 0741 271 3421 – not at your convenience but very soon.'

'Gregory, Tony Watson. Sorry to read about your troubles. So much for the quiet, contemplative life of the creative writing teacher. But seriously, I know how important your pupils were to you and he seemed a nice lad. Now, you'll recall that we vaguely discussed your contributing to *FatherLand*, the little anthology I've been commissioned to put together. That offer's still open and we might be able to do something about the money but, while you're considering that, it occurred to me that you might be interested in a project on men's first sexual experience that we're calling *Losing It*. Sensitive but saucy – you know the sort of thing. We'd be really pleased to have you on board. Give us a bell at my usual number. Cheers for now.'

'Greg, Brian. We need to talk.'

'It's me, your wife. I won't be home tonight but I need some information from you. Something very odd seems to have happened to our account. Perhaps you could ring me at work. Don't forget to feed Donovan.'

'Are you all right, darling? Or have you gone into exile to avoid the publicity. It's Fay. Now listen, I've got a few people on hold vis-à-vis features and I'm really going to have to give them a view a.s.a.p. Are you thinking about it, darling? This is a window of opportunity and you should seriously consider jumping through it or whatever one does with windows of opportunity. Ciao, darling.'

'Don't mess me about now, Greg. It's all been going so well. Wouldn't want things to get nasty. Oh, and how's Doug these days?'

One is, I suppose, inoculated against the terrors of everyday life by immersion in the cauldron of creative endeavour. Thus, while under normal circumstances the unholy chorus of menace and demands contained upon that small tape might have sent me scurrying to the drinks cupboard or the medicine cabinet or both, now they seemed like distant cries of alarm relating to someone who was not me, the writer, but to a lesser person, some sort of minor cousin, to whom I was barely related.

Carefully, I placed the bright, virgin pages of my novel into the box-file which, some weeks ago, I had purchased in joyful anticipation of this moment. I opened the bottom drawer of my desk and withdrew an A5 brown envelope containing £2,000 in £50 notes and put it in my bag beside the folder containing *terpsichore 4:2*. I picked up the telephone, dialled Brian McWilliam's home number and left a message on his machine suggesting we meet that night at his club. I checked the leather shoulder-bag now containing the two packages of paper which, I trusted, would close one door for me and open another, and went downstairs, out of the front door, into the car and headed east.

You will have heard of Fay Duckworth. Whenever there is a public literary *bagarre* (the death of the novel, the overpayment of writers, the decline in publishing standards, a plagiarism spat), Fay will be on first call. Elegant, lethal, funny, queen of the telling sound-bite, she is the lazy journalist's friend, a joy for picture editors. In an age of power suits, high heels and shoulder-pads, she cuts a tall, modishly dishevelled figure, the flecks of grey in her riot of long black curls lending a sort of earth-mother integrity to her striking, matronly good looks. By ruthlessly excluding all but the best from her stable of writers, she has come to represent a steely literary virtue, which justifies, or even entirely obscures, conduct which, in other agents, would be regarded as predatory, unseemly or simply greedy. When Fay broke her contract with the large agency which had established her name to set up on her own, taking with her the more prominent of her clients (myself among them; *Forever Young* had just been published), attempts to take her to court were so successfully portrayed as giantist corporate bullying that her former employers dropped the case for fear of alienating their few remaining authors. When Fay seduced a succession of literary figures into leaving their (usually ageing, usually male) agents to join her, her motives were ascribed to a crusading spirit to acquire the best living for writers she admired rather than anything as base or banal as financial acquisitiveness.

Seduced. The erotic nature of deal-making can rarely have been more evident than in the business manner of Fay Duckworth. She cooed, she touched, she gazed, she gave great phone; even on the frequent occasions when she was angry, there was a piquant hint of intimate, perverse sado-play which only the most torpid of men or women could fail to find curiously arousing. Naturally enough, in a business whose every movement was oiled by the juice of adultery, flirtation and desire, Fay's charm encouraged rumours of a flamboyant and colourful private life – like virtually every attractive and successful media female of her generation, she was said to have had a fling with Martin – but no proof of misbehaviour had ever been found. There was some sort of husband lurking in the background, but no children. Fay's womanly energies, we had begun to suspect, were largely expressed in the coitus of contract, the delirium of deals.

A high-flyer, yet, after this period of low production, she was still my agent. Fay would never actually sack a client. She would simply go very quiet, replying to letters and calls later and later, speaking to clients who were out of favour in an increasingly distracted tone, casually mentioning the vast sum being earned by her for her other, more blessed authors or reflecting with studied gloominess on how publishers were buying fewer and fewer novels of serious intent by the unpromotable, the unlovely, the unyoung. Almost invariably, her victims would huffily resign from her agency, to receive a brief, heartfelt, handwritten note of hurt regret from Fay.

I, on the other hand, had stayed, no doubt to her increasing irritation. After all, if she was silent, then so was I. Contrary to the belief of certain authors, literary agents are but conduits: they play no part in the writing process. What good would it do me to have some ambitious ten-per-center nagging me for work, gently suggesting projects, giving me the benefit of her infernal sympathy? When asked, while attending festivals and launches in my capacity as correspondent for the *Professional Writer*, who my agent was, I could reply, 'Fay Duckworth'. It registered. While Fay represented me, I was still alive as a novelist. It was enough for me.

I had no confidence, for these reasons, that I would actually see my agent when I drove my modest, writerly, saloon car into the discreet, moneyed square in Islington where she lived and worked in two adjacent houses. I rang the bell at the right-hand blue door leading to her office (the other door was a warm and personal peach colour; by such zany, self-mocking devices, Fay maintained the illusion that she had a private life). Within seconds of my announcing myself on the intercom, a tall, willowy, sun-tanned creature with a careful hairstyle and the sort of perfect looks rarely associated with the literary world opened the door to me.

He announced my name more as an expression of the sheer pleasure of meeting me than as any kind of question, extending a languid arm. 'I'm Simon,' he said warmly, then, with a catwalk twirl, led me into a hall whose walls were strewn with items of African folk art. For as long as I had been her client, Fay had been attended by young males more notable for their looks and style than for any marked interest in books or authors. On the circuit, rumours abounded that they contributed more to her than their typing skills and telephone manner but, as so often with Fay, their function was essentially a matter of image. On average, they lasted a couple of years before drifting off into acting or travelling the world or, in the case of the less ambitious of them, becoming book editors.

To my surprise, I was not required to sit for the statutory ten minutes in the reception room decorated tauntingly with flattering, smug photographic portraits of the more eminent of her authors as, through an open door leading to her office, the great agent spoke on the telephone to a succession of clients and punters whom I imagined racked up above her office like aircraft circling over Heathrow. Within a second of Simon putting his head around her door and announcing my arrival, Fay had terminated a call in characteristic manner – 'Now fuck off, darling, someone important's arrived' – and had come billowing out of her office, wearing some kind of purple counterpane, in which, before I could take evasive action, I was enveloped.

'You bastard.' Fay pulled me against her. Inordinately proud of her considerable, free-swinging breasts, she had recently and with much publicity had them renovated so that they now felt alarmingly like two baseballs pressed against me. 'You are a fucking bastard, Gregory Keays. Why have you been avoiding me?'

With a deft scrum-half wriggle, I extricated myself. 'It was difficult,' I said bashfully. 'I've been busy. Working.'

My agent was looking at me, like a mother whose son has just returned from the war. At last she noticed the box-file, peaking proudly from my shoulder-bag.

'Oh, my God, don't tell me. You're not . . . *with novel.*'

I nodded.

From behind me, Simon called from the reception desk. 'Will returning your call.'

'Hold all calls.' Fay spoke evenly, as if, merely by raising her voice, she might scare me and my box-file away. 'Beginning? Middle? End? Not a whole fucking novel, darling? Pass the fucking smelling-salts.'

To avoid another clinch, I extracted the box-file and passed it to her. Over the past fifteen years, various fragments – *Accidents of Trust*, *Adultery in Hampstead*, *A Stranger Here Myself*, *Mind the Gap*, *A/The/Until*, *Giving It Large* and others – had crossed her desk, receiving increasingly wan and sceptical notes of encouragement, so her frank astonishment at receiving an entire work was perhaps not as surprising as it might appear.

'How did you do it, darling?' Reverently, she held the box in front of her, testing the weight of its pages in her two hands. 'Where did it come from?'

I hesitated. There were to be many such moments in the future. The natural difficulty of describing, within the framework of informal conversation, a complex, agonizing, artistic construct was compounded by the fact of this particular work's unconventional provenance. In the end I opted for a formula borrowed from my wife.

'It came from a place I never knew existed,' I said.

'Sure. I read you.' Reverently, my agent lifted the lid of the box-file. '*terpsichore 4:2*,' she said, a touch nervously. 'Postmodern?'

I moved into pondering mode. 'For some time I have believed that much of modern fiction, by obeying the unity of action, is like a narrow street down which the novelist drives his or her characters with a whip,'* I said thoughtfully. 'I've tried to loosen things up.'

'You haven't gone up your own arse, darling, have you? Some of my clients are so far up themselves they could polish their own ulcers.'

I smiled, conveying the merest hint of disapproval at my agent's vulgarity. 'That wasn't the place I was referring to,' I said.

My agent closed the box gently and, for a few seconds, gave me the full burn, gazing into my eyes in a manner which, to one less used to her, would appear like a frank and open

---

* A legitimate borrowing from *Immortality* (1991) by my fellow novelist Milan Kundera.

lustfulness. 'I will read and I will call,' she said. 'In the mean time, I have two words for you.' She extended her right hand and touched my cheek. 'Thank you.'

'Hope you like it,' I said. 'And I think you will.'

I turned and made my way through the hall, allowing Simon to scurry past me and open the front door. I nodded an aristocratic farewell. As the door closed behind me, I felt, for a brief second, overcome by feelings of elation and relief. I stood motionless, my hands clenched, my eyes closed.

I was on my way back into the literary fold.

There are few stranger moments in the novelist's life than when, elated, bereft, he releases the work that has been the living centre of his creative and personal universe for months, years, into the hands of strangers. First, briefly, there's the sheer relief of completion; then, quicker than one would believe possible, a feeling of searing emptiness and loss becomes all-encompassing. Add to this cauldron of conflicting emotions, intense feelings of anxiety and terror and you will realize that, as I drove through the streets of London, a stranger among the ordinary, non-writing people going about their practical business, preparing for a night of mindless clubbing or pubbing, I was in a peculiarly febrile state of being, both intensely of the world and outside it. It was, I imagine, the fact that in a real sense I was out of control, that led me not to Jesters, as I had intended, but to the Agency. Pia was not there but Annabel summoned Anisa, a stringy blonde with a distressingly professional air to her which, on any other occasion, would have made me feel cheap and exploited.

Today, though, it did the trick, just perfectly.

31

It must have been past midnight when I reached Jesters. Parking my car a block from the club, I walked up the Uxbridge Road. People hurried by, not alarmed – to journalists, it may be Murder Mile, but to us it's just home – merely tired and eager to be behind closed doors and off the street. Shepherd's Bush is not a place where you hang out late at night to savour the street life. Good times are rarely just around the corner.

Two men had turned into the alleyway leading to the club. I walked on by, keeping to the well lit main road, giving them time to go wherever they were going, playing safe. Round here, we tend to keep an eye on the Exit sign, particularly when carrying an envelope stuffed with cash to pay off an old debt. When I turned, fifty yards down the road, and made my way back, the path was clear. I rang the bell. Moments later, a low moo of acknowledgement issued from the intercom.

'Greg for Brian,' I said.

There was silence. I waited for the click of the door release. A minute, maybe two, went by – too long to be standing in a dark alleyway, even when you're not making a delivery. I was about to move off when the flaring of a match down the path, some thirty yards away, revealed a figure – small, almost childish – leaning against the wall, silhouetted against the lights of the main road. The other end of the alley was too dark to see anything but it was not beyond the reaches of paranoia to imagine another presence, called up from some nearby rat-hole, gathering in the gloom.

The door swung open in front of me. Brian McWilliam stood in the dim hallway. 'Glad you could make it,' he said, standing back to make way for me.

I held out the envelope, eager to be rid of it. 'Quits?' I said, then laughed at the schoolboy phrase.

Brian looked down but made no move to take it. 'Let's have a drink,' he said.

'It's been kind of a long day.'

Ignoring my reluctance, he turned and made his way into the smoky subterranean gloom of the bar, striding between the tables where men sat in quiet conversation. The place seemed busier and darker than when I had last been here. Apart from Brian, who was wearing a leather jacket designed for man half his age yet looking good in it, most of the members were soberly dressed as if on a night out at an old-fashioned working men's club.

He led me to a corner table and sat down facing the bar. Uninvited, I took the seat opposite. He drank from the glass of wine in front of him, watching me all the while. He put down the glass as if considering, then deciding against, the idea of buying me a drink.

'Greg.' He spoke with a sort of leaden sincerity.

I tapped the envelope which I had self-consciously slipped down the side of my seat. 'Sorry we're a bit late,' I said, speaking low.

'Greg.'

'Been finishing a novel.' Even in this unlikely benighted place, I felt oddly proud of my achievement. 'I just delivered it to my agent.'

He glanced at his watch and, unsmiling, raised his eyebrows.

'And I had to make an important social call.'

'Let me ask you something.' Brian carefully positioned his glass so that it sat precisely in the centre of a beermat. 'Do I look like a cunt?'

'No.' I smiled, glad to be honest. 'You're nobody's idea of a cunt.'

'That's what I had assumed. I'm not saying I'm popular. I'm not even saying I'm nice. But a complete and utter cunt? Probably not.'

As he took another almost ladylike sip of his wine, I smiled disarmingly. 'I'm sorry I didn't get back to you quicker, Brian. I was racing for the finishing line.'

'Three messages. Not one fucking reply.'

'I'm sorry. I just had to go to ground for a bit.'

'The novel comes before me, then.' Suddenly Brian smiled and his even, bleached teeth seemed to glint in the darkness of the bar.

'I just had to finish it,' I explained. 'I couldn't think of anything else.'

'I'm like that,' said Brian. 'Some people call it obsessive. We call it perfectionism, we call it getting a job done, don't we?'

'Yes.' I shifted uneasily in my chair. Now seemed as good a time as any to take advantage of what seemed a moment of good humour. 'Brian, something cropped up tonight. I had to dip in. I'm afraid –' I tapped the bag beside me, '– there's a bit of a shortfall.'

'How much?'

'£300. I'll make up the difference next week.'

'Dipped in. Cropped up.' Brian seemed to leer in the darkness. 'It was an expensive social call, then.'

I shrugged.

'Special intimate celebration, was it?'

Not for the first time, I was startled by how well this untutored lowlife understood, as if by instinct, the artistic impulse. 'Something like that,' I said.

To my surprise, he stood up suddenly, almost as if he had forgotten to do something, walked quickly to the bar, then returned, smiling warmly. Moments later, the barman brought a tray bearing a bottle of champagne and two fresh glasses. With the fixed expression of goofy joyousness you might see on the face of a door-to-door evangelist, McWilliam watched the barman pouring, his belly stretching against a white shirt. He waited a few moments until we were alone, then raised his glass. 'To literature,' he said. 'I hope your book's number one with a bullet.'

I saluted him with my glass. It occurred to me in that brief, odd moment of comradeship, that, in a very real sense, we shared the edgy, honourable status of outsiders, each of us swimming against the tide of accepted behaviour, beyond the norms of conventional society, renegades, outlaws. 'Cheers,' I said simply.

'Don't worry about the money.' McWilliam spoke casually. 'I mean, in your own time. And, when you do, add on a three spot for the drink and petrol.'

'Thanks, Brian. That's – that's helpful.'

'Nah.' He swatted at the air with a squat, well-manicured hand. 'I know how it is when you finish a job. You've done the research. You've looked at how best to approach the thing, maybe tried one way, then another. You've gone for days, weeks, agonizing about the fucking thing. Then, suddenly, you see it. There, before your eyes, is the solution. Now all you can think of is how to get the job done. You're obsessed, driven.'

'Yes, that's exactly how it is.'

'Then, when you've done it – the book, running some little cow into a ditch, whatever – it takes a while to get tuned back in to normal life. You come down slowly. I'm like you, my first need is to get the old ashes hauled. Re-entry, I call it. Guess it's a sort of primal, warrior-returning sort of thing, eh, Greg?'

'Maybe.' Although there were elements of truth in Brian's version of the creative act, I found the idea that, within moments of popping the final full-stop, the writer (Anita Brookner, Kazuo Ishiguro, A. S. Byatt, Harold Pinter, Gregory Keays) became a bug-eyed sex-machine in search of immediate release, somewhat reductive. 'For me, the shag's not obligatory,' I said carefully.

'Writing, murder. It's not that different, is it?'

I tried to laugh but, even to me, the sound that emanated from me seemed nervy, unconvincing. 'I wouldn't exactly put it that way.'

Brian watched me for a moment.

'What was the stuff about running the little cow into a ditch?' I asked, anxious to break the silence.

Brian smiled. 'You're not actually very fucking bright, are you? Not for someone who has read all those books. Not for someone who spends every fucking day fucking cogitating.'

I shrugged uneasily. 'I just hadn't heard the expression.'

'A three spot for petrol. Didn't that seem just a bit on the large side?'

'I'm not very good on the practicalities of motoring costs.'

'Fuck off, Greg, you shit-faced lying little cunt.' McWilliam sat forward suddenly as if he were about to hit me, and the lights from the bar glittered in his eyes. 'You may fool your precious little writing friends but don't you ever try to bullshit Brian McWilliam, all right.'

I remained silent for a few seconds, allowing the moment of

tension to pass. 'So,' I said eventually. 'Why did you need to spend so much on petrol?'

'I was driving round the fucking campus, checking where little Mary went on that student bike of hers. And then running the little cow into a ditch.'

He said the words without dropping his voice. I glanced around us but no one seemed to have heard.

'That was a bit dramatic,' I said. 'Is she –? I mean, which hospital is she in?'

He exhaled, looking, for the first time, seriously pissed off.

'Brian,' I spoke quietly. 'When I said discourage her, I thought you understood what I meant. I was talking about a, well, a dislocation between her and Peter Gibson.'

'She got fucking dislocated all right.' Brian poured himself another glass of champagne. 'Plump little thing,' he said quietly. 'Nice face and all. But the body – oh dear. Not my type. I'm not saying I didn't think about it. No one around. Loads of cover – trees and bushes and that but I couldn't summon the enthusiasm. Struggling with those smeggy, studenty jeans. Puppy fat lolling all over the place. You'd understand all that, being a novelist, a student of human nature. So I just drove on.'

'Where was this?' In spite of the champagne, my mouth felt dry. I suppose that, absorbed in creative frenzy, I had not until now imagined quite how McWilliam would interpret my admittedly vague instructions. Now I saw it all. This trim, neat, grey man standing over Mary's body on a dark country road, the wreck of her bicycle like a smashed toy nearby, the engine of his car murmuring as he considered whether he should take one last prize from her dying body.

'You all right?' Brian smiled. 'You look a bit peaky.'

'I hadn't meant . . . *that.*'

'Don't worry, Greg, it's history. No witnesses. The car had been nicked by a colleague of mine. False number plates. It's in the crusher now. Just one of those tragic hit-and-run accidents.'

I closed my eyes for a moment, then reached for the envelope.

'Not here,' Brian spoke sharply, then frowned, as if a thought had suddenly occurred to him. 'As it happens, I had a proposal for you which might enable you to keep that little brown envelope of yours.'

Somehow I knew that any proposal Brian made would not be one that I would welcome. 'Shoot,' I said with a polite lack of enthusiasm.

He pointed a finger at me. 'Never say that to someone in my line of business. We might think you mean it.'

I laughed wearily.

'No, but what I had in mind was a sort of exchange of expertise. I like to think that, in my small way, I've helped you resolve a problem.' He shrugged. 'Quite why you wanted to eliminate a porky but apparently harmless little girl it wasn't within my remit to enquire.'

'I didn't want her –'

'I know nothing of the ways of creative folk. You told me you needed a bit of an assist on a practical matter. No problem, Greg, I said. And I delivered. Didn't I?'

'Yes. You did.'

'Greg, I want to write a book.'

'Another one?'

'Too right. I like the book business. Easy cash, nice people and – well, you know about the fringe benefits.'

'You've already got a writer.'

'Useless cunt. I know we got some good reviews and that but all the best bits in *Sorted* were straight off the tape I gave him. Couldn't stand the bastard. Sitting there with a snooty look on his fucking face. No, I want someone who understands where I'm coming from, someone who's lived on the edge.'

'I had never thought of myself as –'

'A novelist, preferably.'

'You want to move into fiction.'

'You creative guys – you just sort of see things, don't you?'

McWilliam shook his head nastily. 'Why else would I want a fucking novelist? Thing is, a lot of the spicier stuff – stuff from my past that's a bit on the naughty side – I wasn't able to use in the memoirs. It might be misunderstood, if you take my meaning. So, I was thinking that fiction's the job for me.' He sat back in his chair, and glanced around the room, gazing for a few seconds at a group of three youngish men in big suits and sharply styled yobby haircuts – footballers or hoods or A & R men – who were standing at the bar. As he watched, a girl in a short lycra skirt joined them, one of the men laid a hand on her left buttock and fondled it thoughtfully.

'Well?' Brian turned back to me. He looked older now, and tetchy, as if he had used up what small reserves of goodwill he had. 'Are you up for it?'

Even then, I could see it was not so much a question as an order. I was up for it or I was in trouble, up for it or right in it. I looked away from the unblinking eyes, regretting to the depths of my soul that I had ever become involved with this man, that he had interpreted my vague instructions with such lethal results.

Unwisely, I tried to play for time. 'Norman Mailer says that he writes fiction only to make reality more believable to himself –'

'Greg.'

'But I don't agree with that. Fiction's fiction. It's not some key to the real world – a sort of reality with value added.'

'Greg.'

'Of course, what we would need to do is to go through a few basic lessons in composition, talk about structure, lend you a few of the key manuals – Dorothea Brande's *Becoming a Writer* is an excellent starting point. Then I could read over your material, make suggestions, act as an editor, give you the name of a competent agent maybe.'

'Greg, you are boring me fucking rigid here. I've told you I can hardly write my own fucking moniker. So . . . Are? You? Up? For? It?'

'You want me to write a novel under your name,' I said, a note of despair entering my voice.

'I'm not a writer, Greg. When I say I want to write my book, it's like saying I want to service my car. It means I want to get it done. By a professional.'

'Listen, Brian, I'm very honoured,' I said weakly. 'But this has come at a very difficult time for me. Novel being sold – rewrites, dealing with the publisher. Tell the truth, I'll be pretty flat to the boards over the next few months.'

'For someone who works with his imagination, you can be very fucking unimaginative.' Brian drained his glass and stood up. With a brisk, authoritative jerk of the head, he made for the door. I followed, watched by the barman.

In the alley outside, he half-turned. 'Let me take you by the hand and lead you through the streets of London,' he said softly.

'Brian, it's been a long day.'

He set off towards White City. It was one a.m., we were on Murder Mile, and I was in the company of a professional terminator: somehow, I sensed that turning on my heel and walking smartly towards the lights and relative safety of the Uxbridge Road was not an option. Brian had a quick, surprisingly athletic stride and, even after I had caught up with him, I found that I was almost running as I kept pace with him, like a child trailing in the wake of an adult.

He took a right, then turned up a smaller street towards the big housing estate, looking neither to the right nor the left.

Soon we were walking between two long redbrick blocks of flats, the sound of reggae and jungle music from behind the walls of different flats on each side of us mingling in the night. Round here, it seemed, no one worried too much about the sleep pattern of neighbours.

On and on they went, each block identical, each emanating an air of grimy, menacing defeat. Ahead I could see the neon lights of the Westway. We had been walking for fifteen minutes when we reached waste-ground, a part of west London ignored by even the most optimistic property developer. In the gloom I could see some skeletal timbers, which might have been an abandoned shed or evidence of some misguided attempt by the council to erect an adventure playground for children whose only adventure was destruction.

Brian stopped in front of a row of derelict houses, boarded up, abandoned except for one uncertain light – some kind of gas lamp, perhaps – on the top floor. Music screamed from the open window, shadows flickered back and forth.

'Party time at the crack-house.' Brian looked up at the windows.

For a moment, I was afraid that he was going to take me into this dark, vibrating shipwreck of a building, put me to some arcane, gangland test of endurance. 'You want reality, writerman?' he said. 'Take a fucking peek.'

'Doesn't look like quite my kind of party,' I said.

'These are the kids that time forgot. They're in their own squalid little capsule. They think they are beyond the rest of us, but they're underneath, bottom of the fucking pile. They think they're users but they're used. The whole world uses them for something or other. They're outsiders – even people on the estate think they're scum. You don't get further out than that.'

'Squatters, are they?' My voice sounded harsher than I intended. I was tired, irritated by Brian's tone of fake concern. It was hardly the moment for the musings of a murderous hoodlum on the moral decline of modern youth.

'Squatters, junkies, kids who peddle their arse down the Dilly or give middle-aged businessmen blow-jobs in the company saloon round the back of King's Cross, who'll do anything, nick anything for the old needle, the old pipe, the chance to kill off a few more brain cells. Lost kids who talk their own language with their own sad, scraggy names. Boz. Mole Shagbag. Bollock.'

'Runaways, I suppose.'

Brian glanced across at me. 'Not all of them,' he said. 'Some are just pulled into the scene for a lark – for the crack, as it were.'

'Crazy.'

'I'll tell you one thing, Greg.' McWilliam gripped my arm, the thumb of a muscular hand digging into the flesh above my elbow. 'I wouldn't want a son of mine up there.'

I looked at him, then up at the light from the window flickering in the night. In that instant, I knew why he had brought me here.

'Seen enough?' said Brian.

The Writer Speaks of . . . Good Citizenship

There is no essential incongruity between crime and culture.

Oscar Wilde

You have to have something vicious in you to be a creative writer. God save me from being nice.

D. H. Lawrence

The decision to try to be a writer emanates from similar impulses in which you have a go at various kinds of disorders. You just don't kill anybody at the end.

Richard Ford

Fiction writers may easily begin as persons of character . . . but the likelihood is that in the long run fiction bruises character. Novelists invent, deceive, exaggerate, and impersonate for several hours every day, and frequently on the weekend. Through the creation of bad souls they enter the demonic as a matter of course.

Cynthia Ozick

The good writer is rarely a good man – and only the vagaries of literary humanism once taught in universities would lead anyone to believe that 'moral values' are to be found in literature.

Peter Ackroyd

Being called a 'bad citizen' is a compliment to a novelist . . . If we're bad citizens, we're doing our job.

Don DeLillo

32

The next morning, Fay Duckworth left a message on my machine.

She told me that I had written a masterpiece, a work that transcended banal divisions between the literary and the popular, that, while my novel was gloriously and essentially English in its sensibility, its sheer quality demanded and would reach an international audience, that its synthesis of maturity and surprising youthfulness would, without a shadow of a doubt, appeal both to the callow, lightweight storyhound and to the most sophisticated reader, that frankly – and I quote directly – 'we could be talking fucking telephone numbers here, darling'. In fact, she planned to cancel her lunch in order to finish reading it.

My reaction to this torrent of congratulation was of mild but unmistakable disappointment. A masterpiece? Well, all right – but had it actually changed Fay's life? Did she wake this morning and, as a result of my vision, see the world with new eyes? In fact, come to think of it, how had she slept at all having started it? Was there a single reference in the message to any of the major literary prizes? My agent had signed off with a request for me to call her to discuss tactics and money, but right now I was not in the mood.

Instead, I rang Brian McWilliam. I was leaving a message when he picked up.

'Yeah?' As if to compensate for the absurd smoothness of his message, his tone was more gruff and hostile than usual.

'I've been thinking about our discussion last night.'

'Hm.' There was a wheezy, unpleasant chuckle from the other end of the telephone as if he were impersonating a nastier version of himself for the benefit of a third party. I imagined the elfin figure of Ku, cowering in some corner of the bed. 'I'm listening,' he said.

'Could you turn the tape off?'

'Fucking drama queen,' he grumbled. 'Hang on.' There was a click on the line.

'I'm happy to help you with your work as we discussed. I have a gap in my schedule, as it happens, and I've always fancied the thriller form.'

'Oh yeah?'

'And I sense we have a good creative understanding.'

'Spare me the bullshit, Greg. So you want to make a few bob – nothing wrong with that in my book.'

'As it happens, the money's not that important. I was hoping for something in the nature of practical advice – maybe a bit of hands-on assistance.'

'Hands-on?' The sound of a smack, hand on flesh, echoed down the receiver. 'I'm your man.' He paused. 'It's your boy, I suppose.'

'Yes, it's my boy.'

Affirmation

Today I shall remember that it is in the nature of a writer to live beyond the conventional rules of social behaviour. Actions which might, for anyone else, be 'bad', 'hurtful' or 'immoral' have their own creative integrity. I shall contemplate reality with the pure, unblinking innocence of a child.

33

Soon the telephone began to ring. Fay had shipped the manuscript to the five large buildings in London in which all significant publishing business is conducted. She had asked editors to sign a confidentiality agreement, thereby ensuring that photocopied manuscripts, steaming with forbidden promise, found their way within hours to film producers, scouts for foreign publishers, features editors. Telling a publisher a secret has always been a good way to build up publicity.

I smiled to think of how the tiny village where those who earn their living from books reside would soon be on fire with rumours about a triumphant new fiction which was not yet another gimmicky, over-publicized first novel but a return to the literary fray of one who was almost, but not quite, forgotten. Doubtless, my very character and background would catch the imagination. To think that, all that time, he was working on this! He was one of us all the time! At lunches all over London, editors would suddenly find themselves agreeing that, ever since I had appeared on the Granta list, they had been expecting something rather special from me. Several of the women whose beds I had shared in my undiscriminating youth would dust off their fading erotic memories and let it be known that it was not that long ago when they had been 'seeing' me. Friends, some of whom I had never heard of, would solemnly confirm that they had been aware that I had been working on this major project for many years but had been sworn to secrecy. Before a single deal had been signed, my novel seemed certain to become a choice item of gossip and speculation.

Amusingly, one of the fortunate publishers considering my novel even attempted to pre-empt the auction with an offer which, not so long ago, would have made me weep with gratitude and astonishment. Fay was outraged. *terpsichore 4:2* was a work of literature, not some kind of get-rich-quick futures bond; this vulgar, fiscal bartering would never deflect her from her essential duty as an agent: to find a suitable, serious publisher who would work upon the project in a suitable, serious manner in return for a suitable, serious monetary consideration. She would, out of politeness, make a note of this early offer (she assumed it was firm and unconditional), but she would make no commitment even to discuss it with Gregory Keays. He was a writer, for Christ's sake; he had higher concerns.

At times, when Fay rang me with the day's good news, I wondered whether she was entirely in control of the stampede she seemed to have unleashed but at precisely the right moment, she cracked the whip, corralled the foaming steeds of the media prairie, and accepted the highest offer.

So business was done, on an encouragingly significant scale. A contract, bubbling with zeros, issued from auctions for volume rights in London and New York. Doubtless, within a couple of months, translation deals would follow, including several for languages I never knew existed. A begging letter from at least one leading Hollywood producer was said to have reached Fay's office. *Forever Young* was reissued, causing, according to some reports, a new spasm of public interest in the 1960s.* I was asked to appear as a guest critic on a respected nationwide radio books programme.

Most of this you will know. Within a month, the news of my astonishing return to form elevated the name of Gregory Keays from the occasional 'Where are they now?' column to lead item in more than one arts diary. As a columnist for the *Professional Writer*, I knew better than most the potency of a literary fairy-tale. The struggling author, talented yet alone in his belief that he had a story to tell, the big strike, the moment when the agent calls ('Are you sitting down?), the wild, runaway success. It is a bookish version of the priceless Rubens found in the dusty attic. Everyone, after all, believes that he has an undiscovered literary masterpiece upstairs.

Of course, I was always going to be a good story – better than the kiss-and-tell actress with her memoir or the brilliant, floppy-haired undergraduate with his precociously brilliant novel. My wife was London's most fashionable *feng shui* designer. For years, I had been but a humble teacher, a jobbing journo (in my view, these aspects of my life received an unnecessary amount of attention); now, it seemed, I was about to become a literary superstar. Then there was the whiff of enigma, of sin and controversy, about my recent past.

Pundits of every shade and school analysed my affair with Peter Gibson and meditated upon the connection between my

* 'The surprising return of the *Forever Young* generation' was the headline in *Prospect* magazine.

late-flowering bisexuality and the release of my inner talent. The name of John Cheever was frequently evoked. Sniffing scandal, one reporter attempted to present Peter Gibson as a victim of my brutal ambition. Others tried to reach Marigold Keays, hoping to goad her into some appropriately enraged or heartbroken response. For the first time in many years, she ignored the opportunity for self-promotion. To impertinent questions, her agency responded with a brief, cool statement to the effect that no one could be more delighted than Marigold by her husband's much-deserved success, that she was sharing these happy moments with Gregory in a marriage that, after recent problems, was stronger than ever. Neither she nor our son Douglas would be commenting further.

I, too, remained silent. After one small, unwise move (an over-emphatic rejection of an interview for *Gay Times*'s 'Coming Out for Air' column), I let it be known that I would not be available for interviews until the weeks immediately preceding publication of my novel.

If all these things seemed to pass in a distant haze, as if they were happening to another, alien version of myself, it was because, having finished my novel, I was experiencing difficulties of acclimatization.

Once, when I had first become a writer, I had feared that the parameters of my small study would become a prison. Then one day, a few years later, I realized that it was the real, outside world that had become dislocated and threatening, that the longer I spent in my imaginary kingdom, the more fearsome reality became. Taking my daily walks, east or west, I would ensure that the route I took was familiar. Whereas once I would take lunch, attend clubs, move easily among the city's shoppers, commuters and tourists, I was now daunted by the slightest exposure to urban life. Writing novels, as Martin once said, is all about not getting out of the house. As *terpsichore 4:2* strengthened its grip, I had hidden away in the study, as timid as a little old woman living alone with her cat.

Now there was no avoiding it. I had finished writing the novel; it was time to get out of the house. Making my way to unavoidable meetings with those who were buying my talent with significant sums of money, I blinked, like Rip van Winkle at the brightness and noise all around me. Contemporary life seemed to have accelerated since my last visit; it had become harder and louder. Entire streets had changed. New shops, selling unrecognizable electrical objects in absurd, garish, nursery colours, had sprung up. The last time I had looked, this had been a sleepy place, a country in grumpy, helpless decline; now I saw women and men, confident, aggressive, hurried, solitary yet forever in urgent communication. They talked to themselves as they walked down the streets, negotiated with themselves in doorways, sometimes stood on traffic islands declaiming as the cars swirled around them. It was if the compulsion for crazed soliloquy of the nutters and tramps I used to see on my walks had spread to the rest of the world. There was something exclusive and threatening about the new dependence on contact; even when people met face to face in restaurants, they would leave their mobile telephones close at hand on the table beside them, like gunslingers with their Colt .45s at the ready.

Home felt dangerous, too. Returning from the imaginary world to domestic life, I found that everything was changed. Doug's vacated room had undergone a transformation. The more intimate or extraneous items – ancient, yellowing, encrusted handkerchiefs, empty cigarette packets crammed with ash and butt-ends, hard, grey pellets of ancient chewing-gum – had been removed, while other memorabilia had been arranged in a sensitive designer version of adolescent disorder, porn mags stacked carefully below a marginally less repulsive men's style magazine, anonymous items – a single rollerblade wheel, a cigarette roll-up machine, an ancient invitation to a rave – laid out side by side on the bedside table. On the bed itself, the sheets had been cleaned and the Garfield duvet folded back in heart-breaking invitation.

For the first time in two years, the door was left open. Sometimes, alone in the house, I gazed into the room, trying to remember my son's voice as a child, happy family moments from the early years, but the sights and sounds of the past seemed distant and fuzzy, incomparably less authentic than any fiction. Douglas, Dougie, and Doug were all gone. In their absence, there stood this odd shrine to adolescence, a sort of design exhibit from a lifestyle exhibition, 'Male teenage life at the end of the twentieth century'.

Marigold and I had taken to living parallel lives. At the very moment when my telephone had stirred into life, hers was so silent that I assumed that her calls had been redirected. When she appeared at the house during the daytime, it was to collect something, to change or to consume a quick meal before she disappeared again. Sometimes she would return late at night, closing the bedroom door behind her and leaving for work the next day before I had emerged from my study.

When we met unexpectedly outside the bathroom or in the kitchen, a ludicrously formal exchange would take place.

'What news of the masterwork?

I would tell her the latest deal.

'Good. You must be very pleased.'

'You're not?'

'I simply couldn't be more delighted.'

Once, I asked her to accompany me to one of the fashionable parties to which I was now regularly invited. She rejected me with a curt laugh and a shake of her head as if any further response would be a waste of breath.

She cancelled the monthly allowance she paid into our joint account for my living expenses and suggested that my influx of funds meant I could support myself for a while. When she closed our joint account, I was startled by how sad it made me that we were no longer even together on chequebooks, 'G. and M. S. D. Keays'.

'Why are you doing this?' I asked once as she brushed past me in the hall.

'I'm fine. You're fine. We're a successful modern couple. I see no problem here.'

'So why has Doug moved out?'

'It's a phase. He needs to sort himself out in his own way.'

'You know that?'

'We talk most days. We have longer conversations than when he lived at home.'

But we were not fine. Nothing was fine. It occurred to me that the reason why my wife was still formally married to me merely reflected a characteristic determination not to give the world outside the satisfaction of seeing Marigold Keays, one of modern life's cool winners, in retreat, the victim-wife. She was not, nor ever would be, a cliché.

As if articulating what Marigold was not prepared to say, the house seemed to give up its soul. Where once there had been an elegant vibrancy, there was now a collection of tasteful objects gathered in an imitation home. Miguela and Ned continued to attend to the house and garden, yet, for all their ministrations, a sense of dry neglect descended on the place. More than once, I found myself running a finger along a mantelpiece or examining the surface of a toaster, expecting to find dust.

For the first time, I recognized the tiny changes my wife had made every day to keep the place alive, as the landscape is modified in endless subtle ways by the changing weather. Now, simply by withdrawing herself, she had taken its life. The house had become a neat and desolate prison.

One morning, I noticed that the rice in Buddha's bowl had become yellow, hard and dusty. I tried to be amused that Marigold's much publicized faith could be shaken by such a trivial thing as marital conflict, but sadness defeated any sense of cheap triumph. I missed those absurd, reverent replenishings and took to visiting the fat boy in his bedroom shrine to place a spoonful of shiny, white rice between his upturned hands. Alone in the empty house, I listened out for the gentle ringing of harmony chimes, for the tapes my wife used to play (whale song, the menstruation chants of native American women) but they were never there.

Now and then I would attend a fashionable party. No longer on the fringe with the liggers, spouses and personal assistants,

I was propelled within moments of my arrival into the gathering's hot social centre. Once, while conversing with a literary editor at the anniversary celebration of one of the smarter imprints, I glanced away to find myself staring into the dark, amused, unblinking eyes of an attractive woman. Yet the very openness of the invitation, the easy, unexpressed availability, which I had once found so irresistible, now alarmed me. I saw a trap: with intimacy, even the fake intimacy of a friendly, post-party fuck, comes a lowering of the guard. In an easy, post-coital moment, I might find myself talking about my novel, my new status as an acceptable figure, the speculation over my relationship with Peter Gibson. There was no telling where it would lead. Behind the wall which I had erected for myself, the erotic longing which had always seemed to be at the centre of my being curled up and sank into a deep, self-protective slumber.

I wanted to talk to my wife. I needed to see my son. Yet they had absented themselves at the very moment when I was at last able to hold my head up in the family home as a successful, talked-about, financially secure husband, father and writer. Beside this void in my life, the various treats I had promised myself down the years – parties, celebrity, casual and emotion-free engagements with clever, hard-bodied young women – now seemed tawdry and trivial.

I went south. A few weeks after *terpsichore 4:2* had been accepted, I rang Brian McWilliam and suggested that we should start work on the project he had suggested. When he expressed surprise at my eagerness, I explained that I was creatively written out, that it was the ideal time to research. Besides, I had always liked to clear my debts as quickly as possible. He gave me the address of his house in Streatham.

So I moved into a new routine. Doug-like, I would stay in bed late every morning. I would arrive at Brian's smart yet anonymous terraced house in the suburbs soon after lunch where I would be ushered into the front room. At first I had thought that the place, with its patterned carpets, hanging brasses and Victorian prints must have belonged to Brian's

244

mother but it transpired that this self-conscious, spinsterish neatness was a reflection of his own taste. There, behind net curtains, on each side of gas log fire, we talked about rape, murder, blackmail and the abduction of minors. The link of criminality (murder) between us seemed to have encouraged Brian to be open with me and, apparently unmoved by the fact that he was spilling out the foul detritus of his libidinal past to a man who, whatever his weaknesses, was still (above all) a writer, he reminisced, eyes sparkling, about his past as 'a bit of a Romeo'.

On the few occasions when I attempted in my line of questioning to shape Brian's clammy maunderings into some kind of fictional narrative, he would quickly grow impatient. 'But Greg, that's not how it happened,' he would say, irritated by this interruption of his violently erotic reverie. In spite of the welcome escape the job provided from my own life, I began to feel contaminated, as if this collaboration had somehow slipped from the literary to the real.

The novel's working title had been *Cutting Up Rough* but soon it had become clear that mere violence was the least of my co-author's preoccupations. He began to talk about girls. Soon the girls became teens. Eventually, and with a sort glazed and distant smile, the teens became even younger. Brian explained that in a certain area – 'we're talking erotologically here, Greg' – he was a classic case of arrested development. He recalled the various activities he and the lads used to enjoy at his East End secondary modern, lingering nostalgically over the gangs, the parties, the iffy games they used to play on some of the tastier girls.

'So you still like teenagers.' I dared to inject a note of disapproval into the question.

Brian shook his head with a sort of disgust. 'Teens these days – they're just slags. By the time they're seventeen or eighteen, they've gone, Greg. They've lost that girly nervousness, that purity. They can't be corrupted.' He stared sadly at the fire. 'I do like a spot of corruption, and that's the God's honest truth.'

I waited, somehow knowing where we were heading.

'Angels.' He spoke dreamily. 'Nymphs. Lovely little Lolitas.'

'Nabokov would be honoured.'

'Who the fuck's he?'

'Doesn't matter.'

'They're not kids, Greg.' Brian seemed eager to convey his integrity. 'Only a fucking pervert would do anything to a little twink or a pre. They're different – on the turn, if you know what I mean. They're curious about it all, but still smooth and pure and unsullied. A year or so and they'll just be all sag and hair but now they're still in their own little world.'

I must have looked embarrassed because Brian shrugged defensively. 'I'm just there to catch them before they fall.'

It was a tricky moment. I was the author of a novel that, even before publication, was being widely discussed as one of the year's likely prize-winners. In the small and inward-looking world of books, it was quite conceivable that my connection with McWilliam might come to light. A liberal in the political and social sense, I have always taken a strong line against the exploitation of children. Were I writing my own novel, a level of knowing irony might have provided a defence against misunderstandings on the part of the more literal-minded reader but it was clear that the nominal author did not intend *Cutting Up Rough* (or *Lolitaville*, as he took to calling it) to be that kind of book.

'For legal reasons, it might be wise to add a couple of years to these . . . Lolitas.'

'Fuck off. They wouldn't be Lolitas then, would they. Who's ever heard of a sixteen-year-old angel?'

I thought of Doug, seventeen and still a lost child. 'You'll get slaughtered in the press, Brian.'

'It's a novel, isn't it?' He shook his head, lost in thought. 'They've got that little twitch of adult naughtiness that can be teased into desire.'

I elected not to point out that Brian's Lolitas had invariably fallen into his hands as a result of some sleazy act of blackmail, bribery or coercion. 'I'm uncomfortable with the work,' I said quietly.

Brian sighed. 'Maybe it's time we talked about your boy,' he said.

It turned out that he had been busy over the past week or so. He told me that the house where Doug was living was known throughout the area as the local crack den. As it happened, only the basement flat was used for this purpose, the first and second floors being occupied by a shifting population of squatters, illegal immigrants, dealers and teenagers on the run from children's homes, parents or the police. There were two older men who had lived there for some time, one a dealer and small-time burglar, the other a veteran of what Brian described as 'the adult entertainment industry'.

'Do the police know about the place?'

'They keep an eye on it. Now and then they pick up some idiot white boy living dangerously but otherwise they leave it alone. They don't give a fuck about the various wasted rastas and teenies in there. Where's the point in clogging up the court with losers?'

'I need to get in there.'

'Grow up. The law would have you down the station, a rock in your back pocket, before you reached the first floor.'

'I'm a father. I could explain.'

Brian smiled pityingly. 'You're not too familiar with White City life, are you?'

I shook my head wearily.

'It's not a problem. I'll get him out for you. Arrange a little family sojourn. How does that sound?'

'How soon?' I asked.

'He'll be home before we finish the first chapter of *Lolitaville*'

I sighed and reached for my notepad. 'Where were we?'

34

Now and then, a novel is published which, well before it becomes available to the common reader, captures the collective imagination of the literary world. To have been sent an early proof by the publishers becomes a matter of pride. At the smarter dinner-parties, it is *de rigueur* to have some sort of strongly held, informed opinion about the book and the author of the moment.

terpsichore 4:2 was such a book. Gregory Keays was that author.

Although there were few overt references to the forthcoming publication of my novel in the press, it was clear that something was in the wind. Columnists began to talk of a 'new dawn' within British letters, of the arrival of a new school of 'bleeding-edge fiction', of an uncharacteristic spirit of fiscal optimism within the bookselling community. Behind these various coded announcements lay a sense of intense and undeniable anticipation. *t42*, as it became known among the cognoscenti, was on its way.

At my suggestion, early book proofs had been sent to key members of the fiction aristocracy. It amused me to imagine the changing reactions of my writerly compadres (curiosity giving way to surprise making way to awe-struck, envious despair) as they read. Rushdie would fussily note the book's literary antecedents. Updike would insist, in a lordly manner, that he should be allowed to review the British edition in the *New York Review of Books*. There would be an eloquent, deafening silence from Martin.

Inevitably, a few of the more curmudgeonly critics would already be sharpening their quills. Responding to my triumphant conflations of style and psychology, head and heart, depth and narrative drive as if they were a personal affront, they would now be rehearsing their casual insults, preparing to express their 'sincere bafflement', their 'reluctant reservations', their 'profound sense of disappointment'. As one who has, down the years, paid his dues to Simenon's 'vocation of unhappiness', I felt genuine sympathy towards them. For many of these failed or would-be novelists, angrily living off the scraps of journalism, my triumph would be a brutal reminder of the futility of their ambition, the emptiness of their professional lives.

Yet, at this moment of imminent triumph, I found myself alone. There was no one with whom to share, in an amused, proud yet modest manner, the daily ratcheting up of my reputation, apart from a psychopathic criminal pervert now too absorbed in memories of nymphs and Lolitas to consider weightier, more literary matters. 'Good for you, Greg,' he would mutter when I foolishly confided another triumph. 'Fucking ace. My writer, the champion. Couldn't be more pleased, mate.'

That possessive noun, incidentally, I was by now beginning to find a trifle irksome. Once, arriving early in Streatham, I had encountered a wizened stable-lad type who, to judge by his shifty manner and eagerness to depart was no more pleased to be found in the company of Brian McWilliam than I was. Before this little eel – who went under the name of Jimmy or Joe – had slithered out of the house and back to the shadows, Brian had nodded proprietorially in my direction. 'This is Greg, my writer,' he had said. 'You can trust him. We're working on a project together.'

I had clenched my teeth, not so much in anger as to prevent myself pointing out, self-effacingly yet firmly, that in the great community of authors, the concept of possession has no meaning. It happened that I was temporarily caught in a trap of obligation; yet I was no more beholden to Pussy McWilliam than Peter Gibson had once been beholden to me. As Maugham points out in *Cakes and Ale*, the writer is 'the only free man'.

If I was more than usually tolerant of my collaborator, it was because he had, true to his word, been busy on my behalf. Through the mysterious chain of communication which stretched from the derelict house where Doug was living to Brian McWilliam's grannyish residence in south London, the word reached me that my son was prepared to see me, providing our rendezvous was on neutral territory.

So, six weeks after I had first discovered where he was now living, we met in a brightly lit Tex-Mex bar in Notting Hill Gate. It was a desolate place, decked out in fake saloon-bar pine with lamentable artwork of buffalo, cacti, six-guns and Red Indian headdresses on the wall, and, even though it was early evening when I arrived, it was deserted, apart from one table where a raddled woman gazed blankly ahead of her and smoked a cigarette as her two pale children picked in silence at bowls of French fries in front of them.

Doug lives by a different clock to the rest of the world and has never knowingly been punctual since he was about twelve but, on this occasion, he arrived a mere ten minutes late, entering through the slatted swing doors like some trainee cowboy. When he saw me at the back of the room, he nodded and made his way over to the table, not with his normal furtive scuttle, but with a swagger that was almost adult.

'Owi?' He stood hands on hips, as if considering whether to hit me or not.

I looked up and smiled in a welcoming, fatherly way. His

clothes were as torn and dirt-encrusted as ever, but there was something unavoidably different about him. He seemed less rat-like, more muscular, taller. His skin had cleared and his face revealed the dark beginnings of a beard. For the first time since he was about eight, it occurred to me that he might grow up to be a good-looking, possibly even a handsome, man.

'Doug.' I extended a hand which he shook awkwardly. 'How have you been?'

'Not so terrible, as it happens,' he said, almost amiably. He glanced over his shoulder. 'Tell you what, let's sit by the window, yeah?' Without waiting for my reply, he made his way to a table at the front of the restaurant. I followed and, as I sat down opposite him, I saw why we needed to be seated in view of the street outside. Across the road, parked casually on a double yellow line, was an ancient saloon car. Two men, one black, one white, sat, smoking on the front seats. They glanced occasionally in our direction.

'Have you been accompanied?' I asked.

'Maybe.'

'They don't trust you? Are you being held against your will?'

My son gave an irritated little laugh. 'Fuck off,' he said.

A waitress ambled up to the table. I ordered a beer for my son, a spritzer for myself. Doug took a battered packet of twenty out of his jeans pocket and lit up.

'Given up the old roll-ups then?' I asked.

'Yeah.' He sat back in his chair and exhaled showily. 'So?' he said.

Small talk, a brief paddle in the shallows before plunging into more treacherous waters, did not seem to be an option. 'Look, Doug.' I lowered my voice, as if the two men across the road were somehow able to catch my words. 'I know that I haven't been the greatest of fathers but –'

'You're a writer yeah yeah, blahdy-blah.'

'No. I was going to ask you to put what has happened in the past behind you. I'm not interested in talking about exams or getting a job or keeping your room tidy or smoking or speaking to me or now and then turning up for meals. We're beyond that stage.'

He muttered something and looked across at the sad little family group across the room.

'I want you to come home, Doug. You've made your point. We can work this out together. Things are easier now that I've finished my novel. I've got back my career. I have my own money. I'm me again – your father.'

'Finished your novel?' He looked away. 'Congratulations.'

I smiled. 'It's going to be quite successful, I think. Well, actually, I know.'

Doug gazed out of the window, bored once more.

'I don't like your keeping this company. We don't like it.'

That parental first person plural seemed mildly to bring my son to life. 'We.' He mimicked his father with a skittish contempt. 'So you and Mum got over the old problem about you turning out to be a bit of a bender, then.'

I paused, swallowing back my rage. 'I am not a bender, as you call it. What happened was an aberration. Since all that, and its . . . aftermath, your mother and I have talked about the situation. A lot of it was career pressure. We're better now.'

For the first time for a while, he looked me straight in the eye. 'That's not what she says.'

The waitress returned with our drinks. Doug swigged back his beer and smacked his lips vulgarly.

'And what does Marigold say?' I asked.

'Words to the effect that you're a selfish wanker, basically.'

'Doug.' I felt defeated. It seemed pointless to suggest that Marigold, of all people would never use those words.

'Well, aren't you?'

'I'm not here to talk about me. I'm not the one hiding out in a crack house.'

He smiled and looked away.

'You can talk big and act big,' I said. 'You think you're in control but you can get sucked under. I may not know much, I may appear not to be very good at life, but I know this. Bad company can destroy you. These people are not your friends. They may seem to understand you but they'll just use you for their own purposes.'

'Yeah?' he spoke so loudly that the two children across the way looked up from their plates, their eyes wide with undisguised curiosity. 'So that'll be why you've taken to hanging out with good old Pussy McWilliam, will it?'

Trying not to show my surprise, I started to explain that Brian McWilliam and I had a professional writing arrangement, that in my work, research of the darker aspects of human behaviour sometimes involved personal contacts one might not normally choose for oneself, but, as I spoke, Doug shook his head slowly. 'You have absolutely no fucking notion,' he said eventually.

'I know McWilliam,' I said. 'I've probably heard more about his murky past than most people.'

'Murky past. Shit, man, you talk like he was some sort of joke baddie from an Agatha Christie film. You think that just because he's done a book and talked at a few of your lame festivals that he's straight up, no problem. Oh yeah, like there's been a bit of dodginess in the past, he's a bit rough round the edges, a bit fuckin' murky maybe, but he lives in a nice house now, don't he – basically, he's an all right sort of bloke.'

'I'm not quite as naïve as you may think.'

'I tell you there's people round here, right, who shit themselves when they hear his name.' My son lowered his voice. 'Straight up, he's a psycho, man, one mad fuck. If he's got anything on you – anything at all – you are just so – well, you're fucked basically.'

By Doug's standards, it had been quite a speech. While it may have lacked a certain linguistic polish, and told me rather more than I wanted to know about the attitudes and turn of phrase of those among whom he was now moving, it conveyed genuine emotion and a concern which, at the time, I found rather touching. Disconcertingly, this gruff son of mine, with his snarling voice and gutter language, was making me feel as if I were the innocent abroad in need of worldly advice, as if I were the one who was lost, vulnerable and in danger.

'Just tell me Pussy's got nothing on you,' he said wearily.

'Brian McWilliam and I have a working arrangement –'

'Oh, *shit*. You are such a fucking idiot, Dad.'

In spite of myself, I smiled. It had been a long time since I had heard him call me by that name. 'Come back, Doug,' I said. 'We can help each other out of trouble. It'll be good, father and son. We'll rediscover what we've lost.'

'Sucked under, you said. It's not me that's being sucked under. I'm not the one with the big secret and with an evil bastard holding a gun to my head.'

I looked at my son more closely. 'I haven't had a big secret for a while.'

'Yeah?'

'Yes, Doug.'

He looked across the road to his minders. Then, sighing, he reached into his back pocket and took out a scuffed sheet of paper. Carefully, he unfolded and smoothed it out on the table. It was a sheet of lined A4 paper, filled with the neat handwriting which I now knew better than my own.

'Tell me about this, then,' he said.

Top Five Methods for Overcoming Writer's Block

1. Leo Tolstoy, when blocked, would play a game of cards, usually Patience, sometimes deciding the fate of his characters on the outcome.

2. Franz Kafka would walk out of his study, play with his hair in the mirror, wash his hands three times and return to work.

3. H. G. Wells believed you should take the novel by surprise by writing at odd times of the day or night.

4. Annie Dillard quotes a Washington writer who became frozen with fear as soon as he became self-conscious in his writing. During a story, he would regularly leave his desk to go for a walk. On his return, he would copy out every word he had written in the hope that the momentum would carry him

forward to create two or three new sentences. Then the self-consciousness would afflict him again and he would repeat the process.

5. Kingsley Amis suggested that a writer should compose the day's first few sentences in his head before he reached his desk (in the shower, while shaving etc.).

35

They say that, when E. M. Forster reached his terminal, definitive writer's block, he gathered the characters in the novel he was trying to write at a station, put them on a train, and never saw them again. They disappeared over the horizon, leaving only a trail of smoke drifting upwards into an empty blue sky over the deserted landscape of his imagination. Shortly afterwards, the former novelist dolefully made his way to King's College, Cambridge where he lived out his days, writing books of criticism, dreaming of choristers and, very occasionally, giving half-regretful interviews in which he tried to explain how exactly he had, as he put it, 'gone smash'. It was not that the emotions themselves had dried up, he said, merely that the expression of them was no longer at his disposal.

Only a true writer will understand the pathos of this remark. The fact is that, for us, a life without expression (and publication and readers) is no life at all. It was Martin who articulated his great pity for non-novelists, asking, 'How are you going to live in a denuded world, when you're just living in it, no longer giving it some shape?' Philip Larkin made a similar point when he confessed: 'My trouble is that I simply can't understand anybody doing anything but write, paint, compose music – I can understand their doing things as a means to those ends, but I can't see what a man is up to who is satisfied to follow a profession in the normal way.' For any truly creative spirit, life without art is hardly life at all.

I can perhaps confess at this point that there have been moments in my life when it has seemed disquietingly possible that Gregory Keays might become that pitiable creature, the non-writer; I had 'gone smash' over the past fifteen years as frequently as a demolition-Derby veteran. Now, energized by the assured success of my new novel, I realized that the vast majority of my half-completed novels were not dead, but sleeping. During the few moments when I was not at work on *Lolitaville*, or making preliminary notes for this guide, I found myself returning to the abandoned novels of my past and was pleasantly surprised. A few, it was true, were trapped in the time when they were written – *Adultery in Hampstead* reflected a jaunty, light-hearted attitude to sex which I no longer felt, *Glitter*'s perspective on eighties consumerism was witty but outdated, *Gang Hoot Yer Heeb, Auchtermuchty*'s perspective on the vicious, pie-eyed Glasgow underclass was frankly over-sentimental – but most contained the kernel of emotional and intellectual truth that is the mark of true literature.

Rereading my work with the clear eyes of the successful novelist, I found much that was good and fresh: indeed, I now saw that several of my novels-in-progress had grown in stature during their years in my literary pending tray. *Mind the Gap* presented a vision of the metropolis every bit as witty and acerbic as that achieved by Martin in his London novel, but with a depth of feeling of which he could only dream. My comedy of contemporary male lifestyle *Giving It Large* offered proof of my lighter side after the relative austerity of *terpsichore 4:2*. Several of the stories in *Tell Me the Truth About Love, About Love* retained the powerful resonance which the more vulgar journalists like to describe as 'zeit-geisty'. I looked forward to completing these projects in double-quick order, firing them at a joyful, appreciative market and bludgeoning my formerly smug, would-be literary peers with the sheer heft and fecundity of my work.

· These plans were for the future; my main project during these months was *Lolitaville* and it was taking shape well beyond my expectations. For about a month, McWilliam had talked around his subject, providing background, incident, roughly drawn characterization and the beginnings of a plot, and frequently lapsing into a sort of stream-of-consciousness erotic trance which, while somewhat unnerving at the time, provided some powerful raw material. When I judged that he had contributed all he could, I began to transform my notes and tapes into the real world of fiction.

Utterly different from *terpsichore*, which in its turn belonged to a separate imaginative universe to *Forever Young* (when Martin said a writer needed no more than two or three subjects, he was not speaking for Gregory Keays) *Lolitaville* already contained, in its opening chapters, what one of my recent reviewers has described as 'the indelible water-mark of a natural story-teller.'

Meanwhile my other characters (the characters of my life), last seen chuffing sadly over a Forsterian horizon, were now returning to the station. By a strange paradox, the secret that Doug and I shared concerning Peter Gibson's unacknowledged contribution to my novel provided a bridge across the gulf of mistrust between us. I had suggested, shortly after our meeting in Notting Hill Gate, that, having made sacrifices to my career, my son should share in its rewards, receiving a monthly transfer into a bank account I would open for him in return for which he would come home. Graciously, Doug accepted the offer.

My son, it transpired, had not been a prisoner in the squat but a promising trainee. I was obliged to make a reasonable four-figure contribution to the unofficial landlords on the ground floor of his house as compensation, a sort of transfer fee. It was all somewhat squalid and hole-in-corner but, at the end of it all, Doug was home.

It would be an exaggeration to say that this carefully negotiated return to the fold (the financial details of which we had decided to keep from Marigold) heralded a new dawn of energy and communication on Doug's part. The door to his room remained closed. Many daytime hours were spent in slumber. He had become rather fond of baths and spent much of the day lolling in bubbles, staring ahead of him, stirring only occasionally to reach for the hot water tap. Once, and with the cautious banter which now marked our relationship, I commented upon this new enthusiasm for cleanliness and suggested that he might combine his ablutions with reading a book.

He laughed, a hard, barking, unamused honk, reminding me of something Martin once said about laughter being second only to behaviour 'in the sack' as an indicator of personality. He didn't do books, he said.

Oddly, he didn't seem to do music either these days. I had assumed that, with his new-found wealth, my son would invest in records but now the machine-gun rhythms, the thump of bass and the strangled screams that were once so much part of life at 23 Brandon Gardens were no longer heard. To my surprise, I found that I missed it. I looked back on the days when I could knock on his door in a caringly authoritative manner and ask him to turn the bloody noise down. Doug without vinyl was somehow less the Doug that I knew.

One day, as I descended from the loft for a mid-morning coffee, I detected the unmistakable squeaks and tinny fanfares of a computer game. Through the half-open door of his room, I saw my son perched on the side of his bed, zapping and powing, his eyes fixed on the screen of a monitor perched on his bedside table. My son had invested in a new hobby. Like many parents, I tried to find benefits in the hours spent in thrall to cybernetic mindlessness – his powers of deduction would be honed, his sharpened speed of reaction would be useful in later life – but unavoidably I remembered that Doug's first discovery of hand-held Gameboys and Action Men had coincided with the first signs of social withdrawal. 'How are you going to explain that to Mum?' I asked.

My son's eyes remained transfixed to the screen. 'Gave it to me, didn't you?'

'I did?'

'Surely you remember. Reward for coming home. Thanks, Dad, cheers.'

'You don't think that including me in your little lie is rather taking me for granted.'

'You what? Oh fuck.' He banged the keyboard and groaned. 'I was on Level Four and all.'

While the old-fashioned parent within me was dismayed at the lack of respect, amounting at times to open distaste, which my son accorded me, I told myself that it was a positive sign that we had moved beyond the stage of silence and mutual incomprehension. We had both walked on the darker side of life's highway. For the first time, Doug had a certain authority in his dealings with the adult world. A new ease was evident; companionship would doubtless follow at a later date. My initial fears that he might abuse his position of power over me, drop hints of his secret knowledge, make oafish and insensitive remarks about it, had receded.

He told me that he had discovered the sheet of Peter Gibson's manuscript during a trawl through my office, an activity which, for reasons Doug was unable to explain, had become something of a routine for him. When, with a certain amount of awkward humour, we had burnt the page on his return to the house, he swore that no further evidence of my collaboration was in his possession, and I believed him. The matter was closed.

A few weeks later, I became aware of another development in my son's life, more surprising than his revived interest in computer games. One morning, I was startled to encounter a small, plump, female figure with cropped dark hair emerging form the bathroom. Eyes down, she scurried past me without a word and entered Doug's room. Moments later, I heard giggling.

A girlfriend. It was a surprise, I admit. The idea that any-one, no matter how homely and unformed, could engage in intimate activity with my skinny, callow progeny was diffi-cult to comprehend. Yet this bouncy little thing in jeans that were too tight and a T-shirt which cruelly mocked her lack of womanliness became something of a regular visitor, announcing her arrival with a brief trill on the front doorbell. Often, when I passed Doug's door, I would hear their two voices, hers chattering and gay, his gruff and monosyllabic. What on earth did she find to say to him? What brilliant *aperçu* had my son unleashed which had caused her to collapse into peels of high-pitched and, I must confess, not unattractive laughter? She became less timid in my presence, never actually speaking but darting a brief glance and a half-smile in my direction.

After a few days, I asked Doug about her, taking care to sound neither disapproving nor leeringly over-curious. Her name was Zoe. She did have a second name, something Scottish, but my son was unable to recall what it was. She was sixteen.

'Girlfriend, Doug?'

'She's a girl. She's a friend. Work it out for yourself.'

She was a girlfriend. I could tell that from the way she spent the night. Sometimes, their voices would die down to be replaced first by a sort of mumbling, then by a creaking of timber, punctuated occasionally by a rhythmic knocking of the bed-head against the wall.

Soon any pretence that Zoe was a casual guest, just passing through, was abandoned. Some mornings she would appear in the kitchen, barefoot in her jeans, still smelling of bed. With a muttered greeting, she would make two mugs of tea which she would take upstairs to my son, her lover. Occasionally they would watch television together in the sitting-room. I became used to her presence. It was almost like having a daughter, or at least it would have been had it not been for the fact that Zoe and her weight problem, her clear skin and dark eyes reminded me uncomfortably of the late Mary Kydd.

One night, lying alone in my marital bed, I was woken by a cry. Like any parent – even one for whom the care of an infant is distant memory – I was immediately wide awake and alert. At first, I thought that I was mistaken in thinking that the disturbance had come from inside the house and that some sort of altercation must be taking place on a nearby street outside, but there was no mistaking the next sound, a gasp followed by a groan. I got out of bed and, for a few seconds, stood in the corridor, listening. The groaning grew louder, more urgent, punctuated by yelps, the occasional slap of flesh. I returned to my room and closed the door but Zoe was proving to be a surprisingly noisy lover.

I lay there, disapproving yet uncomfortably aroused. As a liberal parent, I knew I should be pleased by any new sign of my son's burgeoning adulthood but this loud, truculent love-making, only feet away from where I was trying to sleep, seemed oddly derisive and triumphant. I was unable to go back to sleep.

Alone in the marital bed? Yes, it was true. I had returned to the bedroom but, at this time of change and turmoil, when the days were accompanied by the comfort of an endlessly ringing telephone and the nights echoed to the *cris de joie* of little Zoe, Marigold was rarely at home. The influence of *feng shui* design, it seemed, was reaching beyond the purlieus of Greater London to conference centres in Birmingham, hotels in Scotland, stately homes in Yorkshire, upmarket housing developments in the West Country. Suddenly they all required the on-site attentions of Marigold Keays Associates.

Each time she called in to collect clothes and mail, my wife seemed to be more of a visitor, acknowledging me with a tight, formal smile which discouraged conversation. From the way she took to visiting Doug in his room during her brief sojourns at the family home, I assumed that many of the calls he made from his mobile phone were to her. We seemed to have reached an arrangement which was both paradoxical and unfair: I lived with my son, estranged from him yet obliged to support his lazy, expensive habits; Marigold wandered the country, yet was closer to him than she had been for decade.

Even the house and garden, which had once seemed almost a part of her, or at least an outer expression of her character and sensibility, now appeared to be of only passing interest to her. I took to moving objects around, placing the Inca fertility symbol where the Chou hill-jar had once been, in an attempt to goad her aesthetic sense into life. A flicker of irritation as she entered the room was her only response.

'I've been freshening up Buddha's bowl,' I told her one day, catching her in the bedroom during one of her fleeting visits.

She glanced at the godhead. 'How amusing of you,' she said.

'I wasn't trying to amuse. You always said it was important that he had fresh rice.'

'To bring blessing and harmony to the marital room,' she said in a distracted voice. 'That no longer seems such a high priority. Do you have to follow me about like this?'

I left the room. It was true that, as soon as I sensed her entering the house (a slight chill in the atmosphere, a surge of negative *ch'i*), I would emerging from my loft and attempt to engage her in conversation about whichever castle or housing development she was working on, or to bring her up to date, in a tone of jokey modesty, with the latest developments in the triumphant progress of *terpsichore 4:2*. She would respond with cool, distracted politeness, avoiding my eyes. Eventually, she would say, 'Anyway, I had better get on' or 'I want see Doug now' and I would retreat to my work station, defeated once more.

For a while, I had assumed that the logical explanation for this *froideur* and these lengthy absences was that her emotions were still engaged elsewhere. Yet her gypsy wanderings across the country seemed inconsistent with a woman in love. When I made casual reference to the affair which was no longer a secret between us, she reacted oddly, with a sort of scoffing wince, a laugh that contained neither humour nor warmth. As an old hand in such matters, I judged that her arrangement had reached the moment of critical mass at which it either became more public and significant or was terminated in the same cool, well-organized fashion with which it had started. He had returned to his wife, or found someone else. They had 'moved on'.

Perhaps it was my success, my new-found strength, which had alienated her. For years, she had luxuriated in the illusion that, just as her material resources had supported our little family, so her confidence had kept afloat the leaky vessel of my self-regard. The advances in her career, she believed, had given me courage through the dark hours of non-production, of 'work in progress' that somehow never progressed. The monthly contribution she made to my living expenses had established a sort of hierarchy between us: I was the suffering, indigent artist, hopeless in all practical matters; she was the entrepreneur whose gift for making money had allowed me to pursue my demons untroubled by fears of what the next post would bring.

Money – her success with it, my lack of it – had provided a bond, and now that bond was broken. I was free, drifting away from my moorings. It was odd: I had always imagined that, at this moment of financial independence, I would become more attractive to her, but I had been wrong.

I realized that I did not want to lose my wife. I wanted to talk to her about Doug, to share awkward, relieved, parental jokes about his new girlfriend. I missed her neat self-sufficiency, the way that she brought an effortless elegance to her life and surroundings, her generosity of time and spirit towards the dreariest of neighbours, her standing orders at the bank to various carefully considered charities, her quiet, unshowy sense of the correct way to behave, her laugh, her old-fashioned expletives. Goodness. Blimey. Sugar. Good grief. In my mind I would hear her voice and I would smile. I even missed her scoldings. I wanted to take her to bed. I imagined moments when, at some early hour in the morning, we might be roused by the sounds of Zoe in full cry. We would turn to one another, groaning with parental exasperation, and, unable to get to sleep, find ourselves responding with a gentle, middle-aged variation on the same theme. We would fall asleep in each other's arms.

As if to escape more completely from me, she had become different from the Marigold with whom I had lived for all these years. She dressed more casually, moved through the house in a manner that was uncharacteristically deliberate.

For the first time, I could imagine how she would be as an old woman. Oddest of all, and it was difficult not to discern some kind of slight here, her taste in reading had shifted from the popular history and vapid inspirational volumes she used to enjoy to mainstream contemporary fiction: Jane Gardam, Robertson Davies, Penelope Lively.

One day, when she was packing a case in the bedroom (recently, she had seemed to leave for each new project with more cases than she ever returned with; maybe she was shipping herself out of the house in stages), I noticed a copy of Martin's woeful American *policier* sitting up perkily and proprietorially in her handbag on the bed.

'Since when have you been into Martin?' I asked as casually as I could manage.

My wife followed the direction of my eyes. 'He's great, isn't he. I can see why you're always going on about him. Surprisingly good at women, I thought.'

I hesitated, hoping, in my innocence, that this was a good-hearted tease, but she returned to her packing as if nothing particularly unusual had been said.

'*Good? At women? Martin?*' Unable to hold back any longer, I found that I was speaking more loudly than I had intended. 'The policewoman narrator of this overblown *jeu d'esprit*, this painfully elongated short story, this pretentious little sub-Elmore Leonard semi-thriller, is no more feminine than the banal crew of tossers, losers and *faux*-lowlifes to be found in all his other novels.' I picked up the novel and, as I riffled contemptuously through its pages, various irritating Martinian yelps and phrases ('suicide is all over town', 'downward disparity', 'state-of-the-art cynicism', 'I'm sorry I'm sorry I'm sorry') caught my eye. 'In fact –' I lowered my voice, aiming for a note of teacherly authority – 'By opting for an American setting, he has sacrificed the one faintly intriguing aspect of his work – its edgy, Transatlantic linguistic tension. The plot's wafer-thin and contrived, even before he abandons any attempt to tell a coherent story at around page 120, when he falls back exhaustedly on a feeble but lengthy Welsh joke. In a Chicago police story! Talk about hoisting the white flag!'

My wife sat back on her haunches and looked me with faint amusement. 'You know, I had completely forgotten that you were so jealous of him.'

'My critique was entirely objective,' I said, regretting that I had allowed her to goad me into a response that was more heartfelt than the occasion demanded.

'You hate him because he's done all the things that you should have done, written the books that you should have written.'

I allowed a few moments for the full idiocy of this charge to become clear to her. When I spoke again, it was in cool and measured tones. 'As it happens, I had a lot of time for him up to the time of his Eighties novel. No one could regret the catastrophic decline in his talent over the last few years more than I do.'

'Poor Gregory. He's sent you round the twist.'

'In fact, as a fellow author, I feel profound sympathy for the man. When *terpsichore* appears, he'll be finished. Cultural journalist? Of course. Humorist? Maybe. Serious novelist? Sorry, Mart, you're not even close.'

'Well, he just seems like a damned good read to me.' My wife stood up and, unusually, looked me straight in the eye. 'By the way, why can you never bear to mention the title of any his novels? The "London novel", the "Eighties novel". Why don't just say it – *London Fields*, *Money*? Go on – it won't hurt.'

I swore at her (I very rarely swear at her) and left the room.

Later, it occurred to me that this conversation had nothing to do with the small man at all. My wife was provoking me, pushing me into leaving her. I tried to tell myself that, when I was once more the king of the literary pages and the TV arts programmes, she would see me for who I was – Gregory, her husband, the father of her son, one third of our precious little family unit, but I feared that, by then, I would have lost her. Anyway, she had probably never even read Martin.

265

The Writer Speaks of . . . Ego

'As for conceit, what man will do any good who is not conceited? Nobody holds a good opinion of a man who has a low opinion of himself.'

Anthony Trollope

'The good artist believes that nobody is good enough to give him advice. He has supreme vanity. No matter how much he admires the old writer, he wants to beat him.'

William Faulkner

'Writing a book is a horrible, exhausting struggle, like a long bout of some painful illness. One would never undertake such a thing if one were not driven by some demon which one can neither resist nor understand. For all one knows that demon is simply the same instinct that makes a baby squall for attention. And yet it is also true that one can write nothing readable unless one constantly struggles to efface one's personality.'

George Orwell

'I think writers are inclined to be intensely egocentric. Good writers are often excellent at a hundred other things but writing promises a greater latitude for the ego.'

John Cheever

'A confessional passage has probably never been written that didn't stink a little bit of the writer's pride in having given up his pride.'

J. D. Salinger

'To be any good you have to think you're the best of your generation . . . Without that ridiculous competitive pride I don't think you've got a chance, really.'

Martin Amis

36

A month after I had started working, the first three chapters and a full synopsis for *Lolitaville* were delivered to Brian's new agent (sensibly, Barry Storm had been ditched with some of the less desirable baggage from Brian's past) who passed it on to the publisher. She responded with a certain wariness. While she was impressed by the 'brio' and 'narrative energy' of the material, she had expected something rather less racy and more considered. *Sorted*, after all, had offered a serious contribution to the debate on criminality. What was the moral position of the new work? Its tone seemed oddly lenient, indeed almost approving, in its view of child abuse. Was this to be – I imagined her shudder of distaste – some sort of popular thriller? Or had she misunderstood Brian's intentions?

Hearing the news, I cursed myself for my lack of professionalism. In my haste, I had forgotten that we were dealing with book publishers. They had their tawdry reputations, their laughable respectability, to consider. Some light, cosmetic revisions would have to be made.

A lunch was arranged between agent and publisher. The agent, well-briefed by the book's true author, offered his apologies. Clearly Brian's sub-textual intent had been obscured by his enthusiasm for narrative. He had always intended that the full and final version would emphasize a powerful ethical message behind the apparent amorality of the story itself. Its very lack of self-censoring irony would imbue it with the startlingly minimalist contemporaneity of the new Danish film directors who were now all the rage. A mock editorial introduction, of the type favoured by Nabokov in *Pale Fire*, had now been added. The title, Brian had also conceded, might have been ill-advised in that there was a small danger that it might appeal to the very people it sought to expose. He now proposed to call it, with a subtle Shakespearean touch, *Nymph, In Thy Orisons*.

The publisher was convinced. Sensing a heady and profitable conflation of literary seriousness and old-fashioned prurience, she hurried back to her office and, later that day, put in an offer not far short of a quarter of a million pounds.

It would be disingenuous to pretend that I was surprised to find that, yet again, I was responsible for an enviably successful literary project. Yet not for one moment did I consider taking the public credit that was due to me.

terpsichore 4:2 was making its mark. Several of those who had read it had expressed a heartening, if off-the-record, conviction that it was a strong contender for virtually any literary prize for which we cared to enter it. My return from the wilderness and brief flirtation with notoriety following the death of Peter Gibson, had provoked a flurry of interest among features editors. No fewer than fifty copies of my new author portrait (a sultry black-and-white studio-shot taken by an up-and-coming fashion photographer) had been distributed to the press.

In short, no matter how successful and profitable *Nymph, In Thy Orisons* may have turned out to be, my involvement in a lightly disguised paedo-thriller risked taking the sparkle off my now glittering reputation. The question of the novel's subject matter could probably, with careful news management, be surmounted (I was a writer, for Christ's sake) but the collaborative element of the enterprise was more worrying. Had Roth worked with a low-life media criminal? Did Updike ever share joint billing with a non-writer? No. Even Martin had always ploughed his narrow little furrow in solitude. The idea that I should be seen publicly in harness with the notorious wrong 'un Pussy McWilliam would doubtless cause a sensation in the press but, when the fuss died down, it risked dulling the burnish on my public image as an artist and moral arbiter.

So when we dined in at a vulgar West End restaurant for minor celebrities, shortly after the full scale of the financial triumph of *Nymph* had become clear, I was able to give my collaborator the answer for which he had been hoping. 'Forget any author credit,' I said. 'Have it. This one's on me.'

McWilliam narrowed his eyes in a manner that, somewhat gracelessly, expressed suspicion rather than gratitude.

'You helped me when I was in a jam,' I explained. 'It's the least I can do.'

'So what sort of cut do you think would be reasonable?'

'Cut?' I laughed.

'Yeah, Greg. Don't fuck about. You know what I'm saying.'

I shrugged, unconcerned.

'Personally, I think a one-off payment would be tidier,' he said. 'I can pay it off-shore, if you like. We'll take the tax element into account, naturally. Seems only fair.'

'Brian.' I spoke quietly. 'My novel is about to be published here and in New York. Foreign language rights are on offer to publishers all around the world. Hollywood's hot to trot. I simply don't need the aggravation of off-shore funds.'

'It'll have to be readies, then.'

I smiled and said nothing.

McWilliam looked at me sideways, like an amateur dramatic trying to convey an air of craftly suspicion. 'You don't want money?'

I shook my head.

'So what do you want then? What the fuck are you up to, Greg?'

'It's enough to see you happy, Brian. Let's just say that, when I give you the final manuscript, our account will be settled.'

I picked up my glass to toast him again but McWilliam sat dangerously still. 'Don't be a cunt, Greg. Please, for my sake, just don't be a fucking arsehole. Not with me.'

'I am, so far as I am aware, being neither a cunt nor an arsehole.'

'You're up to something, I can tell. I've known a few cold bastards in my time but you're right up there. You're in the wrong business, you know that?'

'I'll take that as a compliment.'

'Listen, Greg. This is me insisting, right? I like a clean slate. And I'm going to have one. End of fucking story. Tell me what you want from me.'

I smiled, victorious as I accepted defeat. 'I'll try to think of something,' I said.

The Top Ten Unusual Writing Techniques of Great Writers

1. Johann Von Goethe used to write his poems on the backside of his child-wife Christiane.
2. Henrik Ibsen hung a portrait of Strindberg over his desk, saying, 'He is my mortal enemy and shall hang there and watch while I write.'
3. Benjamin Disraeli would take time to dress himself immaculately in evening clothes out of respect for his readers.
4. Leo Tolstoy would wear a peasant herder's smock.
5. Edith Wharton wrote in bed and threw her pages on the floor for a secretary to pick up and transcribe.
6. Ernest Hemingway used to write standing up without any clothes on. Only with passages of dialogue would he sit down to type. The rest was handwritten in pencil.
7. Vladimir Nabokov wrote on cards, standing up at a lectern.
8. Peter Ackroyd writes lying down, eyes close to the page, believing that he works best in a state of semi-slumber, occasionally dropping off.
9. Michael Crichton eats the same meal and wears the same clothes every day that he writes a novel.
10. Gregory Keays listens to fifteenth century plainsong as he works to remind him that writing is a form of prayer.

37

Two months remained before the publication of my break-through novel. After an impossible few weeks, I had completed Brian McWilliam's moral thriller. At some point in the future, I would reach for one of my many works in progress and tease it back into life. But right now I was tired of fiction. I turned to the work you have before you.

For some time, I had wanted to examine the creative impulse within me while providing guidance and encouragement to the thousands, possibly millions, of would-be scribes who lack the confidence to invoke their own private muse. I am, after all, ideally qualified for such a task, having both taught the art of fiction and having personally experienced the highs and lows of the literary life. For a title, I resolved to turn to one of the phrases which echo through writing courses across the English-speaking world. *Less is More* seemed a touch lacklustre. *Show, Don't Tell* was inappropriately skittish. In the end, I settled for that old favourite of writing class and film school, *Kill Your Darlings*.

A memoir-manual: even in this golden age of literary cross-fertilization, there will be those who will find in these pages a hybrid too far. Where is the dappled evocation of the writer's childhood of a traditional memoir, they will ask – the fond yet modest account of his later triumphs? What on earth is the point of a creative primer that contains little or no practical guidance as to plot or narrative, irony or closure?

In a sense my unseen critics are right. One day, perhaps, when I am something of a 'grand old man of English letters', I shall set down a full record of my life (*Speaking Volumes: A Writer Remembers* is the title I have in mind). As for a collection of 'tips' for the aspirant novelist, there are countless such volumes already available, thanks to the earnest efforts of hard-working, sincere (but rarely published!) creative-writing teachers.

Kill Your Darlings would be both more and less than the

memoirs of a novelist. It would be a candid account of my sojourn in a writerly heart of darkness and the act of self-rescue which released me, leavened by insights and quotations from our literary heritage. Opening with the events subsequent to the success of my first novel, it would close on the triumphant publication day of my second.

I have worked at speed, putting down in this first draft my most intimate thoughts and deeds as the events of the past year have unfolded, in the knowledge that this is, essentially, a first draft, a 'writer's cut', of what will be submitted to the public gaze. As I near completion, the possibility of publishing these thoughts and memories as they stand has nagged at me: how easy it would be to pander to the current vogue for public confession by presenting myself, naked and vulnerable, serving up my family and friends in bound and printed form. In the end, though, I have elected to hold my peace, for the moment. There are too many people who could be wounded by the truths to be found in these pages to justify publication, too many areas in which the naïve reader might misread the complex imperatives of the creative impulse, for it to be wholly satisfactory as a work of art. The writer's task, after all, is primarily to be understood.

So *KYD*, in its present version, is for me. Once completed, it shall be consigned to a bank vault until the day comes when I shall once more inspect these pages. At that point, I shall make amendments to the more personal material, and certain of my more precious darlings will quietly and humanely be laid to rest. Perhaps, bearing in mind Updike's advice that 'a fiction writer's life is his treasure, his ore, his savings account, his jungle gym,' I shall weave some of the garish, colourful events of the past year into a work of the imagination, confident that their message of inspiration and hope to writers everywhere will remain as clear and bright as a cloudless summer sky.

38

'We tear out a length of gut from our bellies and serve it up to the bourgeois,' says Flaubert. 'Once our work is printed – farewell! It belongs to everyone. The crowd tramples on us.' This morning, as I sit at my desk on the day of publication, I too await the cruel attentions of the crowd. By the end of today, the novel which has often seemed as much a part of me as my spleen or my liver will be gone. Yet, unlike Flaubert, I feel no sense of loss or compromise. *terpsichore 4:2*, now it is completed, belongs to the multitude: it will survive without me, just as I shall survive without it. Like Tolstoy, Gregory Keays believes that the novelist should only write when he leaves a piece of his flesh in the ink-pot each time he dips his pen. Yet, once the work has gone, it is yesterday's flesh. Life-blood that has been lost will be replenished from within and so the process of death and rebirth will be repeated. Such is the lot of the writer.

From the moment when I delivered the manuscript to Fay Duckworth, *terpsichore 4:2* had been drifting away from me. Sold to a publisher, with a price on its head, it became merchandise, to be shaped by the eager, grubby hands of editors, designers, sales folk – people whose job it is to render the personal public, to transform the complex inner turmoil of a soul into a neat, recognizable product.

By the time it was first set up in type and its pages bound into book form, it was already grown. At meetings attended by jaded mediocrities, it had been given clothes, a face, an image to present to the world, a career path. Its future and personality were decided. Some books are fated to be besuited drones which will dutifully but dully earn a small but respectable living; others will be zany mavericks, loved by a small but loyal group of affectionate friends. *terpsichore 4:2* was one of those rare entities whose destiny, from those first meetings, was to be a prince among volumes. Before it had achieved anything, it was a literary over-achiever, walking, like one or two of Doug's friends, a golden path from childhood onwards. Contracts and praise and money had fallen like manna upon its youthful brow. When it was an adolescent, a mere callow proof copy, it had been introduced to people of judgement and influence, members of the élite who could help its progress through the world, or crush it underfoot. They had (according to reliable reports) been impressed by its sensitivity, wisdom and wit. There was, it seemed, something blessed about the young book which made those who encountered it feel as if, merely by turning its pages, they were privately sharing in its good fortune. It had charisma, a politician's skill in making each person it encountered feel privileged and special and want nothing but good things for it.

Today, my novel will be published. There seems no doubt that it will fulfil its promise out there among the ordinary public – good folk whose favourable opinion has, to all intents and purposes, already been decided for them. All that remains is a moment of matriculation, a smiling formality, after which the glittering future will become a dazzling present. A launch party.

I have, over the past month, paid my dues to the bitch-goddess of publicity. I have subjected myself to questions of varying intelligence and impertinence from journalists and profile-hounds, giving a good sense of myself while retaining the central mystery, the living question mark, which is the essence of the serious artist. Bearing in mind Saul Bellow's warning about the danger of modern novelists becoming their own theoreticians, I have neither attempted to explain my work nor engaged in fashionable self-analysis. I have walked a fine line between the showy reticence of the Salinger school of literary hermit and the crude exhibitionism of chart-hungry thriller-writers.

Interviewers were predictably anxious to meet me in the dream house. Unlike my wife, I elected not to deploy my personal life as a marketing prop and, with one exception, have insisted on meeting my interlocutors and their attendant lensmen in one of the smarter West End restaurants or in a room at the Ritz.

The exception was none other than Tony Watson who, at my suggestion, had been appointed to interview me on behalf of the *Sunday Times*. To show the world that there was nothing evasive or odd about Gregory Keays, I had invited him to 23 Brandon Gardens.

Rather touchingly, this commission revealed the full extent of Tony's fall from impish, brilliant young destroyer of reputations to obedient, middle-aged hack. Expressing doggy gratitude that I had put his name forward for such a prestigious feature, he had willingly acceded to the various ground rules which I established: no hint that my marriage was moribund, only a passing mention of Doug, all quotes from friends, former colleagues and fellow writers to be cleared in advance, no undue emphasis on the Peter Gibson episode and, if at all possible, some inclusion of a quote from Martin. As a final bulwark against inaccuracy, I was to have a final, unofficial view of his copy before it was filed to the newspaper.

No amendments were needed. With his usual eye for the line of greatest personal advantage, Tony Watson elected to present himself in print as a loyal friend to the author he was now interviewing, a contemporary who, unlike many others, had continued to believe in my talent through even the darkest hours of the last decade, a fellow toiler in the literary vineyard who was so close to me that, in some inexplicable way, he shared in my success.

It was a sound piece of journalism, from which I emerged as a complex, thoughtful novelist who, while not unacquainted with sadness and disappointment, had deployed the pain of life to the profit of art. There was a lively intelligence to the Gregory Keays that Tony portrayed, but also an unforced sense of humanity. No icy, ivory-towered intellectual, he was above all a human being who had engaged with the real world, perhaps sometimes recklessly, but with the passion and commitment of a true artist. The article, a five-page title feature, was illustrated by a full-page portrait (Gregory Keays at his desk, pen poised over a manuscript, careful dishevel-ment all around, Donovan sleeping on a chair in the back-ground providing a humorous, domestic touch), a small shot of me during my writer's walk (the dosser in a doorway offering a deft indication of the darker aspects of my work), the black-and-white photograph of my family on a beach in Cornwall back in 1982, and, inevitably, the Snowdon Granta portrait, with a long-haired version of myself standing un-easily between Jeanette and Salman.

What of the quote from Martin? Tony Watson would only say my contemporary and fellow writer had been unable to help us on this occasion. It took little effort to imagine the background to this haughty, mean-spirited response. He would have remembered me, of course; *Forever Young* will have been recalled with some subtly insulting compliment – 'snappy exuberance', 'zestful comic brio' or the like. He would have been pleased to hear of my return to form but would regret that he was unable to look at the copy of 'the new thing' which Tony sent to him. He was at a critical point in his own 'stuff' and it was his custom when fully 'cranked up' only to read familiar work by favourites – Bellow, Nabokov, the 'big guys'. Apparently, the sound of 'other voices from other rooms' had a corrosive effect on the 'swing' of his own prose.

Bastard! Snappy exuberance . . . other voices . . . the new thing. I could hear the bored drawl, the hint of a dismissive sneer as he drew wearily on one of his loathsome little roll-ups. Not so long ago, he had boasted in an interview that he would toke away now and then in the evenings at the recreational drug of his choice. It seemed that, while stagger-ing around pie-eyed with a fat joint in his hand had, presum-ably, no effect on the sainted 'swing' of his prose, he was unable, when 'cranked up', to dip into a work of vibrant, intellectually serious fiction with a view to penning a few helpful words. Somehow this niggardly refusal to acknow-ledge the talent of a contemporary spoke more eloquently of the true nature of the man than all his books and interviews put together. In one small-minded gesture, he had confirmed the flaw which will for ever set him among the competent and the workmanlike rather than the truly brilliant: he lacked a great writer's common spark of humanity.

Naturally, I confided none of these feelings to Tony Watson, accepting the snub with the smiling grace of a man for whom the snivelling rivalrousness of a contemporary was a matter of supreme indifference, but later, after my interview was concluded, I found myself afflicted by feelings of justified writerly disappointment. I thought of the countless occasions when I had recommended to my students the Eighties novel, the London novel, even his absurd little police procedural, when I had quoted in class some languid, carefully rehearsed Martinian *bon mot* about style, research or the literary life, when I had drawn upon one of his tawdry *galère* of one-dimensional characters (Highway, Talent, Self, Clinch, Six) to make a point about characterization. We were peers, we had been celebrities on the same list: how much, really, would it have cost him to acknowledge, briefly yet gener-ously, the stupendous success of a fellow writer? But no, that simple act of comradeship was, it seemed, beyond him.

I would rise above the slight but I would remember it. Some time, maybe some time soon, Martin would pay.

Admittedly, I was in a volatile state during those weeks

before publication. As with all major literary events, a certain amount of controversy had attended the general sense of public anticipation. A tiresome scrap had developed within the books industry concerning some ineffably dull 'trade' matter (Price-cutting? Embargoes? Discounts? The details escape me). Because the prospects for *t42* were generally held to be more glittering – and, for those who cared about such matters, more profitable – than most other volumes, it was my book (together with one or two others) which became the focus of controversy in professional magazines and, in one case, the home pages of a national broadsheet.

Although it is not the role of the author to become embroiled in disputes of a squalid, fiscal nature, the name and features of Gregory Keays somehow came to represent at this time the fate of the individual in an age of heartless corporatism. For many people, I suppose, I became a sort of contemporary hero, a living emblem of the fragile yet enduring integrity of an artist whose work is caught up in a business dispute, like a butterfly buffeted hither and hence in a force-ten gale.

Meanwhile, interviews were published, previews appeared. I was 'Face of the Week' in the *Shepherd's Bush Gazette*. Showing unwonted generosity, the *Professional Writer* devoted an editorial to my forthcoming novel, noting solemnly that 'fiction is a long game and, as readers of this magazine know, Gregory is nothing if not a stayer'. My name became something of a fixture in arts-page diaries and gossip columns.

Although the froth of celebrity hardly impinged upon my outlook – like Ford Madox Ford, I am of the opinion that the serious author should eschew personal publicity 'as you would shrink from soiled underwear' – my son had become intrigued by the fuss surrounding his newly famous father. One morning, I took a break from working on this volume to find him in the kitchen, leafing through copies of the previous week's press stories which my cuttings agency had sent me.

'I don't believe this stuff,' he said, staring down at an

evening paper profile in which I was described, if memory serves, as 'the Lazarus of literary London'. He clasped his brow in a mock-comic manner. 'Like, suddenly you're this big news.'

'It's all nonsense,' I said modestly. 'Cyril Connolly once wrote that the serious author should step off the moving staircase of fame and subject everything he creates to the supreme critical court. Would it amuse Horace or Milton or Swift or Leopardi? Could it be read to Flaubert? Would it be chosen by the Infallible Worm?'

'The *what*?' In the past, any kind of bookish reference would have caused Doug to raise the drawbridge, but now he laughed openly and with apparently genuine humour.

'The Infallible Worm. The discriminating palates of the dead. He meant –'

'That your work isn't any cop unless a load of stiffs go for it.'

I smiled indulgently. 'Not quite how Cyril would have put it, but that sort of thing. All this –' I waved a dismissive hand at the pile of over eight or nine press cuttings '– has no significance at all. The writer's duty is to articulate the voice, concerns and sensibility of his generation and to send it echoing down the years.'

'What generation is that then, Dad?' Doug looked at me with open curiosity.

Although I had been absorbed in the complex dramas of my professional life, I had noticed that my son had changed over the past months. He had found words. He conversed openly. His face, less sleepy and furtive, had a new and bright confidence to it. The absurdly apologetic wisps of hair about his chin had materialized into an irritating little beard of the type favoured by trad jazz players or French existentialists of the late Fifties. His shoulders had lost the bony stoop which had made him look like some crushed and miserable refugee. I had tried to persuade myself that this transformation had been effected by the time I had recently spent with him (Marigold's aggressive female exuberance had always seemed to sap the vitality from him) but in my heart I knew that it was his girlfriend, chatty, noisy, randy little Zoe, who had been his saviour. Sex had saved him.

'I was referring to my generation,' I said quietly. 'It may surprise you but critics around the world have come to recognize the talent of Englishmen now in their mid-life prime. The usual naysayers might claim that we are inward-looking, over-absorbed with the tight little circle within which we live but that was doubtless said about Henry James or Scott Fitzgerald.'

Doug was shaking his head. 'How can you? I just don't get it. You really do seem to believe all this shit you come out with.'

'Maybe I'm wrong to make these claims for our generation. But, just as when you're a writer, you have to believe you are the best, so you need to have faith in your peers. Confidence is what gets you to your desk every morning. It's the machinery that mines the ore from your soul.'

'Or someone else's soul.' The words hung in the air for a moment like a threat.

'What exactly do you mean by that?'

'This is me, Dad.' Doug was almost whispering now. 'You're not talking to some sad bastard of an interviewer. You can kid the rest of the world along, but you don't have to kid yourself. You don't have to kid me.' He shrugged sadly. 'Do me a favour and be honest with me at least.'

'I am being entirely honest.'

Doug snorted like a frightened horse. 'Yeah, right.'

'Certain source material was, as you know, made available to me,' I conceded. 'It was absorbed and used in my fiction. As Faulkner said, "If a writer has to rob his own mother –".'

'*It wasn't source material, Dad. You copied the fucker out!*' The words were spoken with the enraged squawk of the old Doug. 'Word for fucking word.'

I paused, determined not to let my son's adolescent ravings provoke me into an intemperate response. 'There's no need to use abusive language,' I said carefully. 'It may be that the page

280

which you stole from my office bore a certain resemblance to a small section in the final version of my novel but that was an unhappy accident.'

'Word for fucking word. I checked. 100 per cent. You ripped that poor dead bastard off.'

'If you had seen the other pages of the . . . source material in question, you would be aware that there were huge variations between the rough notes that Peter wrote and the final version of my novel. *terpsichore 4:2* was mine. It is mine. You have to believe me on this, Doug.'

He was staring at me with what seemed to be an inexpressible disappointment in his eyes. He took a deep breath, as if to speak but then shook his head once more and looked away. 'Your whole life is fiction,' he finally said. 'Every day that you live is a lie.'

'That's a terrible thing to say.'

'What you did was a terrible thing to do. I shouldn't give a toss but, you know what hurts? I'm part of the lie. I'm in on your scam. I'm every bit as fucking bent as you are.'

'It was just one page, Doug.' An unattractively wheedling note had entered my voice.

'Bollocks. You know that's bollocks, and so do I.'

Suddenly I began to understand the source of my son's certainty. 'You had more, didn't you? You gave me one page but there was more.'

He nodded.

'Where are they, Doug? What have you done with them?'

'I burnt them. It's your life. I'm not going to tell anyone.'

'Does Zoe know?'

'Of course not. Don't be ridiculous. What kind of scumbag would I be to lay the guilt on her?' He stood up. 'Relax, Dad,' he said, pushing the pile of cuttings across the table towards me. 'Enjoy your success.'

'You'll come to the launch party?'

'Yeah, Dad. I wouldn't miss it for the world.'

Moments later, I heard him trudging up the stairs and closing his bedroom door behind him.

> **Top Ten Literary Slogans**
> 1. GET BLACK ON WHITE – *Guy de Maupassant*
> 2. SOAK AND WAIT – *Arthur Koestler*
> 3. WRITE FOR YOURSELF – *J. D. Salinger*
> 4. ONLY CONNECT – *E. M. Forster*
> 5. BEAR SERENELY WITH IMITATORS – *Rudyard Kipling*
> 6. KILL YOUR DARLINGS – *William Faulkner*
> 7. IDEAS ARE ACTION – *Gustave Flaubert*
> 8. HIDE YOUR GOD – *Paul Valéry*
> 9. STYLE IS CHARACTER – *Joan Didion*
> 10. DO NOT HURRY; DO NOT REST – *Johann von Goethe*

39

I want him at the party. I want that above all else. At that moment, when father and son stand together on publication day, the world will see a double victory: I will not only be re-established as a significant star in the literary firmament but also, after its recent Strindbergian phase, my family life will be seen to be back on course. I had hoped that Marigold would be open-hearted enough to set aside our differences for one night and play the writer's wife but she has declined my invitation and, to avoid the embarrassment of answering questions from journalists, has become absorbed in a project to transform the *ch'i* of a chateau in the Lot-et-Garonne district of France.

Disappointing as it is that my wife is not prepared to share my moment of success, there will be certain advantages to the situation. The father bringing up a son alone has recently become a figure much favoured by public commentators, While the truth of my situation is somewhat more complex, celebrity paints with a broad brush: I have no doubt that the image of a dad and his boy, united by an awkward but genuine male pride in one another, will play well in the public prints and perhaps speak eloquently to the more fastidious and egocentric of my writerly compadres who have shied from parenthood like a nervous horse from a stream.

The party for Gregory Keays is to be a major event, perhaps the most significant social celebration the literary world will see this year. Encouraged by a series of none-too-subtle hints from Fay Duckworth to the effect that it was far from certain that the next Gregory Keays novel would be offered to them, my publishers have elected to mark the publication of *terpsichore 4:2* in a gratifyingly extravagant fashion.

Through my freelance publicist, I had suggested that a suitable venue for the party would be stylishly dark and subterranean. The publishers have obliged with Paradise, a Soho Club whose three-floor design is a louche but amusing reworking of the Fall. Last month, I inspected the premises and found them entirely acceptable for our purposes. There are moments when a certain vulgarity is *de rigueur*.

The guest list posed a more formidable challenge. At most gatherings of people connected with books, a whiff of mediocrity and disappointment hangs in the air; often, they are little more than apologetic, low-budget imitations of the grander and better parties held in the smarter quarters of Media Village. I therefore proposed that the usual army of good-hearted losers (booksellers, jobbing reviewers, middle-order librarians, 'trade journalists', arts diarists, wholesalers, compilers of bestseller lists, foreign rights sellers, publishing line managers, deputy culture editors and so on) should be excluded in favour of real, non-literary celebrities.

Soon we had a crop of high-credibility thespians anxious to be seen in the right social circles. Film folk from Hollywood to Soho quickly fell in line, followed by the bigger names from TV and Westminster, a couple of media magnates, and, to lighten the mix, some of the more amusing chefs, sports presenters and glossy mag aristos.

Finally, we opened the sluice-gates of the literary world a few inches to include Frayn and Stoppard, the Pinters, A. S. and A. N., Rushdie and a few of the Granta gang whose reputations were still in credit. Updike, we discovered, was making a rare visit to London and might be prepared to put in an appearance, the glad news of which we carefully leaked to one of the diaries. At my insistence, invitations were sent to members of the international socialite-author set – Vidal, McInerney, Easton Ellis and one or two others – and I was confident that at least some of them would ensure that their next visit to London coincided with the big launch. A rumour circulated that one of the world's famous literary recluses was an admirer of my novel and the more excitable scribblers began to speculate that Cormac McCarthy, Thomas Pynchon or possibly even J. D. Salinger was about to come out of hiding.

Then there was Martin. How could he stay away? Not to be seen at my party would be professional suicide. Spiteful tongues would discuss whether he was afraid of being up-staged by a more successful contemporary or, unthinkably, that he had not even been invited in the first place. I had discovered from Tony Watson that the small man was in town and made sure that his invitation went out a few days after the rest.

I was naturally delighted when he accepted. In a sense, today's event is as much for him as it is for me.

Affirmation
My story is an echo asking a shadow for a dance.

40

It is a matter of writerly satisfaction that I shall be able to close this account with a party, a glorious and scintillating set-piece worthy of Tolstoy or Fitzgerald, in which the preceding drama, with all its colour and character, will be brought together in one last spectacular social moment. Tonight, with the regrettable exception of Marigold Keays, all the survivors from this great adventure will be there to celebrate the coming of age of my novel: Doug, Zoe, Tony Watson, Anna Matthew, Brian McWilliam, Fay Duckworth, Martin. I have even, after a certain amount of deliberation, included Pia in the guest list: she may be tempted, in time-honoured fashion, to cash in her chips and exploit her knowledge of certain intimate aspects of my past, yet somehow I doubt it. She has a certain pride and to present herself to the world as a common whore, albeit a part-time and very beautiful one, will do more harm to her reputation than it would to mine. Indeed, were I a cynical man, I might even welcome the revelation that, even during the temporary aberration that was my over-affection for Peter Gibson, my essential heterosexuality was still being expressed on a regular basis.

A book written in blood shall be launched in an appropriate fashion. I found a way for Brian McWilliam to repay his debt.

Tonight, as the champagne flows and the name of Gregory Keys is upon everyone's lips, there will be an uninvited guest in Paradise. At around nine o'clock, speeches will be made, the significance of *terpsichore 4:2* noted, my future success toasted. I intend to reply with a modest expression of thanks to all those who have helped me – my agent, editor and, above all, my dear wife, Marigold, who would so much liked to have been here tonight. I shall dedicate the evening to the memory of a promising student and a dear friend, Peter Gibson, whose passing was an abiding reminder of the price all writers pay for their work. Having allowed a couple of beats for the emotional force of my comments to reach the alcohol-addled brains of my congregation, I shall thank my many friends and distinguished guests who have made tonight such a memorable occasion. They will all be welcome to spend as long as they like at the party: drink, food and music would be available throughout the night.

The dancing will begin. Some of the gathering will move from Heaven to the first basement, Limbo, where there will be dappled lights and jaunty middle-of-the-road sounds from a Venezuelan guitar combo. Others will descend yet another flight to the thud and darkness of the lower basement. What would Paradise be without Hell?

The uninvited guest will mingle, awaiting his moment.

Aesthetically, I would have liked the final act of closure to occur before midnight but, in the end, I have decided that there are certain occasions when one must leave details of timing and method to the experts. If it happens an hour or so into the day after publication, then so be it; often it is the flaw in a pattern which reveals its full artfulness.

He will wander from Heaven, where I intend to hold court throughout the evening, to the easy Latin sunniness of Limbo and down to the heat, darkness and noise of Hell. He will choose his moment and, to tell the truth, it would not have worried me too much if he had chosen his subject as well. In a sense, almost everyone in Paradise – coke-brained film exec, scurfy critic, sneeringly resentful writer – is worthy of his attentions. An irritatingly supercilious look here, a drink-spilling jog of the elbow there, and that would be it.

But no. I have created the work. Why should I leave the life (the loss of life) to the whim of a psychopathic stranger? He might end up taking out some publishing executive, a point-less and demeaning act of bathos that would be a cruel enactment of the very downbeat ending which publishers famously loathe.

One hour a day, you have to hate everybody. Down the years, I have obeyed Martin's injunction. Pia. Tony Watson. McWilliam, Doug. My agent. My editor. Virtually any pub-lished novelist who is my age or younger. Martin himself. They have all played their part in the creative flowering of my hate. Now, as they dance and laugh and drink upon the soul of my work, one of them will pay.

The anonymous guest will choose Hell. He will move into the heaving, thumping, wild-eyed throng. Swaying and smil-ing like any other zonked-out reveller, he will watch his prey through the blackest of dark glasses. He will see Pia, making up to the man whom her trained professional eye has identi-fied as being of most professional interest to her. Doug will be there, pacing the floor in the absurd silver trainers he has bought for the occasion. A flash of almost phosphorescent white from Martin's proud new teeth will catch his eye. The music will be pumping, urgent, loud. Sweat and laughter will be in the air. He will move closer, so close that, for a fraction of a second, his subject will know that something really rather terrible is about to happen. Too late. He will make sure that, when they come, the two quick, muffled detonations will be perfectly syncopated to the beat of the music. Dg. Dg. By the time, the partygoers realize that the figure crumpling to the floor is not demonstrating the latest clubland dance step – the Jerk, the Sag, the Totter, the Bleed – my guest will be on his way, the cool night air outside against his face.

Up in Heaven, I shall hear the first scream. Then the music will stop. There will be another scream and raised voices.

And I will know that, at last, my work is truly published.

I can hardly wait to write it all up.

The Writer Speaks of . . . Writing

A great writer is just simply a martyr whom the stake cannot kill.

Honoré de Balzac

A writer's true gift is his temperament.

Ford Madox Ford

Never trust the artist. Trust the tale.

D. H. Lawrence

Fiction is written in last year's blood.

Bernice Rubens

We write books because our children aren't interested in us. We address ourselves to an anonymous world because our wives plug their ears when we speak to them.

Milan Kundera

All plots lead to death.

Don DeLillo

It was not muffled at all. It was more of a sort of dry crack, they said – like someone treading on a branch in a forest. And it was not in the darkness of the basement in that sad, Eighties-throwback club but on the ground floor near the entrance. No one thought to come downstairs and stop the music until about a couple of minutes after it had actually happened. I was chilling out on one of those floor-level sofa things, drinking a beer and wondering when it would be all right for me to get the hell out of the place, when suddenly the DJ kills the sound and says, 'We're gonna take some time out there because there's been some kinda accident upstairs.'

'Dad.'

According to Zoe, I actually said that word. For sure, I thought it. I stood up and ran for the stairs. I just knew, as you do, that, if something bad had happened, it would be to my father. He had been walking the edge for too long. Sooner or later he had to fall.

I made my way up the two flights in double-quick time. On the ground floor, I noticed that people were making their way towards the door – like, don't let's get involved in any unpleasantness, darling – but, in the far corner, there was this little cluster of guests looking down to the floor, one or two of them kneeling. A thin stream of blood was trickling across the floor.

Even before I pushed my way through, I knew what I would find.

He was on his side. The jacket of his precious cream linen suit was a dark crimson mess. His face was against the floor as if he were listening really carefully to something that was happening downstairs. His skin was all pale and glassy and the only sign that there was any life left in him was a slow twitching movement of the jaws, like he was trying to say something, to squeeze just a few more words out before he went. Soon his eyes glazed over and there was a sort of shudder of his whole body from head to toe, then stillness. Someone behind me was pulling at my shoulder. I heard a voice saying that I was his son. Zoe and some woman I have never met led me away. When I looked back, they were laying a table-cloth over him. What a way to go.

I knew it. I had told him that Pussy McWilliam was a psycho. He thought he knew better. He could handle it. Just because he wrote stories, he seemed to believe he could control things in real life. Different rules applied to him.

Later, I heard that some of the other guests had commented that he seemed to be unusually hyper during the evening, like maybe he was on something. They said he had been chatting away in that corner when he noticed someone across the room. He became agitated because this bloke – a small, wiry type in dark glasses – kept glancing at him and started moving closer. They say that Dad looked confused. Then, when the guy in the shades walked quickly towards him, it was if he knew what was about to happen. He turned to face the man but didn't say anything, just gave a sort of weird smile. The guy pulled a piece out of his pocket, raised it to chest height and shot him through the heart. As Dad fell back against the wall, the man turned, pocketed his gun and, cool as you like, made his way out of the club before anyone could do anything.

Poor Dad. No wonder he was freaked. It was only Jimmy Rose, the man he had once seen round at McWilliam's place, one of Pussy's most experienced removal men. Rose was not exactly part of the book set. He could only be there for one reason. Only, instead of going down to the basement, he went up where he was. Then he made his move.

He was never stupid, my Dad – innocent, yes, stupid, no. I guess that, in those few moments, he realized that I was not the only one in possession of a dangerous secret. He knew about Pussy's past. He knew that his media career was built on a scam.

No reason to kill someone, you might think. But Dad had gone too far. He had taken a liberty. When he had suggested to Pussy that the debt owed to him might be repaid with a bullet, Dad did something which few people have ever managed to do. He shocked Pussy McWilliam.

In many ways, Pussy is a just traditional geezer. As bent as you like, he has his own warped sense of right and wrong. He was always a great believer in family. So what Dad proposed was just the worst thing he had ever heard. Who did this author bloke think he was? What kind of scumbag did he take him for to think that Pussy McWilliam would stoop to such a thing? No, when Dad asked Pussy to arrange the assassination of his only son, he signed his own death warrant.

Yes, it's true. Dad had got his precious success at last. The way he saw it, the only person who could take it away from him was me. I had told him that no way would I blab his big secret around the place but somewhere along the line he had forgotten how to trust people.

The morning after he was murdered, the police came round to the house. They took his diaries and files and were interested to find a manuscript of Brian McWilliam's *Nymph, In Thy Orisons* on a shelf beside his desk. But they ignored the contents of his work-in-progress drawer, including a box-file marked *Kill Your Darlings*. What good was that to anyone? It was just one of his stories, wasn't it?

I read it. To tell the truth, I'm not too into books and Dad's stuff has never been much to my taste (although I quite liked *The Lonely Giant*, right enough, when I was a kid). But there it all was, in back and white, the truth at last. Possibly the first completely honest thing he has ever written.

Not that he could quite bring himself to admit, even to himself, what he was going to do. When I showed Mum the last pages of the manuscript, she seemed to think that it could have been the prostitute he had been seeing who was the target, or even that Martin bloke he was always so obsessed by.

Yeah, right, definitely. That really made sense, didn't it?

It was me. It was always going to be me. I put in a call to the police and told them everything I found in his book.

They fingered Jimmy Rose within hours. They knew that he had done work with Pussy in the past. His face and method of operation fitted the description of witnesses. But old Pussy was already one step ahead. One of his contacts in the force tipped him off and, by the time the squad cars had rolled up at his gaff, he was on his way to the airport. They say he's in Rio with all the other old lags.

Word got out. Suddenly poor old Peter Gibson's novel was tainted goods. Booksellers took it off display. The publishers quietly let it go out of print. Mum agreed to pass over a whole stack of money to Mr and Mrs Gibson. The porny thriller that Dad wrote for Pussy came out in paperback and hit the book charts, no problem. All the cash it's making is going to the Barnardo's Homes. And they say that publishers have no sense of humour.

As for Dad's very last work, I read it again shortly after Jimmy Rose had been tried and sent down for ten years, then gave it to Mum. Between us, we decided that, for all his faults, Gregory Keays deserved to have his side of the story told. The publishers were a bit iffy but, when they heard that all proceeds of the book would go to the dead author's poor little son, they agreed to take it on. It was Mum's suggestion that I should bring the story up to date.

Sometimes I sit in his little office and look through the work that had become my father's life: his unfinished novels, his articles for the *Professional Writer*, his little ra-ra affirmations, his precious quotations, his half-completed lists, 'Ten Great Red-headed Authors', 'Top Five Literary Hermits', 'Five Worst Cases of Writer's Block', 'The Flying Fist: great writers and self-abuse'. It makes me sad, the way he was sucked under by all those words written by other people, by the way he needed to compete with Gustave, Leo, Martin and whatever, his obsession with that good old infallible worm.

Once he had been all right. I remember how, years ago, he told Mum and me that sometimes, for an hour or so, he would copy out a few pages from his favourite books and pretend that he had written them himself, just to ease the log-jam in his brain. Now, in an unmarked folder, I found page after page after page of his work. *The Good Soldier* by Gregory Keays. *The End of the Affair* by Gregory Keays. *Something*

Happened by Gregory Keays. *The Counterlife* by Gregory Keays. *Money* by Gregory Keays.

For a short while, I thought about getting something down myself, my memories and thoughts of a man who lost it for literature, my poor dead dad. The kid bites back. Then I glanced through the pages of his little creative primer and decided that there was a world out there, a life to live, and that it was best to leave the last word to Gregory Keays.